Jan

CW00508812

Matt's Passion

For Lynne,

Who taught me love.

Song

O mistress mine, where are you roaming?
O stay and hear, you true love's coming
That can sing both high and low.
Trip no further, pretty sweeting;
Journeys end in lovers' meeting-
Every wise man's son doth know.

What is love, 'tis not hereafter,
Present mirth, hath present laughter,
What's to come is still unsure.
In delay there lies no plenty,
Then come kiss me, sweet and twenty;
Youth's a stuff will not endure.

'Twelfth Night'
William Shakespeare

Matt's Passion

Exposition

He stopped abruptly in the doorway, frozen by a sudden vision; a vision both unexpected and audacious, which flooded his senses with immediate emotions – desire, awe, wonder.

A naked young woman, asleep, dreaming. A sensuous face, full lips slightly open, heavy eyelids voluptuously closed. Her head lay towards him, the turn of her neck extreme and tantalising.

He let his eyes wander over her body, investigating her soft curves and delicate crevices. His heart was thumping in his chest. She lay before him like an offering, like a goddess, ripe, expectant.

He stepped into the room, a floorboard squeaked. He froze stupidly mid-step, but still she slept.

He swallowed, calmed himself, felt the trickle of sweat down his back.

Reassured, he moved softly towards her, drawn by the erotic line of her leg, the exquisite arch of her back. Her skin was limpid, smooth, enticing.

He longed to run his hand down her throat across her breasts and down to her essence, her tumescence. And still she slept.

Yet didn't he know her? Know these soft curves and familiar folds, that languid look, that breath-taking beauty? How, when, where? Who was she, this vision of purity, this semblance of reality? Hadn't he fashioned her in his mind before sometime, some other time, and known her? Known her, oh so intimately? Or was he imagining it?

Time hung suspended.

He hardly breathed, loathe to break this resonating moment shimmering with electricity.

He craved her, drugged now with heavy desire and this feeling of déjà vu.

He tried to look away, but not for long; he couldn't look away for long. She dragged his gaze back to her, to her glowing skin, bathed now in golden evening sunlight glinting low through a side window.

"The museum will close in five minutes...." the Tannoy splintered the space, shattering the moment.

Chapter 1

The sudden quick coldness of the air hit his lungs as he arrived outside the museum, as if he'd caught a whiff of ammonia or solvent, and he coughed dryly, instinctively wrapping his scarf around his neck with habitual deftness. His vocal cords felt dehydrated – he must get a drink of water.

It had been raining, leaving the pavements glassy and smooth, the lowering black-grey clouds piling eastwards after depositing their load. Looking the other way he saw another bank approaching, underlined by a jagged ribbon of fluorescent orange near the horizon as dusk drew on, that shaft of sunlight which had moments ago pierced the room now curtained for the night. Other museum- goers randomly rippled past him in groups and twos, variously chatting or not, obliged to circumnavigate his rooted form which partially obstructed the exit.

Matt stood, swaying stupidly, as if with vertigo. His mind had gone blank, or rather teemed with an image so bright, so radiant it excluded thought. Where was he? How to get back to his hotel?

He looked down the road, straining to glimpse a landmark to jog his memory and remind him of the layout of this part of Gothenburg. He tried to picture the map he had recklessly left in his room thinking it was too easy a route to have to take it with him. 'Just use your brain' he'd said to himself. 'Think, memorize, don't be so mentally lazy!' So then he had looked it over, drilled a couple of street names into his head and sallied forth with a smug feeling of superiority over those who needed maps! Now he couldn't remember anything. Total blank. What a prat!

After a few moments recapping his progress to the museum two hours earlier, he pieced together the return route and began walking and allowed the heady vision of her image to flood his senses with the delicious freedom of uncensored thought. As his footsteps mechanically took him along the pavement his mind danced recklessly over her supine body, investigating every nook and cranny, drinking in her cool torso and indulging his wild infatuation. Yes infatuation. That's what it must be, but sprung from a pure desire; a clean, honest lust. He smiled in his elation, realising he was nurturing a clandestine obsession with an inanimate lump of marble. How could a piece of stone conjure such an emotional response in him? How could a lifeless combination of curves and hummocks so inspire him with desire and passion and an almost religious awe?

He was used enough to the stimulation of the naked female form. Whenever he saw his girlfriend Maggie sprawled negligently across her Tracy Emin bed in the morning, he never failed to be aroused, often with delaying consequences, which had required outrageous fabricated excuses when he used to be late for class at college or now, occasionally, for rehearsals at the Royal Opera House. But that was living flesh, warm and breathing, undulating rhythmically and smelling of sleep and sex. This was a frigid, frozen female form, incapable of response, yet inspiring in him a response so strong it made his heart race and his mouth dry, just like on his first date with that skinny girl all those years ago in Walthamstow, when he was fifteen and she was – oh don't think about it – and he was so excited he thought his heart would burst out of his chest and his cock out of his pants! When it came to it, he recalled wryly, the fulfilling of that excitement had been somewhat short of expectations, as he had by that time discharged his manhood uselessly into his boxers and the combination of her gaucheness and the sickening sweetness of her buttermilk moisturiser had by then rather deflated his ardour.

It was almost dark as Matt tramped through the centre of the city under the now bright street lamps, finding his way back to the hotel his agent had booked him into; conveniently situated for both the rehearsal venue and the concert venue, Peter had said. Convenient yes, he had to agree, and comfortable and classy, but totally characterless.

How much more preferable that rather seedy, side-street albergo in Rome he'd booked into when he had gone to audition for the opera house there, where the old Signor at the reception desk, chain smoking and always with an espresso at his elbow, had talked endlessly about the great singers he'd heard – di Stephano, Correlli, even late Gigli, always tenors, and of course Pav.? Then he'd suddenly launch into Nessun Dorma or a favourite Neapolitan song, his voice belying his years and the effects of cigarettes and coffee, a clear clarion tenor, so naturally and instinctively produced, ringing in the foyer with the sheer joy and exuberance of Italian extrovert passion. Contrast this with clinical Scandinavian efficiency and Matt sighed for a bit of grubby laissez-faire.

"Good effening, Mister Chamberlain, did you haf a good day?" ingratiated the receptionist when he arrived in the foyer, glad to have just missed the sudden torrential shower outside.

"Yeah, fine thank you," he automatically replied, as the image of the sculpture flashed in his mind and he wondered what this clone would make of his experience.

"Um, is there a good place to eat near here?" he asked, expecting to be handed his room key, but immediately remembering that he had the entry swipe card in his wallet and they didn't use such outdated, technically primitive systems here.

"Yes, if you are not wanting to eat in the hotel, you go just round the corner here there is a very nice restaurant where you can get a variety of meals. It's just five minutes walking."

He went up to his room to change his shirt which was still damp from his rush of emotion in the gallery and had been making him feel chilly. He decided to have a quick shower whilst he was about it to warm up and flicked on his laptop to check for emails. There was one from Peter about the possibility of auditioning for Santa Fe opera next week after he got back from Sweden, various Facebook invitations to poke someone or sign up to some stupid appreciation group, and one from Maggie, obviously in a frisky mood.

"Hi Matt Babe. Missing you. How you doing? Did a screen test for a Pepsi ad today an thought I had a good chance, but too old. Can you believe it? Wanted some teen dude I guess. Feeling a bit horny. Naughty girl needs big daddy to sort her out. Write me soon...XXX M"

Standing leaning over the machine with nothing on in preparation for his shower, Matt felt an involuntary surge in his loins as the vision of Maggie in provocatively abandoned posture sprang to mind. They had a very healthy sex life, if 'healthy' can be used to describe activities which one wouldn't exactly own up to at a dinner party but which for Maggie opened the doors to heightened pleasure. He had found it all very exciting and new to start with and had gone along with her various desires, but as it had progressed he had become increasingly concerned for her safety and wasn't sure how flattering it was to himself that she seemed to need this extra stimulation. It kind of called into question his sexual prowess, which is never a question a guy likes to have to face.

He stood for a moment part stimulated, with flashing images of Maggie writhing in ecstasy, but felt grubby and tainted when he thought of the pure erotic experience in the museum. Was it a more noble lust he felt for the statue, that emulation of innocence and purity, that fabrication in stone fabricating emotions and responses?

It was a lie, he thought, a deceit, a conjuring trick to elicit such emotions from base rock. At least Maggie was alive, a tangible responsive being capable of interaction, intercourse. This statue was really a high class piece of pornography masquerading as art. Where was the difference between him yearning over the lustrous, smooth sheen of polished marble in an art gallery and fingering the cool, glossy pages of a porn mag.? Both evoked an arousing response. Both were images of naked reclining female forms. In both the subject seemed to be experiencing some mental or physical ecstasy. Where was the difference?

He suddenly thought of Bernini's sculpture of the Ecstasy of St. Teresa which he'd seen in Rome and that look of abandoned supplication, that swooning, adoring, transported gaze which so reminded him of Maggie when she came, mouth half open as she whimpered with the convulsions of her climax. Was St. Teresa transported in some similar fashion? Bernini certainly seemed to have thought so or why would he have given her an expression of such excruciating physical pleasure?

The shower was hot and fast, zinging his skin, making it feel clean even without soap. He took the opportunity to sing a few phrases in the humid air and richly flattering acoustic of the fully tiled bathroom. King Philip's aria from Don Carlos always took his fancy when he indulged the singer's constant need for reassurance that the voice was still functioning. He smiled, reassured, grateful for his charmed life; loving parents, a well-paid career doing something he loved, travelling. What more could he want?

King Philip metamorphosed seamlessly into Puccini's Bohemian Colline singing about his coat, a role he had sung at college and would soon be singing at the ROH. What an opportunity for a young bass-baritone, to sing a main role at the premier opera house in the land at the age of twenty seven! Many singers had to wait years for such a chance, if it ever presented itself.

Refreshed and glowing Matt ignored the silly bathrobe and rubbed down with the pristine white towel the size of a small sheet and sauntered to get dressed. In the bedroom he noticed the courtesy light flashing on the bedside phone, indicating that a call had been missed. It must have been whilst he had been blasting away in the shower. He rang down to reception and was told that Erik Eriksson had called to say that the possible rehearsal tomorrow afternoon was cancelled. The confirmation of this reprieve sent a quiver of expectation through his stomach; a gleeful twitch of excitement as he realised what an opportunity this window of time afforded. He knew where he'd be. He'd be with 'her' again, gazing at that sublime form, drinking in that pure image to indulge his desire.

He felt excited with the anticipation of tomorrow as he dressed, telling himself at the same time that this was totally ridiculous and he should stop being so childish; it was only a lump of marble! But he nonetheless beamed idiotically and an occasional chortle of delight interrupted the snatches of humming which accompanied his investiture.

Just as he was about to leave his laptop pinged an email notification, another email from Maggie. 'Thought you might like to see what I ordered from the mail shop!!! Can't wait til you get back and we can try it out...X' He clicked on the attached link, which after a few seconds directed to a catalogue page in one of Maggie's favourite websites. As the image scrolled across the page, his mind's eye replaced the model with Maggie's voluptuous body and his imagination began to play out a scenario. But he clicked out of the site, controlling himself and forcing himself to the task in hand, namely satisfying an increasing hunger of a different sort which was making his stomach gurgle.

He spent a rather lonely evening in the restaurant, but he knew this was 'par for the course' with these foreign gigs, so much time on your own away from home in unknown cities with unknown people. But the meal was good; some excellent very fresh prawns served warm in a large bowl followed by sea bass in an interesting piquant sauce. He allowed himself a couple of small beers, nothing that would impair a rehearsal in the morning, just good relaxation. He didn't in fact have very much to sing, but there were parts of the Christus in Bach's St. Matthew Passion that needed absolute poise and technical excellence in order to do justice to the exposed baroque lines which, he was only too aware, involved great care for his voice type.

As he dallied with a crème caramel he reflected on what an unusual engagement this was, rehearsing the day before the concert. Usually it was a run through on the day, nothing more. But the conductor had insisted and his fee reflected the extra time spent, so he was happy.

It occurred to him, as he settled down in bed that night, that it was perhaps more unusual that the man singing the part of Christ in Bach's St Matthew Passion in Holy Week, should be reading Richard Dawkins' book 'The God Delusion' and he smiled at the deliciously subversive irony.

Chapter 2

Matt sat in front of the choir and orchestra looking out on the empty church and let the waves of sound wash over him, the oscillating strings of the bass instruments vibrating through his back to his core. He tried to work out whether the music was triumphant or tragic, the vacillating major and minor struggle suggesting first one then the other, until he decided, maybe, it was both. Had Bach managed to encompass the emotional extremes of the Passion even in the first few bars - the tragedy and crime of Christ's death which would lead to His glorious ascension to eternal life; the darkness of the cross leading to the light everlasting; our grief at His suffering but our joy at His resurrection? Was it a musical portrayal of the indivisibility of opposites? There could not be the one without the other? And this was as true as the inevitability of Christ's death, 'as foretold by the Prophets' and which now must come to pass, as the reiterating basses insisted. The lamb must go to the slaughter as in Old Testament tradition, but now not as an offering to a jealous God, but to bear away the sins of the world, the sins of us mere mortals who, however hard we try, will always be sinners.

Matt didn't subscribe to any of this, he just sang it. Sang it with passion and conviction, appreciative of the import it had for those who believed and for he who had composed it; respectful of the tradition from which it had sprung.

Matt now stood up and reminded the disciples that in two days time it would be Passover and he would be handed over to be crucified. He sat down again feeling that this was going to be a Passion to remember. The acoustic in the church was fabulous, resonant but clear with not too much reverb, so that none of the detail would be lost, although as he well knew that effect could change once there was an audience. The orchestra sounded clean and tight, the conductor organised, dynamic and incisive, leaving no doubt as to his intentions, which promised a solid, trustworthy direction but with subtlety, nuance and above all sensitivity.

Once he'd sung all his part except the final 'cry from the cross', Matt took the opportunity to leave the stage and walk out into the nave of the church and listen to the rest of the rehearsal from there. It was one of the perks of the job, he thought, to listen to other musicians making amazing music. The line-up of soloists was impressive. The Evangelist of Gerhardt Munch as he'd already discovered was intelligent, musical and attuned to the inherent drama of his part, setting the scenes and pacing the recitatives well to match the ensuing numbers. His voice had a reediness and clarity which suited the narration and his enunciation was faultless. He was 'marking' a lot of his music down the octave this morning, which didn't surprise Matt – it was a huge sing and he had the responsibility of driving the drama forward all evening.

The other tenor, Ernesto San Juan, singing the two fiendishly difficult arias was the complete opposite, a heroic, full-voiced Italianate sound which suited the more operatic nature of his music, although Matt felt certain that Bach would not have heard it sung like that. But in keeping with the conductor's 'no holds barred' interpretation it was appropriate. What amazed Matt was that a voice of this weight and power had the dexterity to cope with the florid coloratura passages which went at a furious pace. But this diminutive young Spaniard seemed to have no problems and Matt imagined him being perfectly at home as the Count in Rossini's Barber of Seville.

The alto part was sung by a Mezzo Soprano and not a Counter Tenor as would have been the case in Bach's time, but Matt presumed that this also was a personal preference of the conductor. Ionela Ciobanu, a rather surly, unsmiling, smouldering Romanian certainly had a heck of a voice, rich, round and plummy, like a well brandied Christmas pudding, but Matt felt it was a bit overdone, a bit unsubtle for this music, excellent though her technique was. A competitive interest and a proprietorial feeling for the repertoire always coloured his appreciation of basses. The tall, older Latvian Artis Ozolins however had the most amazing sound; cavernous, woody and with a resonant buzz. But he had an enviable facility to lighten the voice off at the top which enabled him to sing the higher passages with apparent ease. These were particularly demanding a semitone higher than baroque pitch, which is what Bach would have heard, and Matt knew how Bach arias are notoriously challenging in the width of their range. But the Latvian's easy descent to the lower register in those falling phrases, which so often end up being an unintentional fade because a singer just lacks tone there, were wonderful to hear as it sounded like he could have continued on down for another octave, so rich and resonant were the low notes. Matt reluctantly had to admit that he was rather good and he would have happily listened to him all day.

However it was the Finnish soprano who really took his breath away, and not just for her singing. She was very pretty with a ready smile, gorgeous huge bright blue eyes and a seemingly very jolly disposition. But when she opened her mouth such a stream of silver sound was loosed, and of such intensity, that this alone elicited an emotional response. He remembered a girl at college who had a similar voice and he had been amazed in masterclasses that just the sound of her voice had moved him. Something to do with the frequency and intensity of the note, the way the tone was honed to an almost unbearable purity, cut straight to the heart and caused goose-bumps to rise and eyes to smart. Caterina Jokela had this quality but even more so. Matt sat listening to the two oboes dropping tears beneath the grieving, lamenting flute whilst her angelic, keening 'Aus Liebe' poured sadness over him. It suddenly stopped as the conductor cut to the last few bars to segue into the violent chorus that follows, and Matt realised he'd have to wait to the evening to hear that magic again.

"That was really beautiful," he said, knowing how trite that must sound. Caterina had come to join him in the pews after her aria and was sitting next to him.

"Thank you so much. I was really worried a few days ago as I had a bad cold and I thought it might go in my throat and I would have to cancel. But lucky for me it went away quite quickly."

"Yes getting an infection is the curse of the singer's life, isn't it? I'm really glad I don't have children; they always seem to pick things up and pass them on."

They were speaking in lowered voices whilst the rehearsal continued and were leaning towards each other in what would otherwise have seemed an intimate and private moment.

"That's right," she breathed, "and I may have got the cold from my little girl because, you know, these kindergarten they breed them and all the time there is children with the running nose."

Faint wafts of perfume escaped from her hair as it brushed his shoulder, little puffs of body-warmed fragrance that cut through the musty smell of wood and old incense.

"How old is your daughter?"

"Oh she's three and a half, quite exhausting but really beautiful."

"It must be in the genes, right?" Matt replied with a grin. She blushed and smiled wistfully. "So what happens when you're away?" he continued. "Does your husband look after her or do you have an au pair?"

"Well my husband he is always very busy. He's away a lot with his work – conferences, meetings, often travelling - so I can't rely on him. She's with my mother right now. This is why I don't do the opera for now. It is better to do these concert works so I'm not away for long." She fingered her score and gazed at the orchestra, although not seeming to focus on it. He watched her profile, her faraway look, and wanted to pry, wanted to know more.

The angular dotted rhythm of the introduction to the third bass aria began, played on a cello, not the viola da gamba. The cavernous bass entered so gently with the delicate phrasing of 'Komm susses Kreuz', belying the power and strength of his instrument, like a six litre Ferrari purring in idling mode, that Matt couldn't help being hugely impressed. Was there nothing this singer couldn't do?

"What does your husband do?" he asked her.

"He's a chemical engineer. His company designs the chemicals for industry. I don't understand any of it." She smiled and looked at him appealingly as if asking if he would. He noticed her eyes were moist. She blew her nose on a paper tissue which she took from her handbag. He noticed she carefully zipped it up again.

"So where are you staying?" She looked directly into his eyes and he was stunned by the amazing blue of the irises, clear, bright and searching.

"At a hotel near the square. It's very comfortable, you know, but a bit grand."

"I love hotels; all those clean towels and little bottles to choose from. I can spend hours taking a bath. I tell you when you have a child it is luxury to have time for a good soaking."

An image appeared in Matt's mind of her face surrounded by bubbles like in one of those 'because you're worth it' ads. It was a pleasing image.

"I find them a bit sterile, but I suppose a bit of luxury is very enjoyable occasionally. See how the other half live."

It was nearing his final outcry from the cross so he whispered he had better go up on stage again.

"What are you doing after the rehearsal? Would you like to go for some lunch?" There was the smallest note of urgency in her hushed voice, as if she really didn't like the idea of eating alone.

"Yeah, well I hadn't planned anything, but that sounds cool. I'll see you after."

He walked up to the front feeling that he had just been propositioned, but persuading himself that she was just a bit lonely and wanted some company. The music of the alto recitative brought him back to the Passion and he took his place next to Gerhardt. He looked back onto the church and saw her still sitting there, a compact form, the pale face and hair offset by the tan fake fur collar of her coat. She was staring at him. He smiled slightly and saw her features relax. She was very sweet.

They met outside the church and sauntered across the open space in front of it. The sun was almost unbearably bright after the dimness of the church and reflected up into their faces off the light pavings.

"Do you know of anywhere to eat near here that is good?" She took his arm in the comfortable way that a girl might link arms with a girlfriend, but he was slightly taken aback, this not being something he was used to in England from such a short acquaintance. But he supposed it was a continental gesture, rather old–fashioned, but he found he rather liked it. It made him feel protective. Maggie never took his arm; she was too fiercely feminist to subjugate herself in public, whatever she might do in private.

"I really don't know Gothenburg at all. I only got here two days ago so I haven't had a chance to suss it out. We could just walk and see what we find."

"Yes that's fine. I think I remember if we walk over there we find a street with many shops and restaurants. So tell me about yourself. If I am not being rude you must still be quite young."

"Well I suppose I am really, twenty seven next month."

"Oh my goodness, a baby!" and she laughed a cascade of notes down a scale, or so it seemed, and squeezed his arm. Her familiarity took him by surprise, but her manner was easy and unaffected, confident and uncluttered by inhibition.

"But your voice is really very mature for a bass," she continued, serious now, "it doesn't sound like a young singer, so this is very good for you because so many of your roles are of the old men. I'm sorry, I am presuming you are doing opera."

"Oh yes of course, but there are younger parts I can do like Figaro and Colline. I don't want to be an old man too soon." He looked down at her with a broad grin which she returned with smiling twinkling eyes.

"Of course, and you have your whole career before you to play the old men. No point in being old when you're young."

"Did you do much opera?"

"Yes, I was really busy with that before I had my daughter. I loved it. The stage work it really suited me and I loved the rehearsals, discovering a character and working out the motivation etc. I think I am more of the stage animal than the concert singer," she added ruefully.

"But you sing Bach so incredibly well, I'm surprised you haven't been specialising in early music all along."

"No. I could have done that, it's true, but I suppose I didn't want to restrict myself. You know, I had a wonderful teacher." She suddenly stopped walking and faced him, as if what she wanted to say was too important whilst casually walking. "She said that technique was the most important. If you had the perfect technique you can sing anything, so we work on exercises and method and you know I can sing anything in any style. It might not sound right because of my voice type, but I can sing it. I am very grateful to her for that because I can always rely on my technique and I know it will never let me down. Never forget your basic technique."

She accompanied this injunction with such a serious and searching look that he smiled with awkwardness, like a naughty schoolboy who was about to chuck all his technique books away in an act of reckless defiance.

"I'm sorry," she laughed, once more taking his arm and marching him forward, "I don't mean to be bossy, but I hear so many young singers coming up with beautiful voices and in a few years many of them are struggling because they have forgotten their basics."

By now they had come into a main street where there were shops and restaurants and they walked along looking in the windows.

"Don't worry about me," Matt suddenly said, "I'm very aware of the pitfalls in the singing profession. But thanks anyway."

"Of course. You have a beautiful voice and a good technique I can hear, but it is so easy to go wrong when you are under pressure. Anyway, enough of that, what about our stomachs? Where should we go? I don't want anything too big. What about Italian?"

"Sounds good to me."

They went into one that they had just reached and were shown to a table by the window. It was late for lunch so the place was almost empty. They ordered and then sat sipping mineral water and watching the passing pedestrians.

"You're not married?" she asked suddenly.

"No, no, footloose and fancy free. Well I've got a girlfriend, but no ties." Matt suddenly realised the double-entendre of what he'd said, although of course it was lost on Caterina.

"That's the best way if you want to lead this sort of life, I think. This is why I don't do it much now."

"But you miss it?"

"Oh there are compensations. I have my daughter who is so beautiful, and a lovely home. But I miss the excitement of the first night. I miss being in a company and working on a piece all together. I miss being with people who think the same way, who share the same emotions, who express these big emotions. You don't get that at home. It's very different." She trailed off looking out at the street sadly.

"Maybe you'll be able to get back into it when she's a bit older and is at school; you know, she'll be more self-sufficient and won't need so much attention. I mean my sister has a girl and she's really great.

She's eight now and she's so independent. Does everything herself – gets her own breakfast. Tidies her room. Yeah, she's a really good girl."

"I know, but they still need you to be there. They need their mum emotionally, and with my husband always going away I will need to stay at home."

"Well it's really good you can get away sometimes to do these concerts. You know, keep you in the loop."

"Oh God, I tell you, it's like, like….what's that word in English, you know when food gives you goodness…"

"Sustenance? Nourishment?"

"Yes, nourishment, that's it. When I do a little job like this I realise how much I miss it, and how much I need it. You know, at home with your child can be so beautiful and you discover all these mother instincts and it's a great journey, but eventually a lot of it is very boring. Cleaning, washing, cooking, going to nursery, talking with other mothers about children and toys and bedtimes and parenting and…oh God it can drive you crazy it's so boring. And then occasionally I can sing a concert like this and I discover who I am again. Not the mama who is there to do everything for my child, but who I really am. Caterina the singer. Caterina who won the gold medal at college. Caterina who sang Papagena when she was only seventeen in a professional company. Caterina who has a soul and a voice and a need to express emotions…I'm sorry, I didn't mean to cry."

Matt waited, awkwardly, as she again found the tissues from the bag and attended to her eyes and nose.

"Look," he said, "no worries. Don't mind me. Let it all out, as my dad always says. Best not bottle it all up inside." He put his hand out and gave her forearm a squeeze across the table, which made her laugh briefly between sobs.

"I'm sorry, I'm being embarrassing."

"Nah, nah you're okay."

She collected herself, taking a couple of deep breaths. The meal arrived and they set to, applying black pepper and parmesan liberally. She smiled at him between mouthfuls.

"Mm this is good. I didn't know how hungry I was."

"Well it's a long time since breakfast. This should keep us going through the concert."

"Oh yes, and then they normally have some food afterwards."

"You've obviously worked here before."

"I've done two concerts here, one last year and one two years ago. It's nice to be asked back."

He noticed a fragment of Bolognese sauce had caught at the side of her mouth which she was unaware of and, although he tried not to stare, it became the tantalising focus of his gaze whenever he looked up from his plate.

"Do you live in a city in Finland or are you out in the country?"

"We live on the edge of Helsinki, which means we get a bit of both. It's very convenient and there are excellent facilities, especially for children."

"I'm embarrassed to say that I don't think I know anything about Finland, except Sibelius." It moved precariously when she smiled, but refused to be dislodged.

"Oh don't worry. We are just a little country. We don't have much influence in Europe. We keep ourselves to ourselves and love our traditions. And you, where do you live?"

"Always lived in London, never known anything else."

She took a last mouthful and the pink tip of her tongue flitted out between her red lipsticked lips and snatched the sauce from his sight. She drank some water and dabbed the corners of her mouth with the napkin.

"I'm sorry I cried like that. It was nothing. I'm very happy really. It just hits me sometimes – missing the opera." She smiled weakly in reassurance and again gazed outside.

"Do you want coffee? Or tea?" he hazarded, beginning to be aware that time was moving on and if he were to have enough of it to get to the museum and then back to the hotel to have a rest before changing for the concert, he mustn't be too long.

"Yes tea would be wonderful."

He ordered it for her, and a coffee for himself.

"Now what about you," she turned a beaming smile on him, "what else are you singing?"

Matt told her about his up-coming roles and what he had already done but could not fail to notice the initial look of interest gradually become wistful and faraway, so that he began to regret listing his engagements. Even when she was sad she was immensely beautiful. The vivacity which animated her features when she smiled gave way to a near tragic mask when she was upset or moved, but she made congratulatory noises and encouraging comments at the right moments in his catalogue. They finished their drinks and paid and again found themselves blinded by the bright outside.

"What are you doing now?" she asked.

"I think I'll just ....go for a walk around the city for a bit and then go and have a lie down back at the hotel. What about you?"

"I must go and find a little present for my daughter. If I go away I always try to bring a little something from where I've been, so I look in the shops for something Swedish from Göteborg."

"Well thanks for the company and I'll see you at the concert."

"See you Matthew." She gave him a beaming smile and a squeeze of the arm and then quite abruptly stepped forward, leaned up and kissed him on the cheek. He watched her daintily cross the road and skip up the step of a shop and disappear, and continued staring after her in confusion. It was totally unexpected and he wasn't at all sure what it meant. Was she just naturally coquettish and enjoyed flirting with him or did she mean something more? As he turned and walked the other way he reminded himself that although she was unbearably attractive and it was a very tempting opportunity, she was married and it was just a bit stupid to make out with a woman perhaps ten years his senior and the complications that might entail. But this thought didn't prevent him from turning over in his mind the possible delights that another twenty four hours in Sweden might afford with such a potential lover. She had a sophistication which he hadn't tasted before but had seen in other opera singers; a maturity and suggestion of wealth which suggested the Marschallin in Der Rosenkavalier rather than Maggie's chaotic bohemianism.

As he turned, he reflected on the intangibility of attraction. What was it about Caterina that was so attractive? Apart from her stunning looks and gorgeous figure there was something else, some vibration that resonated in him and felt 'right' that he couldn't pin down. Just an empathy with a like-minded artist he reckoned, but he missed that with Maggie, however much fun she was. 'Ah life's rich tapestry' he thought, and then set about directing himself to visit one of its threads which at the moment had totally wound its way into his heart.

Chapter 3

He strode out in the direction of the museum, filling his lungs with the cool late March air and squinting in the low-glancing sunlight reflecting off countless passing windowpanes.

As he walked towards the scene of yesterday's euphoric experience his anticipation grew, his senses primed by Caterina's tantalising looks and gently exuding perfume. Why was he now crunching his way across this gravel square eager to revisit those rushes of emotion which had fled through his body yesterday, when there was an equally goddess-like form browsing through a gift shop ten minutes away, apparently eager to visit some similar emotions with him? What power drew him from Caterina's captivating charisma to the silent stone in the museum? He didn't know, but knew only that he was now hurrying there again full of expectation to indulge this wild fantasy. Flashes of images darted into his brain, snapshots of the blinding white statue in a subdued room vied for his attention with glimpses of Caterina's haunting visage framed with fur.

He hurried up to the entrance whilst extracting his wallet from an inside pocket and paid the admittance fee in the vestibule. Walking up the stairs it was difficult to gauge whether his increased heart rate was more attributable to the exertion or his sense of anticipation. Again he experienced that dryness in his mouth and by the time he reached the entrance to the room the adrenalin was certainly pumping. He stopped at the door as before and sudden disappointment cut his mood, felling his high expectation at a stroke. There were people in the room. He was shocked. In his mind's eye the room was empty, as it had been yesterday, and he'd foolishly assumed that it would be the same today. He somehow hadn't conceived of the possibility that there might be other visitors, but had projected this desirable ideal into his imagining, that he would have her all to himself, that he would be able to commune in sacred solitude with the object of his passion.

The spell was broken. The sanctity of his intimacy had been violated by these predators who now greedily soaked up her image, feasting their eyes on her delicate nakedness, soiling her image with their gloating glances. His irrationality in this was, he realised, spectacular, like some peevish four-year-old jealous of a treasured toy which he will not share, despite the parents' embarrassed imprecations. The loss was almost tangible, a bubble of joy burst by a mundane reality, his silly little make-believe world, conjured from a ridiculous obsession, squashed under the foot of the pragmatic present.

He went into the room sulkily, resentfully watching the people dawdling around her, hating their peering necks and leaning, scrutinising heads. He just wanted them to go, to leave him alone with her. It was childish, incredible and pathetic he knew, but this fragile, shimmering image had taken on an iconic status in his thoughts and seeing its original so unceremoniously scoured by crude culture-lust cut into him. As he perambulated around them they began to disperse, disjointedly drifting out to the adjoining room. A stillness crept into the room and flowed over him as he breathed more freely and began to relax, reassured of his intimacy now. He tried to recollect yesterday's atmosphere, to summon her aura and inspire those keen tender rushes of sublime ecstasy which had electrocuted and infected his reason. He approached the plinth tentatively, taking in once again the tantalising torso and breathless purity. Occasional torn threads of elation stimulated his sensual memory, ragged snippets of emotion that began to patch together the fabric of yesterday's experience and reassemble that radiant experience. A calmness fell over him as he let his eyes float over her, the glow of the glossy surfaces of her skin suffusing with an ever more intense light. The more he looked on her the brighter she grew, her face seemed to relax and her muscles loosen to a limp lethargy. He breathed slowly, quietly and deeply as the suspended silence settled.

A dull distant cacophony echoed in the corridor outside, a growing, swelling rumble of tramping feet and excited voices with a single more strident commanding voice pitching above the rest. In a jostling ungainly surge a group of children spilled into the room with a teacher chivvying them. Matt drew back from the plinth, shocked by the sudden activity. The children began to crowd around her, pointing and grimacing, nudging each other and winking. Some of the boys facing her front started giggling and pushing each other, craning to get a view of her exposed intimacies and then falling back snorting with lascivious delight. The teacher managed to quieten them and began apparently, because Matt couldn't understand what she was saying, explaining about the work, pointing and gesticulating whilst the kids appeared interested, bored or amused. She cursorily indicated parts of the statue, the legs, the arms, the angle of the body and then drew attention to the area around the figure, which Matt couldn't see for the press of bodies. Some of the children started making hideous grimaces and laughed at each others' faces whilst the teacher tried to hold their attention. Realising that she was losing this battle she herded them, yelping and whooping, off into the next room.

Again he was left in the room with her, the atmosphere now torn and ripped, any chance of finding those precious feelings seemingly hopeless. He edged towards her, curious to see what the teacher had been pointing out, and was amazed to see what he had completely missed the day before. He must have been so engrossed in the figure that he had failed to see the setting and what surrounded it. He now saw that the figure reclined on a raft which was tied by a length of rope to a post which was supposedly sticking up from the surface of some water. Not only that, when he came to look closely there were ugly, leering faces and parts of faces emerging from the water. He was troubled by this new context in which she lay which changed the dynamic of the piece, suggesting alternative stories and hidden meanings. But this no longer seemed to matter. What mattered was that he'd been robbed of revisiting that special place he had discovered yesterday. The statue that now lay before him no longer resonated, no longer held that power to imbue him with extraordinary passion and euphoria. It had been violated first by the thoughtless, careless scrutiny of uncaring adults and then by the lurid thoughts and ribald jeering of mindless adolescents. He felt she had been raped, her aura destroyed, her sanctity adulterated.

He thought her face now seemed anguished. What he had taken to be ecstasy now seemed agony and the body was taut and stressed. The muscles appeared strained whereas before they had been languid, the head turned in hurt not rapture. How could he have mistaken, misinterpreted her expression? She was writhing in agony at the ogling faces protruding from the water, gloating at her vulnerability. It was a gesture of shame, the eyes closed with self loathing and the head turned askance to hide from the probing looks.

As he was about to leave, he noticed a small brass plaque fixed to the sloping side of the plinth:

"Näckrosen" designed by Per Hasselberg

Made by Christian Eriksson 1896

Näckrosen, Matt wondered what it meant. Rosen was possibly a rose, as in German, but Näck? He'd come across something similar in German meaning Nixie, another form of pixie or sprite? Possibly it was something like that. He turned despondently away and headed out of the room, out of the gallery.

He was about to stomp straight out of the museum but something made him pause and turn into the shop. He flicked through the cards on the stands, mostly of paintings, but couldn't see one of the statue. He was again about to leave but then decided to ask the assistant at the counter.

"Excuse me, do you have a card of the statue on the top floor. It's a reclining female nude...19th century I think?"

"Ah yes, Näckrosen." She sighed. "It's very popular. Just a moment." She turned and looked through a long drawer behind her and shortly turned back with a postcard.

"Here you are," with a forced smile and knowing look that suggested she knew exactly why he'd want that particular card and why they kept running out on the stand; because men are all the same and can't resist a picture of a nude woman.

Matt paid and left, annoyed that he'd succumbed to his whim of buying it and angered that he should allow himself to feel shame at having wanted to. He returned to the hotel feeling empty. Once back in his room he slumped down on the bed and took out the postcard which passively stared back at him, plain and cool. No emotions, no auras, just a photograph of a lump of marble, skilfully sculpted into smooth scallops of form. Näckrosen. What was that? A nymph? 'Nymph in thy orisons, be all my sins rememb'red'. Hamlet's words hit him and he somehow felt guilty. Sins. Was it a sin to be stimulated by such an image?

He looked again at the postcard. A technical exercise in 3D, an anatomical masterpiece conjuring still life. But life that is still isn't life. Life moves and changes, evolves, adapts. Dawkins and Darwin had told Matt so and he believed them.

He stared at the postcard in his hand and looked at the expression on her face. He couldn't say what it said to him now. Ecstasy? Agony? Maybe it depended on what you wanted to believe. Maybe it depended on the context. Maybe it meant different things to different people. Maybe it didn't mean anything at all. Maybe it didn't matter. Maybe nothing mattered.

Actually, something did matter and that, he reminded himself, was that he had to sing the Christus in an hour's time, and if he didn't he wouldn't get paid, and that mattered! So he forgot his scruples and took a shower preparatory to donning his tails and walking round to the church for Bach's "Passionmusik nach dem Evangelisten Matthäus", where there would be, after all, the pleasure of seeing the beautiful Caterina's sublime face and hearing the beautiful Caterina's sublime soprano. He perked up suddenly and King Philip once again reverberated in the flattering resonance of the shower cubicle.

Chapter 4

The first sombre chord ushered in the opening chorus and the celli and basses pulsed out their unerring beat as the bars of the Passion inevitably surged down the church over the sea of faces facing Matt. He was comfortably nervous; that is, excited enough to spark a dramatic performance yet absolutely in control to deliver a vocally accomplished rendition of his part. The other soloists had been predictably low key before the concert, being practised and professional they seemed not nervous, except for Gerhardt perhaps, whose role was so taxing. Caterina was looking breathtaking and had greeted him cryptically, neither suggestive nor demure, rather leaving every opportunity open and potential. She was all in black, very suitable for a passion, with a full length pleated silk skirt which helped to make her look taller. Above she wore a gorgeous open-weave latticework jacket, with small sparkles at the intersections, over a black silk bodice. The effect was both sober and glamorous, but the fact that you could see through the outer jacket to the figure-hugging bodice lent a certain frisson to the ensemble. Matt found it decidedly attractive and found it hard to keep his eyes off her.

He shifted slightly in his chair, the restriction of the tail coat and waistcoat, an ever present aggravation in these concerts, requiring occasional relief. The antiphonal choirs questioning and answering each other set up a reverberation down the church, their anxious staccato interjections thrown out into the nave over the tripleting swell of the orchestra, the whole over-arched by the long legato lines of the 'Ripieno' boys' choir from the gallery. Matt allowed himself to be swept up in the river of sound, the sonorities surging around him and buffeting his senses with irresistible force. As he got up to sing he felt joyful, inspired by the genius of the writing and the perfection of the music. He felt his voice flow out of him like a length of dark velvet as he relished mouthing the rich round vowels of the German text. He felt strong and defiant, a Christ with attitude who combined fierce confrontation with charismatic compassion. The muscular moving harmony of the accompaniment provided the strong framework over which his weaving vocal line wound, allowing for so much colour and interpretation in the sinuous dissonances of the word 'gekreuziget' – crucified.

He sat for the following chorale and looked out over the audience, which in Bach's day would have been a congregation. Funny, he thought, how words hold so much connotation. Congregation surely just means collection, gathering, but has a distinctly religious association. Audience, conversely, suggests theatre and spectacle.

Well, he supposed this was a spectacle really, certainly in its epic quality. As his eyes took in the rows of faces in front of him, many following the words in the programme, some with eyes closed, others gazing into the roof or investigating the musicians on the podium, his view passed, stopped and then re-viewed an upturned face. A pale, oval face whose eyes stared straight at him, apparently with astonishment. For the brief second of their locked look a thrill passed through his body, a fleeting shock of recognition, before he had to shift his gaze as if he hadn't caught her eye. Would he look again? He looked at his score and tried to refocus on the Passion.

'Then assembled together the chief priests, and the scribes, and the elders of the people, into the palace of the high priest who was called Caiaphas, and consulted that they might take Jesus by subtlety and kill Him' sang the Evangelist. Matt ventured another look. She was reading the programme and he was able to observe the top of her head, with its central parting of blonde hair swept back over the ears and tied behind. She looked young, maybe late 'teens, with intelligent questioning eyes. He looked away not wanting her to catch him viewing her and prepared to sing his next interjection. When he stood he noticed out of the corner of his eye that her eyes were fixed on him, and thought that when he sang she sat more upright. He rebuked his disciples for suggesting that the ointment the woman poured on his head was a waste; it was for his burial and her action was good.

He sat again and saw her eyes on him, an expression of deep concern and warmth emanating from them. He dared to hold her gaze which she unflinchingly maintained and it seemed an eternity before he self consciously had to look down. He felt a glow suffuse his head as if her eyes were radiating a halo of light around it. He tried to recall what it was he recognised about her. Something about her jogged a nucleus in his memory, but he couldn't think what it was. A sensation, a taste, a tiny remembrance of a feeling was evading capture in his mind and he couldn't search it out. When he again lifted his eyes out of his score, she was sitting with her eyes closed and her face slightly elevated, a frown on her forehead and a tension in her neck.

'Buss und Reu, Buss und Reu' the rich-voiced Alto sang, 'Grief for sin, grief for sin, rends the guilty heart within.'

Now he was able to study her face without fear of detection and appreciate that she was very attractive in an unsophisticated way. Her skin was very fair and clear and the features subtle and perfectly proportioned. There was nothing that stood out to catch attention but the whole effect was of natural simple beauty, untarnished by the application of cosmetics and artifice, striking in its purity.

'May my weeping and my mourning be a welcome sacrifice.'

As he watched, her features responded to the music, faint flickers of movement, denoting washes of emotion, sporadically flitting across her face.

A member of the choir stood up to sing the part of Judas, asking what he would be given to betray Jesus, and the thirty pieces of silver were agreed as the murder money. Matt looked across past the conductor to where Caterina now stood to sing the ensuing aria, and he was again struck by her stunning looks, enhanced by subtle make up, expensive coiffure and designer couture. She radiated cultivated elegance and as she began to sing the church was filled with that crystal clear but full throated bubble of sound, shimmering with heart-rending pathos. Matt looked back to the girl in the audience, who was sitting quite upright and still, looking above his head at something behind him. He realised this would be the huge crucifix suspended above the altar. She was staring as if transfixed, her eyes unblinking in total concentration. 'Blute nur du liebes Herz' – Now bleed, beloved heart – Caterina's voice soared higher, then held a long E natural on Herz, the tone scintillating in the acoustic, as Matt watched a glistening tear spill from the girl's eye and pearl down her cheek.

He was mesmerised by her hypnotic look. It was like watching someone in a trance, in a state of suspended animation, and he found himself concerned for her. But she remained peacefully pouring out some pent up grief, letting the flood of sound unleash some deep emotion that only she could know and explain. Caterina had started on the 'da capo', repeating the opening phrase even quieter than before and with a concentrated intensity as of someone privately crying a lullaby for comfort.

Matt had to recollect himself quickly when the Evangelist again stood to sing as there was only a short chorus before his next piece. When he delivered his forewarning recitative to his disciples he felt her attention fixed on him, and catching glimpses of her between phrases, saw that she was watching him with an intense expression. When he invited the disciples to eat his body and drink his blood, he found himself addressing her with his long arioso lyrical lines, assuring her that he wouldn't again drink wine until he would drink it with her in heaven.

He sat down and saw her radiant elated face shining a look of such ecstatic joy that he had to look away, sure that someone must notice this electric energy flickering between them. But as he took in the audience and those of the performers he could see, of course, they were completely oblivious to this interplay, which to him was so blatantly obvious. It was as if there was a supercharged highway between them in full view of hundreds of people, but completely hidden from them. He was unable to resist gazing into her uplifted face and she returned his gaze with a look of such extreme gentle devotion that he found it exquisitely difficult to concentrate on the performance.

Ich will dir mein Herze schenken
Senke dich, mein Heil, hinein!
Ich will mich in dir versenken;
Ist dir gleich die Welt zu klein,
Ei, so sollst du mir allein
Mehr als Welt und Himmel sein.

I will give You my heart,
Sink into You, my Saviour;
Wish to meld myself in Thee.
This world's too small,
But You, for me, shall more
Than earth and heaven be.

Caterina's spinning tone flew joyfully, dancing over the phrases whilst the two oboe d'amore chased each other underneath her, like two excited children encouraging each other in some wild, exuberant game.

After the initial excitement of the realisation of this apparent mutual attraction, Matt managed to calm himself and control his breathing to the extent that he felt again in command of his senses. The alternation of action and reflection, chorus and chorale, recitative and aria progressed the plot forward through Jesus' prediction of Peter's denial, the prayers on the Mount of Olives and culminated in the betrayal and arrest. Throughout his singing, Matt felt he was inevitably performing for her and when he wasn't he watched the delicate interplay of emotions move across her face as the story unfolded, each step on his road to Calvary registering as a tiny prick of pain.

She followed the text hungrily then would look up, either at the crucifix, a soloist or directly at Matt, and then often closed her eyes in reflection. When she did so, she often turned her head to the side as if she found it unbearable to continue listening, or maybe found the experience too moving. It was when she adopted this posture in the final benedictive chorus of the first part, with her head tilted and her pale neck stretched out and her skin seeming to glow with a cool luminous light against the background of dark coats and dimly lit pews, that her likeness resonated in his brain. The look of pain or hidden joy with eyes closed and lips slightly parted, that aura of private ecstasy, that purity and vulnerability so open and yet so secret, sent his thoughts racing back to the gallery and the euphoria of yesterday came flooding back with the realisation that she was 'her'. The face, the hair, the expression were hers and here was the warm, living, breathing, sentient manifestation of that cold, smooth sculpture, with hot blood coursing through her veins and myriad nerve endings, sensitised by the harmony, vibrating with emotion.

A subdued, respectful applause broke the atmosphere, the sound ricocheting off the walls in waves. Matt stood automatically when indicated by the conductor, but in a blur. He saw that she didn't clap, but crossed herself and knelt to pray. He left the stage without realising what he was doing and didn't really hear anything that was happening around him. It was as if he were wearing ear muffs and when Caterina approached to congratulate him on his performance he only heard her faintly and it was as much as he could do to return the compliment.

"Are you okay, Matthew?" she asked, concerned.

"Yes, I'm fine. Just feel a bit dizzy. Must have got up too quickly," he managed to reply.

"Will you be alright? I'll get you some water." She went off while he sat down on a convenient chair.

She's alive! The statue's alive!

Chapter 5

The seat was hard and unforgiving; stout, one hundred and fifty year old pine, worn smooth and shiny by the sliding off and re-seating of years of penitent parishioners kneeling to pray. But this discomfort didn't disturb her, merely acting as a gentle goad to alertness against any temptation to distraction.

Not that in her case there was any chance of that. She was totally involved in the proceedings, rapt in awe and devotion and an increasing feeling of destiny. She gazed humbly up at the enormous crucifix leaning at a precarious angle towards her. It seemed to be falling away from the wall but was somehow magically frozen in the act.

It was illuminated from either side by two cross lights showing the glossy sheen of the polished wood. The girl was fascinated. It was so beautiful, she thought, so amazingly life-like, the way the head fell lolling to one side with the thorns of the cruel crown piercing it; the slump of the body sagging under the exhausting weight; the legs crumpled together looking so painful.

She studied every detail of His body, the way the shadows fell in the gaps between His ribs, the tension in His arm muscles taking the strain of His torso, the stomach awkwardly collapsed inwards as if it had been punched by an enormous fist.

Poor Jesus. She could almost hear His gasping breath, could almost feel the pain. As she stared unblinking, her eye welled and a single tear pearled down her cheek. She wiped it away self-consciously and looked to see if anyone had noticed, but it was okay, no one had seen.

The music ebbed and flowed hypnotically as a background to her thoughts. Occasional wafts of incense enveloped her and she felt a bit sick, but she continued to stare at the cross. He had put up with His pain; she could put up with feeling sick.

It was the beginning of her commitment to Him, to suffer some discomfort, however small. She couldn't let Him do all the suffering for her sins. She must take some of it herself. And she would.

She wanted so much to serve Him, to make her life good and pure and devoted. And this was the beginning, when He would become a part of her.

Suddenly aware that there was a shuffling in the pews as people were preparing to get up, she knelt quickly to say a final prayer to her Lord Jesus; to forgive her sins; to free her from blame; to accept her as His loyal servant.

She hastily crossed herself before rising to queue with the others. Standing in the aisle she looked to where her parents were sitting and saw them beaming at her with encouragement and pride. Their little girl taking her first communion! She smiled, embarrassed, and looked away. They didn't understand how important this was for her. They thought it was just like when anyone else had their first communion, something that every Catholic child inevitably went through. Like her school friends standing in the queue. But it was different for her.

The priest was intoning as he blessed each bowed head and then gave the sacrament. As her turn approached, she became physically nervous, her legs shaking and her hands cold and clammy. She looked up at the cross again, at the rich brown wood of the carving and His sad face staring down accusingly it seemed. And she knew, knew as strongly as she knew anything in her little life, that this was her destiny.

The line of receivers moved forward step by step and she tried to concentrate on her Lord, but it was difficult when the others were shuffling and looking around with excitement. Why wouldn't they keep still? Sister Agnes had told them that they had to behave and not turn round. All Katya seemed to care about was her dress which she'd been bragging about for weeks, how her mother had taken her to this very expensive shop and how they'd bought the most beautiful one there. She knew that for Katya it was more important to look good.

The celebrant stood in front of her, the Host held in the Trinity of thumb and two fingers on the edge of the golden goblet.

"Signe" the acolyte whispered, reading off his list.

"Signe, receive the Body of Our Lord Jesus Christ which is given to you for the remission of sins". She crossed herself and he crossed her symbolically with the Host in the air and placed it in her uplifted con-cupped hands.

She could hardly feel it, this gossamer-thin, translucent wafer resting in her palm, light as Spirit. She murmured a final prayer then lifted the Body of Christ to her mouth and moved to the side to let the next communicant approach.

It wasn't at all what she had expected. She had thought it would dissolve, maybe effervesce slightly, like one of those sherbet surprises. But it just stuck like damp cardboard to the roof of her mouth.

She worked it with her tongue as she returned to her seat and managed to free it and chew it dryly. She swallowed the awkward lump which caught somewhere down her oesophagus causing her to repeat the action a few times to try to get it to go down, but with little saliva it was a slow progress.

Christ becoming part of her had been so far from her dream of how it would be that she was quite upset. She didn't feel any different.

Back in the pew with the others she knelt in prayer to try to recapture that special feeling she had had before, but it didn't come back.

"That wasn't too bad," Irma nudged her. "I didn't think much of the bread though. It was horrible wasn't it?"

"Ssh, we shouldn't be talking," Signe cautioned.

"Oh it's alright. Did you see the priest though? He was really weird. His eyes were all funny. He looked like..."

"You mustn't say that. It's blaspheming," Signe whispered urgently.

"No it isn't. I just said he looked weird."

"Yes but he's God's representative on earth, so if you say he looks weird you're saying God looks weird."

" No, but he ISN'T God."

"Yeah, but he's like God, because he works for God on earth and God's working through him," chimed in Kajsa in a loud whisper, who was sitting on the other side of Irma.

"Yeah but he's not God," repeated Irma.

"No, but God's inside him, doing the things he does," insisted Kajsa.

"What, all the time?"

"Yeah."

"Like when he goes for a poo?" She sniggered....

"Sssshh!"

"No. The big things he does, you know, like helping people and saying the Mass."

"But He can't be inside him all the time. What about the other priests?"

"He's inside them too."

"What all of them?"

"Irma, didn't you understand any of the communion classes?" intervened Signe, who didn't want to be part of this silly argument, but she couldn't just sit there whilst they got it all wrong!

"Course I did. But how can He be inside hundreds of people all at the same time!"

"Because He can. He's magic. He's omnivorous. Anyway, it's because of communion when we eat His body. So now He's in you too."

"And you."

"But He didn't taste very nice!" put in Kajsa.

The first communicants having all partaken of the feast, the congregation were now filing up for communion, and Signe's parents winked at her as they passed . Why would they DO that?

"Does that mean you're God now and I'm God?" Irma hazarded.

"A little bit. Well there's a bit of God inside you," said Signe.

Kajsa looked at her dress. "D'you think God likes wearing a dress? I bet He's really embarrassed!" she giggled.

"Maybe God's a girl." wondered Irma.

"Don't be stupid! How can He be a girl? They call Him He, so He can't be a girl. Anyway Jesus was a boy so that proves it!" said Kajsa triumphantly.

"Yeah but the Virgin Mary's a girl," retorted Irma.

"Yeah but she's not God. She was just ordinary before the pronunciation."

"But she's more important than Jesus."

"No she's not. It's just because she was His mother."

"Yeah but if it wasn't for Mary, Jesus wouldn't have been born, so she must be more important than Him."

"But if it hadn't been Mary it would have been someone else."

"How do you know?"

"Anyway, she wasn't pregnant."

"Yes she was. She just wasn't...you know...she didn't do it with anyone."

"Yeah, so she wasn't pregnant."

"Yes she was. It was a spectacular connection."

"No stupid, it's a miraculous inspection."

"You mean the immaculate conception," corrected Signe.

"Whatever. Anyway God did it to her by magic." assured Kajsa.

"What, because He was inside her all the time?"

"I suppose so," conceded Kajsa.

The last of the congregation had returned to their seats and the celebrant was finishing up any remaining crumbs and washing them down with a chalice of blood.

"Had she had first communion then?"

"Must have done," said Kajsa. There was a pause.

"Does He still make people pregnant by magic?" asked Irma, obviously concerned.

"Nye, He's too old now," Kajsa said confidently.

Their theological deliberations were summarily interrupted by the tinkling of the bells signifying the end of communion.

"Dominus vobiscum," he intoned.

"Et cum Spiritu tuo." they replied.

****

She flung off her coat and ran up the stairs.

"Signe, don't be long. They'll be here soon," her mum called up the stairs after her.

She slammed her bedroom door and tore at the buttons of the silly dress, ripping it over her head and furiously throwing it on the floor. The crisp, cold sheets shocked her skin in that way she loved before the cotton responded to her body heat, the duvet suffocating her warmth in its downy depths. Under the duvet with Jopi she curled herself into her usual coil with him in the crook of her arm and the middle fingers of that hand rammed between her teeth. The outer fingers gently stroked either side of her nose which calmed her as she suckled.

She remembered the first time she had got into pure cotton sheet and duvet cover after she had got that rash that wouldn't go away. A skin specialist they had taken her to had advised trying natural unbleached cotton, which her mum had to iron or it was full of wrinkles, and the rash had got better, so now she always had crisply ironed, coolly crinkling cotton next to her skin.

She didn't like her pyjamas. When her parents had kissed her goodnight she would take them off in the glow of the lava lamp and slip back between the pristine sheeting. She loved to feel the weight of the toggy duvet pressing the pure material against her body, like a big fluffy cumulo nimbus resting its soft heaviness on her.

It reminded her of the nun at first school who had hugged her into her starchy white pinafore when she had fallen in the playground; an almost brutal embrace, crushing her face into the crackling white bib of her bosom which absorbed her fought-back tears.

Since then she had associated crisp white cotton with sanctity and purity; the priest's vestments, the altar cloths, the stiff white serviettes of the celebrants, the nun's habits. They all had that rustling purity.

Now as she lay cocooned in cotton, she felt she was purified and she relaxed her tensioned muscles. Jopi was slowly released from the intense scissor-clamp of her arm lock and the fingers eventually re-appeared.

"It was all wrong Jopi. It wasn't supposed to be like that," she whispered, holding him to face her in the dimness of the luminous under-cloud. "There were so many people and the girls were fooling around and not taking it seriously. Sister Agnes will be so angry and I hate it when she gets upset. She said this is such an important day and now they've gone and spoilt it all."

Jopi looked back at her noncommittally in the gloom. He didn't say anything. He never did, he just was there, her silent confidant for all her problems and secrets. He'd heard it all over the years, the tears, the fears; the joys, the ploys. He never teased her like Lars, told her off like her Dad or made her feel bad like her Mum. He just listened tacitly and was there for her and that's what she loved about him.

"Signe, come on, Uncle Mats and Auntie Agi are here. They want to see you," her Mum's voice echoed up the wooden staircase and muffled through the duvet.

Signe's face screwed up and Jopi involuntarily head-butted her as he found himself pulled into her violently.

"Not Uncle Mats," she moaned, "he'll just get drunk again and tell those stupid jokes." Jopi suffered the usual indignity of having his nose rubbed against her forehead, re-polishing its already shining patina. "And I don't like Marta; she always makes fun of me because I'm shorter than her although we're the same age."

"SIGNE....."

She realised it was no good and she'd have to go down. Jopi fell on the floor as she threw off the covers and pulled on her favourite jeans and jumper. She only ever wanted to wear these, whatever the weather. They were 'her'. They were the way she felt normal – not that stupid dress! Her thick blond hair was a mess after rolling under the duvet and she dragged a hairbrush through it, forcing the splines to separate the strands. Her brushing became less vigorous as it de-tangled and she stroked its rich thickness, arranging it around her shoulders, watching herself in the mirror.

She stumped down the stairs as more people arrived – neighbours, friends, family. It was the usual social occasion, like Christmas and Birthdays, when her mum insisted on having lots of people round and spent the previous few days fretting about preparing the food, baking traditional recipes and worrying about whether there would be enough. Her mum and dad always ended up having an argument about it. He always said, why did she go to all the trouble? Why didn't she just buy ready-made stuff from the supermarket and save all the work? She said, because that wouldn't be right and her mother had always done things properly and she was going to do the same. Then they'd start shouting at each other, although afterwards they said they were just arguing and having a discussion, but they weren't, they were shouting!

When she was little she would hide with Jopi under the sideboard and tell him she was never going to get married. She would live with him in a little house by a lake and an elk would come every day and bring them milk and Gwendolyn cakes. She loved Gwendolyn cakes because they were the best cupcakes and had hazelnuts on the top. Her mum always made them for special occasions. There would be some today, which was one of the only good things left now.

"Oh Signe, why have you taken off your dress?" her mum cried as she walked into the kitchen. "It looked so lovely and we wanted some pictures with everyone."

"It was itching," she lied. She had prepared that fib as she knew her mum wouldn't argue about it.

"Oh that's a real shame, darling. Never mind. You looked lovely in the church."

"Hi Aunt Agi."

"Hello darling, you looked really beautiful," Aunt Agi gave her one of her big hugs.

"Now just take these and put them on the table, there's a good girl." Her mum continued fussing with the arrangements. Signe turned with the bowls and went into the dining room.

"Well, look who it is. Here's the girl of the moment! Hey, brown eyes, why did you take your dress off? You looked so nice."

"They're hazel, not brown," she said.

Uncle Mats finished off the bottle of beer and put it down before giving her a chest hug, scrunching her nose into his tie. "Now you, young lady, were a star in the service. A real little angel. Hey, Elizabetta and Marta are in the den." He took another bottle from the table and turned to Mr Munsen from next door, who said "Hi, Signe."

She didn't want to go to the den, but she felt she had to. That's what she was expected to do. Kids were supposed to go 'play', as if that was something really exciting. They always ended up getting some toy out they'd played with tons of times before or played a game on the Wii they had all done to death. It was boring. What they really wanted to do was look at YouTube or watch a DVD, but they weren't allowed to because it was a social occasion.

"Hi, Marta."

"Hi. Where's your dress?"

"Took it off."

"Oh."

"What you doing?"

"Nothing."

Signe sat on a beanbag. Marta was lying on the futon; Elizabetta was playing a game on her mobile on the floor.

"Your priest's weird." Marta announced.

Signe knew Marta would want to get at her somehow and immediately felt defensive, anticipating a criticism of the service and therefore an opportunity to score points.

"He's not my priest. He's just here doing the First Communion. I've never even seen him before."

"He's still weird."

There was a pause. Signe didn't want to fight with Marta. She wished they could be friends.

"What was your first communion like?"

"Never had one."

"But you're Catholic right?"

"Well, we started off being, but Mum said we didn't have to go anymore if we didn't want to."

"Really? So you're not anymore?"

"Don't know. Suppose not."

"But, what about when you die?"

"What d'you mean?"

"Well what happens to you then, where do you go?"

"Dad says we come back as someone else. Like a different person."

"Why?"

"Don't know but that's what he believes."

Signe felt worried for Marta, because if she didn't go to church anymore she'd surely go to Hell. "Does that feel frightening?"

"Sounds kind of fun. D'you want to play on the Wii?"

"Sure."

Chapter 6

The applause sputtered out as the soloists filed into the vestry for the second time after taking their final bows. There then followed much embracing and back-slapping. Mutual admiration was rife and acclaims of each other's vocal prowess met with protestations of humility in the presence of a greater artist. And so the friendly massaging of egos was mutually enjoyed and by common consent the concert was hailed as a triumph.

"Are you okay Matt?" Caterina looked up into his face, concern in those eyes. He wanted to kiss her, enfold that enticingly packaged body with his arms and taste her mouth.

"I'm fine thanks." He couldn't tell her that the second half of the concert had banished the thought he'd had in the interval, namely that he'd imagined those looks in the first half. In the second half she had definitely looked directly at him and he had returned her look. They would hold each other's gaze until one of them had given in and looked away. It had become a game of dare in which the frisson was delicious. How long could they lock eyes? How long could they dare to stare?

"So are you going to escort me, my handsome Jesus?" Caterina slunk her arm through his after the general post-concert chat had subsided.

"But of course, my fair Madonna, where would you like me to take you?" Matt responded, taking up the theme.

"Why, to feasting and making merry my Lord!" she replied with a wicked smile.

God, her eyes were just amazing he thought as he looked down at her. When they shone like that and laughed at him it was such a come on. Did she mean to be so forward?

"Did My Lady have a particular restaurant in mind?" he said, feeling slightly disconcerted now that she seemed to be expecting him to make the decision and not quite sure where this game was going.

"No, silly, just to the reception naturally. Remember I told you there would be food for us?" She squeezed his arm and chortled her descending arpeggio in affectionate teasing.

Matt felt stupid, having completely forgotten their conversation at lunch, other things having rather filled his mind in the intervening few hours.

"Hi everyone, they arrange some cars to take you to the reception. They leave in about five minutes," maestro Kalput announced, coming into the choir room with a bundle of orchestral parts which he slid into a folder.

"Where's the reception then?" Matt queried.

"Oh it's just down in the harbour on the Barken Viking ship. You must have seen it, opposite the opera house."

"Oh yes," he said, remembering the unmissable four-masted sailing cutter dominating the view at the end of the main shopping boulevard.

"Let's walk," Caterina suggested excitedly. "It's only about ten minutes and it's a lovely evening." He looked at her smiling face, like a little girl with a new idea eagerly wanting a parent's permission.

"Yeah, I'd like that too."

"Markus, we're going to walk. We'll see you there, okay?"

"Yes, okay. We see you there."

They donned their coats and clicked across the marble floor of the all but empty church. The audience had gone and there was just a man clearing the orchestral chairs and music stands. After the acoustic upheaval of Bach's music flooding the space, the church had now settled back into its accustomed vaulted stillness, broken only by the reverberation of reverent steps, hollow coughs and whispered benedictions.

Issuing out of the main doors they were greeted by the lights of the shop fronts and houses across the canal which ran in front of the church, the reflections glistening on the still surface of the water. It was an unseasonably balmy evening for spring, but as Matt had been told, Gothenburg was often called 'Little London' as the weather was very similar – changeable, wet and very different from the expected Scandinavian archetype further north.

They went down the granite steps to the roadway by the canal side and wandered along its edge.

"This could be Venice," she said and sighed as she leant on his arm. "Beautiful."

They wandered onto the bridge spanning the canal in front of the church and leant on the balustrade and looked up the length of the waterway, so still and peaceful. The lights in the church illuminated the stained glass windows like open advent calendar doors in the dark mass of the outlined building. Minutes passed and Matt again caught wafts of her perfume on the delicate breeze as she nestled next to him.

"What are you thinking?" he said, desperately wanting to kiss her.

"We had our honeymoon in Venice," she replied dryly.

The silence that followed was awkward, pregnant with possible meaning that he felt he couldn't presume to question. He expected every second that she would expound in some way, shed some light on that barren statement that she had left hanging in the air. He was just on the point of trying to pry out some further information when she said "We'd better go," breaking the stillness, "or they'll be waiting for us," and she steered him off the bridge and along the street. They walked along the canal side, she linking his arm again, but seemingly withdrawn, melancholic. A tension had suddenly come between them and he found an awkwardness in breaking through it. He had to make an effort to broach a subject.

"Who are the sponsors?" he ventured. He'd seen their name all over the programme with a caption, but as this was all in Swedish he was none the wiser.

"Oh they are Scania Investment Bank – SCIB. They used to be called Scania Allied Bank and this is part of their re-branding this year."

Matt thought quickly and laughing hollowly said, "If they had used the same form of abbreviation, I'm not surprised they wanted to change their name!"

"Why is that?" she said, not getting it.

"Well if it was Scania Allied Bank presumably it would have been abbreviated to SCAB which isn't very flattering, but appropriate for a bank these days," and he laughed again.

"What is scab?"

"It's a very insulting term – usually shouted by union members on strike at colleagues who cross picket lines." She looked like she didn't completely understand. "Strike breakers? But it's actually the word to describe the dried blood which covers a cut. You know, it falls off eventually."

"Ah yes, I know, Rupi in Finnish. We have another word for strike –breakers, Rikkuri. I see what you mean. Yes scab would not be good for a bank." She giggled. The atmosphere had passed.

They rounded the corner as they came out of the square onto the main boulevard and "There it is, the Viking," she chimed, delight again in her voice, and he saw the rigging illuminated by floodlight against the inky sky. She seemed again excited by the thought of the reception and started chattering about how she'd been on the boat before and that it was also a hotel and that she'd love to stay there sometime. Blue trams whooshed past them, the pedestrian warning bells clanking by the crossings and the wheels rattling in the rails. Glimpses of passengers passing in the sudden brightness of the lit carriages reminded him of a Hopper painting and the fleeting transience of the caught image.

When they reached the end of the street the opera house loomed out of the night, its profile like the ghostly prow of the Flying Dutchman's ship, cutting across the sky. Its sleek modern lines of glass and brushed aluminium challenged the old cutter moored across the harbour which faced it, like some impotent old relic of a slower era. But it was to the erstwhile ocean-goer which now housed a hotel, not to the opera house masquerading as a ship, that they now made their way, crossing the roadways down to the harbour front to the oily water lapping idly in the still night.

The spars of the masts rose majestically above them as they crossed the gangway into the vessel.

They were greeted by a SCIB representative and directed up the stairs to a reception area thronged with people. It was a small space and they had to squeeze their way through to where the sponsors had formed a receiving line at the far end. They were introduced and given drinks and it was unfortunately 'stage-managed' such that the soloists were shared out into different groups, so Matt wasn't able to flirt with Caterina anymore. He stood surrounded by enthusiastic Swedes all eager to use their excellent English. Some were associates of the bank, some were their guests and some local dignitaries.

Matt found these receptions were normally tedious, with the usual endless questions about the singer's life and comments about his good fortune in working at something he loved and most people only enjoyed in their leisure time. But although he was irritated by them, he always had to remind himself, as in the concert, what a privilege it was to work in such an environment. However, the usual trivialities of conversation turned to the more interesting topic of Bach and baroque performance, period instruments and the merit of authentic interpretation as against modern rendition. This was a subject Matt knew about and enjoyed discussing, and the elderly gentleman who brought it up was well informed and had some good points to make. He said he preferred performances at baroque pitch on period instruments with their mellower sound. He had found the bright sound of the orchestra too romantic.

"Yes, and of course it makes quite a difference for a singer when the pitch is higher," Matt replied. "It may not seem much, but that semi-tone can make quite a difference to the technical ease of a piece and there are natural limits to the range of a voice which don't really apply to instruments."

Matt found he was getting quite hot, now onto a second glass of this punch thing which seemed to be a Swedish speciality, and he availed himself of his 'special concert handkerchief' to wipe his face and looking around noticed that the room seemed even more crowded. Then, suddenly, there she was, in the doorway, gazing at him. He couldn't look away. God she was so pretty, so natural, so innocent.

".....don't you think?" His elderly friend was leaning towards him earnestly. Matt had completely missed the whole of this last sentence.

"Er, yes. Exactly," he said, as he forced himself back to the conversation.

"But you see for me, this is the end of live performance. It's no longer so special. We can get a performance whenever we want it at the touch of a button. Think of the people in Bach's time. It was so special for them. No recordings, so this music was a big day for them, a big event......"

The old gentleman prattled on, now well into his stride and enjoying his topic. Matt nodded and occasionally put in a 'yes' or 'absolutely', but fortunately he didn't need to say much as his companion was quite happy it seemed airing his opinions to the small group. They, who had been a little out of their depth in the baroque pitch evaluation, apparently felt more confident to join in now that the subject had turned to classical recording generally and then more specifically to i-players, downloads and the various wonderfully convenient ways one can now appreciate music.

He hardly concentrated on the conversation, just nodded and smiled, his mind dwelling on other images. So she was here. Would he meet her? Would he get to talk to her, find out what it was that moved her so much? She was obviously religious, but he'd never seen someone quite so engulfed by a performance as she had seemed to be. And why had she stared at him so? She was quite young. Did she find him attractive or was it more the story of the Passion that enthralled her? But she had just locked eyes with him again. It was intriguing and tantalising.

He looked to where she had been by the door, but of course she wasn't there any longer and a quick search of the room above the heads of the crowd didn't find her. He would maybe try to see her later, manage to bump into her accidentally and initiate a conversation. He had no idea how, but he desperately wanted to meet her face to face. It would complete his little narrative, his silly obsession and it titillated his imagination.

The conversation in the group began to flag and it was therefore opportune that they were at this point called away to a private party with the other soloists. They were ushered down two flights of stairs into the hold area of the ship where one of the conference rooms had been made over to a dining room. The other soloists were there with a selection of 'suits' of both sexes and it became apparent that there were to be some speeches before the food. He found himself standing next to the tall Latvian, Artis, who whispered in his ear as quietly as his enormous voice could manage, "This is the boring bit" and winked. Matt looked around, hoping that no one had heard this not very successfully private comment and then smiled back and murmured, "Yes, looks like it". Caterina was just across the room and smiled at him, raising an eyebrow slightly, he thought as if to say "Ah, there you are, handsome. I'm over here. Why don't you come and get me!"

Jeez, what was it about that woman? She was just playing it so hot! If she didn't want him to seduce her, she was certainly giving him completely the wrong signs. That double bed in his room was just crying out for him to throw her, giggling mischievously, onto its generous covers and discover her secrets.

His lascivious musings were interrupted by a tray of full champagne glasses which had appeared in front of him. He and Artis both took one, toasted each other and had a swig, before realising that they were supposed to be waiting for a toast which apparently was about to be made by a grey-haired suit standing at a microphone on a lectern which had the SCIB logo in a vinyl graphic emblazoned across its front.

"Mina damer och herrar..." He spouted forth in Swedish for a while, Matt amused, as always, by the occasional English word or phrase which jumped out incongruously - 'fiscal deficit, austerity'.

He eventually changed to English, thanking the soloists for their wonderful singing and the conductor for such a moving concert. He was proud that SCIB had been able to fund the concert. The bank was keenly aware of their social duties in the city of Göteborg and wanted to help promote a platform for great music to be heard live in the city. He would like to take this opportunity to announce funding for the choir for the next year, something about concerts in the coming season, at which point Artis leaned into Matt and gravelled quietly "This is all very interesting. What he doesn't tell you is these bank was in the news not long ago. They, how do you say.....make a bad deal with property developer. He was bad man and the bank they pretend they don't know about him, but the authorities they investigate and find the bank they must know the deal was dodgy. They find bank would have make big money selling mortgage through property developer. Now they try make bank look better again putting money in local choir. You know, image, working in community. Is not so nice as you think, eh?"

"Ah, I see" Matt whispered. "Bit of a PR exercise!"

"What is PR?"

"Public Relations. You know, how the company appears to the public"

"Yes this is it. This is very important for them, specially now. Many people don't like banks."

"No, or bankers either. In English it rhymes with a rude word!"

"Yes?"

"Yeah," Matt gave a very subtle rendition of the international gesture for those of the self gratification inclination!

"Ah yes! Wankers!" Artis said, which as he was starting to laugh came out rather louder than the rest of the conversation.

The effects of the champagne combined with the formality of the address and the need for decorum then of course had the reverse effect and made them collapse into schoolboy giggles and they had to turn away to the wall with shoulders heaving.

At that moment there was applause for the speaker, who then was answered by the conductor who wanted to say his thanks on behalf of the choir and orchestra, for the concert funding and for the commitment for the future. He spoke at length during which time Matt and Artis managed to control themselves, wipe their eyes and turn round once more.

Looking across the room Matt caught Caterina's eye, or rather both eyes with both eyebrows raised this time, apparently commenting on their bad behaviour. Matt was by now so well-oiled with the champagne, which had again just been re-charged, that he wanted to say to her 'Look, sweetheart, if you think that's bad behaviour, you just come back to my room and I'll show you bad behaviour!' which he fancied he in part conveyed, as she appeared to reply with a twitch of the mouth which seemed to say 'Ok, big boy!'

Finally the speeches were over and after further applause everyone sat at the tables. They were allocated places and Matt got to sit opposite Caterina and could flirt silently across the table.

They began with salmon in the Scandinavian style Matt recognised as Gravad Lax and then went on to a cold chicken platter, rather like coronation chicken he thought, and he had to chat to the 'banker' on his right who was okay but a bit uptight. His big interest was fishing, which for Matt was about as interesting as observing the desiccation of Dulux, but he hoped he made the right noises in the appropriate places. He was actually a bit pissed, he had to admit, and also was being distracted by playing a surreptitious eyebrow game with Caterina. It obviously began with her one eyebrow raise, but by now had taken on extreme notions of suggestion which they played out wickedly across the space between them, whenever the opportunity allowed. It was supremely playful, suggestive and erotic and Matt found himself in a state of excitement throughout the meal.

Eventually Matt found he needed the toilet and excused himself just before the dessert. Getting up from the table he found he had to adjust himself to avoid embarrassment. He winked at Caterina, who returned it with a flash of her eyes as he passed. What a woman! He found he had to go up to the next deck to reach the toilets and had a certain amount of difficulty manoeuvring himself to get the pee directed into the bowl. Women just have no idea how difficult it is to pee when a bloke's in the ascendancy, he thought, as he gave his John Thomas a few good old pulls to clear his throat.

When he emerged he thought he'd see if he could get a bit of fresh air to clear his head. The toilets were on the entrance level so he took the lift up to the top deck and opening the metal door was greeted by a fabulous cool breeze. There was a fine moon up and a wonderful inky black sky with the brightest stars glistening their multi-million-miles' lights.

Every time he thought of those astronomical figures he was stunned by the enormity of the universe, the billions of stars and millions of galaxies, the unbelievable numbers of space and time.

And to think that until comparatively recently in Man's history they believed it was all created about two and a half thousand years BC.

He stepped out across the deck to the rail and took some deep draughts of clear cold air and felt fresher. It was one of those nights when the moon casts distinct shadows and captures the crystalline outlines of every object. He looked out across the quay to the city lights and took in the glow of the city's nightscape. It was good to be alive and feel such vigour in his body and he revelled in the chill of the air and the infinity of the firmament.

He had been there a couple of minutes he supposed when suddenly the door he'd just come through opened and turning he saw a form flash briefly in the light-spill from the corridor before the door swung to again, returning the scene to moonlight. He could see a figure in the shadow of the ship's bulk, the moon being away from it. It seemed to sway slightly and then proceeded to walk out across the deck away from him and as it did so the moon illuminated the fair head and small stature of a young woman. She obviously hadn't seen him, as Matt was standing some way to the left of her, further along from the door.

She began talking to herself, disjointedly, but of course he couldn't understand what she was saying. She followed an erratic path and appeared to become increasingly unsteady as she walked further. Matt thought she looked imminently in danger of falling over and so moved out into the open ready to assist her. She was not looking in his direction but seemed to be making for the rail at the other side of the boat. He followed her, getting closer, and in his concentration felt more sober himself. The moon shone a silver beam across the water in the harbour and she was a dark outline in its midst. He felt he ought to make sure she was okay and so moved quickly towards her.

"Are you alright?" His voice echoed slightly in the still space before the reverberations died. She stopped and turned to him, shocked maybe at finding she wasn't alone. She looked at him, he thought, as if she'd seen a ghost, with a mixture of fright and surprise, which turned to wonder and relief. He stood facing her in the moonlight, her face in shadow, with his arms slightly raised and turned out, questioning, unsure what to do, not wanting to invade her privacy but indicating he was there to help if she needed him. She murmured something unintelligible and Matt, anticipating instinctively that she was about to fall, rushed over the few feet between them to catch her as she fainted.

What to do now? he wondered. Better find somewhere to lay her down. With an effort he scooped her up, not easy for a tall man getting underneath a collapsed body, which, as he soon found, appeared incredibly heavy. When she was lying in his arms and he turned to go back towards the body of the ship the moonlight fell right across her face and he saw that it was her.

His whole body flooded with electricity. He was holding her, the statue, the girl in the audience, the being with whom he'd shared so many secret glances and so many locked-in looks. It was a miracle. What was she doing out here on her own, wandering about as if drunk and then fainting in his arms?

Looking about he noticed that there were cushioned benches along the sides of the ship's house with awnings above. He went to put her down on one and as he moved she stirred, murmuring again, and her head rolled in his arm towards his chest. He looked down at her face, the alabaster skin glowing in the moonlight and the image in the gallery flicked into his mind. Here was the living, breathing, sleeping reality in his arms. He took in the contours of the clothes covering the curves of her body, the folds in the loose jumper and full skirt. But he knew those contours, knew every curve and cleft, so keenly etched in his mind's eye.

The temptation was too great and he leant down and tasted those parted lips, drank in their soft sweetness and felt her exhalation caress his cheek. He knew it was wrong – she was drunk and comatose – but being somewhat drunk himself and certainly drunk with lust having been primed by Caterina and now fired by this chance encounter, he was bursting with contained passion. He drew back slightly to view her face again. Her lips had parted and were now suffused with a delicate pink which was colouring her cheeks as well. He could just see the tip of her tongue glistening, hiding behind her pearly teeth. It twitched slightly with each breath, tormenting him, tempting him to taste its tenderness. He held his breath, hardly daring to hope she'd lie thus for longer, his heart thumping in his chest. Could he just steal another kiss without waking her? Could he slip into her mouth secretly like a moth in the night to steal her nectar and slip away unnoticed? Time stood still. He pulsed with expectation. It would have to be gentle – oh, so slow and gentle.

His muscles trembled with the strain of holding her so long as he again descended to her upturned face, tantalising himself with deliberate slowness and welcoming the soft cushion of her lips meeting his. With agonising delicacy he allowed his tongue to slide smoothly through her parted lips and find the hidden tip of hers. He felt a ripple of response in her body and as he withdrew she opened her eyes with a look of complete astonishment, wide-eyed, unbelieving, trying desperately to take in what she saw. Sweat trickled in the small of his back. Her eyes struggled.

Sudden recognition swept her face, her eyes filled with tears and she clasped his face with both her hands and drank deeply of him in an embrace which was at the same time fiercely passionate and excruciatingly tender. He responded with shocked but enthusiastic reciprocation, lowering her onto the bench and settling himself gently upon her. Their kisses were deep and desperate, she shuddering with enormous emotion as if releasing a lifetime of suppressed desire, clinging to him with a passion that took his breath away.

In the wild gentleness of their embraces he managed to fumble open his fly and free himself to lie next to her, his practised hand gently sliding her skirt up. She was fixated on his face, cupping his cheeks and franticly engulfing him with her love. He pushed upwards, caressing her curving haunches – *My God she's wearing silk underwear.* His senses thrilled as he yearned upwards to his desired spot. He became restricted in the slippery garment, his excitement now welling up uncontrollably, when she suddenly screamed, a piercing hysterical scream that shattered the night, as she pushed him with incredible force off the bench to land heavily on the deck.

Panicking, he grabbed himself together and tried to shush her, pleading with her to be quiet, but she continued to scream uncontrollably, writhing as if she had been stung, oblivious to anyone or anything.

Suddenly, running shoes clopped on the wooden deck boards and immediately two silhouettes dashed around the corner of the ship house, a girl and a man.

"Si...Si," the girl jabbered away in Swedish, kneeling down by the girl on the bench, who was now curled in the foetal position, clinging to herself and wailing a wolf-wail of utter despair.

Matt was reeling. He'd hit the floor hard and jarred his head and bruised his shoulder. He gathered himself together as best he could, getting up off the floor.

"What have you done to her?" the black-haired girl shouted at him in English.

"I......I didn't hurt her." He blurted. "She's not........hurt" he repeated. He couldn't think how to say it more accurately, but delicately. The man just stood there, apparently not knowing what to do, but occasionally said something to the dark-haired woman who jabbed short sentences back at him.

Suddenly more people appeared on deck and Matt was immediately aware of his compromised situation. His tailcoat was all awry, his white waistcoat skewed round with the back buckle showing and his bowtie had come undone and hung limply down his front.

There was now quick-fire conversation between the black-haired girl and the persons who had just arrived. Questions and answers, questioning looks, shrugs, accusatory looks at him and questions to the girl on the bench who was still keening and rocking herself.

"Si, Si," the black-haired girl kept repeatedly asking her a question to which she made no reply.

One of the persons who had come, now rushed off as if a course of action had been decided upon. Matt stood there hardly knowing what to do, what he **could** do. He was incapable of thinking straight. What had happened? Had he penetrated her? He had certainly come, that was obvious and tangible. But she had wanted him. She had engulfed him with her ardour, dragging his face into her, desperate to love him.....

"Si....Si," again the repeated question at which the girl this time replied with a hoarse yell, "Ya, Ya" and collapsed into uncontrollable, shuddering weeping.

The black-haired girl glared at him with ferocity and again fired some staccato sentences at the other three persons and the man she was with. They looked at him coldly.

"Matthew I don't know what has happened here, but we need to sort this out," the man said. "I have to ask you to stay here."

"Absolutely," Matt stammered. He suddenly recognised the man as the cellist from the orchestra. "I'm sure I can explain everything. She's...she's okay. She's not......hurt, you know. I think she's a bit drunk, and shocked. I found her wandering about and brought her here to lie down. I think she got quite a shock when she saw me. She was, well, she'd kind of fainted or passed out or something and... and when she saw me she screamed."

He felt a bit more in control. If he could just get them to believe that she was drunk that might save him. Various thoughts had been racing through his head, 'how old was she?' being foremost.

Now more people gathered around and there was a great deal of talking, the dark-haired girl again apparently explaining the situation. Of course, she had been in the orchestra too.

Caterina appeared, saw him and took in the rest of the scene. She spoke to the dark-haired girl, then came over to him, her eyes serious, hard and concerned.

"What the hell are you doing Matthew? Are you mad?" she whispered.

"Look, I don't know what they said to you. It's not what it looks like." Lowering his voice he went on urgently, "Caterina, I didn't do anything. I just lay her down here. She'd fainted and, I was just seeing she was okay... put her on the bench there and...." he couldn't think how to say more, especially to her. It was too complicated.

"But Matthew, you must have done something. She would not cry like this if you just brought her over here. She's having the hysteria now."

"I know, I know. I don't understand. She just opened her eyes and started screaming. I must have terrified her.....I don't know."

Caterina's eyes softened, the concern increased and in a lowered voice, "This could be serious for you Matthew. They said you raped her. They asked her if you raped her and she said yes."

"It's not true. Oh God, Caterina, you can't believe that. You can't believe I'd do that can you?"

At that moment there was a disturbance and two police officers approached, a man and a woman, both efficient looking and brusque. Again there was much explanation and questions back and forth. One of the officers then radioed via the device on his lapel. They conferred, got some of the people to leave and then the male officer approached Matt, Caterina still standing beside him.

"I understand there is an accusation against you. I have to ask you questions to find out what happened," he said in heavily accented English. "Who are you?" this to Caterina.

"I'm a friend. We have been singing this concert together."

"Okay if I can ask you to stand away for now please."

Caterina squeezed his arm and withdrew, and the officer took him to the far end of the deck and pulled out a notebook.

Chapter 7

They're going for a picnic. Dad's driving. It's a bright sunny day and her brother Lars and she are fooling about in the back of the car. Lars keeps tickling her and she's laughing so hard she can't breathe. Stop Lars, stop. But he doesn't, he keeps on tickling, faster and more tickly until she's suffocating and gasping for breath.

She's drowning; there's water everywhere, in her mouth, her eyes, her ears. She has to get out. She pushes up with all her strength and bursts out of the water, panting with huge breaths as the water splashes everywhere.

She can stand. It's not deep and her toes are in the squidgy mud. A dog rushes down to the edge of the water wagging its big fluffy tail and barking at her. It's Lars. He's become a dog. He's smiling and shaking himself. He barks again saying 'come and chase me'. She walks out of the lake and the picnic is still there by the shore but there's not much left. They ate it already. Lars is jumping about and barking, still wanting her to chase him.

She can't see her mum and dad and a small panic grabs her tummy. Have they left her alone? She begins searching all around for them, running this way and that, then going further to some long grass under a tree. She hears a woman crying, sobbing, and a man panting and grunting. She goes closer to where the sounds are coming from and peers over the tall grass. There's a woman lying on her back with her white blouse torn open and her breasts shaking in the sunshine. Her arms are stretched out sideways and her hands are grasping tufts of grass. Her face is frightening, her mouth grinning over her teeth which open rhythmically as she cries out "Yes, yes". The man is lying on her, jerking his hips forward, supporting himself on his arms and his face is red, so red and angry. And he keeps on hurting her and she keeps on crying out.

Signe wants to run away but she can't. She hates watching but she's got to stay. The veins in his neck are bulging and sweat's pouring off his face. He goes faster and the woman's shouting now. Her eyes open and she looks straight at Signe. She looks angry and happy at the same time, like a witch with her hair all wild and her mouth snarly. He shouts, then groans and collapses on top of her, both of them panting and moaning. He rolls off and she sees him, sees the ghastly bloated, pumping beast of him stretched out, glistening with slime.

She's going to be sick. She has to get away. She turns and runs. Runs fast, as fast as she can – faster. She's going so fast everything is whizzing past her. She has to get away, away from that horrible sight.

She's panting now and her legs get heavy. She's trying to run so fast but her legs are heavy. They won't move, they're stuck in thick mud and she can't drag them out. There are tree roots growing around them. She's in a big forest. The sun is way up above the trees which arch over an open space in front of her, their branches fanning out to touch each other in the middle, only allowing sparkly bits of sunshine to flicker through, like stars.

There are big pictures hanging on the trees. There's St Sebastian tied to a tree with the arrows going through his arms and legs. And St Jerome with his lion, looking at a skull he's holding. They're the pictures in her bible, but they're huge. Like real-life size. There's a sudden swish of wind and an arrow streaks past her across the clearing and sticks into St Sebastian's ribs. He cries out, and she's crying too, trying desperately to free her legs from the ground. The lion roars and pulls on its chain which is attached to a stone column. They are in a church. The tree trunks have become the pillars in church and there's Christ on the cross above the altar. His body is slumped down hanging from the nails in his hands. Blood splashes in huge drops from his wounds onto the altar. He suddenly shouts out "My God, My God, why have you forsaken me?" and writhes in agony on the cross.

There's a picture from her bible right next to her of Eve in the Garden of Eden. She's standing by the tree and the snake's coiled round and round the trunk from the top with its head next to Eve's naked body. Its tongue flicks out of its mouth and it coils out of the picture and around Signe's body. She struggles but her body won't move. The snake slides round her, its body glistening and smooth and its head wicked and cunning. She tries to cry out but her throat's blocked. The snake slips down around her knees and then slides up inside her skirt, higher and higher. She's screaming and screaming but nothing's coming out. The lion roars and charges towards her, pulling so hard the pillar collapses and the whole church starts to fall down. She screams as hard as she can.

She screamed and screamed, gasping for air between screams.

Her mum rushed into her room. Her hair was all dishevelled and she was wrapping her dressing gown round her.

"Okay okay Signe, it's alright darling. Ssh, ssh." She held her as Signe clung frantically to her.

"Kill it, stop it, take it away," she shrieked hysterically before collapsing in violent crying.

"What's the matter?" her dad shambled in, "Is she alright?"

"She's burning up here. She's got a fever and she's hallucinating.

Get a wet flannel or towel or something. There, there, ssh, it's okay. You're alright now. You've just got a temperature. It's okay, it's okay. Mamma's here. Ssh."

She went on calming Signe, who clung to her, crying and wailing.

"You've had a bad dream. One often gets bad dreams when you have a high temperature. You're alright now. It's all okay. Ssh. You've taken your 'jamas off again have you? You funny little thing!"

They found she'd wet the bed too, so they had to strip it all off and change the sheets. She sat on her chair shivering in a towel.

"We'd better give her a quick bath to wash her off," her mum said. "I'll do that if you can go and find the calpol. We need to get this fever down."

Her mum took her to the bathroom and ran her a warm bath.

"Here, come on, in you get quick. We need to get you back to bed."

"What time is it?"

"It's the middle of the night. Must be about one o'clock I should think," her mum slooshed her with a sponge. Signe noticed her mum was just wearing her dressing gown, she hadn't got her 'jamas on. Her dad shuffled in with the calpol.

"Did you bring the measuring spoon?" her mum said.

"Oh damn, I'll go and get it. Is it in the drawer?"

"Yup."

She noticed her dad's 'jama bottoms were inside out – the label was flapping about at the back. He had scratches on his shoulders.

"Come on, missy, out you come!"

Her mum lifted her up and gave her a big cuddle in the soft towel.

"I'm sorry I woke you," Signe said.

Her mum looked strange for a second. "Oh you didn't wake us. We were just going to sleep. Come on then, let's get you tucked up."

Snuggled in her bed with the clean sheets and the insisted-upon pjs she took her dose of calpol. She winced as it went down and her eyes teared.

"It really hurts to swallow," she whined.

"Let's see. Open your mouth and say ah." Her mum scrutinized her throat, moving Signe's head to catch the light in the right place.

"Ooh yes, you've got a nasty inflammation there. I'm sure that's really painful. Never mind, the calpol will stop it hurting. Settle down now and have a nice sleep. I might have to ring the surgery in the morning and get you some medicine."

"Mum, why do you get nightmares?"

"Oh goodness. Well it's your brain working when you're asleep; like when you have dreams."

"But why does it want to scare you?"

Her mum took a deep breath. "Well, I don't know that it **wants** to scare you. I think it's just thinking of things, and sometimes they're scary things."

"Are they true things?"

"Oh I don't think so. Sometimes your brain just plays sort of games with you and tries to scare you with things you're frightened of. But it's only tricking you; it's not real. Now come on, let's get some sleep. I'm tired too now. We'll talk about it in the morning."

"Do you get nightmares?"

"Of course. Not so much now, but I used to get lots when I was your age."

"What were they about?"

"Oh I don't know, robbers breaking into the house and stealing my favourite toys. Getting lost. I can't remember most of them."

"Do they make you a bad person if they're bad dreams?"

"No of course not. Some people think they're a good thing because they help you to face up to your fears which can help you be braver when you're awake."

Signe suddenly looked worried. "I'm not going to tell you my dream. I can't. I can't tell anyone."

Her mum took this in for a moment. "That's okay, you don't have to tell anyone unless you want to; only if it makes you very frightened. Then you can tell someone if you want to. You can always tell Father Francis if you don't want to tell me."

Signe looked terrified. "No, I couldn't tell Father Francis, I couldn't tell **him**."

"Okay, okay, you can decide if you want to tell anyone, but now let's settle you down."

"Where's Jopi?"

"Ah Jopi. Yes where's Jopi gone? Jopi! Jopi! Where are you hiding?"

"There he is," Signe cried, pointing under the chair.

"Oh Jopi, there you are. What are you doing under there, you silly Jopi!"

"Silly Jopi!" Signe repeated, smiling and hugging him to her.

"Nightie, nightie."

"Nightie, nightie."

Her mum gave her a squidgy kiss on her nose and turned the light out, leaving the night light burning in the plug socket. Signe heard her pad down the landing and go into her bedroom and the door squeak to. There were muffled voices as she heard her parents talking, probably discussing what had happened; mainly her mum, with her dad grunting and occasionally asking a short question. Eventually they stopped and she heard the click of the light being switched off.

Silence.

The shadows of the chest and wardrobe loomed on the ceiling like dark mountains. Were they asleep yet? She waited a bit longer until she heard the light snore of her dad like a regular puttering fart. It sounded funny. Yes, they were asleep so now she could risk it. She quickly flipped back the duvet and pulled off her pjs, chucking them on the floor beside the bed away from the door where they were out of sight. Then she pulled back the crisp new white sheets and loved the feeling of their pure texture against her skin. She felt clean again and clutching Jopi to her she settled into their soft caress.

But as she lay there the nightmare began to creep back into her head and made her shiver. All those horrible pictures started moving again and as much as she tried to think of good things, those pictures kept taking their place. Was she full of badness? Why was she having such horrible thoughts? She must have a very bad mind if it wanted to scare her so much.

She thought of Sister Agnes and how kind she was and she tried to think of God and good thoughts, but then she thought of the crucifix in the forest and the blood dripping on the altar and all those horrible thoughts came back. And she knew the snake would come back too and curled her legs up to stop the awful feeling in her belly. She clutched Jopi harder and told him he had to protect her from the snake. But she didn't believe he could, knew that Jopi couldn't help. She'd sort of grown out of Jopi and he didn't make her feel safe anymore. She felt more alone now.

She clutched the duvet around her like a magic cloak to ward of the evil thoughts. She tried to believe its soft whiteness would protect her from her dark thoughts. But the black mountains peered over the duvet cover, bending down towards her and frightening her with their sinister shapes. If she hid under the duvet she knew they would still be there and they were probably leaning closer and pouring over the bed. Then she was sure she felt something pressing down on top of her. She braved a quick look out; there was nothing there except the shadows on the ceiling, but now she was really scared again.

She quickly jumped out of bed, put on her 'jamas and hurried down the landing to her mum and dad's room.

"Mum, can I sleep with you? I'm scared," she whispered loudly.

"What.....? Oh Signe! Alright, come on then, in you get. But no wriggling!"

She snuggled up with her mum. The dark thoughts wouldn't be so bad here. She thought her mum smelt different, a bit like when she used to suck Jopi's paw and stick her fingers in her mouth and rub her nose with it.

But it was nice; cosy and close.

Chapter 8

She stopped in the doorway, frozen by a sudden vision. There he was, haloed by a small group of admirers who were dwarfed by his stature. She hadn't realised how tall he was when he had been singing as he had mostly been singing by himself and the orchestra of course had been seated, but now surrounded by members of the audience he towered above them, his face glistening and radiating a rich glow.

In the second that Signe stopped in the doorway, momentarily transfixed by this image, he drew a pristine white handkerchief from his pocket and dabbed his forehead and temples, at the same time glancing across the heads of the assembled disciples. She knew he must see her as his gaze moved like a lighthouse beam across the room, and in those micro-seconds of thought her mind contemplated turning around and walking away or looking down and pretending to get something from her handbag. But actually she already knew she wasn't going to do either of those things and she willingly let the atomic clock of fortune run its milliseconds' course until his panning gaze locked contact with her unblinking eyes and a laser beam of recognition again ignited between them. It lasted less than a second but seemed to hold eternity before each broke the moment, thinking that everyone else must have heard the whip-crack of electricity which had seemed to ring in their ears.

"Si...Si. Come on. There won't be any food left." Irma had half turned whilst trying to get through the throng, which wasn't easy, hampered as she was by the cumbersome cello case slung over her shoulder on a strap.

Signe stood immobile. That fleeting moment had just heightened her already emotional state. The performance had taken her to a place she had never been before, to a place she had no idea existed. It had lifted the lid on a well of feelings she couldn't have plumbed without the intensity and purity of the music. She had tripped to another reality of sound and sense, drugged by painful and poignant emotions which resonated to the depth of her being. She stood there incapable of moving, with people passing her, brushing against her unaware form.

Christ is dead, Christ is dead, but is risen. Disparate strands of the Passion jostled to be heard again, crowding into her consciousness from her short-term memory banks. 'Grief for sin', 'Grief for sin', 'Blute nur du Liebes Herz', 'Take, eat, this is my Body', 'Let him be crucified...', 'My God, My God, why hast Thou forsaken me?'

Christ is dead, but is risen and has just gazed at me.

"Signe, come ON!"

Signe snapped out of the moment and forced herself to focus through the blur of teeming thoughts. She followed her friend to one side of the room where there were a series of trestle tables laid out with finger food of various sorts. She glimpsed rye bread, smoked salmon, herrings, pickles, cheese - in fact a usual smorgasbord. Irma located a corner of the room which had been taken over as a general repository for bags and instruments of the orchestra and went to add her cello to the heap. Signe watched her find a space by moving a few bags to one side so that she could stand the moulded case upright by the wall for safety, and then turn as another cellist came up to where she was with the same intention. Irma started chatting to this player, who was considerably older than her, as were all the members of the orchestra, and Signe envied her easy confidence and relaxed, assured sociability. But Irma had always been like that. She was her best friend but they couldn't be more different, she reflected. Irma outgoing, confident, theatrical and musical; she shy, nervous, bookish and academic. Not that Irma wasn't intelligent, she thought, she just hid her innate intelligence under a bubbling and extrovert exterior which gave the lie to her depth.

Whilst they were talking and she was left standing a few metres away, she couldn't help now turning to look again in the direction of the haloed Christ, feeling safe in the knowledge that she was hidden from his view by the press of people around the smorgasbord. By shifting her position occasionally she could glimpse him through the crowd, now engaged in talking to an eager elderly man who appeared to be slightly deaf, as he kept leaning in and turning his head to one side to hear the singer's part of the conversation.

"Hey Si, this is Karl. He played the continuo. Signe's my oldest friend; we've known each other since kindergarten." Irma and the cellist had come up behind her.

"Hello Signe. Nice to meet you" said Karl, smoothly taking her hand. Then to Irma, "Shall I get some drinks? What would you like?"

"Oh, I'd like a Kopparberg pear if they have one," said Irma, "What about you Si?"

The usual minor panic seized her whenever she found herself put on the spot in public to make a quick decision, and she felt the blood rise to her face.

"Do they have a hot chocolate?" she hazarded and immediately saw a look of mild surprise and possible doubt flicker across Karl's face. "Sorry, I'm feeling a bit cold. Probably from sitting in the church," she added by way of explanation.

"I'll see what they've got," he smiled generously and went off in search of the bar. Irma grabbed her friend's arm and squeezed it hard.

"Isn't he awesome? I'm absolutely in love with him, and d'you know what? He said he'd give me a consultation lesson." Her eyes were glittering and Signe felt her excitement.

"What does that mean, you want to have lessons with him?"

"Of course, wouldn't you?"

"Well I suppose that depends how good a teacher he is," Signe always the practical, level-headed one, couldn't help damping her friend's ardour with mature advice.

"Si, he plays first desk with the Göteborg Symphony and he teaches at the Conservatoire. He's only playing today because it's a one-off gig – you know just a made up chamber orchestra kind of hand-picked by the conductor. Probably he's a friend of his or you know, like me, invited in because my teacher knows him..."

"Okay. Well he sounds good," Signe smiled at her friend with assurance, realising that maybe she had been a bit cold about it. "Just could be awkward if you get to fancy him too much. Don't get involved like with Jan."

Irma barely flinched, then rejoined confidently, "That was totally different. He was so, like, full on. I couldn't breathe. He owned me and I had to get out. But you know all about that..."

"Here we go," Karl reappeared and gave Irma a glass which she took with gushing thanks, flashing her eyes at him and wrapping him in her generous smile. "That was quick," she said.

"Ah well, you've got to know how to attract a barmaid's attention," he said with a twinkle, which had Irma simpering "Oh, I see" and winking at Signe.

"They didn't have any hot chocolate I'm afraid," he turned to Signe, "so I got the next best thing," and he handed her a glass of Glögg.

"Oh I don't really drink," she flushed. "I'm sorry...."

He looked concerned and sympathetic.

"Don't worry," he said. "It really won't be like drinking alcohol. You know, they cook this stuff for so long they boil all the alcohol off anyway. It'll just be like drinking spiced berry juice. Go on, it'll warm you up."

He smiled so disarmingly that she couldn't say anything so she accepted it with a small thank you, deciding to have a sip and leave the rest.

"Well, how did you like the concert?" he continued to Signe, as he sipped his red wine.

Put on the spot again Signe squirmed internally and had a quick sip of punch to give herself time to formulate the right answer. To her surprise it tasted really nice, not like her dad's which always smelt really strongly of brandy.

"Oh it was beautiful. I really enjoyed it," she replied. What had she said? Was that the biggest understatement anyone had ever uttered?

"And you must be very proud of your friend Irma here, playing like a true professional."

Irma simpered in pure ecstasy.

"Of course. She's brilliant. I could never do something like that," Signe returned, but kind of hadn't meant to say the last sentence out loud.

"Oh I'm sure you could. Do you play an instrument?"

"No, I don't. I'm not musical at all."

"Well you don't have to be musical to appreciate music at least. What are your interests?"

Again Signe felt cornered and flashed a look of 'Help' to Irma who didn't notice, as she was still wrapping Karl with an overgenerous smile which was being helped by the cider which she had already nearly finished. Signe fought to find a suitable answer. What were her interests?

"Well I read a lot....and..." she faltered.

"Perhaps you play sports?" he guessed.

"I'm more of an intellectual," she blurted out and realised immediately that wasn't the word she had meant. Again that avuncular smile. "I love plays," she said trying to redeem herself and, realising that Irma was beginning to be irritated by his persistent questions to her, added "and I've been to see Irma loads of times at the Drama Centre. She's a really good actress."

"Ah, an actress as well as a fine cellist," he turned at last to Irma and Signe felt a huge rush of relief as the spotlight focused away from her. She took a large gulp of Glögg, which was nice and warming and calmed her panic.

Irma soaked up the attention hungrily, managing to combine an apparent embarrassed modesty with a ready ability to list all the plays she'd been in with the parts she'd taken, embellishing it all with little anecdotes about each particular production. Signe enjoyed the opportunity to just smile occasionally when needed and corroborate certain interesting details when asked to by Irma. Karl listened patiently to it all until –

"Ah, there you are darling. We've been looking all over for you."- and Irma's mum gushed into the conversation, inundating her daughter with a theatrical embrace."It was marvellous. We had excellent seats and could see you very clearly darling. Isn't it long though. Hello Signe darling, did you enjoy it? Oh Irma the Thorsteinssons are here, I saw them across the church and waved but I don't think they saw me."

"Mum, this is Karl Hanson. He was leading the cello section," Irma managed to interject.

"Oh how do you do. Very nice to meet you. Isn't she good!" and she carried on talking to Karl excitedly as her husband trickled into the group, giving his daughter a tired peck on the cheek, nodding at Signe and – "yes meet my husband" – shaking hands with Karl.

Irma's mum babbled on hysterically for about five minutes, apparently without the need for oxygen, as she didn't come up for air, during which time Irma's dad asked everyone through the medium of sign language if they would like another drink and noted the reorders, Signe declining and his wife seamlessly interpolating " a dry white wine, but make sure it's cold, darling" mid-sentence as she careered wildly from the size of the orchestra, the advantages or otherwise of organs and what **is** a Ripieno choir? (which it transpired was a rhetorical question as she certainly wasn't going to wait for an answer), through, why does anyone want to play at Baroque pitch anyway and if they do then they might as well all dress in 18th century costumes and wear wigs? to wigs in general, to wigs specifically and the difficulty of amateur companies finding and funding costumes and wigs on limited budgets, until she finally caught sight of a friend and with "Ah there's Monica, I must just catch her to talk about the curling club party" she rushed off, pushing through the crowd to assault Monica just as Irma's dad arrived back with the drinks.

It seemed as if a raging torrent had suddenly been dammed up leaving a still pool into which occasional embarrassed drips of conversation plashed.

"Sorry. Mum's a bit over the top when she gets excited."

"Thanks," Karl said receiving his glass from her dad. "That's okay."

Irma's dad sidled round to Signe. "I got you another Glögg. You look cold. It won't do you any harm."

She took it, unable to refuse his gentle insistence. She really liked him. He was always kind to her in his reticent, shy way and she felt a kindred spirit in him. They never exchanged much of import but she felt a reassurance in his quiet companionship. She surmised that he probably craved some periods of peace.

Irma was now talking to another couple who had joined them and they seemed to be discussing technical details of the performance.

"How are your parents?" He always asked after her parents and she always said "fine". This was part of their comfortable conversation.

They looked around the room whilst they sipped their drinks, he vaguely trying to catch sight of his wife who seemed to have disappeared. The Glögg was warmer than the previous one and smelt spicier. They must have made up a new batch, she thought, as it tasted quite different. A bit more like her dad's, but it was still nice and warming.

"Did you enjoy the concert?" she ventured, thinking she ought to break their silence.

"Well, Bach's not really my thing," he said simply. She always liked his honesty. He never said anything just to please you.

"What kind of music do you like?" she returned, realising that despite their long acquaintance she had no idea.

"I like jazz. You know Oscar Peterson, Charlie Parker... that kind of thing?"

She didn't know, but nodded anyway and noticed she wasn't as honest.

"Did you enjoy it?"

"Yes, it was really good." She realised this was the second time in only about half an hour that she had completely understated her response to the Passion. "Irma was brilliant," she added.

"I can't say I really heard her," he said facetiously, "but she seemed to keep in time!" He smiled mischievously then looked towards Irma. Signe could tell he was very proud of her even if he didn't like the music or understand the genre, and it pleased her to see his love.

He suggested they get something to eat and signalling to the others their intention they pushed over to the now not-so-laden tables.

"Have you decided what to study at university?" he suddenly asked.

The glow of the Glögg and the soft sleepiness seeping into her head were interrupted by the question. She had known someone would ask her soon but hadn't as yet thought out a suitable answer and was now caught unprepared. She couldn't tell him. She couldn't tell anyone, well not yet anyway. Except Irma of course. She'd told her ages ago and sworn her to secrecy.

"I'm not really sure. I'm kind of thinking History, maybe with Literature and Ethics." It had come as a flash of inspiration – Ethics. That was good and true really when you thought about it. What she wanted to do was all about ethics.

Irma's dad grunted a vague response, preoccupied as he was in charging a plate whilst also trying to deal with his drink and that of his wife, which he now realised he as yet hadn't delivered to her. There being no table space available to conveniently park his wine glasses he had been constrained to holding both in his left hand together with the paper plate and trying to load with his right, but had quickly found he had run out of fingers.

"I think I'd better take this to Anna," and before Signe could offer to help he shuffled off with a smile of apology in search of her.

Signe, although not particularly hungry, moved slowly down the length of the tables looking out for anything which might take her fancy. Cheese straws were a favourite and she caught sight of some at the far end and headed in that direction, picking up occasional carrot and celery sticks on the way. As she was helping herself to a handful of straws and noticing a dish of grapes nearby she found her glass was topped up by a large lady with a jug, saying "A drop more Glögg my dear. That's it, help me finish it up. That's the last of it now." She was next to a table with an electric ring and saucepan for heating the punch which the server had obviously just emptied into the jug. She tried to remonstrate and refuse but she already had a full glass.

"Oh sorry, my darlin', didn't you want anymore? Oh well, never mind. Give it to someone else. Can't waste it eh?" and she fussed about behind the heater, clearing up.

Signe turned away from the tables, not sure what to do, as Irma's dad hadn't reappeared. She looked for Irma. Her head spun a bit as she turned and the room moved strangely, rather like she remembered when she was young getting off the carousel seat in the playground and feeling dizzy. She caught sight of Irma, now surrounded by more musicians it seemed, laughing wildly and leaning too familiarly into Karl, who didn't seem to mind.

She didn't feel she could join them and cast about for anyone she might know in the crowd, but no familiar face presented itself. She looked towards where 'Christ' had been when she first came in, but he wasn't there. A tiny fear clutched her heart which she hardly dared to acknowledge. Had he gone? Wouldn't she see him again?

She absent-mindedly took a gulp of Glögg, which was now very sweet and heady. It felt like hot treacle pouring down her chest. She negotiated her way across the room with no clear purpose except perhaps locating Irma's dad. Reaching the other side, after excusing herself around various tightly-packed, smiling, voluble groups, she found a number of chairs sprinkled along the wall, a few of which were vacant and one of which she gratefully slumped into.

It was nice sitting there unnoticed, vaguely catching conversations of the nearest groups of people and letting her mind range over the concert and the different images and musical moments still resonating in her mind. She found pictures flashing through her head, the huge crucifix, the choir standing to sing, the different soloists singing arias and duets, the towering roof of the church, the dramatic Evangelist and, yes, the beautiful Christ. These images mixed with pictures she had known all her life from her mum's old edition of the Children's Bible; romanticised representations of the fishermen on the Sea of Galilee, the Sermon on the Mount, the turning over of the tables of the money-changers in the temple. They had informed her perception of Christianity, had moulded her mind's eye and conditioned her visualisation of the events of the Old and New Testaments such that when she re-heard the familiar stories these same images sprang into her mind.

Throughout the concert as she had followed the translation of the German text, those friendly colour-washed glossy plates had formed the background and starting point of the film narrative that was generated in her mind as the Passion played out. The muscular Peter with a reddish beard and curly hair; the amazing folds of the dress of the woman kneeling to wash Jesus' feet with ointment; the severe expression and weird hat of Pontius Pilate as he passed judgement and Jesus Himself, benign with flowing hair and a light blue gown, bathed in a shaft of light which shone from a slit in the heavenly billowing clouds. These images had been seminal in her religious journey and were indelibly printed in her mind.

She reached into her bag and took out the programme which Irma had given her before the concert and which she had followed so closely. Turning over the pages of explanation and translation she came to the section at the back which she hadn't looked at before, containing the biographies and photographs of the soloists. Some of the photographs didn't really look like the singers she'd just seen, they looked younger and were taken at strange angles which altered their appearance. She paused at the entry for 'Christus – Matthew Chamberlain' and read:

'Matthew Chamberlain was born and brought up in London. His vocal talent was discovered whilst at school and was nurtured at Trinity College junior department before he received a scholarship from the Royal College of Music. After graduating with honours he was accepted at The London Opera Studio where he studied under Edward Silson and coached with Jeremy Fleming and Edwina Rauchmann.

He was subsequently invited onto the Royal Opera House Young Artists' Scheme where he has covered Timur in 'Turandot' and Il Commendatore in 'Don Giovanni'. He is shortly to make his debut singing Colline in Andrew McRector's new production of 'La Boheme'. He has recently performed Nick Shadow in Stravinsky's 'The Rake's Progress' with Amber Opera, Villotto in Haydn's 'La Vera Costanza' in Lyons, France, and created the role of Bodkin in the world premiere of Whistlebirt Harrisdink's new opera 'Flibbertigibbet' at the 'Glasgow Kiss Festival'.......

Signe stopped reading and looked back at his photograph. The list of operas and roles didn't mean anything to her, although she recognised Don Giovanni, and she had lost interest. His calm features stared back at her with an expression of cool confidence mixed with ....amusement was it? Could she detect a tiny curl to the edge of his upper lip and the suggestion of a raised eyebrow above that left eye, or was she imagining it? There was a touch of the Mona Lisa about the photograph and she found herself looking first at the eyes and then at the mouth trying to decide. But the eyes on their own didn't smile and then when she looked at the mouth alone it didn't seem to either. It was only when you looked at the whole expression that the amusement crept into his face.

Signe was intrigued and now looked at the photos of the other soloists to see if a similar effect occurred there. No, each one she examined was singular in its expression, some smiling, some serious, but none both at the same time.

She looked back at Christ, the Saviour of the world, who now gazed back at her with the seriousness of His Passion- His Agony, tempered by the smiling generosity of His unbounded Love for her and His forgiveness of the Sins of Mankind. Her heart warmed as she gazed at His Beloved Face, her head filling with the myriad bible texts, bible pictures, prayers and treasured images of her life and mixing with the music of Bach's Passion which even now reverberated in her mind. This was her Lord, her Saviour, her Redeemer and she wanted no other. She would cleave to Him and renounce all others. She would not falter but embrace His love for always and forever. Her eyes filled with tears of joy.

Chapter 9

Matt woke with a start and was immediately aware of a number of things which simultaneously claimed his attention. The most insistent of these, presumably because it was causing the most grief, was that the whole of his body that he could feel ached and his torso was stiff. The part he couldn't feel he was lying on and had lost circulation. As he began to move, his body informed him of the extent of the trauma, updating him with startling shooting pains and isolated sharp twinges. Concurrently he was aware that what he was lying on was far too hard to be a bed and that this must be partly responsible for his physical state. This observation, combined with the stark, blank, painted wall which hit his eyes when he opened them, suggested that this probably wasn't a bedroom and that therefore his having slept here was unnatural and possibly alarming. Various explanations presented themselves in a cascade of ideas – he had been drunk and had fallen over; he'd crashed at someone's house; he'd fainted and been knocked out; he'd been assaulted and robbed.

His view travelled from the blandness of the wall to the length of his body as it painfully uncurled itself and he took in the disarray of a tail coat creased, an un-tucked, crumpled dress shirt and, further down, some dirtied dress trousers. The events of the time he was last cognisant jumbled into his mind and he was hit with such a feeling of dread that he heard himself gasp a dry, abrupt exclamation. He managed to half turn to look at the austere small space in which he lay. Slowly he began to piece together the sequence of events which had brought him here; the reception, the mortification on the deck, Caterina's searching accusatory look, the scream of the girl, the hostility of the police.

It took some time for all this to sink in and for him to come to terms with the reality of the situation. The reality was apparent enough but his memory of the concert and what followed it was incomplete. He remembered laughing with Artis and drinking glass after glass of champagne. And flirting with Caterina across the table – God those eyes! But what happened then? How did he end up on the deck with people crowding around him? It was all confusing. Had he fallen over? Had he been drunk? The dark-haired girl glaring at him. What had he done? God, he couldn't remember the sequence of events.

He was interrupted by the viewing window in the door being unscreened and the sound of the door being unlocked. Two policemen came in.

"Good morning. Mister Chamberlain, yes?"

"Yes."

"You know why you're here? You remember last night?"

"Well, actually.....I'm rather confused to be honest," Matt rasped; his voice was raw.

"Yes. I can believe this. I think you have too much to drink last night," the same officer observed. "I must ask you to confirm that these things are yours." He opened a plastic wallet and began pulling out all Matt's personal possessions, wallet, keys, phone, hotel entry card etc. Matt nodded.

"You were not making lots of sense last night, so I just have to make sure."

"How long do I have to stay here?"

"We hold you here in the police station for maybe two days, then you go to a long term unit."

"But what's going to happen? Have I been charged?"

"We have a serious allegation of rape which means there has to be a court hearing."

"Oh God!" he ran his fingers through his hair. It was as bad as he had imagined.

"You have the right for a lawyer and as you are a foreign national also a translator. He or she will come and see you here before you are transferred."

"How long before the trial?"

"The lawyer will tell you everything you need to know. They'll bring you some breakfast soon."

With that they left with a clank of the locks and jingle of keys.

"Christ," he grimaced. The irony wasn't lost on him.

He looked at the cell. There was nothing to see; oblong, small and empty except for the 'shelf' he sat on. You couldn't call it a bed! The whole thing was surreal. You see these things on TV or in a film and they look fairly austere, but actually being in one for real. God, it's brutal, he thought. The bareness of the room and its lack of anything at all was numbing. Numbingly awful.

In prison in a foreign country, with nobody near. He felt very alone.

What would he do? Phone Maggie, his agent, his parents? He didn't want to tell anyone, it was all too humiliating. And besides, what would he say? He couldn't still quite work out exactly what had happened, so how would he explain it? 'I got banged up because this girl said I raped her, but I don't think I did, and anyway she seemed to want it and I thought she.....' Oh God, it sounded pathetic. So predictable and grotesque and sordid. And lame.

Caterina. He had to explain to Caterina and make her understand, make her realise that he wasn't some perverted paedophile preying on any innocent young girl who happened to come his way. He had to explain the whole thing, exactly what had happened, the order of events which led up to... whatever it was that had actually happened.

But first he had to try to figure that out.

Breakfast interrupted that immediate plan, with a noisy opening of the door. A policeman deposited a tray on the 'bed' and was about to leave.

"Excuse me, can I....will I be able to call someone, you know, get in touch with people... let them know...?"

"You can make one phone call to a family member to let them know your situation. Otherwise no contact, except with the lawyer of course."

"What? Just one call?"

"Sorry. These are the rules for police custody," and he was gone.

Matt surveyed the tray. Orange juice, cold ham, hard- boiled egg, pack of dry toast. Hardly appetising. In any case he wasn't hungry. If anything he felt nauseous, but this could be on various accounts; alcohol, shock, nerves. The orange juice was the most palatable and at least helped to sooth his raw throat.

No contact. It wasn't getting any better.

He spent the next hour piecing together what had happened after the concert and most of the important facts eventually fell into place. He remembered seeing her in the entrance to the reception when he was talking to the old man. He remembered the excitement knowing that she had noticed him and held his gaze. He remembered the speeches downstairs followed by the meal and the frisson with Caterina, then going upstairs to the toilet, yes, that was it. And then he went on deck. 'The millions and millions of stars', Dr Brian Cox's smiling voice echoing in his head. The stars, the water, a silhouette in the moonbeam across the deck. Lifting her up and her white face irradiated by moonlight.

His mouth tingled as his mind's eye focused in on her parted lips and he felt again the exhilaration of her breath on his mouth. It had been an exquisite second in time before he had given in to the primal urge, the desperate need to rend her with his lust and violate the sanctity of the moment. The tang of forbidden fruit loitered on his tongue.

But it wasn't just him; he felt again her hands cupping his face, dragging him into her hungry embrace, her eyes searching his with ardent, dilated pupils, urging on his passion.

He knew he wasn't wrong. He knew that was the truth, but would anyone believe him? She had screamed for help, screamed to be released from the situation. Accused him of rape. Yes, reduced that precious interplay of febrile erotic energy to the level of a violent, vicious crime, a hedonistic attack on the sanctity of an individual, not the sensual, consensual synthesis of souls.

The bitch. The bloody fucking two-faced whore of a bitch. Fuck her. Fuck her to hell.

He wanted to smash something. He felt such violence in his body that he wanted to smash his fists into the wall, throw himself against it – wreck his body if need be, but find some outlet to vent this unbelievable fury.

Jesus, how could she do that? How could she lead me on like that and then fuck me over? Bitch. Fucking, fucking Swedish bitch.

He hated her, hated her with more passion than he had felt for anything or against anything. He couldn't formulate words suitably ugly or violent to satisfy his desire to execrate her sufficiently. He dug his fingernails into his hands and drew blood. And it felt good. He wanted to hurt himself if he couldn't hurt her. He needed to inflict pain and if it had to be on himself, so be it. It vented his ire, released the unbelievable and sudden velocity of his hate.

Then he saw her. Saw her uplifted moon face in his arms, her eyes searching his soul, her mouth gasping puffs of moist breath which caressed his lips, and his anger melted into heaving sobs. He wept. Freely and uncontrollably he wept, pitying himself and hating himself for his self pity; loathing his lack of self control, yet incapable of stemming this outpouring of grief that forced itself through his frail resistances. But there was that within him that he couldn't deny, something so precious and pure that the loss of it was tearing him up.

Simply, he loved her. That was all. But, that was, all. Everything. In this moment, it seemed to be all and everything that mattered, and to lose it was unthinkable.

Yet, it was lost, he realised. It had gone. Whatever was contained in that moment of singularity was gone forever. It could never be redeemed, never be brought back to that pristine state of innocence. Its nature had changed, had been savaged by circumstance and unwitting wilfulness. Human nature's hunger for satisfaction had wrecked the promise of perfection. He reflected sardonically that he epitomised Man's overriding capacity, whilst ostensibly striving for perfection, to destroy it. In a fleeting second, in a swift careless moment of indulgence, he had smashed his heaven to pieces and scattered it into the firmament like so much space dust amongst the millions and millions of stars.

He struggled himself into a sitting position, hunched over, and attempted to clean himself up, wiping his eyes and sniffing back the tears. What a mess. Him *and* his life.

Time dragged.

There was no daylight in the cell and without his watch or phone he had little idea where he was in the day. Sometime, he reckoned it must have been about 10am, he was allowed to use the phone. As it was international it had to be short. He had already decided to ring Maggie as being the less involved option.

Her mobile rang for a bit, then the familiar "Hi, it's Maggie. Sorreeeee, can't pick up right now but leave a message and I'll get back soon as." Beep.

"Hi Mags, it's Matt. Really wanted to talk to you but I'll have to leave a message. Look things are a bit weird here. I've got to stay in Sweden for a bit to sort something out. It means I won't be back when I said, so everything's on hold. I can't ring again and my phone's not working so you can't contact me at all. But I'm fine, don't worry, it's just going to take me a few days to sort out. I should be able to ring in a couple of days and then I can explain everything, ok? Love you".

It was totally not good. That was just such a rubbish message, but he hadn't been able to think how to put it and getting the voicemail had really thrown him. He had expected her to pick up. She was normally just getting herself together mid-morning. Maybe she had had a last minute job, some extra work again and had had to be on site for 6am and she was on set right now doing a take. Whatever, she at least had the message that he wouldn't be back. He was glad he hadn't contacted his parents, they would only have panicked and tried to get involved. If he got off they'd never need to know.

Maybe.

If.

****

"Mr Chamberlain, hello, my name is Christer Bergstrom. I'm here to represent you."

"Hi."

They shook hands and Matt self-consciously made room for him on the bed.

He watched him take out a file from his briefcase and sort through some papers. He was youngish, very young actually for a lawyer, Matt thought, with sandy-coloured hair and a freckly complexion.

"Ok, so you are English, in Sweden on business, correct?"

"Absolutely."

"Now, I tell you, for today I am just here to make some notes to be sure I have the main facts. We will be making another meeting soon when we will have a translator for you, to be sure you understand everything and in case there are things I need to be sure about. Is this ok?"

"Of course, that's fine," Matt felt relieved that this guy seemed approachable even if he was rather 'cut and dried'.

"I just need to ask you a whole lot of questions which I'm afraid you have probably been asked already, so please forgive me if I am asking them all again."

Matt gave his age, address, nationality, occupation, marital status etc and explained what his business was in Gothenburg and about the concert.

"Now, you understand the reason you are here is because there is an accusation of rape against you?" Matt nodded. "I need to know if you want to challenge this or if you accept the accusation."

"I didn't rape her," Matt said. "She encouraged me. She was kissing me."

"So you wish to challenge the accusation."

"Yes."

He looked at his notes. "The police report says you were drunk and were shouting when they put you in the cell."

"Right."

"Does that mean you agree?"

"Well, I don't think I was so drunk I didn't know what I was doing. I drank some champagne at the reception, but I wasn't out of control."

"Mr Chamberlain, you do realise there is going to be a trial. I have to prepare a defence for you. I have to know as much as possible from you so you need to remember exactly what happened so that I can make a convincing case. Do you think you can remember?"

"Of course."

"Fine. Now I can't do more now until we arrange the translator; it's important that everything we say is fully understood by you and me. I speak fairly good English but we cannot afford misunderstandings which is why we give you a translator."

"No that's fine, thank you."

He began packing his things into his case.

"Hang on, wait a moment, are you going already?"

"There's nothing more to do until next week."

"But, I need to know, what happens to me? I mean, presumably I can get bail until the trial?"

"Well, that is only in two weeks maybe so this is not usually granted, and as you are a foreign national this would not be allowed, as we can't be sure you come back for the trial."

"Two weeks? The trial will be in two weeks? But doesn't it usually take months for these things to come to court?"

"In the UK maybe. Here in Sweden we process court cases quickly, particularly when there is not so much evidence to collect. Yes, you will be transferred from this police station early next week to a custody unit where you stay until the trial."

"I see. And, I don't want to be rude, but could I get a British lawyer to represent me?"

"Of course. You can do as you like, but it may be expensive for you. I am paid for by the judicial service to give you a fair trial, but if you want to get someone else in you can, but this will be your expense."

"Yes, I understand. And how do you think you will be able to defend me? I mean, what kind of a chance will I have?"

"I should warn you that this will not be easy to defend. A young girl's word against yours in this type of case, the judge, the jury, they will usually take the side of the victim. We will wait on the forensic report and the medical evidence before we decide how to proceed. So, I will see you in a couple of days and then I will need to go through the events as you remember them. I suggest you ask for some paper and a pen to write down as much as you can before we meet again."

"Of course."

"Here's my card and they will let you ring me if you need to discuss anything. I am the only person you can talk to right now."

"Yes, so I discovered."

"Is there anything more you want to ask now before I go?"

Matt thought for a moment. "How long am I not allowed contact with anyone?"

"While you are in this unit, but I think you can send emails when you are transferred to the holding unit. I will check for you. So, until next week," and he offered his hand, which Matt shook automatically, and knocked on the door to be let out.

Chapter 10

Signe watched the old priest shuffle in carrying the silver cup with the strip of virgin white cloth over the top of it with the tasselled ends hanging down each side. He clasped the cup with his right hand, clamping the white square down over the cloth with his left whilst carefully going up the three steps to the altar. He hardly stopped as he genuflected before continuing towards the altar.

Signe was suddenly aware that when he rounded the side of the altar he would face down the church as he placed the cup and would therefore inevitably see her watching his every move, so slipped quietly to her knees, hiding her face in her hands in prayer to save the embarrassment. Through gaps in splayed fingers she then watched him shuffle to the little door in the far wall of the church behind the altar, haul a bunch of keys up from the depths of his vestments on the end of a cord, and unlock the little door. From the cupboard he took another, bigger silver goblet which he took to the altar and decanted a number of hosts from it to the smaller goblet, before returning and carefully replacing it in the cupboard. Next he brought two little glass bottles with glass stoppers and placed them on the altar next to the silver goblet, before returning to the little door and closing and locking it, each journey accompanied by small inclinations of the head.

Signe enjoyed the ritual, the little gestures which accompanied each foray to the cupboard, the minute inclinations of the head and body which denoted deference to the solemnity of the moment. She became aware, as the ritual progressed, of the church gently ricocheting sound from its walls, the sounds of footsteps, as a sprinkling of parishioners entered, sauntered to seats, genuflected, knelt to pray, as a prelude to mass. She loved the hushed reverence of the church, where small sounds were magnified by the amplifying volume of the space; where a pew edge struck by a careless shoe caused a dry hollow report which glanced reverberations off the ringing stonework, as if calling the perpetrator to account; where the microphone-enhanced incantations of the celebrant at mass resonated with increasing magnitude as the echoing sentences chased each other around the concave acoustic of the sanctuary; the clinking chains of the thurible as it was lifted to make the sign of the cross towards the altar, belching heavy puffs of billowing incense, setting up a sibilant cacophony in the still silence. She loved each and every facet of the life in the church; the beautiful lacework edge of the celebrant's surplice; the way the sun shone through the stained glass windows and caused a kaleidoscope of colour to seep across the blank walls; the wispy dance of the snuffed candle smoke eerily rising; the heavy heady must of incense hanging in the void. They were like a big warm embrace to her little body, a huge soft duvet to cocoon her soul.

She sat through the mass, going up to kneel at the steps with the other communicants, but not lifting her head like them to receive the host on their tongues through parted lips, but keeping her head bowed to indicate her unconfirmed state. The priest laid a hand on her head and murmured a short blessing. She loved the weight of his hand there, pouring a benediction on her. She thought she could feel God's love flow from that pressure into her body, like liquid gold filling her with glowing goodness. What would it be like to share in His body? She dared not think. That was an excitement to look forward to at first communion, not far away now. She crossed herself and returned to her place in the pew to pray.

She had let the rest of the congregation leave before she got up and wandered down the church. She could go home straight away, which was only a hop and a skip across the park, ten minutes at the most, or she could walk the Stations of the Cross round the church first. She liked doing this. They started at the back on the right hand side just after the dish of Holy Water stuck into the wall, where people dipped their fingers before making the sign of the cross on their foreheads when they entered and left. It was a long time before she could reach it and her Dad used to make the sign for her or, later, lifted her up to wet her fingers so she could do it herself. She'd been able to reach it for a long time now.

The first station was Pilate condemning Jesus to death. Jesus was standing on the left in a long white gown with His hands crossed in front of Him. Pilate was sitting on a chair in a long red skirt and a white T shirt it looked like. The colours were glossy paint and the figures kind of stood out from the picture to make them more real. Her Dad said they were 'relief' pictures, which means they stick out. Pilate was looking at Jesus but his hands were to his side over a bowl. Her Dad said this is because Pilate is washing his hands of Jesus' death. She didn't quite understand why he had to wash his hands because Jesus was going to die, but her Dad said it was symbolic; so that everyone would know it wasn't Pilate's fault. Because everyone else had said He should die. She didn't understand that either, because she thought He was the king of the Jews and they all loved Him. But apparently some of the people didn't like Him and they persuaded everyone to say He should die. Pilate had asked them who they wanted to die, Jesus or Barabbas the thief, and they had said Jesus, so he was washing his hands to show it wasn't his fault.

She had tried this once when she and Lars had had a fight in the kitchen and a mug had got broken. He said she'd started it and she said he hadn't done what she'd said and he'd pushed her and she'd fallen against the table and knocked the mug off with her arm. He said it was her fault because she knocked it off and she said she only knocked it because he pushed her, and then she'd gone and washed her hands to show everyone it wasn't her fault, but her Dad said that wasn't the same because it wasn't symbolic. Lots of things in the bible were symbolic. They often meant something else which was quite confusing. But she liked the Stations of the Cross.

The second one was Jesus carrying the cross. It wasn't a very big cross and it was leaning on His shoulder. It didn't look very heavy although she knew it was meant to be, and Jesus didn't look too unhappy about it, He was just standing there holding it with one hand, the other by His side, facing out as if saying 'well this is what it was like'. There was a man with a big grey beard in a long yellow robe standing behind Jesus holding a rolled up piece of paper, but she couldn't remember who he was. In the next one Jesus falls for the first time and a different man in a short blue dress holds His cross for Him. He falls three times altogether, each time lower to the ground showing how tired He is getting. Apparently this is symbolic too, showing the weight of the sins of the world were getting heavier for Him and weighing Him down.

"Signe."

"Uh," she jumped out of her skin and couldn't stop herself letting out an involuntary cry of fright with the surprise of finding someone right beside her. It was the priest, Father Francis, whom she hadn't heard sidle up to her.

"Oh Signe, I didn't mean to frighten you. What are you still doing here?"

He was looking a bit red in the face and his eyes were very bright and shiny. She thought maybe it was the wine from the communion which she could smell on his breath mixed with his funny old man smell which reminded her of their cat's basket.

"I was looking at the Stations of the Cross, father."

"Ah yes, the Via Dolorosa! Our dear Lord's final journey." He cleared his throat, some phlegm rattling briefly. "Shouldn't you be going home now?"

"Oh it's ok. Mum knows where I am," she replied brightly.

He looked at her strangely, like he was trying to understand her and then smiled showing his yellowy teeth.

"Shall I walk round with you?"

She didn't reply, but they began to walk around the walls of the church, she fiddling with the tails of the belt of her dress, he shuffling along beside her with his hand on her shoulder. He made little grunting comments about each station they came to, not exactly explaining it, she thought, but just reminding her what they were about. She liked Father Francis and his hand on her shoulder was reassuring, like it had been on her head when he had blessed her.

"I've got a miniature version of the Stations of the Cross in my room. Would you like to see it?" he said, when they came to the end.

"Oh yes," she said, "I love miniature things."

He seemed very pleased that she wanted to and led her towards the sanctuary and through a door to the left, which is where he always came from before mass. He pulled his keys up again and unlocked a dark wooden door which he closed and locked behind them.

"We don't want anyone disturbing us, do we?" he winked and giggled.

The room was a bit messy and unorganised she thought, with books piled up here and there, a cassock and surplice on hangers hooked on the window frame, a couple of dirty mugs on the desk, one half full of cold coffee. It smelt fusty, with a mixture of incense and cigars, but was also secret and special; Father Francis' private room which he was allowing her to see.

"It's just in the drawer here," he shuffled around to the other side of the desk, plonked into the leather armchair there and slid open the middle drawer. He moved a few things around which she couldn't see and then drew out a dark brown leather folder. It was about the size of one of her exercise books and quite thin.

"This is so you can carry it around with you when you go away," he explained. "You can have it with you all the time."

She held it carefully when he placed it in her hands. He helped her un-flip the leather band from the loop and open it out to reveal the fourteen little pictures of the stations around a central much larger one of the Saviour on the Cross in a blaze of light streaming in shafts from heaven, with the words Via Crucis underneath. The pictures all around were much more real than the ones in the church. There were more people in them and they looked much more like photos although she could see they were paintings. The pictures of Jesus carrying the Cross really showed how heavy it was, and the women were really crying and the roman soldiers looked very cruel. The colours were very pretty, and she thought it unspeakably beautiful.

"What does that mean?" she said pointing to the inscription.

"Ah, that means The Way of the Cross. It's just another way of saying the Stations of the Cross or the Via Dolorosa, the way of sadness."

"It's very beautiful. Is it very old?"

"Well, it's nearly as old as me," he winked, "which means it must be very old! My parents gave it to me when I was ordained."

He had come around the desk and had sat down in the only other chair in the room, a big leather armchair, rather battered and worn, which she thought looked like it might have come out of Hogwarts. Still holding the folder she turned to him, inquisitive.

"What's ordained?"

"Come here and sit with me and I'll tell you."

Signe felt very special. He had brought her into his private room and was telling her all sorts of interesting things she didn't know. She happily approached him and he gently lifted her to sit on his leg, supporting her around her waist with his arm. He was breathing heavily and she saw his face was quite red with little droplets of water on his forehead.

"Being ordained is what happens when you become a priest. First you have to do a lot of studying at a place called a seminary where you learn all about the bible and Jesus' teachings in great detail." He had to pause to cough the rattle from his chest.

"Like a school for priests," she chirped, pleased with her idea.

"Exactly," he said, recovered now, "a school for priests. But it's really more like a university. And when you finish at the seminary you're ordained by the bishop."

"Is it like getting a 'stificate?"

He smiled and she thought he looked pleased. His left hand was on her knee below her light summer dress and he gently stroked her soft skin.

"Oh, it's much more than a certificate. You see, ordination is being appointed by the church to be God's representative on earth. Ordination has been going on for hundreds of years since Jesus ordained Simon Peter as the leader of His church. And Simon Peter ordained people to the priesthood after that, each one ordaining others in an unbroken line from Jesus right down to the present day."

Signe's eyes had got bigger as she understood what he was saying. "So the line of priests goes right back to Jesus."

"Yes, absolutely," he said, giving her a little squeeze. "Jesus started the line of priests, bishops and popes and there's an unbroken line of connection right back to His ministry in the Holy Land."

Signe was staring at the ornate silver crucifix hanging on a chain around his neck and wanted to hold it too, but was still holding the folder. This man who she was sitting on and who was caressing her thigh was her direct connection to Jesus. She could see Jesus' hand on Simon Peter's head and the liquid gold pouring into him. And then Simon Peter pouring liquid gold into the other disciples and the bishops and popes doing the same down all the ages and the gold pouring in an unbroken stream until Father Francis poured it into her. Like the shaft of golden light which was pouring from God onto the head of Jesus on the cross in the big central picture in the folder she was holding in her hands.

"Now Signe, you're going to have your first communion soon aren't you?"

"Yes father. I'm doing classes with Sister Agnes."

"Well, one of the duties of a priest is to check that all those who are accepted into God's church are pure and spotless. Are you pure and spotless Signe?" There was a quavering in his voice and his hand was a bit shaky now.

"Yes father, I pray every day and ask Jesus to keep me pure."

"Well. Just be a good girl and take your dress off so I can check for Jesus."

He helped her off his knee and took the folder from her. Signe felt it was odd he had to check her, but she so wanted him to see that she was pure and spotless, that she didn't question it.

She undid the three little buttons of the simple thin summer dress she was wearing and pulling the shoulders off let it slip to the floor, so that she was standing just in her knickers. Father Francis was breathing heavily now. She was sure he would be pleased with her pure body.

"Oh yes, Signe, you're a very good girl I can see." His eyes were very bright and his face had got very red. "Now just take your panties down for me."

Is this right? Signe didn't know, but Jesus must know and Father Francis was working for Jesus. She pulled down her knickers and stood in her innocence before him.

He grunted as he moved himself forward in the chair and began stroking her body with cool leathery hands.

"Oh yes, Signe, you're a very, very good girl." His voice was quavery. She was delighted, but felt something was wrong.

"And do you say the Lord's Prayer?"

"Yes father." His hands were stroking her chest.

"And do you say your Hail Marys?"

"Yes father." His hands moved down to caress her hips.

"And do you pray for the unbelievers and the sinners?"

"Yes father." One hand had slipped around her back to cup her buttocks while the other was investigating her pee-hole.

"Father Francis?" There was a loud rap on the door.

He shuddered with fright, as did she, and whipped his hands away. "What is it?"

"The lady is here about the flowers for the wedding."

"Okay, Stefan, I'll be with you in a minute." He looked at her standing shivering before him and a gentle smile spread over his face, which reassured her. "That was a surprise wasn't it?" He patted her bottom. "That's all fine, Signe, you're a very good girl. You can get dressed now. You don't need to tell anyone I've inspected you. I have to inspect all the first communicants. It's important, but we don't talk about it."

She was quickly pulling on her dress now, eager to leave. "I'll let you out," he said, standing shakily.

"Thank you for showing me your things."

He unlocked the door and opened it cautiously, looking to see if anyone was outside. "Off you go and remember your Hail Marys."

She walked along the little corridor to the church, her thin sandals spatting on the stone floor. When she got to the corner she looked back and saw him still standing in the doorway, his fingers to his nose, watching her. Then she turned and quickly crossed the church, only just remembering to genuflect and cross herself, before rushing out of the church and racing home across the park.

Chapter 11

She lay on her back, her head turned to the side, her eyelids screwed closed to avoid the hateful scene.

Why is it taking so long?

Her legs lay limply in the separating stirrups, the futile gown ridden up leaving her shamefully exposed and vulnerable.

Why did I agree to this investigation?

Her breath shuddered feebly through her pain-pouted lips in the exhausted aftermath of trauma. Her resistance was spent. She lay supine, sedated, subjected to the final indignity of internal investigation.

"Okay, Signe, I'm just going to take a little look now."

She felt the latex-gloved fingers efficiently splay her labia and probe a cold speculum.

It's Irma's fault. She insisted, persuaded me. Told me it would give the proof necessary to get a prosecution.

"The hymen's intact, no penetration."

What? That can't be right.

"But that's impossible. He raped her." Irma's voice was quick, clear and decisive.

"Well, I'm just telling you what I find here. Your friend has not been penetrated. There may well have been attempted rape, but I see no evidence for rape having taken place."

*He did, he did. I felt him. He was on me. He pushed up, hard. He was hot, hot against me. The snake....*Signe retched.

"Are you ok Signe? I'm nearly finished here. I just need to take a couple of swabs to test for semen, then we'll be done. Okay?"

Signe couldn't reply, she was choked.

"Are you quite sure?" Irma had lowered her voice, but Signe could still hear her whisper, "She really hasn't been raped?"

Is she disappointed? Did she want me to have been raped?

"Quite sure. It may have been close, but he can't have entered her fully otherwise I would see evidence and damage to the hymen."

"It's ok Sig, she's nearly done now. You're alright." Irma stroked her forehead and although it didn't ease her discomfort, the action, the gesture was a comfort mentally. She was cared about. And she craved some sympathy and understanding even if no one could possibly understand how she felt.

I'm intact. I have not been defiled. I am still complete. But how? How was it possible? He was on me, pressing into me. How could he not have entered me when I felt him so close?

"There we go, all done," the investigating doctor stood up and carefully placed the swabs in a plastic wallet and sealed the opening, writing on the designated reference space. "You can take a shower if you want and we can give you some clean underwear." She released Signe's legs from the stirrups and walked away to make notes at the worktop across the room.

Signe curled onto her side and put her hand over her face.

"Excuse me, what happens now?" Irma had followed the doctor.

"Oh yes, when she's dressed she needs to speak with the police officer who has to take her statement. Then she can go."

"Can't she give the statement in the morning? I don't think she's in a fit state to do any more tonight."

"Well, you can ask the officer, but I think she'll need to take some kind of statement tonight. This is the usual procedure."

"Okay, thanks." She turned back to Signe who was lying foetus-like on the gurney.

"Come on Si, let's get you in the shower. You'll feel better when you're all cleaned up."

I'll never be clean. "He raped me." Her voice was a monotone, stripped of emotion.

"Well, I think he tried to, but you must have fought him off before he was able to."

"He won't get away with it, will he?"

"Oh no, I'm sure he'll go to prison for a good long time. I think trying to rape someone is nearly as bad as actually raping them."

Irma was by now getting Signe off the trolley and towards the shower room.

"But they'll believe me won't they? I mean just because he didn't rape me they'll believe he tried to?"

"You bet, Si. There were witnesses. It was pretty obvious what was going on. But what happened? Why were you up on deck? Had you gone out there together?"

Signe stopped, trying to remember, but it was all hazy. How had she ended up on deck? She'd no idea. One minute she was sitting looking at the programme and the next thing she could remember was screaming with him on top of her. It was frightening. "I don't know."

The jets of water were sharp on her goose-bumped skin, ricocheting a haze of spray onto the glass cubicle. She could have turned the temperature down but her body craved heat and the exfoliating pressure felt cleansing and therapeutic. Her legs were jittering as she stood there, cupping her crotch with one hand as if protecting herself, watching the rivulets of water cascade over her hard nipples. As she watched, the heat of the water suffused her nipples with blood and the change in temperature sensitised and swole them, sending small electric shocks across her skin and tingling beneath her cupped hand. Despite herself her body seethed with desire, his image forcing itself into her mind no matter how she tried to resist it. She loathed herself.

"Si, you okay?"

Sudden anger swept her into violent rubbing. She had to wash his presence from her, wash his smell and skin from her skin, cleanse herself from his violation.

"Yah, I'm fine. Just coming."

Irma was there to receive her, steaming and dripping and shaking still. Irma rubbed her in the towel. "There you go....all nice and clean....that's better."

Sitting at the table in front of the policewoman with Irma at her side she felt odd, dislocated; she was suspended in another world, occupying another body. This body wasn't her body. Her body was light, white, clean; pristine, perfect, pure. This body she was now in was soiled, dirtied, besmirched. Its purity tainted by passion, the passion of desire.

Chapter 12

Hey Mags,

You must be wondering what's going on 'cos I haven't been mailing you. Don't know how to explain, but I've been accused of rape and I'm in a police station in Gothenburg. They've let me use a computer here to send this – I'm hardly allowed to speak to anyone and this will probably be screened.

I can't believe it. It was a mistake. I'll explain when I see you.

They've given me a lawyer, a nice young guy who thinks it'll be ok. He knows I didn't rape her. We just got a bit drunk and it kind of got out of hand. Now she claims I tried to rape her.

I'm stuck here in a remand centre until the trial, which will be in about 2 weeks. I don't want anyone else to know about this obviously. Can you tell my agent that I've been taken very ill with something – like one of those hospital bugs or jaundice or something, so I have to stay here? He'll have to let people know at ROH and for that Stabat Mater next weekend. But it's only Solihull. He'll have to find someone else.

Tell my parents the same thing, but make sure they don't think it's serious – they'll only panic and try to get involved. Actually I think they're away now on Easter break to my auntie's in Peterborough, but no one must know 'til it's all sorted.

You won't be able to reply to this as I can't receive emails or anything and anyway they've got my iPad and phone. Sorry. It's a big fuckup. Shouldn't have got so pissed, but you know how it is.

Miss you babe. Don't worry I'll be fine. See you when I get back. I'll ring as soon as I'm released.

M x

Chapter 13

"Ok, settle down, please. Kurt take that thing off your head!"

"It's not a thing, miss, it's a beanie," Kurt challenged.

"Thing, beanie, it doesn't matter what you call it, you're not to wear it in my class, thank you."

"Oh miss, come on, it's cool. And anyway it's my self-expression."

"Your self-expression is limited to answering the questions I ask you, not turning my classroom into some kind of teen fashion fest!"

"But that's against my human rights, miss, stopping my self-expression!"

"Kurt, if you continue to cheek me and don't take that thing off, the only right you'll be left with is to stay in for detention at lunchtime; the choice is yours."

There followed jeers at Kurt and "Woos" of admiration for Miss Neilson who had 'won out' the situation. Kurt removed the beanie and stuffed it into his pocket, not too put out really; it had wasted a few minutes of biology at least!

"Right, you remember last time we were talking about genes and variation." Murmurs, some of recognition, others more akin to groans. "So who remembers what an allele is? Yes Anne-Sophie."

"It's the different versions of a gene."

"Yes, that's right, the different versions of the same gene or characteristic. Now, most of the time you have two alleles for each characteristic – one from each parent. You remember that during sexual reproduction twenty three chromosomes from the sperm combine with twenty three chromosomes in the ovum, making a complete set of twenty three pairs of chromosomes in the new individual."

"Miss?"

"What is it Axel?"

"Can we do a practical in sexual reproduction, Miss?"

There was a general disturbance in the room, snorts and suppressed laughter.

"Well let's see Axel. How old are you?"

"What Miss?"

"How old are you? It's a simple enough question."

"Fifteen Miss."

"Right, well it would be legal at least! Hands up anyone who would be happy to provide Axel with twenty three single chromosomes, gestate the resulting foetus and then give birth to the baby so that he can take notes of how many of his alleles have passed on?"

A degree of mayhem then broke out, various girls giggling and screaming loud horror at the thought of allowing Axel's DNA to come anywhere near them. He then play-acted heart-broken and appealed to the class, whereupon Henrik put his hand up with a stupid grin on his face, to rapturous applause.

"Well, Henrik, that would certainly be a miraculous conception, unless you happen to have an ovum and womb about your person and a fair amount of oestrogen pumping through your body, which does seem rather unlikely! Okay everyone, settle down. We've had some fun, but let's now concentrate on the syllabus. Anyone who interrupts with inappropriate comments will get an immediate detention."

She went to her laptop and initiated a PowerPoint display on the screen while the excitement bubbled down to a tolerable level.

"Okay, quiet please. So genetic character traits are governed by alleles, which are passed from each parent. Now alleles can either be dominant or recessive and the combination determines the resultant phenotype. Remember the phenotype? That's the characteristics an individual displays, like whether they have blonde hair or long legs."

"I like the phenotype with both of those Miss" – snorts of approval.

"That's your last chance Axel, I'm serious."

"Sorry, Miss."

"So, you remember we looked at the determination of the sex of an individual caused by a female parent having two X chromosomes and a male parent having one X and one Y chromosome. These were neither dominant nor recessive so were equally probable for male or female."

She brought up a diagram.

"This is a punnett square diagram showing the possible offspring from the combination of male and female chromosomes and as you can see we have two possible outcomes for female and two for male, an equal result. Generally alleles for character have an unequal result, seventy–five percent to twenty-five percent, because dominant alleles, as the name suggests, govern the outcome.

"So let's say that we have an allele which in squirrels governs tail length. The dominant allele, which we write as a capital, is responsible for normal tail length. The recessive which gives a long tail we write as small case. So parents both have one B and one b, one dominant and one recessive and if we do the punnett square you can see the result of the mix is BB, Bb, bB and bb. The first three will be normal tailed squirrels and only the final bb will show a long tail. Therefore there's only a twenty-five percent chance of having a long tail. What's so funny Alex?"

Alex was shaking helplessly and hysterically in noiseless mirth. His male near neighbours then also snorted and buried their heads in their arms, unable to control themselves.

"I thought we'd grown up a bit now that we'd reached grade ten, but obviously there are those that are still amused by childish humour," Miss Neilson was getting a bit ragged now and turned back to the projection.

"Miss?"

"Yes," she said whirling around, "What is it, Sara?"

"What happens if you have a dominant and a recessive to start with?"

"Ok, we'll all work it out using the punnett square. Put the BB along the top and the bb down the side and see what you end up with. This method always gives you the combinations."

"All dominant Miss."

"That's right, Hagan, the recessive is not seen at all in the possible offspring, because every possible combination is governed by the dominant allele."

She turned back to the laptop and clicked onto the next PowerPoint page. "Now an interesting and very apparent characteristic in humans which we can easily observe is eye colour. As you know there are lots of different eye colours, but originally Homo sapiens all had brown eyes and indeed brown is the dominant allele for eyes. In fact eye colour is said to be inherited polygenically, that is, it is controlled by a combination of different genes. For our purposes we are going to talk about the basic dominant brown gene which governs most eye colour and the recessive blue gene which gives only blue, grey and blue/grey eyes.

"So, as with the dominant allele in squirrels, brown dominates as a determinant of eye colour in humans and will therefore proliferate over blue eyes. So we have quite a few blue-eyed people in the class, so hopefully we can see this in action. Eva, you have lovely blue eyes. What colour are your parents' eyes?"

"Well, my mum's eyes are definitely blue but my dad's are kind of browny grey."

"So we can see that your mum is bb", she wrote on the white board, "and your dad is Bb and therefore you are the twenty-five percent chance of getting the two recessive genes like your mum and therefore inheriting blue eyes. What about you Erika?"

"My mum and dad both have blue eyes," Erika smilingly replied.

"There we are," cried Miss Neilson enthusiastically, glad to have the theory so quickly and clearly demonstrated. "The two recessive parents **have** to produce a blue-eyed offspring. What about your parents Christoph?"

Signe was preoccupied with drawing a very neat punnett square diagram in her book. She was always meticulous with anything she entered in her school books and her attention was distracted. *What did Miss Neilson just say?*

"Ah, my mum's kind of got dark browny green and my dad's are..." Christoph appeared a bit embarrassed. "... I don't know, I think they're probably light brown really."

"Good, so we can say that your mum and dad are both Bb and again you are the twenty-five percent with the recessive genes."

*"The two recessive parents **have** to produce a blue-eyed offspring. Was that what she said?"*

"Right, so let's look at non blue-eyed people and see what colour their parents' eyes are."

Signe panicked. *Don't let her ask me.*

"Madalena, what about you, you have, what, hazel eyes?"

Signe breathed, but her heart was clenched as she reviewed the information. *Blue eyes, recessive allele. Both parents blue-eyed HAD to produce a blue-eyed child. You didn't even need to do the punnett square for that, it was blindingly obvious. To have blue eyes you had to have two bs and if you mixed two blue-eyed recessives the only possible outcome was a recessive offspring as there were no Bs possible to dominate.*

"Ya, I guess. My dad has greyish eyes and my mum says hers are green, but I don't think they are really," Madalena said, smiling doubtfully.

"Ok, well women like to have green eyes. They're more unusual and actually sometimes hazel eyes can look more green, but the point is they would be the dominant allele and when mixed with your dad's recessive, you are the seventy-five percent chance of none blue eyes."

Why didn't she have blue eyes?

"Miss, what causes all the other eye colours?" Greta asked.

"Ah, well, this is where it gets complicated. Eye colour isn't perhaps the best example of genetic traits, but it's a very apparent one which is why we're looking at it, but in fact eye colour is determined by other things than genetics and can even change over time due to certain conditions like diet and stress."

Signe clutched at this possibility. *Maybe it was one of these other reasons....*

"Of course when Caucasian babies are born and 'til they are about a year old they have blue eyes and the colour comes in later. It's to do with the make-up of the stroma and the content of melanin it contains which affects the absorption or reflection of light. However, that is a big subject and not really to do with genetics. The point here is that blue is recessive and all other eye colours are dominant."

But Miss Neilson just said again, blue is recessive and all other eye colours are dominant. Lars has blue eyes just like mum and dad, so why don't I? Signe wanted to ask, but couldn't in front of everyone. *What could be the reason? There must be a variation, an exception to the rule. Or else I'm a freak, a genetic mutation.*

"Now, for us in Scandinavia the blue eye colour is a very interesting trait. Can anyone think of anything strange about the fact that the blue allele is recessive?"

Signe could only think of one thing. *How can I have brown eyes when my parents both have blue?*

"Think of the percentage probability of brown eyes dominating and then think of the number of people in Sweden with blue eyes," Miss Neilson prompted.

"Miss, is it that most people in Sweden have blue eyes, but if brown is dominant then you would expect about three quarters of the population to have brown eyes?" Hagan ventured.

"Absolutely. So this is a very strange phenomenon. Why, when you would expect only twenty-five percent of the population to be blue-eyed do we find the majority to be blue-eyed? In fact in Estonia ninety-nine percent of the population have blue eyes; in Germany seventy-five percent; in Sweden eighty percent. Well, there was some interesting research done at the University of Tromso in Norway to try to understand this anomaly. They took a random sample of men and women and tested their preference for attractiveness by using photos of people with different eye colours and extraordinarily they found that blue-eyed people invariably preferred blue-eyed people, whereas people with other eye colour had no discernible preference."

"Miss, but maybe these people just found those women or men attractive anyway. Maybe it had nothing to do with their blue-eyes."

"Good point, Eva, but they thought of that and manipulated the photos in the experiment. They replaced brown eyes with blue ones and vice-versa and the blue-eyed men still preferred the blue-eyed women."

"Wow, that's amazing. So what do they think the reason is?" Greta was obviously intrigued by this, and the rest of the class were seemingly also switched on by the idea, as it had become very quiet.

There was another possibility. Signe's stomach somersaulted as it occurred to her. *Her dad was not her dad!*

"Well they're not absolutely sure, but it seems to suggest that blue-eyed people have developed an unconscious favouring of the recessive trait, recognising a similar genetic type and thereby protecting the weaker recessive allele."

"But Miss, that kind of goes completely against random selection doesn't it?"

Miss Neilson was on a roll! This was the moment all teachers craved; to have the class in the palm of your hand having managed to capture their imaginations and know that you had their undivided attention. She just needed to keep dropping little pieces of information for them to greedily feast on and the rest of the period was a piece of cake.

"Well exactly Georg, it would seem to. But you know, we are beginning to find that there are some inherited behavioural characteristics in various animals which seem to suggest a gene's ability to preserve itself and this may just be another. Normally we find genetic characteristics selected, as you rightly point out, by the 'survival of the fittest'. The animal with the traits most suited to the environment it's living in will tend to survive and those traits will tend to prevail in subsequent generations. Or the animal which appears to be healthiest, either by its winning looks or its strength, agility or speed for instance will win the race for a partner."

"But, miss, what you're saying is that some genes seem to have an intelligence to survive and they manipulate the person they're inside to help them survive. That sounds pretty weird, like you're being programmed to act in a certain way."

"Yeah, like you're some kind of machine."

"You **can** think of the human body as a machine which is programmed by its genetic make-up which influences character and therefore to a certain extent behaviour. You just have to allow that maybe the genetic make-up might influence behaviour more directly than we had previously thought, so in this instance of eye colour, it appears that the gene is protecting itself and its characteristic by influencing behaviour..."

At that moment the bell went and there would have been the usual stampede had not Miss Neilson managed to contain them with a shout of "HOMEWORK!" followed by a general groan. "Now for homework, it's really easy, I just want you to make five punnett square graphs for five members of your family – can be you and four others. If you don't have many relations just do friends whose parents you know. Write down eye colour of parents, suggest probable alleles and show offspring with probable alleles for their eye colour. By next lesson please."

The usual pandemonium then ensued of a whole class erupting into conversation as bags are picked up, chairs scraped back, books smacked together and the general clatter of exodus to morning break proceeds.

Signe hung back whilst Miss Neilson was tidying up, sorting out her laptop. When everyone was gone she sidled up to her desk.

"Hi."

"Oh Signe. You okay?"

"Yup. I was just wondering. You know you said eye colour was polygenic?"

"Ya."

"Well, that surely means there could be lots of different ways you could end up with different coloured eyes."

"Of course. But the polygenicity only affects the variations of eye colour, not the basic eye colour. The dominant brown and recessive blue alleles still govern basic colour and this is an unchanging rule. We'll go into variations a bit more next class, ok?"

It was obvious Miss Neilson was eager to get to her coffee, so Signe thanked her and left. She walked outside into the bright sunlight. It glanced obliquely down through the pine trees, dappling the playground, casting deep shadows in places and in others blinding the eye with its dazzling reflection off the sandy ground. There was the usual coterie of enthusiastic basket-ballers rushing side to side, bouncing the ball, jabbing, feinting and thrusting passes across the space til one could make a shot in the millisecond when he was suspended between the ascent and descent of a leap.

Beyond, another ball was flying into the net of a football goal as a triumphant yell went up. Groups of girls ambled aimlessly, some arm in arm, gossiping loudly or sniggering at a whispered secret.

Signe didn't want company and made her way to her favourite spot up behind the school, above where it had been hewn into the hillside. Granite boulders and outcrops sat fatly between the pine trunks which rose at various angles from their cramped root boles. She liked this elevated place away from the noise of the play areas where you could look down on the school buildings and hear the wind soughing in the branches. A water tower stood sentinel to the left, its white concrete sides lifting seamlessly into the sky above the surrounding pines like a lookout post in some Middle Earth fantasy world.

She sat on a rock which was encroached by moss and grasses and tried to begin to understand what it all meant. If both her parents have blue eyes, she should have blue eyes. Lars has blue eyes, why didn't she? It could only mean one thing – her dad wasn't her dad. That thought was horrible, and as it wormed its way deeper into her brain it spawned other thoughts which wriggled and claimed attention, thoughts which were painful to contemplate and harrowing to deal with. If her dad wasn't her real dad, then who was? How did it happen that he wasn't? Was he actually Lars' father or not? Does her dad know he's not her father? Did her mum have an affair and not tell him so that he thinks he's her dad? But her mother couldn't have had an affair; she's so proper, religious and strict. She wouldn't have let herself, would she?

She thought of the rows her parents sometimes had and imagined them separating, maybe for a few months and then getting back together again, by which time her mother was pregnant by someone else. But she couldn't have, wouldn't have.

She kicked a few twigs at her feet and pulled her fingers through her thick tresses of hair, twisting them together and turning the ends, distractedly looking for splits. Oh how she hated genetics! The moment they'd started it she knew she'd feel threatened. It always happened when there were discussions about the origin of life and the infinity of the universe. She felt they challenged her belief, called into question the validity of the Written Word and stacked piles of irrefutable scientific evidence against the tender wisdom of her faith. It was so difficult to square her faith in God with the myriad facts she was faced with at school. Each scientific theory she learnt about, with its premise, practical experiment and provability was like a body blow to her belief and sometimes she struggled to maintain her commitment to Him.

It must have been so much easier when mankind didn't know so much, she thought, when the mysteries of the world were so numerous and inexplicable and Man was helpless in the face of disease, natural disaster and the elements. But now that science has conquered so many diseases, explained away so many complex systems and alleviated so many of the difficulties of life, people didn't think they needed God anymore. They were now trying to explain how the whole universe began using the LHC, calling it the God Moment. She bit her lip, fighting back her anger. Why were people so arrogant? Why did they think they knew better than God? Their vanity only strengthened her resolve and her determination not to be swayed by the easy embrace of scientific fact over spiritual belief.

There was a sudden clap and splatter of wings as a collared dove fluttered down from the trees overhead and landed a few feet from her.

It looked at her with its glittering pin eye as she remained motionless. It seemed to realise she posed no threat as it proceeded to peck about in the leaf litter, flicking unwanted pieces here and there whilst giving her an occasional beady glance. It was so close that Signe could see every detail of its creamy white plumage; the soft blush of the lightest chestnut in its breast feathers, the sudden blackness of the ring at its neck. And each covert feather, as she had learned, composed of a quill with countless lateral veins all zipped together with minute hooks to achieve an amazingly light, air-resistant paddle which, when arranged with others along an articulated aero-dynamic arm, creates the perfect blade for flight. And all those feathers grow according to the genetic code in the cells; the down feathers fluffy and insulating, the flight feathers hooked and water resistant, the neck feathers grey and short and only black at a particular point to make the collar. All this dictated by genes passed down through generations, (or was that gene rations?), dictated by natural selection and the chance mutations of cells over millions of years.

That was just too amazing, too miraculous a sequence of events to arrive at this fantastic creature strutting about before her, confident in its particular behaviour. There had to be a Divine hand in this, she was convinced. And that programme she'd seen on TV recently about the Fibonacci sequence; the pure perfect mathematics which applies to all aspects of the natural world couldn't be a force of chance, a 'bit of luck'. God's hand was obviously there, His fingerprint coded in all life, at every point, if you could just read it.

The dove had found a spindly birch twig which it was turning and dropping and picking up again. Then, apparently satisfied with its selection, with a clap of wings it scattered off up into a nearby pine tree where Signe could just make out the beginnings of a nest high up in the crux of three branches. How did it know how to build a nest? How did it know which twig to choose? How did it know that such a twig was just the right one for the nest? Its parents never showed it. It had been off by itself long before they built another nest the following year. Yet somewhere, programmed into its very nature, it inherently 'knew' the process required to create a dove's nest. Genetics? Instinct? God!

She offered an impromptu prayer of thanks as the bell rang for the end of break time and, with sudden energy, she grabbed her bag, sprang off her perch and flew away to physics.

Chapter 14

"Dear Lord, we thank you for the fruits of Your gracious bounty and for the gift of Your Son our Saviour Jesus Christ, Amen".

Gustav Larsson crossed himself fleetingly with practised humility before Mrs Larsson served out the spaghetti and meatballs which was the staple Thursday night meal. Normally she eschewed 'shop-bought muck', as her mother had called it, but because she was always out all day on a Thursday volunteering at the Catholic bookshop attached to the Cathedral in Göteborg, she made a concession to her husband's favourite frozen brand from the supermarket, 'killing two birds with one stone'.

Two large helpings of spaghetti crowned with a glistening pile of tomatoey meatballs arrived plumply in front of father and son, followed by a very different arrangement carefully constructed on Signe's plate, the spaghetti to one side and the meatballs to the other separated distinctly by a line of pure unadulterated plate. If the spaghetti was 'infected' by the tomato sauce it wasn't possible to eat it!

Having waited whilst Mrs Larsson served herself her usual minute portion, which she used both as a tacit visual protest against the meal and as a useful weight-watching aid, they all set to in their various fashions. Signe's dad preferred using just a fork, expertly twirling the spaghetti through the centre of the mound, thereby gathering a good coating of the sauce with every mouthful, and alternating these with a pronged meatball well rolled in sauce. Lars adopted the spoon and fork combination, attempting the fork roll but mainly scooping as much of everything onto the spoon as possible and cramming this swiftly into an overstretched jaw, hoping to avoid the usual admonishments from his mother in respect of decent table manners. She in contrast managed to make her small portion last as if it were ten times the size by dissecting each meatball, cutting the spaghetti into tiny lengths and combining the two in delicate forkfuls. Signe followed her ritual of eating all the spaghetti first with extra butter melted on the top, carefully rolling the fork in the spoon without touching the tomato sauce, and when, only when, all the spaghetti was gone could she embark on the meatballs, which she stabbed with the fork and ate little nibbles from, re-dipping in sauce until each ball was gone.

"How was hockey practice? Did they sort the front line?" Signe's dad always had to get the latest update on the junior team from Lars.

"Ya."

"And? Who did they put in?"

"Henrik."

"They moved Henrik from wing to centre? So who's on right wing now?"

"Dag."

"But he was a defenseman wasn't he?"

"Yup," this all through a large mouthful.

"Lars, really! Come on, some table manners please," his mum urged.

"But Dag hasn't played there before has he?" his dad continued, as if his wife hadn't spoken.

"Nah."

"Is he fast?"

"Ya."

"What's his shooting like? Has he scored many goals before?"

"He's ok."

"So what's happening in the right defenseman position? Who's replacing him?"

"Mateo."

"Mateo? Who's he?"

"New kid."

"One of Mr Svenson's scouting recruits?"

"Yeah."

"Is he good? Have you played with him?"

"Pretty good."

Mr Larsson began to experience the usual frustration with the near monosyllabic replies he received from his son when talking about anything. Why couldn't teenagers hold a conversation? Was it computer age syndrome, gaming? He was sure he hadn't been like that. He'd always argued every point with his parents, fought to listen to pop music and asserted his individuality, backing it up with spiky rhetoric about freedom of thought and personal destiny. Lars didn't seem to have an interest in anything except hockey, and even then he seemed incapable of having a conversation.

"I suppose they wouldn't break up the second line."

"Nah. Can I leave the table?"

"Lars, there's dessert, and we haven't finished yet," his mum's plate was only half eaten.

"But they're announcing the new Indians line up for next season on TV."

Mr Larsson looked at his wife, raising his eyebrows and compressing his lips in that 'it's up to you dear but it's the only thing he's interested in and quite frankly he's not much of a conversationalist so why not let him go he'll only be a pain if you make him stay' expression.

"No Lars, you stay til we've finished eating please."

"God that's so unfair. None of my friends even have to sit and eat with their family. They can eat in their rooms."

"Well, Lars, isn't that a fine indictment of the twenty-first century; the breakdown of the family unit, everyone eating by themselves. Well it's not going to happen in this family so you can just sit there 'til we've all finished and have some consideration and respect."

When Mrs Larsson 'went off on one' like this, no-one challenged her; meal protocol was her domain!

There was silence for a minute as this cloud passed.

"So Signe, what did you learn today?" Her dad often shot that question at her out of the blue, challenging her for a ready answer, but also seemingly checking up on the education system to see if the policies of the new government were resulting in detrimental changes on the ground.

Usually Signe fended off these sallies with an astute reference to something reasonably complicated which inevitably silenced him, as although he was no fool and had done well at school, being an older parent his education had involved very different subject matter from the present school curricula and he wasn't versed in the detail she was familiar with. But he enjoyed challenging himself and airing his knowledge.

"We were doing genetics in biology," she said.

"Well, that's a big topic," he answered confidently, "chromosomes, the double helix, twenty-three pairs," he put in, just to show he knew. Then, warming to his subject, "Actually, I was reading an interesting article about cystic fibrosis and how it's often inherited through two people who never knew they were carrying the disease. It's a recessive gene which is normally not seen, but if two people with it have a child that child has a chance of getting the disease." He expounded a bit further about how they were trying to find ways to deal with the genetic material to find a cure, which is what the article had apparently been about. Signe fiddled with her food, hesitating whether to broach the subject or not. What would happen? Would her mum break down? Would there be a scene? Would they refuse to talk about it? Was she brave enough to go through with it? But she had to find out; had to know whether she was imagining things or whether genetics was the catalyst to revealing a truth about her life, which although it might be painful, she had to know. "....we've got so much to be thankful for that we don't have to deal with terrible situations like that," her dad finished up.

Signe waited a couple of beats. "Yes, we were looking at inherited characteristics too, including recessive genes," she said, looking him in the eye and not sure if she detected a flicker of fear as he glanced at her mum, who hadn't been paying much attention to the conversation, lost in thoughts of her own.

"We were looking at recessive genes in eye colour," she continued, determined now to go through with it. "Did you know that statistically blue-eyed men are more attracted to blue-eyed women than to women with other eye colours?"

"Well that certainly seems to be the case here," her dad blurted out with a laugh and smiled at her mum, who began to be aware what the conversation was about and smiled back. "But that's nothing to do with genetics."

"Hold on," Signe held her hand up. "Lars, what colour eyes has Astrid got?"

"What?"

"Astrid, what colour are her eyes?"

"Dunno," Lars answered with a shrug. He hadn't been following the conversation; the iPhone he'd sneaked out of his pocket under the table taking his whole attention.

"What? You've been going out with her for, what is it, two weeks, and you don't know what colour her eyes are?" her Dad exclaimed incredulously.

"I think they're blue," Lars eventually offered, lamely. "Why?"

"There we are," said Signe. "It's weird isn't it? Apparently most blue-eyed men just *are* attracted to blue-eyed women." This was the calm before the storm. "Because otherwise, there wouldn't be so many blue-eyed people." Did her dad begin to look worried? She couldn't tell. "Because the gene for blue eyes is recessive." Her dad had got it. "If both parents have blue eyes, it's impossible not to have a blue-eyed child." She hadn't expected Lars to cotton on, but her mum was obviously still in the dark, despite her dad giving her meaningful looks.

She'd said it. There was a long pause only interrupted by the staccato metallic tapping of her mum's knife and fork. She finally finished and pushed her plate to one side.

"Is that your iPhone you've got under there, Lars?"

"Mum, did you hear what I said?" Signe blurted out, as the tears would come.

"Yes darling, but I was never very good at biology, so I'm afraid it doesn't make much sense to me. Why are you getting so upset?"

"It's not difficult to understand," Signe almost shouted, the anger and frustration forcing her to attack, which startled her mother. "If both parents have blue eyes they can only have blue eyed children. Now d'you understand?" she practically screamed and then collapsed into shaking sobs.

"I don't see why you're getting mad at her." Lars suddenly piped up. "So, blue eyed parents have blue eyed children. What's the problem?"

"Because, in case you hadn't noticed in fourteen years, I've got brown eyes, dumbo!" Signe shouted.

"Hey hey, come on you two, calm down," her dad interrupted, but then stopped short. Her mum was biting her lip and fiddling with her placemat. Lars' brain was still processing the information to the only possible conclusion.

"So..... why's Si got brown eyes?"

Mr Larsson looked at his wife, "I said it would come out sooner or later. Are you going to tell her?"

"Tell her what?" Lars was all attention now, sensing an imminent revelation.

Mrs Larsson hesitated, her bottom lip quivering, but then dove in.

"I didn't want you to feel lost or rejected. I just wanted you to be a happy normal little girl, so I didn't want you to know. I didn't want anyone to know. I didn't want them to treat you differently."

"What are you saying mum?" Lars pressured.

"Hang on, hang on," their dad now interjected. "Let's go right back to the beginning, ok Melissa?"

She nodded.

"When your mum and I wanted to start a family we found we couldn't and so after some time we went to have some tests at the hospital to find out why. It turned out I have a very low sperm count and they said realistically there was only about a one per cent chance we could conceive. Right Mel?"

She nodded again. "So we decided to adopt," she continued, "and we signed up at the adoption agency for a baby or a very young child, to bring up as our own."

"After going through all the meetings and assessments," her husband continued, "we were accepted onto the programme as eligible adopters and a few months later they told us a little baby girl of ten months old needed a home."

Mrs Larsson was sitting motionless with her hands clasped on the table in front of her, gazing at Signe, the tears gently gliding down her cheeks. Signe was still hugging herself, looking down at the table.

"We were so happy to have our little girl after so long wanting a family and you made our lives complete. But then, eight months later, a miracle happened and your mum found she was pregnant. The one per cent chance of a baby had unbelievably happened and six months later Lars was born."

The silence that followed was hollow and hung heavily.

"Why didn't you tell us?" Signe looked at the woman across the table who was no longer her mother.

"When?" she answered. "When could we tell you? When is a good time to tell your child she is not really your child? When you were three? Six? Twelve? We had a happy family, living a normal life. What was the point of shattering that reality and upsetting you unnecessarily? You were our daughter, you **are** our daughter and we will always love you just the same."

Signe looked in her direction, but actually stared through her. "But I'm not your daughter. I'm someone else's daughter. Someone I don't know, and who doesn't know me. Who are they? Do you know them? Do they live near here?" she said quietly, rationally, apparently without emotion.

Mr Larsson said gently "We don't have any contact with them and don't know where they are. They weren't very well when you were rescued...."

"Rescued?"

"They were....having a bad time; didn't have anywhere to live or the means to support you. We were able to offer you a secure home which they couldn't. It was for the best, really."

"Did you meet them?"

"No. We weren't allowed to. That's not how it's done."

Signe sat quietly, drained of emotion, grappling with the implications.

"I'm going to my room," she said.

"Signe, honestly, we tried to do it the best way we could, what we thought was right." Mr Larsson caught her in his arms as she passed and squeezed her to him. When he released her she walked mechanically out to the stairs. They heard her footsteps trudge up each tread and the door of her room click shut.

Silence ensued. Lars looked at his dad standing where she had left him, his mum sitting motionless.

"So we're not related. She's not actually my sister."

His mum tidied herself up, regaining her composure. "Of course she's your sister. You grew up together, you're just not blood-related. But she's still your sister. Nothing's changed."

Lars got up from the table, walked off into the snug and turned on the TV.

She took her clothes off, laying them neatly on the chair by the bed, and slunk into the sheets, welcoming their cool embrace. She lay on her back with her arms by her side staring at the ceiling.

Adopted.

The word had so much connotation; orphaned, abandoned, impoverished broken relationships, abuse....

She felt defiled. The clean orthodoxy of her life was now sullied by a mess of questions. Who were her real parents? What were they like? Did she have real brothers and sisters? Before she was adopted, what had happened? Where had she been? Who had she been with?

It was like she had suddenly lost part of herself. Those months that most people don't remember anyway, but which are explained by first photos and treasured accounts. And yet it explained something she'd always found weird, that there weren't any photos of her when she was a baby, whereas there were pictures of Lars. She remembered she'd asked her mum about that once and she'd said they'd lost them or something.

She tried to see if she could remember anything at all of when she was a baby, anything which might give her an idea or picture of those first eight months, maybe a smell or taste. Nothing. It was a blank.

But that wasn't surprising. She had never had any recollection of anything different, of being in a different environment with different people. What about dreams? Did any of her dreams give a clue of that time? She tried to think of any dream she had regularly. There was the one about Christmas; the one when she was dressed as a Maundy Thursday witch and flew away on her broomstick, but that always got mixed up with the middle of a quidditch game and racing Harry Potter; and the one about swimming with dolphins. Then there was the snake one – well that was a nightmare really, but it kept coming back. She gripped her legs together, recoiling as the images insisted playing through her mind. The couple in the long grass, their faces contorted in ghastly pleasure, were they her real parents? It was a horrible thought, but it was a possibility; something she might have seen when she was very young. Otherwise where did that image come from?

Adopted. Why hadn't they told her? They'd been lying to her all these years. All these years they had let her believe she was their child and Lars was her brother. How could they do that? How could they have lied to her when she had trusted them? A tap on the door interrupted her thoughts, and her mum crept in, only she wasn't her mum.

"Signe, are you alright?"

She couldn't speak. She felt she was suffocating. Her 'mum' moved the clothes onto the back of the chair and sat on it next to the bed.

"I know it's hard, but nothing's changed really. You're our daughter and we love you. Nothing's going to change that."

Signe lay tense, confused, not knowing whether she wanted her to go or stay.

"Maybe we should have told you, but we didn't want to spoil things, upset you. We only ever wanted you to be happy and not worry about things."

Signe swallowed back the urge to cry. "I don't know who I am," she croaked.

"You're Signe Larsson, a very beautiful, talented and precious girl."

"But that's what you've made me, not what I truly am. I need to know the real me." Signe turned her head and searched the face of the woman sitting next to her, this woman whom she knew so well, but whom she now knew better, as not her mother. Her whole thinking was now so radically altered, looking at this face in front of her the words in her head screamed 'this is not your mother, this is Lars' mother, not yours'.

It hurt; the feeling of having been deceived. The feeling of loss of that which you had known and which now proves to have been a lie. A whole unravelling of all that you had believed in and which now wasn't - 'Uncle' Mats, 'Auntie' Agi and 'cousins' Elizabetta and Marta. All lies. She turned her head back to look at the ceiling again. She didn't want to cry, but she felt the soft tears slip gently down her temples.

"I'm so sorry, Signe, I really am. It may have been selfish, but we were just doing our best. We hadn't done this before – it was new to us. It was a difficult time, Gustav had a new job, there was so much to do, and then, I think, it was too late."

She stood and leant over and kissed Signe on the forehead before quietly leaving the room and closing the door behind her.

Chapter 15

"So, Mr Chamberlain, you were very drunk and you went up on deck to try to sober up and you found the victim asleep on a bench."

The look in his eyes told Matt that this guy was a terrier. He wouldn't let anything go and would jump on anything he said that didn't corroborate.

"No, I ....well, yes I was a bit drunk..."

"One of the waiters, Mr Forstein, says in his statement, I quote, 'Mr Chamberlain was giggling in a drunken fashion during the speeches and was reeling when he left the room'."

My God, he's even interviewed the staff. "I was a bit drunk, but was still in control of myself. I left the dining room to use the toilet which was on the deck above and when I came out I thought I could do with some air."

"As I said, so that you could sober up. And when you arrived on deck you saw the defendant asleep on a bench, which presented an ideal opportunity."

Matt could feel himself getting wound up and looked across to his lawyer, who closed his eyes and nodded briefly, encouraging him he thought, to keep calm and carry on.

"No, when I went on deck I didn't see her...."

"Not at first maybe."

"If you let me finish, she wasn't there. The deck was empty, deserted."

"Well, I don't think that's true, because a few moments later when you attacked her, two witnesses arrived in seconds when they heard her scream. They were also on deck as they say in their statements."

Matt took a deep breath. "Well, obviously they were there, but I didn't see them."

"So it wasn't deserted."

"Well, I thought it was."

"How convenient. So this gave you the privacy you needed."

Matt felt the sweat prick under his arms as he began to feel flustered. This guy was impossible. He could twist anything any which way.

"So, we've established that you had no idea whether there were people on the deck or not, so I put it to you that you arrived there completely unaware that the victim was asleep on the bench, but then you saw her and assumed the deck was deserted."

"No," Matt raised his voice, and immediately saw a small look of triumph in his interrogator's eyes. *Damn.* "Please let me explain."

"With pleasure," he smiled without smiling and looked to the jury with a raise of his eyebrow.

"I arrived on deck and didn't see anyone. I walked towards the front of the ship and then moved across to the right and leant on the railing. There was a full moon shining on the water; a beautiful evening."

"How romantic!" There was a titter from someone.

"So I put it to you that here you are on deck on a beautiful moonlit evening, drunk, and lascivious thoughts enter your mind because, Mr Chamberlain, you are by nature a highly-sexed individual are you not?"

"Madam Chairman," his counsel was on his feet. "I feel the prosecution is making leading suggestions."

"Sustained Mr Bergstrom. Please modify your questioning Mr Thorne or substantiate your assertions."

"With pleasure, Madam." Matt's attorney looked worried when he shot him a glance. "I would never," the prosecution continued smoothly, "make such an assertion without hard evidence and I feel sure the court will take note of this revealing piece of information." He made a performance of finding some sheets of paper and brandishing them in the air. Matt was non-plussed. *What the hell's he talking about?*

"I have here in my hand graphic evidence of the type of thing the accused is interested in. Mr Chamberlain, do you recognise these pictures?"

He gave the papers to the court clerk to show to Matt. He was confused. They were pornographic pictures of women in various bondage outfits. He thought he recognised them, but couldn't place them.

"These pictures," the prosecution continued, "are screen captures from Mr Chamberlain's computer which the police seized in his hotel room. The pictures are from a website which was linked to him in an email two days before the assault took place and involve sado-masochistic activity and dominance-featured role-play."

Matt was stunned; *Maggie's dirty email about the latest addition to her wardrobe.*

"I would suggest, Madam Chairman, that this revelation casts a certain light on Mr Chamberlain's character not unrelated to the case we are considering."

The judge nodded as she was shown the photos which were then passed to the court.

Matt was mortified. His counsel looked questioningly at him, then looked away shaking his head. *They've been through my room and all my things. God, there's no privacy.*

He looked across at the jury who were passing the pictures from one to another and grimacing. It didn't look good. He could almost feel the antagonism build against him. What would his counsel say in defence? It's not a crime to have pictures of fetish gear, but it doesn't paint a good picture.

"Furthermore, Madam Chairman, I have another exhibit for you. In addition to the contents of the laptop, this card was also found in the hotel room. It would appear the accused visited the Konstmuseum, but out of all the cards he could have chosen to buy, it seems this was the only one he chose, a sexually explicit photograph of an erotic sculpture, further evidence of his sex-obsessed nature."

With a complacent smile he passed this evidence to the court clerk who handed it to the judge, who, Matt thought, looked at it for a surprisingly long moment before handing it back with a strange expression – eyes glittering and cheeks flushed. Was she embarrassed? Surely the bondage gear was more embarrassing? She was a good-looking woman Matt thought, in that very collected and austere Swedish way, straight blond hair in a bob, clear almost translucent skin and oblong glasses perched on a thin nose.

"I presume, Mr Chamberlain, that you don't deny that this card was purchased by yourself before the assault."

"No."

There was a small disturbance at the back of the room as the doors were opened and someone was shown into the public area. Matt didn't notice much as he was trying to concentrate on his cross-examination.

"No, Mr Chamberlain, how could you deny that? And no doubt you also won't deny that you are by nature predatory to women, seizing any opportunity to lure them into your power."

"What?" Matt blurted out, "How can you say that? You're just making things up." He looked pleadingly at his attorney, who just raised his eyebrows.

"Well, Mr Chamberlain, if it's evidence you want let's just look at the situation. Do you have a girlfriend?"

"Yes."

"Yes, Maggie, the equally highly-sexed woman who sent you the link to the pornographic pictures. But not content with having an active sexual partner at home in England, when you're away and the opportunity arises you waste no time in trying your luck with any woman who falls in your path."

Matt couldn't believe what he was hearing. He was trying desperately to keep his cool and looked away from his inquisitor towards the public gallery where he became aware of someone waving at him. *Mags? Maggie? Here in Gothenburg? How? When? She must have been the one shown in. God. Mags here at his trial! How did she know where to go? What did she think she was doing?*

"Mr Chamberlain, on the day of the assault you had lunch with Miss Caterina Jokela at La Riviera restaurant on Postgaten, and the same night after the concert you were seen to behave in a very familiar manner towards her at the reception. I put it to you that this further establishes your character as a womaniser with a predatory nature. Do you deny this?"

"I had lunch with Caterina certainly, but I reject your accusation that I'm a womaniser. We were colleagues eating together. It's ridiculous to suggest that this means I'm a womaniser." He gave an appealing look to his lawyer who now stood.

"Madam Chairman, I find Mr Thorne's line of approach insinuating and based on pure conjecture. I feel he's attempting to discredit my client using flimsy and circumstantial evidence."

"Madam Chairman, I am merely trying to gather a picture of the defendant's state of mind and natural appetites, to put the assault in context. My intention is to show that the assault was not just a result of drink, but is based on the defendant's obsession with sex and women."

The judge removed her spectacles releasing the full penetrating gaze of her blue eyes. "Mr Thorne, don't let your desire to paint a true picture of the accused stray into the realm of fiction. More facts please."

"Madam Chairman, I would humbly submit that Mr Thorne's questioning and assertions are trying to portray my client in a bad light more than trying to prove that rape has taken place, which I believe is what the trial is trying to establish."

"Mr Bergstrom, thank you for your helpful comment, but I'll decide what is and what is not relevant to this case." She replaced the glasses. "Please continue, Mr Thorne."

Matt looked across at Maggie. She had settled herself and was sorting out a mess of two or three tangled scarves which looked like they were threatening to strangle her. She was flushed and bright-eyed. She must have been running and was dishevelled but radiant, and strangely beautiful from where he sat, her dark hair wildly Amazonian around her dark skin.

"I think the court will by now have a picture of the accused in their minds which is perhaps rather different from the smart young man in front of them. Things are not always as they seem. To go back to the details of the assault after this small but important diversion. So, Mr Chamberlain, you are on the deck and apparently there is no-one else there. Continue."

Matt promised himself to keep calm. "As I said, I was leaning on the ship's rail looking at the water, when I heard a door slam behind me. I turned around and saw a figure lurching across the deck...."

"Lurching? What do you mean by lurching?"

"Well, walking unsteadily, from side to side. She looked drunk."

"So you could tell the figure was that of a woman."

"Of course. She was wearing a skirt."

"And did you think she was attractive, alone on this deck, in this romantic evening?"

Matt paused and breathed slowly. "I couldn't see her face. She had her back to me. She was wandering towards the front of the ship."

"But I thought that's where you were."

"Well, I had been, but I had moved to the rail at the side."

"Ah, so you moved from the front to the side."

"Yes, there's no rail at the front. The rail goes down the side of the ship, you see," Matt said sarcastically.

"There's no need to patronise me, Mr Chamberlain. I'm just trying to establish the order of events."

"Madam Chairman, what has this to do with whether rape actually took place?" his lawyer was standing.

"I would ask you once again to let me be the judge of that Mr Bergstrom."

"Thank you, Madam Chairman," the prosecutor continued. "So how did the victim, according to you, end up on the bench?"

"I was concerned for her safety, as it looked like she was going to fall over, so I went towards her asking if she was okay. She just looked at me and collapsed, like fainted, when I managed to catch her."

"So what did you do then?"

"Well, I picked her up and saw there was a bench against the wall and so I thought I'd lie her down there 'til she recovered."

"But as soon as she was in your arms another thought entered your head. A beautiful young girl fainted in my arms and no-one else close by. What a prime opportunity!"

Matt hesitated, the image of her upturned face and full-blooded lips in the moonlight cramming his brain. *This guy isn't far wrong, but I never intended to rape her, just kiss her.* "I lay her on the bench and as I did she woke up and looked straight at me and kissed me. Full on the mouth, very passionately."

"I see. So this very young girl, who is rather drunk and whom you have saved from falling, is now lying on the bench unconscious. She comes out of her faint, is totally confused and bewildered and in her confusion kisses you, which you take to be a tacit agreement for sexual intercourse."

"No, I..."

"Did it not enter your head, Mr Chamberlain, that this vulnerable young girl was not in complete control of her senses? She'd just fainted, she was inebriated and you took her confused actions as an invitation to have sex with her. And in your sex-crazed mind, this was all the encouragement you needed to take full advantage of her compromised situation without further thought."

"NO!" Matt shouted, "Sorry, no, it wasn't like that."

"What **was** it like, Mr Chamberlain? Persuade us that she asked for it," he purred, sure of his prey now.

Matt felt it was like the lamb to the slaughter; whatever he said could be twisted and made to sound sordid. "She didn't exactly ask for it," he said with an effort, "but everything she was doing suggested she was enjoying it, that she wanted to kiss me. And she did, passionately."

"A fifteen year old innocent girl kisses you, a stranger she's never met, and you take that to mean she wants to have sex with you. Ladies and Gentleman of the court I put it to you that Mr Chamberlain, considerably drunk and in a position of power, found himself alone with the victim and determinedly and wilfully forced himself upon her in the absence of any agreement by her."

"She encouraged me," Matt blurted out. "D'you think I'd have gone ahead if she hadn't?"

"That's exactly what I'm suggesting," the lawyer said smoothly. "Did you ask her if she wanted to have sex with you?"

"No."

"So she obviously couldn't have said 'Yes'."

"No she didn't."

"She didn't say anything."

"Yes," he said, remembering suddenly, "she did. She said 'It's you'."

The lawyer hesitated for a moment, obviously surprised by this information, but he quickly regained his composure. "Mr Chamberlain, can you think of any reason why this young Swedish girl, whom you have never met, would say 'It's you' in English?"

"Well, only that she'd been at the concert and seen me singing."

"So she said 'It's you' in English, just like that, for no reason. When was this?"

"As soon as she opened her eyes. She looked at me, said 'It's you' and then kissed me again and again."

The lawyer wasn't done.

"But you took this to mean 'I want to have sex with you'."

"No, I just thought she was..... agreeing to...to.... I don't know, it all happened so quickly...."

"It always does, Mr Chamberlain, but that's no excuse for deciding to have sexual intercourse without prior consent. As it turns out she decidedly didn't want to have sex with you, as when you attempted to rape her, she screamed the place down and has been suffering severe trauma ever since."

He had turned to the jury during this last speech, punctuating each phrase. "If further proof were needed, Madam Chairman, the forensic report states that semen with a DNA match to the accused was found on the victim's clothes." He held up another sheaf of papers which were passed first to the judge and then to the jury.

"Madam Chairman, I have no more questions for the defendant, but hope to have shown fairly conclusively the nature of the attack and the defendant's intentions. The fact that he didn't succeed in those intentions was down to the victim's presence of mind and courage in raising the alarm, enabling people to intervene."

The prosecution sat down with apparent satisfaction.

"Thank you Mr Thorne. Mr Bergström, please."

"Thank you, Madam Chairman. Before questioning my client I would like to comment on revelations concerning my client brought by the prosecution. I hope you will allow me to refute some of these aspersions which I feel are prejudicial to his character."

The judge inclined her head.

"The prosecution has attempted to show my client as someone who is obsessed with sex and of a predatory disposition. He referred to the email found by the police on his computer from his girlfriend containing the link to a fetish website which he claimed showed 'sado-masochistic activity and dominance-featured role play'. I would like to remind the court that, one, this is a private email between two adults in a relationship, and two, this is a legal website for the purchase of sexual aids for and by consenting adults. As you would verify, Madam Chairman, to cast aspersions on my client's character by referring to what he does in his private life and his personal sexual preferences, is no basis for character analysis. As the court well knows, sexual preference between consenting couples in private is not a criminal offence. Various members of the public might be personally offended by knowledge of their activities, but they should not form the basis of negative character analysis and the court should be reminded that they are strictly legal within the context of the law.

"Regarding the prosecution's other claim, that my client must have perverted tendencies because he has in his possession an image of an erotic work of art, I would suggest that he would need to censure half the world's works of art in that case. It is ridiculous to base a character evaluation by reference to someone's taste in the visual arts and I would urge the jury to be mindful of the danger of going down that route. I find the prosecution's approach totally objectionable and unhelpful in this case."

He referred back to some papers and then with a fresh smile approached Matt.

"Mr Chamberlain, what is your profession?"

"I'm a singer."

"And what kind of singing do you do, pop, rock, jazz?"

"Classical singing – opera, concerts."

"And where do you usually sing?"

"Well, opera houses, concert halls, churches and cathedrals," Matt said, wondering where this was going.

"And would you say you were successful? Are you doing well in your profession?"

Matt blushed. "I suppose so, yes. I'm very busy."

"And what kind of level do you work at. Is it generally local venues in the UK or are you international?"

"Oh no, it's international, like this. I mean most of my work has been in Britain, but increasingly I'm working in Europe, America and around the world."

"Oh, so even though you're only twenty-six years of age, which I believe I'm right in saying is young for a singer, you are already an international singer. And presumably you are working with the best conductors and directors?"

Matt felt he was being asked to 'big himself up' for whatever reason, so decided to go with the flow.

"Yes, my last job was with Christian Williams in Paris, who is probably one of the world's most respected baroque specialists and before that I worked with Sir Robert Settle in Berlin." It felt good for his self esteem to reel off these names, although he realised that they probably meant nothing to the legal people here.

"So, an up-and-coming successful young singer, already highly respected in the profession and carving an international career, would have everything to lose by risking taking advantage of a young girl in a public place? Much more so as you are so in the public eye, as opposed to someone who doesn't have your high profile job."

Matt felt he hardly needed to answer this question but murmured affirmatively.

"So ladies and gentlemen, I would suggest that the prosecution's contention that Mr Chamberlain was intent on finding a suitable female to seduce has no substance. Here we have a very successful professional person in the public eye, who is in an ongoing relationship, and has everything to lose by following such a course of action. He has no need or reason to be seeking sexual satisfaction outside of his relationship with his partner, which, as has been demonstrated, is sexually active and apparently mutually fulfilling. I would further remind the jury that the medical evidence attests that rape didn't actually take place."

He paused for a moment to refer to some notes and then turned to Matt again.

"Mr Chamberlain, have you ever done any first aid courses or had instruction in first aid?"

What's he on about now? His mind raced back to school, the school hall and people lying around on the floor with bandages.

"Uh, yes, I did a course before going on an outward bound trip in year nine."

"And would you tell us what one should do when a person is unconscious."

Again his mind raced. "Um, you should lay the person in a comfortable position, well ideally the recovery position. Make sure that the clothing is not restricting their breathing and the airway is clear and they're not in danger of choking."

"And this is what you did with Miss Larson. You carried her to the bench and lay her down to recover from the faint, staying by her to make sure she was breathing properly and wasn't in danger."

Well, kind of. "Yes."

"And when Miss Larsson regained consciousness she held onto you, said 'It's you' and repeatedly kissed you."

Matt felt himself blushing as he remembered the moment and realised he was being given the opportunity to make his case.

"Yes, she clung to me as if she was desperate, as if her whole life depended on it. She kissed me again and again, very passionately and I was completely stunned and didn't know really what was happening."

"Did she seem to be in a dream or was she definitely awake?"

"No, she was definitely awake. She kept looking deep into my eyes as if she was trying to tell me something, like she was, imploring me to, to, I don't know....to love her." He said with a final effort.

It was the truth. He'd said the truth. He'd left some bits out, that was also true, but he hadn't lied. It's what's called 'being economical with the truth' isn't it? He'd answered what he'd been asked; there was no need to offer information he hadn't been asked for, like 'Did you kiss her when she was unconscious before she woke up?' He'd truthfully answered the questions put to him. If he'd been asked to relate every minute detail of his actions and thoughts from the moment she fell into his arms, that would be a different matter. 'The truth, the whole truth and nothing but the truth' in that case would have been a bit more difficult to put into words and justify.

"To love her," his counsel echoed. He looked to the jury. "She seemed to be imploring you to love her. This girl or young woman whom you had never met before." He paused, turning back to Matt. "But Mr Chamberlain, you had **seen** her before had you not?"

"Yes, I noticed her in the audience at the concert."

"This was the concert you were singing in which immediately preceded the reception where the assault allegedly took place."

"Yes."

"And what made you notice her during the concert."

"Well, she was staring at me."

"But isn't that what an audience does, Mr Chamberlain, they watch the entertainment?"

Hang on, I thought he was supposed to be on my side.

"Yes, but she stared at me constantly. I thought people would notice. It was like she was fixated," he felt himself getting more confident. "Normally if you catch someone's eye and you don't know them, that person looks away, you know, it's a bit awkward otherwise, but she just kept staring openly at me and I looked away. But whenever I looked back she was still staring at me."

"And how did you feel about this?"

"Well, I was surprised at first and then when it continued, I thought it a bit unusual and strange." *Again, economical!*

"And what did you think it meant?"

"I didn't know what it meant. I thought maybe she was in a daydream or perhaps" and he gave a self-deprecating laugh, "she fancied me."

"You thought perhaps she fancied you. By this you mean that she appeared to find you attractive and desirable. There was a look in her face that suggested to you that she was encouraging you to flirt with her."

"Well," Matt hesitated, *this is the nub of it*, "she was looking at me so boldly and openly that I found it difficult to concentrate on the concert because I was trying to understand what it meant."

"You found her attitude forward, might one even say provocative?"

"Well, yes." What else could he say? She'd put him in this position after all.

"So Mr Chamberlain, when you were later up on deck and saw this same girl, drunk, fall into your arms and subsequently kiss you passionately, this just confirmed your suspicions that this girl in the audience fancied you, and coming out of her faint saying 'It's you' further underlined her intention to pursue relations with you?"

"Yes." *Neatly done.*

Turning again to the jury, his counsel continued. "Ladies and gentlemen, I put it to you that Miss Larson, although young and inexperienced, overtly encouraged my client to believe that she was very attracted to him and immodestly encouraged him physically when she recovered from her faint. I would further suggest that it is not unreasonable to assume, on the strength of her bold behaviour in the concert, that she noticed him go up on deck and followed him there with the express purpose of meeting him in private to pursue her personal agenda. I would further suggest that it is not beyond the bounds of possibility that she fabricated the faint to throw herself in Mr Chamberlain's way so that he was forced to help her and this gave her the opportunity for kissing him."

"Madam Chairman, leading questions and conjecture."

"Mr Thorne, I note your objection but I'll hear this one out."

"Madam Chairman, I'm not suggesting that Miss Larsson had criminal intentions, just that young people with a little alcohol inside them can get carried away with romantic ideas and sometimes act in a rash and headstrong way, not realising the consequences of their actions. I suggest that she encouraged my client to believe that she wanted relations with him and it was only when the reality of the situation hit her, that she realised her mistake and raised the alarm. An unfortunate series of circumstances led to my client being caught in an invidious situation which portrays him as a callous opportunist, when in fact the reality is that he was encouraged by a young lady who had no idea of the consequences of her actions and who wasn't really sure what she wanted from the situation. I would go so far as to suggest, that contrary to my client being accused of attempted rape, the jury should rather consider whether the victim didn't in fact seduce him by forcing herself on him when lying on the bench, as my client testifies, kissing him again and again. The messages he was being given were tantamount to a green light for sexual activity."

There was sudden uproar in the courtroom, the prosecution counsel standing and objecting to the judge, the public gallery erupting into noise and the members of the jury leaning across and talking animatedly to each other.

"Mina Dame och Herrar" the judge claimed control of the outburst.

Matt's lawyer sat down, satisfied with this sleight of hand in which he had neatly turned the charge on its head. Matt admired his skill, but had he gone too far? The judge removed her glasses once more.

"Ladies and gentlemen of the jury, in respect of Mr Bergstrom's assertion, which, I should add, is circumstantial, suggestive and unsubstantiated, I must remind you that you are required to consider the charges as brought in this case, namely of rape on the part of the accused against the defendant. It is not your duty to consider an alternative charge, only whether the accused is guilty of the charge as brought. The court will adjourn for lunch."

The courtroom bustled into activity. The judge grabbed her sheaves of papers and strutted out through the door to the rear of the room while the lawyers stood and sorted through files and documents. Matt hardly had time to think before he was hustled away by a court official. He managed a brief glance to Maggie who mouthed a kiss and waved. The door to the holding cell behind the courtroom banged shut and all was silence.

Maggie! He still couldn't believe it. How had she known? How had she found out about the trial, the date, time, place...? She was normally so disorganised and chaotic. He couldn't imagine that she'd sorted it all out, booked a flight and managed to get here, to be with him. He was shocked, truly shocked, and immediately also felt guilty. He had never credited her with that kind of concern and dedication. He felt humbled that she had made such an effort, had spent the money, had made such a commitment. He had under-estimated her and presumed he knew her and she had completely surprised him.

He realised that over the last few days he had hardly thought of Maggie, had, in effect, forgotten her. He'd been obsessed with Caterina and the statue/girl. Now she was here which complicated things.

The door was abruptly unlocked and swung open to let his lawyer in who immediately congratulated him.

"It's going as well as we can hope," he continued. "Unfortunately the judge is a bit of a feminist which doesn't help. She should never have tried to influence the court like that, saying they shouldn't consider an alternative scenario. Of course they should consider it, that is what doubt is about, the possibility of an alternative. True, they have to consider it in the context of the present charge, with the evidence etc, but she shouldn't suggest they needn't consider other possibilities. At least the prosecution is annoying her a little, which is to our advantage."

"Yeah, well thank you, you're doing an amazing job, even suggesting that **she** seduced **me**!" Matt forced a laugh. "I hope that wasn't going too far."

The lawyer smiled. "So do I. But you know sometimes I think we have to be bold when we have the back against the wall. Sugges-ting this to the jury in what they probably see as the cut and dried case is good, because it sows a seed of doubt for them. Doubt is all we need in law for a prosecution to fail. Just enough doubt for the evidence not to hold together."

Matt hardly dared to hope there was enough doubt to let him off, but he had to believe in some hope.

"Did you see the girl who came in late, long dark hair, dark complexion?"

"Not really. I was aware of someone being shown in."

"My girlfriend, from England. She's just turned up. I had no idea she was coming."

"Oh, the one who sent you the pictures?"

"Yes."

"I see," he paused, thinking. "I wonder. This might be useful. Do you think she would take the witness stand?"

"I'm sure she would, but how would that help? She can't exactly say anything that will change the evidence."

Christer Bergstrom didn't say anything immediately in reply. He was lost in thought, his left hand to his mouth, the thumb gently rubbing the skin below his bottom lip and his eyes unfocused on the floor. "No, I know, but we have to use every possibility to help us out. I will think about it over lunch. What's her name?"

"Maggie. Maggie Ruffini. Her dad's Italian."

"And what does she do?" He was taking notes now.

"She's an actress. Not in a show right now, but she does extra-work and some adverts and things. She also works in a bar." He didn't say what sort of bar, but that probably wouldn't help.

"How old is she?"

"Er, hang on, she must be...twenty nine I think, few years older than me."

"And how long have you been together?"

"Two, three years?"

"That's good. So you live together."

"Yup."

"Ok. I'll think if I can use this. Maybe she can help, maybe not. We'll see." He finished writing some notes. "This thing she said, the girl, which you never told me, 'it's you', when she woke up."

"Yes, I only just remembered when he asked me, I'm sorry."

"It's okay, but are you sure she didn't say anything else?"

"I don't think so. It was kind of mumbled, but that's all I heard."

"Ok."

There was a pause, both of them thinking.

"So, what else do we have on our side?" Matt asked.

"Well, not much it seems. I think it is lying in the hands of the gods, as you say." He got up to go. "I'll see you later Matthew."

In the hands of the gods. Yes, that's just about how it feels. Let's hope they're in a good mood.
* * * * *

When Matt was returned to his place in the courtroom, he immediately noticed that Maggie wasn't in the public gallery. He wondered if Christer Bergstrom had found her and was going to get her up to answer questions. But what questions could possibly help? His eyes wandered to the jury who were taking their seats again, a woman and two men, all dressed conventionally. They gave nothing away, government appointed jurors, as Bergstrom had told him, a completely different jury system than in England.

His lawyer scooted into the seat beside him just as the court official shouted out 'Court will rise' and the judge entered, dabbing the sides of her mouth with a tissue which she then pocketed. Only just finished her coffee, Matt thought enviously. He'd only been offered water or juice.

"Mr Thorne, I have no notification that you wish to bring witnesses."

The prosecution lawyer stood immediately. "No, Madam. I felt the evidence was so compelling and overwhelming that I didn't want to waste the court's time by having witnesses confirm what has already been accepted as fact by the police and professional investigators."

He sat with a self-satisfied smile and a smug look at the jury.

"We thank you for your consideration Mr Thorne. I'm sure none of us want to drag this out longer than necessary."

Matt's counsel sighed audibly beside him, obviously not liking the inference.

"Mr Bergstrom, I have just received a late request from you to bring forward a witness."

"Yes, Madam Chairman, it was only at the last minute that my witness was able to attend."

The judge was looking at her papers. "And this witness is here now and ready to give evidence?"

"Yes."

"You may call your witness."

"Thank you, Madam."

He nodded to the court clerk who indicated to the man on the door at the side who exited. Matt felt nervous and looked quizzically at Bergstrom who whispered to him.

"Don't worry I had a talk with her. I think we may be able to score some points here, but it's risky. Depends whether it comes out right. I just hope she doesn't say too much. She's very up-front isn't she?"

"Yeah, I know," Matt smiled as Maggie was shown to the witness stand.

"Maria Magdalena Ruffini," she said in a clear voice, looking Matt straight in the eyes with that defiant, independent look which had first attracted him to her, so feisty and edgy. She repeated the oath still looking at Matt with those deep chocolate eyes, steady, confident and so sexy. She emanated strength and confidence and Matt felt reassured. It was so different from the look he most often held in his mind's eye of her, subjugated, frightened, yet wildly excited.

Bergstrom approached her. "You are the partner of the accused, correct?"

"Correct."

"Miss Ruffini, would you say that you are a moral person?"

She looked coolly at Bergstrom. "It depends what you mean by morality," she replied steadily.

"Well, you know the difference between right and wrong?"

Matt detected a slight twitch at the corner of her mouth which he thought denoted pleasure – she was going to enjoy herself. But what was Bergstrom getting at?

"There are many rights and wrongs, it depends on the context." This was a topic they'd touched on a few times and he knew how passionate she was about it.

"Okay, let me put it a different way. Do you do things in your life which, although legal, many people would consider immoral?"

"I do lots of things in my life that some people would consider immoral."

"But you don't break the law."

"Yes."

"Right, so although some of your activities might appear immoral you don't break the law?" Bergstrom seemed pleased that he now seemed to be getting somewhere.

"I do."

"I'm sorry?" Bergstrom hesitated, "You do what?"

"I break the law," she said defiantly.

Matthew was desperately trying to understand what was going on here. Bergstrom took a few seconds to collect his thoughts.

"Alright," he said, "you occasionally break the law. We all do that. Occasionally we break the speed limit, bump up our expenses a bit, 'forget'", and he gestured the parentheses, "to log some part-time earnings, but you're not a criminal, you haven't been to prison for it."

"I have," she said triumphantly.

Matt's heart sank. He realised Maggie was in one of her 'warrior moods' as he called them. When she was like this you couldn't win an argument or bring her round. She was completely obstinate in her self-righteousness. He looked at the prosecution who was smirking with satisfaction that this witness was furthering his case. Bergstrom was desperately trying to extricate himself from this approach which had obviously gone completely wrong. What was Maggie trying to do, ruin him? Bergstrom took a deep breath.

"Miss Ruffini, I'm not wanting to delve into your past or bring up information which has no bearing on this case, I'm just trying to establish that your present activities, although seemingly immoral to some people, are not illegal."

"And they're not immoral," she replied, tossing her hair from her face and flashing a look at Matt.

Bergstrom looked to the floor for a couple of seconds before re-approaching her. "Do you have a good relationship with Mr Chamberlain?"

"Yes."

"Do you have a healthy sex life?"

"Very."

"And would you say that it was normal?"

"It's different, maybe."

"For the benefit of the court would you explain exactly what this involves?"

Maggie hesitated for a second and looked at Matt before looking back coolly at the jury.

"It's bondage. I enjoy being tied up and humiliated. I find pain exciting."

There was a tangible atmosphere in the court now, an expectant hush.

"And did Mr Chamberlain instigate this, was it his idea?"

"Oh no, I'd been into it a long time before I met Matt. He doesn't get off on it like me. In fact he's rather uncomfortable with it."

"So he's never forced himself on you, or forced you to have sex?"

Maggie smiled. "It's normally the other way round. I have a high libido and can be quite demanding."

Matt squirmed, feeling that dirty washing was being aired in public.

"Miss Ruffini, on the twenty fourth of March you sent Mr Chamberlain an email containing a link to a website which sells fetish equipment. Why did you do that?"

Maggie was unabashed, even looking exhilarated as she answered.

"I was excited. I'd just bought some new gear and was imagining using it with Matt, so I sent him the link to show him."

"Have you ever known the accused to be violent?"

She paused, thinking. "Yes. When Arsenal lost to West Ham."

"These are football teams if I'm not mistaken. And what did he do?"

"He threw his can of beer and broke the telly, but he was a bit drunk."

"But he's never been violent to you?"

"Not violent enough, most of the time. But that's how I like it."

"And would you say Mr Chamberlain is promiscuous? Does he lust after other women?"

"Well, I guess he likes looking at women, which is only natural, but I don't think he'd do anything about it; he's normally too tired," she added with a knowing smile, which caused a titter in the court.

"Thank you Miss Ruffini, that's all." Matt's counsel sat down not looking too pleased.

The judge, who had been staring at Maggie all the time, now replaced her spectacles on the end of her nose and glanced at her papers, at the same time saying "Mr Thorne, do you have any questions?"

"Yes, Madam Chairman." The prosecution lawyer rose to his feet. Bergstrom breathed out with a grunt of frustration. It seemed he hadn't anticipated the prosecution cross-examining Maggie. The prosecution approached Maggie thoughtfully, his hands together in front of him, the finger pads touching and rubbing gently backwards and forwards. Matt noticed that his cufflinks, just peeping from his jacket sleeves, were little silver crucifixes.

"Miss Ruffini, you said you were sent to prison. Would you tell the court why?"

"Certainly," Maggie was unruffled, enjoying playing to the gallery, "for affray, breach of the peace and assaulting a police officer."

"And why was that? What had you done?"

"Chained myself to a tree. It was a protest to stop them building a road through a wood. I ended up hitting a policeman."

"You don't seem ashamed of this, in fact I would suggest you seem proud of it."

"Of course I'm proud of it. It takes courage to face up to police in riot gear you know. It's not a walk in the park."

"I'm sure. I just want the court to appreciate that you are someone who is proud of attacking police officers."

Maggie's eyes flashed dangerously and Matt could see she was really angry now. "Look mate, I don't go around hitting policemen for fun, right? This was a peaceful demonstration to save an SSSI which the government had decided wasn't important anymore 'cos the road was more important. So we tried to save it with our bodies. You probably think people who take direct action are just a group of nutters, anarchists who just want to fight authority. They're not. They're actually people who think deeply about morality and are prepared to stand up for what they passionately believe and do something about it. Not like most people who just shake their head and say 'Oh it's not right, but what can you do?' When have you stood up for something you believe in?"

The judge intervened, "Thank you, Miss Ruffini. Mr Thorne have you any more questions?"

"Yes, Madam Chairman." There was a glint in his eye. "Miss Ruffini, you sent explicit pictures to the defendant together with comments of a highly sexual nature?"

"Is that a crime?"

"Just answer the question please."

"Yes."

"Miss Ruffini, what is your profession?"

"I'm an actress."

"And what are you working on at the moment? Are you in a production?"

"No...I'm resting. I do occasional extra work, but haven't had a break yet."

"And how do you support yourself while you are 'resting'?" he said this pointedly, ironically.

"I work in a club as a waitress."

"And what kind of club is that?" again the glint in the eye.

Maggie hesitated for the first time and a look of quizzical concentration gripped her face, but still with defiance she said, "It's a private club for a minority interest group."

He smiled, snake-like, "And would that be to do with your interest?"

Maggie wasn't going to be ashamed and, ever the fighter, came out with "That's right, it's a club for sadomasochists and the dress code is bondage wear."

The effect on the court was electric.

"It's common knowledge, isn't it, that in such clubs, waitresses don't just serve at the table, they serve their clients in other ways?"

"What the hell are you suggesting?"

"That you have more in common with your namesake in the bible than you are admitting to."

"With all respect, Madam Chairman, the prosecution is just asking leading questions of a speculative and defamatory nature." Bergstrom was on his feet.

"I agree. Mr Thorne is that all?"

"Yes, Madam Chairman."

"You were there," Maggie suddenly blurted out. "I recognise you now. The Swede who wanted to be crucified..... Oh my god. Now it all makes sense.... you dirty shit."

"Thank you, Miss Ruffini, I'll ask you to be quiet or I'll have you removed from the court."

"Your honour, he was there." Maggie's eyes were blazing.

The prosecutor was flushed but smiling and gesticulating incomprehension.

"Miss Ruffini, I don't know what you're referring to, but it has no relevance to this case. Please escort the witness out." The judge took a drink of water.

Maggie was hustled from the witness stand, still objecting and shouting 'hypocrite' and 'lawyer scum' at Mr Thorne as she went.

Bergstrom was hunched over his desk, lips compressed together. It was a disaster Matt realised. Maggie had been a liability when it came to it and he now truly wished she had never showed up. What the hell chance did he have now?

Chapter 16

"The court will be aware that unusually we have heard the defendant's evidence first, due to the indisposition of the plaintiff. Rather than commute the case I chose to adopt this alternative procedure, hoping that she would be able to give her evidence soon after, and happily I gather she is now able to do so. So please proceed with the cross examination of your client Mr Thorne."

"Please give your full name," the court clerk was brusque and business-like.

"Signe Maria Larsson."

"And what is your age?"

"Fifteen." *Why can't I control myself, it's so embarrassing? I hope they don't notice I'm shaking.*

Uncle Dirk came across to her and smiled briefly giving her one of his winks that no-one else could see, to reassure her. He wasn't really her uncle but he'd always been 'Uncle Dirk' to her and Lars. It was because he was Gustav's oldest friend, they said when she'd questioned it – like an honorary uncle. She liked Uncle Dirk. He had always been funny and picked her up and teased her in a friendly way when she was little, but treated her like a lady now she was older.

"Ladies and gentlemen of the court, it is often the case that victims of violence find it difficult to give evidence in their defence in open court, and my client is no exception." He looked at Signe who was looking down to avoid every gaze. "Despite having been so traumatised by her experience that for ten days she couldn't speak, my client has managed to be here today to be sure that the aggression and violation she suffered is publicly recorded and the perpetrator duly punished. I think you will agree that after such an ordeal this shows considerable courage." He looked along the jury bench like a magician who has just discovered the missing card up his sleeve.

Oh why did I agree to this? I wish he hadn't insisted on me giving evidence. Why does it make so much difference in public?

Signe dared not look up. Dared not look at the jury, the judge...him!

There was suddenly spontaneous applause and looking up quickly Signe saw people in the public gallery clapping, as well as some of the jury. She caught sight of her mum and dad and Irma.

"Ladies and gentlemen, silence in the court please," the judge smacked down her gavel and the sudden noise ceased, only broken by murmurs and movement in the public gallery.

"Please continue Mr Thorne." The judge replaced her glasses.

"Thank you Madam Chairman." Uncle Dirk turned to Signe. "Miss Larsson...." *It sounds weird Uncle Dirk calling me Miss Larsson* "...forgive me for asking you personal questions but please try to answer as best you can. Do you have a boyfriend?"

I hate this. "No."

"Have you ever had a boyfriend?"

"No." *This is so embarrassing.*

"Do you find boys attractive?"

Signe looked at her interrogator appealingly, begging him not to ask these questions. "Not really. They don't interest me."

"What does interest you, Signe?"

Why is he asking these questions?

"Well," she hesitated, *I can't say 'Him'. I can't say God.* "History?"

"Yes, anything else?"

"Literature......philosophy?" *Is that what I'm meant to say?*

"Right, academic subjects in other words. And you're very intelligent aren't you? In the top percentile for every subject?"

"Yes." She felt herself colouring.

"So one would presume you're planning on going to university?"

Again she hesitated, "Yes."

"Do you know which university you want to go to yet?"

Why does he need to ask that? What does it matter? "Stockholm?"

"And what would you study?"

"Philosophy?"

"Philosophy."

What's he doing? I thought he was just going to ask what happened at the reception, which would have been bad enough.

"So ladies and gentlemen, here we have a very intelligent young lady who isn't, and never has been, interested in boys and is in fact far more interested in an academic career, yet whom the defence suggests tried to seduce his client. At the tender age of fifteen against his mature twenty six years, this would hardly seem a rational proposal, even supposing Miss Larsson is telling the truth."

Signe's heart missed a beat. *What is he saying?*

"Because although my client is giving evidence here in court, I don't think she is being completely honest about her true intentions."

Uncle Dirk has gone mad. Or is he trying some kind of legal trick? What am I supposed to say?

"Miss Larsson, I put it to you that you have a secret, a closely held secret that you have kept from everyone, even your parents, for some time now."

Signe looked briefly towards her 'parents' in the gallery, who were looking anxious and stressed.

What's he going to say? I'm not a lesbian. A feminist, yes, but not a lesbian. Irma and I sleep together sometimes but we're not gay.

"You know that this secret would upset your parents and probably be frowned upon or ridiculed by your friends, so you have hidden it from everyone until it will be too late and they can do nothing about it."

Irma. Irma has betrayed me. She's told him everything.

Uncle Dirk was referring to some notes. "Would you tell the court where you were on the weekend of the twenty-first January when your parents thought you were spending the weekend with your best friend Irma Olsson?"

So that's it. I've got to tell them everything." I was in Vadstena."

"And what were you doing there?"

Signe looked quickly towards the public area and saw Melissa's expression of surprise.

"I was meeting the Mother Superior at the Convent."

"And why was that?"

Signe took a deep breath, realising there was no going back.

"To register my desire to join the Bridgettine nuns, to devote myself to Jesus and to renounce all earthly pleasures." She'd said it. There was a gasp from the gallery as Melissa cupped her hands over her face.

"But you're not in your majority, you would surely need your parents' permission."

"I told them my parents are dead. I'm adopted. I have no parents." There was no way to spare them. They'd lied all those years. It's their fault it's come to this.

Uncle Dirk turned to the jury. "Ladies and Gentlemen, the reason for taking this rather roundabout route in questioning Miss Larsson was to show you beyond doubt that there are no grounds to entertain the defence's suggestion that Miss Larsson encouraged the defendant in any way. As is now absolutely clear, Miss Larsson has one intention in life and it has nothing at all to do with trying to seduce men, if that suggestion was ever taken seriously. If anything her intentions are the total opposite and I hope you will appreciate the absurdity of that claim.

"What we have here is an innocent girl who was violently assaulted in an unprovoked attack, which the defence should be ashamed for suggesting was in any way encouraged. Ladies and Gentlemen, before asking Miss Larsson about the attack itself, I should inform you that she has suffered post-traumatic amnesia, that is, her mind has blocked out the event to a large extent as an emotional protection. Some of this memory has recently come back, but she struggles to recall all of the events."

He turned to Signe, "Now Miss Larsson, if we could turn to the night of the twenty-fifth March when you went to the performance of the St Matthew Passion at the Christ Church on Hamnkanalen. You went to the concert alone, correct?"

"Well. I went with my best friend Irma, but she was playing in the orchestra."

"So you were sitting by yourself."

"Yes." *No, I was sitting with Him. He's always with me.*"

"And you enjoyed the concert?"

"Yes." *YES, YES. I adored it. It changed my life, deepened my understanding and brought me even closer to Him.*

"And this man here," he indicated towards the defence desk, "you saw him performing in the concert?"

Signe slowly raised her eyes and moved her gaze to her right, and beheld him again. *'Nehmet, esset, das ist Mein Leib'* – *'Eat, drink, this is my body'* she heard again that velvet, dark brown voice, full-throated, caressing the phrases over her body. He wasn't looking at her. His eyes were lowered, the eyelids hooding those dark pools of light, but she could see the line of his jaw, the curve of his neck, this man who had tried to rape her. This man who spoke to her in His Agony, in His Passion, forgiving her sins and offering His Body as a blessed sacrament to sustain her, His Blood to wash away the sins of the world. *Jesú.*

"Shayzoo." She whispered.

"I'm sorry?" Uncle Dirk said.

The defendant moved abruptly, looking up at her with a startled expression, their eyes colliding in a flash of recognition, distrust, embarrassment, anger? He leaned over and whispered to his lawyer as Signe recoiled, stung by the sudden pain of his look, the dart of hate she detected in that brief second.

"Miss Larsson, are you alright? Do you need some water?" Uncle Dirk was leaning into the witness stand, concern in his voice and anxiety in his face.

"Yes, yes. No. I'm alright thank you."

"Take your time. I know this is difficult. Don't worry, you're doing fine. I just wanted you to confirm that you recognise this man as the one singing in the concert."

"Yes." Signe took a sip of the water she'd been given. *I can't bear that look. I can't bear him to hate me. Please don't hate me. Please be the beautiful man who sang to my soul, who transfixed me with your passion, who incarnated my religious fervour.*

"Okay. And you had never seen the accused before the concert?"

"No." *Except in my heart, except in Him.*

"And so you heard the concert, and afterwards what happened?"

Oh, what happened! "Er, Irma asked me to go to the reception with her."

"On the Barken Viking hotel ship."

"Yes."

"So you are at the reception with Irma. Can you describe to us what happened?"

He still wasn't looking at her. He deliberately kept his eyes elsewhere when she occasionally stole a look in his direction.

"Well, we were having some drinks and talking, and then Irma's parents came and joined us." *Irma was flirting with Karl. She was quite drunk. Karl was nice. Talked to me.*

"Carry on. What did you do next?"

"Oh yes, Irma's mum went to look for a friend and Mr Olsson and I went to get some food."

"Right. So you and Mr Olsson ate together."

This is when it goes weird and I can't remember the order. "No, we didn't eat together. I think we somehow got lost. I mean I ended up in a different part of the room, and...." She hesitated, nervous, unsure now.

"You're doing fine. Just try to remember what happened next."

"Well, all I can remember was sitting on a chair, looking at the programme. *His dear face smiling, or not smiling. I can't remember which...*

"And then what do you remember?"

A breeze, a silver shaft of light glistening on the water "I don't know... I think being on the deck of the ship. It was dark. *It was bright.*

"Yes, carry on."

A bright white line. Arms outstretched. Him. A crucifix. Him crucified. 'Kruezigen. Lass ihn kreuzigen' – 'Let Him be crucified.' The chorus swelled in her head, the aggressive staccato voices stridently shouting for blood. Then nothing. "The moon was shining. It was very bright. I think I turned...." She searched for the memory. Nothing.

"And?"

"I don't know." *'You only have to answer what I ask you, that's all' is what Uncle Dirk had said when I'd begged him not to make me do this. 'Don't worry it won't be bad. But it will be the best way to really nail this guy, have you up there so that everyone can see you and how evil he is and what he tried to do to you. If he'd succeeded in raping you there would be no question, but because he didn't succeed, there might be some question, some doubt, and I want to be sure to tie him to the mast on this one.'*

"I don't know," she said again and looked towards the defendant. He was looking directly at her with those clear blue eyes. Not angry now, still, calm and deep as lapis lazuli. She swam into his eyes, locked in his gaze and submersed in his aura. *His dear head is in my hands. 'Trinket alle daraus – Drink ye all of it' and I drank of His love. My yearning was fulfilled and He flowed into my body in His Passion, His close embrace. Who could resist such Divine joy, who would resist it? His kisses were deep, dredging desires I hardly knew I had. I was ecstatic. It was sublime divinity, exquisite pain....*

Did this happen? What happened?

"The snake," she cried out and stifled her outburst with her hands.

"It's ok Signe, it's ok. You're doing fine. Take your time." He paused, letting her recover. "A snake? You said a snake?"

"No, no, sorry. I had a dream once, a nightmare. It's nothing....I'm ok, thank you." *Was it a dream?*

"So can you remember anything else?" he said gently

No. Yes. But is it a memory? Is it imagined? It didn't seem real, but I have such a ...physical memory of it? I can feel him, feel his breath on my mouth, taste his tongue on mine....

"Miss Larsson?"

"I can't remember anything else," she blurted out, breaking her look and into tears simultaneously.

"Thank you Miss Larsson."

"Court will adjourn for fifteen minutes," the judge rose and retired. *What have I said? What have I done?*

Chapter 17

Matt watched the glasslike droplets slither down the window, leaving a trail of smaller beads in their wake. They chased each other irregularly, jerkily but frequently as the gusting winds threw handfuls of spattering rain against the unmarked police car negotiating its way along the London streets. He didn't know this part of the city at all, particularly by road. He must have travelled through parts of it on the tube or overground he supposed, but the road system bore no resemblance to that seen from an elevated railway flashing its overview of the city or cutting through high walls or embankments. Occasional road signs, glimpsed diffracted through the prismatic effect of the globules on the windows, informed him of rough orientation – W4 and SW15 suffixing Road/Street/Crescent, Villas/Drive/Rise.

It was with a continuing sense of incomprehension and disbelief that Matt again considered his situation, now bored even more starkly into his brain by the handcuffed transfer from the Swedish police station back to the UK. The whole procedure had been chillingly smooth, efficient and impersonal; he was an article of freight which needed to be conveyed from one holding area to another through the necessary interface of public transport. The different stages of the journey had interlocked like clockwork, from the form-filled discharge in Gothenburg attached to the plain clothes police officer, to the car to the airport where they were transferred through a private entrance and boarded the plane through the rear door after all the other passengers to sit in the rear two seats attracting no notice. At Heathrow he was removed from the plane last, again via the rear door and collected off the tarmac with again a lengthy transfer of documentation and change of handcuffs from one minder to another. At no time did anyone speak to him except to tell him to come, stay or go. He felt like an unloved dog, one of those miserable things in a rescue centre, abused and agonised by abuse into a cipher of what a dog should be. He felt that the way he was being treated was diminishing his humanity. It must be how street people felt in large cities every time someone walked past them ignoring their broken Styrofoam cup and plea for 'any change'. He understood their helplessness now, their feeling of subservience and indignity. How many times had he done just that, walked on by?

For once, he thought, the British weather was doing what it was supposed to do in April, for now, as suddenly as it had started, the rain was gone and a blinding burst of sunshine exploded off the mirror-glass of an office block making his eyes ache. Pavements which moments ago had been deluged were now steaming with the sudden ferocity of the sun's rays. People who had been using copies of the

Metro as umbrellas were now walking normally, just avoiding the many puddles which havocked the walkways. He watched them going about their various businesses, some rushing for appointments, some ambling listlessly, some intent on a mobile phone, some gazing vacantly at a shop front, none knowing his hurt, all locked in their individual experiences oblivious to the concerns of others. Not that this could ever be different, he admitted to himself, but, though 'No man is an island' we are all surrounded by a sea of personal experience and present concerns which necessarily isolate us from the currents of others' misfortunes, which only actually impinge on us when washed up on our shores.

He lifted his arm to scratch his head, forgetting the attached officer, jerking his hand also, apologising and feeling a surge of anger and frustration. What was he going to do, fling open the car door at speed, do a James Bond roll and miraculously disappear into the crowd sending pedestrians flying? Run at breakneck speed down narrow alleys, stall-holders wares cascading off shelves til he finds a sudden door which reveals a massage parlour where he instantly adopts a prone semi-naked pose with the unbelievably attractive masseur rubbing soothing oils into his shoulders whilst the pursuing cops charge past panting and shouting? The police of course have to guard against such a scenario since he's a violent criminal, a rapist who sings Matthew Passions and then ravages young girls whom he compulsively preys on.

Two years. His sentence. Sentence – subject, verb, object. Matthew Chamberlain goes to prison. Full stop. Complete sentence. That one short sentence had put a full stop to his life. No qualifying clauses providing mitigating circumstances, no future conditionals promising let outs or reviews. Matthew Chamberlain, convicted rapist, two years. Gavel down, sent down, two years. FULL STOP. These last few weren't true sentences even though there were full stops; but they were his sentences, his full stops.

In all his life, of all the possible things he might do, in all his nightmares or forebodings or imaginings, going to prison had never featured. True he had had friends who were now probably banged up somewhere knowing the kinds of things they'd got up to, but he'd left that far behind and had never been involved in their nefarious dealings. Fortunately for him music had kept him away from the pitfalls of the teenage years. But now it seemed music had done for him. If it hadn't been for music he would never have been in Sweden, he'd never have seen her, never have wanted to love her. Because isn't that all he'd done, tried to love her? They'd just gone about loving each other, in that moment, in that ecstasy of mutual recognition.

He'd gone over it so many times, examining and re-examining the day, the concert, his actions, and each time he couldn't believe that he deserved this; that that exquisite moment of mutual passion had left her to carry on her life as if nothing had happened and delivered him to penal detention for two long years with a criminal record as a sex offender. It made no sense and the feeling of such gross injustice seethed in his head however hard he tried to suppress it. But suppress it he knew he must if he was to survive the next two years, which seemed to stretch away ahead of him like a brushed-steel corridor to infinity.

The car nosed up to the solid doors of Wandsworth prison and sat expectantly, engine purring, for half a minute as another shower of rain splattered the windscreen before they slid smoothly inside. The security guy in the glass lodge hadn't moved and hardly acknowledged their passage through the gate. Matt presumed the car's reg. had been logged in advance to allow them access.

Arriving at the reception he was officially discharged from the charge of the transfer officer to the prison service, who went through the usual protocol of confirming his identity etc.

"Ok Mr Chamberlain, these your things?" She gestured to his case and a clear plastic bag of personal possessions. He nodded. He'd been given an exchange of clothes back in Gothenburg and his tail coat etc had been taken away and packed up with all his things from the hotel.

"You want to be in the VP wing?"

He blinked. *VP? Violent Prisoner?* He had no idea.

"Er, I don't know. I've never done this before. Whatever you think."

"Yup, I think that's best. It's for your protection. You'll be in cell 268, second floor. You get £2.50 a week for the privilege of being here – isn't the government generous! You can spend it in the canteen or buy stuff from other prisoners. If you want to make a phone call you have to book it through the system in advance. You'll get to know the ropes pretty quickly. Keep your nose clean and you'll be ok. Steve, take Mr Chamberlain through will you."

The thick-set prison warder unsmilingly unlocked the gate with the huge bunch of keys on his belted chain set and locked it shut behind them. Matt was numb as they trudged along endless corridors unlocking and re-locking gates as they went, his minder exchanging mindless greetings and meaningless banter with other warders along the way.

Matt dragged his voice from deep in his chest, "What's VP?"

"Vulnerable person, mate. That's you now. People who've done what you've done.... other prisoners don't like it, know wot I mean. An' if they don't like it, they take it into their 'eads to teach you a lesson. Like prison's too good for yer, yeah?"

"Right," Matt grunted. *Lowest of the low. Same level as a paedophile. Same stigma.* He was a marked man, protected from the outside and the inside, grouped together with his kind. The kind that prey on vulnerable people now vulnerable people themselves. The hunters turned hunted. Was this really him? Was this what Matt Chamberlain had come to? His soul howled silently in the pit of his being. It was all he could do to stop himself breaking down and keep walking.

"'ere you go. Ricko'll tell you how it works. You'll 'ave plenty of time to find out all about it."

The door shut behind him and the lock clicked. He was in a small room; bunk beds, hand basin, urinal.

"Awigh'?"

He looked up to the top bunk to see a tousled head of hair topping a swarthy face with keen dark eyes.

"Hi" he said, almost apologetically he realised, feeling he was invading this guy's space, but then reminding himself that was stupid; it was his designated cell too. But he was the new boy and that was the difference.

"Hi" he said again, "I'm Matt."

"Ricko."

Matt was unsure whether to offer to shake hands but in the absence of any movement from Ricko who continued to watch the TV, quickly decided that wasn't the way. He was unsure what to do. It was awkward, suddenly arriving in this space which was partly occupied by this person he didn't know but with whom he now had to share this intimate existence. He sat on the bottom bunk leaning forward, elbows on knees, hands clasped against his mouth breathing into his palms. What now? Moments passed as, he envisaged, they inexorably would.

"Wot u got?"

"I'm sorry?"

"Wot u got? How long?"

"Oh, two years. You?"

"Five. Fucking shit, righ'?"

"Yeah". What else could he say? Is this what it was like, would be like for two years? Christ! Matt waited for the inevitable question – Wo' yu in for? – but it never came. Instead

"U got any burns?"

"Any what?"

"Burns. Smokes. Ciggies, yeh?"

"Oh no, sorry. I don't. Haven't got any."

Matt couldn't work out where he was from. He looked foreign but spoke with a crumpled cockney accent overlaying some eastern European inflection. Romanian? He'd no idea.

"So welcome to another edition of 'Under the Hammer' where we look at the bargains you can pick up at auction, providing you get the price right. Today John and Paula are looking to buy a one bedroom flat in Earls Court as an investment to do up and let, but will they get the bargain they're after?"

The presenter was introducing the couple and discussing their criteria, the usual glamorising of an otherwise mundane subject, Matt thought.

"Pity that, s'good t'have burns. Can get stuff. Y'know, bargain like."

"Oh, right. I see.... no sorry." He didn't know why he was apologising. Why should he help this jerk he didn't even know? New boy syndrome again; he needed to feel accepted, to feel part of this place just to fit in and go unnoticed, not draw attention to himself, keep a low profile. God, if he was going to be here for two years he needed to find some solace, some security.

"So let's see how John and Paula did at the auction." They'd seen the property and evaluated its potential and now the shot was the auction house with a full room and the auctioneer starting the bidding at four hundred and fifty thousand. It rapidly went up by five thousands, sticking at five hundred thousand when the gavel finally came down, a sound that took Matt's mind racing back to another gavel coming down so finally. John and Paula had secured their one bedroom flat in Earl's Court for a mere half million. Cross fade to them standing smiling triumphantly outside the block of flats followed by re-runs of footage of the cramped dowdy interior for which they'd paid so much, with its miserable view of the building site across the busy road.

"Fuckin' lucky rich bastard," Ricko observed from above. Matt said nothing, not wanting or needing to get involved. The presenter cited the advantages of the area, the proximity of the facilities, the convenience of the public transport system and the potential of the area, the camera panning across swathes of rooftops, then closing in on a shopping centre and buses to emphasis the points. But what would John and Paula do to capitalise on the potential and would they make their investment pay? Very soon the camera was showing the conversion, cross-fading shots of before and after room by room. The transformation was resplendent, all the dowdy decor and tired colour schemes replaced by state of the art kitchen and bathroom and sophisticated minimalist understated chic throughout. It reminded him of the hotel room in Gothenburg. The presenter was euphoric, praising the clean lines and anodyne sparseness, claiming that this was what people wanted, muted tones and a pristine finish. Maybe, Matt thought, but it was still a poky flat with tiny rooms and a horrible outlook. Next, estate agents are brought in to give their assessment of potential letting income and increase in equity value. It transpires that John and Paula have done well; they could let the miserable space for about two thousand a month and expect to sell it for about seven hundred thousand.

"Fuckin' rich bastards," Ricko said again, and flicked over to another channel where some environmental officers were discovering rat faeces in the store room attached to a restaurant in a rural town. It was gripping stuff, the officers decked out in hooded protective clothing, masks and gloves as if investigating a nuclear leak or epidemic crisis.

Two years. Of this?

Matt lay down on the bed facing the wall and, with Ricko moving occasionally above and the TV droning on, felt more alone than he'd ever felt.

He had been lying there for only a couple of minutes he reckoned, tracing the various scratch marks in the paintwork of the wall only inches from his eyes, before he realised Ricko was talking to him. He had thought it was part of the inane drivel emanating from the TV.

"Sorry, what was that?" he called up. *Apologising again!*

"You done time before?"

"No," and he gave a short cough of a laugh, "first time."

"Ah, you get use to it. You jus' godda know de system, y'know wo'ameen?"

"Sure. I'll keep out of trouble, don't worry."

"Yeah, you in trouble already, man, you don' wan' any more fuckin' trouble."

Ricko snorted some snot from the back of his nose and trajected the resulting gob in a practiced arc into the sink on the opposite wall where it landed with a satisfying splat. "Keep owt de way o' Stevie, right?"

Although Matt couldn't say he was enjoying the conversation, he was eager to glean any survival techniques, so was happy to keep it going to learn as much as possible from his hospitable cell mate.

"Who's Stevie?"

"He'sa fuckin' crazy guy on de udder side'. He fuckin' crazy. He try to hang hisself, cos 'e thought dey transfer 'im to some udder place, nicer. But dey jus put'im in anudder cell, right? So 'e still fuckin' crazy."

"So, they told me we can make phone calls, but you have to book them first; what's that about?"

"Dey gotta check who you phonin', you know wo'ameen. Dey don' wan' you phonin' de person you inside for, de victim, right? An' you might ring de sister or der brudder, you know wo'ameen, like it's aggravation. So dey check it ou' first' to be sure, right? You can't do a fucking' thing in 'ere 'ardly without dey know wot you do."

"Right."

"An'dey listen, you know, dey listen to wot you say. You can't say anythin' cos dey recordit right? So don't say nuffin' you don' wan' dem to hear. You gotta have mobile phone for dat."

"But they've taken my mobile phone. I didn't think you could have mobile phones inside."

"Yeah, but people dey got mobile, right? You gotta be friend wid someone who got mobile an' maybe he let you make de call."

"How have they got mobiles?"

"Der famlee, dey smuggle dem in, you know wo'ameen?"

"Really, don't the warders search them?"

"Nah, sometime maybe, but dey clever, you know wo'ameen? Dey know de screws and which one dey can get dem past, yeah? I tell you dey clever."

"So," Matt wanted to turn the conversation to other things, "what happens all day? I mean do we just stay in here all the time or...?"

"Depen' what you wanna do. Some guy, dey do job in prison, you know, dey clean stuff, or work at some shit, so dey earn some money, right? Fuckin' stupid bastard."

"Why's that? I mean, why's it stupid to work, if you get paid for it?"

"Dey pay dem fuckin' sixteen pounda week, you know? I no' goin' to fuckin' work for de bastard for sixteen pounda week, you know wo'ameen. Fuckin' bastard."

"So what do you do?"

"What you mean? I fuckin' in prison, right? I can't do nuffin'. I not going to work for dey fuckin' bastard for sixteen pounda week."

"So you just hang out here and watch TV and stuff?"

"Yeah. I go talk to my friend when dey let us out. Dey from Brazil as well. We meet here in London. Dey good friend now." *Not Romania, Brazil!* "Dey come wi' dinner now."

Cell doors clanked and a bustle of activity could be heard outside. Their door duly opened and a warder stood holding it while a guy entered holding a tray.

"Chicken tikka wrap."

"Yeah mate."

"We got cottage pie 'n veg for you mate as you wasn't 'ere to order yer meals, right?"

"Yes fine, anything. Thanks." Matt took the tray with the plastic cutlery. The cell door slammed shut again, the key clunked the bolts across. Ricko flicked over to another channel, BBC news 24, the anchorman reporting on the beheading of a western journalist by ISIS whilst other news teletexted across the bottom of the screen; a gas explosion in a factory in north London, the government's new initiative on immigration control, UKIP's increasing membership and its likelihood of beating both conservatives and labour in the upcoming by-election, more jobs but worse wages in real terms, the latest scandal in the Australian rain forest as some unknown celebrity slags off a fellow contestant for failing a bush tucker trial.

Life going on. Out there, life going on as usual. But that was out there. Here, 'inside', Matt took a mouthful of cottage pie and acknowledged that he was not part of that 'going on as usual', for two years. This was now what 'usual' would be. As usual, he would be in this room or one similar, staring at a screen or a wall, having meaningless conversations with someone he didn't want to talk to, endlessly, for two years; seven hundred and thirty days. Or was that seven hundred and twenty nine now? Although he was hungry, he also felt nauseous, that feeling of dread seeping into his stomach again. How could he tell his parents? They who had invested so much time, love and care in his upbringing, who had sacrificed so much to enable him to follow his chosen career and who now fostered such high expectations of him. How would they react to the knowledge he was in Wandsworth prison, a convicted rapist and sex offender? It didn't bear thinking about. It was the apogee of shame, the nadir of humiliation.

He swallowed down the pie, more out of a sense of duty than need, not knowing when the next meal would be. It was surprisingly good and he surprised himself by finishing it, but then he hadn't had anything since very early that morning in Gothenburg before the flight. He lay down on the bed again. What else was there to do? He couldn't believe that the prisoners just lay about in bed all day. There must be some activities, some respite from being cooped up in a cell. If there wasn't, he'd have to get a job; doing something would be preferable to incarceration with Ricko all day. Surely you could do courses? He thought he remembered hearing of prisoners coming out with degrees. And then there were singers and actors who went into prisons and worked with the inmates, they even did shows there. God, what if someone he knew came in, saw him here? As yet he didn't think the news had got out. His agent had cancelled his immediate work, thinking him ill in Sweden, but that couldn't go on indefinitely. They'd have to know sooner or later – sooner probably. His agent would have to drop him. His career would be over. You can't just disappear for two years and then walk straight back into the profession and carry on as if nothing's happened.

Damage limitation, that's what he needed. But realistically, how can you limit that kind of damage? It's total and all embracing, affecting everyone and everything. It would leak out, the truth. Inevitably the profession would know. It would be the latest bit of juicy gossip in dressing rooms throughout the opera world.

'Did you hear about Matt Chamberlain?'

'Yeah, raped a girl in Sweden.'

'I know, fancied himself as Don Giovanni.'

'Should have stuck to Leporello.'

'Ha ha, yeah, good one!'

He rolled onto his side and reviewed the wall again. It would happen. He'd have to suffer it, not in person, but knowing it was happening in his absence, whilst he whiled away his potential in here. But his parents. He couldn't bear the thought of letting them know. He'd already decided he would tell them he'd landed a contract somewhere miles away, the other side of the world, doing some prime roles he couldn't turn down. That would give him a few months' grace to work out how to break it to them. The thought of them visiting him in prison was totally out. It would be horrific. In fact the thought of anyone visiting him now was out. He didn't think he could deal with the shame and the sympathy. Once they heard his side of the story he was sure everyone would be sympathetic, but that would just be worse. What good would it do? It wouldn't change anything.

As he lay there with these thoughts tumbling about his mind and the TV droning on in the background, he felt an utter exhaustion come over him, accompanied by a depression that seemed literally to bear down on his body and crush him. He was cut off from everything and everyone he valued and loved and was thrown out into the wilderness, a place barren of comfort and love, to be starved of life. There was no other way to see it. His situation was a catastrophe with no redemption. He was tempted to pray, but to whom or what? The more he dwelt on it the heavier the negative feeling oppressed him, and these self-feeding thoughts crowded his mind ever more densely til his head was a seething mass of gloating self-pity and he hated himself more than he could have thought possible. For his parents, for his friends, for Maggie, for all the people he had let down, he loathed himself completely.

But this self-loathing which obsessed him was then spiked by the huge injustice of his situation and he thought of the girl happily leading her life in Sweden, and his monstrous loathing transformed itself into an anger that was so furious he didn't know how he contained it. It swept through him like a tornado of hate resisted only by him locking his jaw and clenching every muscle in his body til he was shaking with intensity. After a minute he managed to relax as the wave passed and he broke down in helpless shivering, the emotion wracking his body.

"You alright mate? You not fuckin' wankin' down there? De whole bed shakin' man. You gotta do dat in the fuckin' toilet, you know wo'ameen?"

Matt controlled himself as best he could. "I fell asleep. Had a nightmare."

"Fuckin' ell, I hope you not goin' to do dat ev'ry fuckin' night. Jesus!"

"Sorry."

Ricko turned the volume on the TV up. There was some football on – European cup semi final, Bayern Munich v Real Madrid. Matt lay there recovering, shuddering slightly. Normally he'd have watched it but now, right now, he didn't give a toss about football. The feeling of exhaustion returned which he welcomed and he let himself drift away into a fitful sleep, punctuated by occasional yelps of delight or dismay from above.

Evangelist:	*And the Governor said*
Pilate:	*Why, what evil hath he done?*
Soprano:	*To us he hath done all things well*
	The blind he made to see
	The lame to walk
	He told His Father's word
	He sent the devils forth
	The mourners he comforted
	And sinners too he forgave

Otherwise my Jesus nothing has done

Matt's breathing was shallow and short, his face concentrated into a frown that lined his features and squeezed his eyes tight shut. The music played through his head and his mind's eye saw Caterina, her torso shimmering and sparkling in lace-encrusted diamantes, whilst that pure skein of silken sound thrilled his whole being.

Soprano: Out of Love my saviour now is dying-
Of sin he knows nothing-
But so eternal damnation
And the sinners rightful fate
Shall not rest on my soul.

The jury returned to their places after their deliberations and the foreman of the jury stood at the judge's instigation. She removed her glasses and gently wiped them with a smear-clear cloth from her glasses case.

"Ladies and gentlemen of the jury have you reached a decision in this case?"

"We have, Madam Chairman."

"Do you find the accused guilty or not guilty?"

"Guilty."

Evangelist: When Pilate saw that he could prevail nothing, but that rather a tumult was made, he took water and washed his hands before the multitude, saying

Pilate: I am innocent of the blood of this just person, see Ye to it

Evangelist: Then answered all the people and said

Chorus: His blood be on us and our children

"Matthew Chamberlain you have been found guilty of sexually assaulting Signe Larsson on the twenty-fifth March. You will serve a prison sentence of two years starting immediately with the option, as you are a foreign national, of serving the time here in Sweden or after repatriation in the UK."

Chorus: Behold the Saviour standeth bound
Now scourge they him and smite and wound him

Evangelist: Then the soldiers of the Governor took Jesus into the common hall and gathered into Him the whole band of soldiers and stripped Him and put on Him a scarlet robe...

The dark blue Volvo slid deftly through the streets of Gothenburg on the short journey to the holding unit. His arms ached, strapped behind him as they were with the cuffs which bit into his wrists. He was bundled out unceremoniously and stood shivering by the car whilst the Stasi-style police saluted and jabbered away in staccato voices.

"Fucking wankers," Artis gravelled close beside him. He was standing in the shadows by the wall sniggering to himself, whispering loudly. 'Rhymes with bankers.' He became hysterical, no longer trying to be quiet. 'Wankers"', he shouted, 'fucking banker wankers.'

The police didn't seem to hear him, or if they did they inexplicably ignored him. They grabbed Matt and marched him through a doorway and down a long stainless-steel corridor to a desk. The judge was standing behind it and slowly removed her glasses, slipping the end of one arm into her mouth and slowly sucking it through pouted bright-red lips.

'Oh Matthew, you are such a naughty boy,' she said, with a thick Swedish accent. 'What **are** we going to do with you?'

She walked around the desk and Matt saw that she was dressed as a dominatrix, thigh-length stiletto boots, wasp-waist taut with restraining leather corset, breasts heaving against the strictures of the tight décolletage. She flicked him with the scourge across his shoulders. 'Take off his clothes,' she purred.

The Stasi officers peeled off his tailed coat, one grabbing it and putting it on over her leather waistcoat and white cuffs. It was only then that he noticed they were all in fetish gear of different persuasions, some leather, some rubber, some silk and lace.

When he was naked, the judge walked round him and delivered a stinging lash across his buttocks.

'No, not me,' he whimpered, 'I'm not into that. It's Maggie...'

'Oh, but we have to discipline you,' the judge continued, delivering a vicious cut across the tops of the back of his legs. The pain was burning and he could feel welts rising in a searing line across his skin. His heart was pounding with the anticipation of the next lash and his vision was full of the judge strutting in her squeaking boots before him.

'How many lashes should we give him?' she demanded of the officer beside her, who turned to reveal Maggie in full regalia smiling debauchedly at him.

'Oh lots. He's not the son of God, he's a very naughty boy.'

The scourge scythed ferociously into his flesh, drawing blood immediately under his right pectoral muscle and he winced at the heat of the pain. Before he could recover, another cut whipped into his right upper arm and the judge yelped with delight. Despite the searing pain he was aroused and became even more so when the judge suddenly pounced on Maggie and devoured her mouth hungrily in a frenzy which Maggie reciprocated with equally lustful aggression. They completely ignored him, so involved were they in their carnal desire, but the officers pushed him forward through iron gates and flung some prison fatigues after him before locking the gates and clip-clopping away. He hurried to put on the clothes to cover his shame and again heard yelps of delight from the judge echoing down the corridor, no doubt whipping another internee or possibly in her own ecstasy with Maggie......

He woke to a yelp from above and a roar from the television. He grappled to recall dream shadows vanishing from his memory faster than he managed to catch hold of them, the reality of the cell now crowding his conscious mind before he could glimpse his dreamings. Real Madrid had scored and looked likely to win. What was his dream? Dark shadows hovered at the edge of memory teasing him with a flavour of eroticism but without detail. The more he tried to remember the more the phantoms fled his grasp and he was left with the frustration of unfulfilled expectation. The players leaped on top of one another, a heaving mass of muscle, sweat and lycra in an orgy of goal-lust as the Madrid fans went wild, grimacing at the camera and shaking their flags and scarves with aggressive, tribal, victory-kill euphoria.

Matt shuddered, suddenly feeling cold in sweet/sour post-sleep disjointedness. The dream he couldn't recall felt like a loss and he was left with a taste of excitement and something tantalisingly illicit which he wanted to re-visit. The harsh reality of the cell only compounded this longing for escape. Is this how he'd survive here, living vicariously through dreams where he could escape the pressing reality of the four walls, the proximity of his cell mate? It was such a negative attitude to have to adopt – avoidance, denial, damage limitation. That phrase again. Limitation. Wasn't that the very nature of incarceration, being totally limited of everything but boredom? He couldn't further limit himself, he must do something positive, constructive to...

"Hey mate, you like football, yeah?"

"Yes, sure."

"What team you support?"

This could be tricky, but hey, no point in damage limitation here.

"Arsenal."

"Right. Dey good team, man. Dey jus' fuckup sometime, you know wo'ameen?"

Matt felt a kind of relief at the bond of interest, but at the same time a reluctance to give in to too much familiarity with this voice from above.

"I support Chelsea man. Dey gotta play Atletico Madrid next week, you know? Das goin' to be some match man."

"Yeah right. That'll be tough."

"Dey got injuries, you know. Ah, dey going to let us out now." He jumped down from the bunk and adjusted his trousers before going to the shelves and fiddling with the contents. He was stocky and tough-looking; worked out in the gym, Matt guessed by the unnaturally over-developed biceps and the pecs punctuation the T-shirt. You wouldn't want to mess with him.

"You stay here, right? I go see my friend."

"Sure."

"You don't wanna leave dis place empty. De guys here, dey fuckin' take ev'ryfing outa your room, you know wo'ameen, so we never leave der room empty when dey letus out, right?"

"Okay, I see. How long do they let us out for?"

"Depen'. Sometime jus' one hour. Sometime two, free, depen' how dey feel about it, depen' on de screw, you know wo'ameen?"

The keys clinked and jangled and the door clanged open.

"Okay Ricko, off you go. Hallo hallo? Who've we got 'ere. New boy is it?"

"Hi I'm Matt."

"Jus' come in this mornin' did yer?" the warder seemed nice enough, quite chatty.

"Yup."

"Oh right. Welcome to the funny farm, mate. We all 'ave a good time 'ere, don't we Mike?"

Mike grunted, disinclined to join in the banter.

"I'm Barry. You'll see enough of me righ' enough. You gotta couple of hours to mosey about if you want."

"Er, is there a, like a library or somewhere to get a book, you know, reading material?"

"Oh blimey, we got Melvyn bloody Bragg 'ere! Wot d'yer want Shakespeare? Wotsit, Charles Dickens? Doskiteski?" He laughed. "Nah, don't mind me mate, I'm jus' kiddin' yer. Yeah, you can gedda book when the libree's open, wensdi an satdi... Alright, Samir, shutup, I'm getting to yer, alright?"And he moved off to open the cell next door where there was a deal of banging and raised voices.

So some of them were okay; you could have a chat at a certain level. It wasn't relentless oppression. He could do with a different cell mate tho' – Ricko twenty- four seven was going to be hard work.

He found the remote for the TV and flicked through the channels to see what was available, settling on a repeat of a Simon Schama programme about Hadrian's Wall which turned out to be very interesting. Some sort of relief anyway.

Chapter 18

Signe lay on her bed. She was staring at the ceiling which was white and bare except for the central light fitting with its IKEA shade and a crack in the paintwork which wiggled its way from the right hand wall to about halfway across her bed. She remembered her mum – Melissa - had been very annoyed when it had appeared only a few months after her room had been decorated. Natural movement of the building, the decorator had said when queried about it. He could come back and open it up, fill it, rub it down and repaint the area, but it was a half day's work and they hadn't thought it was worth it, and Melissa was still annoyed.

Signe found she could let her eyes defocus from the crack and almost look through it. When she did this the ceiling seemed to lower towards her. In fact by relaxing her focus and then refocusing the ceiling appeared to raise and lower, as if it were breathing.

She was lying here in bed, well on her bed, because she didn't want to do anything, didn't want to see anyone. Her head was full of thoughts and feelings which chased each other round her brain trying to understand each other, yet she felt totally empty. Spent. Drained out. 'Today I don't feel like doing anything, nothing at all'. Bruno Mars' song lyrics ear-wormed into her mind, but unlike in the pop song it wasn't just that she was an indolent teenager who wanted to veg. out; she felt physically exhausted, emotionally rung out.

The trial had done it. It was days ago now, but she was still reeling from it, trying to come to terms with what had happened, trying to understand what she felt about it. Everyone in her family had been euphoric. Uncle Dirk had been ecstatic – he'd got his man – 'Nailed him, tied him to the mast'! They had celebrated the verdict at their house, Uncle Dirk holding forth about the justice system and how it needed more convictions on people like this, the scum of the earth who so often got away with their filthy obsessions and debauched behaviour. This time they'd got him, put him in a cell and rolled the stone across. He wouldn't be coming out for a good long time. Let him rot in there and think about what he'd done. Filthy pervert.

She'd hated it. It had been all wrong, celebrating. How can you celebrate someone's conviction, someone's sentence to years of incarceration? 'Schadenfreude'. Her German lessons had taught her that concept, a fairly revolting idea she'd thought, of revelling in some else's misfortune.

Sounds of the house filtered up to where she lay, pans and crockery clashing and clinking in the kitchen as someone emptied the dishwasher. Must be Melissa; Lars and Gustav would be at hockey practice. It was Saturday morning and the clock twenty centimetres from her face displayed 11.43 in its boxy blue illuminated numbers. She would normally have been at church in the office, manning the telephone for Father Stefan, her Saturday job for which she was paid. It was really easy, all she had to do was answer the phone if it rang, giving people any information they needed – 'Father Stefan's out, can he call you back later? Would you like to leave a message?', 'Mass is at eight and ten on Sunday mornings', 'The church is open for private prayer and contem-plation from seven in the morning til nine at night'. It suited her completely. Although usually shy when meeting people face to face, on the phone she didn't have a problem. She was talking to a disembodied voice which she didn't find threatening. No eyes boring into her, no threatening body language, just the voice. And mostly the phone didn't ring and she had nothing to do except her homework and got paid for it. It wasn't a lot of money, but all she had to do was sit there. Occasionally they asked her to do some filing or update the church website, but it was all easy and well within her comfort zone.

She hadn't been to church since... it had all happened. They had had to cope without her. Everything normal in her life had stopped and everything was different now. It was all referenced by what had happened and the trial. Things happened before the event or after it. Like BC and AD. Her life could never now be the same because of it, because it had happened and everything else had followed on from it, like the domino effect.

She decided she must see Irma. She reached for her mobile. 'Hei, wotsup. Must c u. Can i come over.' As soon as she'd pressed 'send' she remembered that Irma did some music thing on Saturday mornings. Was it quartet? Yes, that was it. Something about how she was in love with the music of some guy called Haydn. Apparently he wrote millions of string quartets and they were all brilliant. Better than Mozart whom she'd heard of at least. Signe felt anxious now, not remembering when the practice ended or what Irma did afterwards. Was it all morning til lunchtime? She couldn't remember and was now annoyed with herself for not having contacted her earlier.

Rolling onto her back again and putting her arms behind her head she caught a strong whiff of BO and realised she'd been sweating with nerves. She went to have a shower hoping Irma would reply to her text. In the bathroom she locked the door and took off her clothes, automatically cupping her hand over herself, a reflex that had started when it had all happened. She didn't fully understand why she did it but it felt safer, reassuring. She had clamped her hand there after she had forced him off in her panic, she remembered that. Her hand had been aching from the pressure she had applied in that desperate act of self-protection so that Irma had had to force her to release it so she could take her clothes off for the shower in the police station. She'd had it clamped there all that time, terrified.

She caught sight of herself in the long bathroom mirror, pale and cool in the diffused light of the drawn-down blind. This body which she had treasured as pure and chaste until a month ago was now defiled, its apparent unblemished purity now besmirched with invisible dirt. No matter how she soaped it and scrubbed it with her exfoliating glove, til the flesh was pink and raw, it would still be sullied in God's eyes. Before it had happened she would stand quite happily in the locked bathroom shyly admiring her naked body, not with pride, but with a simple joy at its fascinating beauty, which she would keep for Him undamaged by sexual contact. There had been no compunction to hide herself in her hand, her eyes hunted and haunted by those terrible thoughts.

When she got back to her room she activated her phone and saw there was a reply from Irma sent at 12.17. 'Hei jst fnshd 4tet class. Off to nandos wth guys. B home@2, c u then? X'. The time was now 12.42. She thought for a moment. 'ok can i stay over?' She needed to get away from home, from the claustrophobic stifling atmosphere of indulgent uncomprehending concern. It was well meant but she needed space and was fed up with staring at the walls in her room.

Having made the decision she suddenly felt free, as if a cloud had lifted which had been suffocating her like a huge pillow pressing down on her face. It was such a relief to have made a decision and have a direction, even if it was just going to Irma's. She would be able to talk, unburden herself, let it all out. She was almost happy.

No, that was too strong a word. Positive would be more correct, something she hadn't felt for ages. Not that it immediately solved any of her problems except her torpor, but that was something.

She clumped down the wooden stairs in her strawberry clogs. Melissa wasn't in the kitchen which was a welcome surprise. She put two bagel halves in the toaster and grabbed some orange juice from the fridge. She scraped butter onto the bagels, carefully covering every millimetre of the lightly browned surfaces and not dropping any down the central holes. Then she applied a thick layer of Nutella in a similar fashion, before taking it all into the sitting room to nibble away at whilst doing the difficult Sudoku in the Göteborgs-posten. She had begun to figure the eights when she heard the back door slam and movement in the kitchen, and realised Melissa had probably been hanging out the washing. Within seconds she was in the doorway.

"Ah, Si, you're down."

Why do they always say the obvious? She never used to call me Si, only since it happened. She always called me by my full name. Why Si? Lars calls me Si and so do my friends. Not them. She's trying to be sympathetic. "Uh huh."

"How are you feeling?"

Crap, dirty, embarrassed, guilty. GUILTY! "Fine."

"Did you sleep okay?"

No. I had nightmares, I woke up sweating, then I couldn't get back to sleep for ages because I couldn't stop thinking about everything and I felt DIRTY! "Yup."

"That's good. I'm glad to see you're eating."

I've been eating Melissa. If I hadn't been eating I'd have died. I only weigh 50kilos. "I'm going to see Irma. I might stay the night."

Melissa hesitated before answering, obviously thinking. Signe had worked out where most of the sevens and ones had to go, but obviously the threes were going to be a problem.

"That's good," there was disappointment in her voice overlaid with enthusiasm. "Will you come straight to church from there tomorrow? The ten o'clock?"

"Sure." *Ah, fours can go there and there...*

"I guess you haven't seen Irma for a while, so it'll be good for you two to get together again."

"Mmm." She knew Melissa was desperately trying to keep a conversation going, but she didn't feel like talking. She knew it was rude, but she wished she'd just go away.

"Signe, as the boys are out...*boys...* maybe we could talk a little, you know, about what happened, I mean, how it's affected you." She was struggling to say it right, Signe was aware, but she wasn't going to help her. She didn't know why. She kind of wanted to make her suffer too, so she knew what it was like a bit.

"Yeah." The sixes were beginning to fall into place.

"I'm not wanting to pry," Melissa continued, coming to sit gingerly on the arm of the settee, still holding the peg bag, "but I need to know you're ok, Si ..*Si again....*that you're... coping, you know, with it..all?" she managed. Her question hung in the air.

"Ya, ya, it's fine. Don't worry. The therapist is helping lots." If she could work out the last six it would help the rest of the lines.

"Ok, well I just wanted to....be here, you know, if you wanted to talk, if it would help... at all..." There was silence. She tentatively put a hand on Signe's shoulder. Signe didn't react, just kept staring at the paper and twiddling the biro between her fingers. Melissa gave up and wandered away.

Signe felt cruel. She knew Melissa meant well, it was just that she didn't want to talk. Well, not with her anyway.

Her phone vibrated and a glance showed "Sure" with a winking, smiley face. The six worked in all directions now and suddenly it all fell into place, bam bam bam bam. She scribbled the rest of the numbers into their inevitable places and chucked the paper down as she got up.

She went upstairs and got a few things together. She couldn't believe how much better she felt just doing something. And she couldn't believe how much she desperately wanted to see Irma, her best and oldest friend. In fact, probably her only real friend. It didn't take her long to throw a few things in her messenger bag – earphones, book, clean knickers, hairbrush, sanitary towels. She was strangely late with her period, about five days, which was weird, as she was usually spot on, so she was sure they'd be necessary. She bunged in her huge slouchy XXL Indians strip shirt which she'd nicked off Gustav and used as a nightshirt. It was her only association with the obsession he and Lars had with the local team.

She clomped down the stairs again and shouting a 'bye' to Melissa but not waiting for a reply, slammed out of the front door. It felt amazing to be out of the house, out of that vegetative tape loop of self analysis and self loathing. At last the cycle was broken and she almost skipped across the park to catch the bus.

Spring was definitely breaking through, the sun was gaining intensity and the first few flies scattered away from her path as she walked. She plugged in her earphones for the first time in ages and chose a Pro Green number from the i-list – 'Read all about it'. This was the only kind of music she listened to really. It suited her lack of musical education and was fairly neutral and cool. She liked its un-sophistication and obvious beat.

She was slightly nervous when she got on the bus that she would meet someone she knew who might know what had happened. Would they say anything? What would she say? To her relief she didn't know anyone; an elderly couple, a young family with an annoying little girl who kept crying particularly when prevented from pressing the stop button, and a smattering of individuals spread around.

Her mind was clearing now and she felt she might be able to think straight, the music in her ears blocking out the accusing voices which had been there for so long. For the first time she felt slightly positive.

The thought of seeing Irma by herself combined with this beautiful spring day had given her a fillip which she readily acknowledged and allowed to impregnate her mood. The music beat through her head. She liked the way Emeli Sandé's smooth lilting voice alternated with Green's aggressive rap – it seemed to embody her own self pity and anger at her predicament and she felt her head nodding with the beat. It was a hypnotising beat, a strong basic rhythm which had a confidence and inevitability about it which added to her positivity. When she got off at the stop for Irma's house she felt a new vigour in her body which reassured her, because although she was excited to see her friend there was something she had to confront her about which had been making her nervous. Irma had broken a confidence, which Signe was really upset about and she was hoping this wasn't going to be a problem, but it had to be talked about, and now she was feeling stronger to do that as she walked across to Stjernsköldsgatan.

She was about to knock on the door when she heard a shout behind her and turned to see her friend crossing the road having just got off a bus which was going in the opposite direction.

"Hei. I was running late," she puffed as she came up to Signe. "We went on longer than I thought and I suddenly realised what the time was. How you doing?" She gave Signe a big hug and looked searchingly in her eyes.

"Oh, you know....ok."

Irma was holding her by the shoulders, not letting her turn away.

"I didn't believe any of your texts saying you were fine and all that. You can't lie to me Si, I know you too well. I've just been so busy with cello and school and stuff....I'd have come to see you, but..." she shrugged. "Come on, let's go inside."

She opened up the house. It was apparent no-one was in except Caspar the Olsson's elderly Labrador who bowled over and fussed about, wanting to be petted and whacking their legs with his flailing tail. The Larssons didn't have a dog and Signe loved old Caspar whom she'd known all her life.

"I'm going to have a coffee, d'you want one?"

Signe didn't really drink coffee. She preferred hot chocolate, but she knew Irma's household didn't have it.

"Sure," she said. She sat at one of the stools at the breakfast bar in the kitchen while her friend got out coffee and charged the coffee maker.

"You look tired Si, have you been sleeping? Don't lie to me."

"I keep waking up and can't get back to sleep 'cos everything's going round in my head." She absentmindedly picked up a straw of sugar from the collection on the counter that Irma's dad picked up from Starbucks whenever he went there. He'd come in and empty his pockets and say "Well they can afford it, the amount of tax they avoid" if anyone commented. She twisted off an end and poured the grains into her hand, licked a finger and transferred them to her tongue.

"I'm sure that's only natural. It's going to take time Si. You've had a huge shock. That bastard's got a lot to answer for." Irma got out a couple of mugs as the coffee maker burped and gargled, and fetched milk from the fridge.

"Irm, I've got to tell you something." Signe didn't know how to go about this, but she had to somehow.

"Yeah, what's that?" She was looking around in a cupboard above the counter. Signe knew she was looking for the biscuits; all Swedish kitchens were pretty much laid out the same way.

"I don't think he tried to rape me."

"What?" Irma's face as she swung around showed that she was both stunned and uncomprehending.

"I've been thinking about it all," Signe hurried on, wanting to get it out now that she'd started before she changed her mind and clammed up, "and I'm beginning to remember more about what happened and.... it's not quite like how it came out in court."

"What are you saying Si? All that stuff in court was lies? Don't be stupid, I came and found you and you were screaming. What do you mean he didn't try to rape you? I saw him lying there. Why are you trying to say he didn't now?" Her eyes were blazing with indignation. Signe felt she was going to cry.

"Don't shout at me Irma, I'm trying to explain to you."

"Ok ok. But, shit, Si, you can't start changing your mind now. I asked when I found you was he trying to rape you and you said yes."

"I know, I know, that's what's crazy about it. But now I'm remembering stuff and I don't think it was like that." The tears were beginning to come now and she couldn't stop them.

"Oh Si, what the fuck's going on in your head." Irma came over and hugged her. Signe cried freely into her shoulder, relieved at the embrace, welcoming the physical reassurance.

"I don't know," she whispered between sobs, "it's all so confusing, because I couldn't remember at the time, and now it's all come back." She sniffed and sobbed, trying to control herself. "At the trial I wanted to say something, I wanted to explain that I thought it was different from how Uncle Dirk was saying it, but...it was kind of decided by then. I couldn't say I'd made a mistake. Not then...oh God, I feel so terrible."

Irma hugged her again and then held her shoulders. "Why do you feel terrible? He did try to rape you, you know. He forced himself on you."

"No Irma, you don't know," she wailed, "that's what they said in court. That's what everyone thinks, but it wasn't like that. I...." and she looked searchingly into Irma's eyes, plucking up the courage to tell her, "I....I kissed him Irm. I wanted to kiss him. I wanted him to kiss me.....I thought he was someone else. I ...." she struggled to find the words. "This is going to sound **so** stupid and you're going to think I'm weird or something, but I was drunk and I think I must have been dreaming or something. If I tell you, you won't tell anyone? Promise you won't tell anyone – on your life."

"What? This is crazy."

"Promise Irma or I can't tell you."

"Ok ok, I promise. God!"

Signe hesitated, trying to weigh up whether she meant it, but she was her best friend, she wouldn't cheat her. "I thought...", she sighed with embarrassment. "Please don't laugh at me." Irma shook her head, serious. "I thought he was Jesus."

Irma just looked at her and Signe couldn't tell if she was trying not to laugh or was merely non-plussed by the revelation. She thought she should hurry on and explain.

"Irm there's a whole lot of stuff I've remembered, which started coming back at the trial but I couldn't say anything, 'cos I wasn't sure if I was imagining it or whether it really happened; you know, like when you have a dream and to begin with you can't work out if it's real or not."

Irma nodded. "But that doesn't change..."

"Just let me tell you what happened and then you can say what you think, ok?"

"Ok." Irma was about to sit down, but then jumped up again, "Oh the coffee. D'you want some now?"

"Ya, thanks." Signe wiped her eyes and blew her nose on kitchen towel. Irma poured and they took the cups and biscuits into the sitting room.

"Ok Si, tell me all about it." Irma settled herself on the settee at right angles to Signe on the armchair, sitting on her legs.

It felt more difficult to start back into it now there had been a pause, but Signe took a breath and blew it out before launching in.

"It began during the concert. I was just looking at him as he was sitting there and suddenly I noticed he was looking right at me. I mean, I think I'd been staring at him for some time without realising and then, suddenly he was staring at me. It was so weird. I felt really embarrassed when I found he knew I'd been staring at him, so I looked away, but when he sang again I couldn't help looking at him again and he was singing right at me. And his voice was so, you know, like, powerful and masculine. I found it very exciting when he sang and I got a bit carried away because of it being Good Friday and everything." She paused, not sure whether she wanted a reaction, but Irma was quiet. "And don't you think he's very good looking?"

A look crossed Irma's face and the faintest smile curled the corner of her mouth. "Ya, I think he's very good looking. But Si, he raped you."

"Wait, you've got to listen to what happened. Anyway, all through the concert I kept catching his eye and I found I couldn't look away. It was like he hypnotised me and all the time that amazing music was playing and I got emotional about the Passion. Honest Irma, it was really awesome. I never realised classical music could do that to you, like really make you cry."

Irma smiled indulgently and gestured agreement.

"So then we went to the reception and I had that Glögg which, you know, I don't drink really so I wasn't used to it and, wow, it really made me feel weird. And then somehow I was outside and the moon was shining on the water and I turned round and suddenly there he was again, in the moonlight, staring at me and holding his arms out like a crucifix. And then, I don't know how it happened, but the next thing I remember was lying on the bench and opening my eyes and his smiling face was right in front of me with those amazing blue eyes and I felt I wanted to....I just desperately wanted to kiss him, Irm. I don't know why. I don't know what I was thinking. It was all a blur and I don't think I'd have done it if I hadn't had the Glögg and if his voice hadn't been so amazing...." She broke off, struggling to put into words what she was trying to say, which she wasn't even sure of.

"So, you kissed him." Irma said, matter of factly.

Signe looked at her blankly, "Ya".

"He didn't force you to, you wanted to."

"Ya."

"But what d'you mean that you thought he was Jesus?"

Signe's eyes were wet again and she used a sleeve to wipe them.

"When I opened my eyes and he was so close I was really confused and I didn't know where I was or what was happening, and all I remembered was him singing "Take, eat, this is my body" and I was so happy I just wanted to kiss him....in gratitude... and he kissed me back, and it was beautiful. And I felt he was a part of me and that it was right. But now I know it was all wrong and I shouldn't have done it. He didn't understand what I meant by it and now he's in prison and I'll never see him again." Signe broke down, the tears streaming down her cheeks and her coffee spilling in her lap. Irma jumped up, took the mug and rushed to the sink to find the cloth and come back and mop up.

"Oh, I'm sorry I'm sorry. Oh shit I shouldn't have told you. It's not your problem."

"Shut up, Si, don't be stupid. Look, you're my best friend, right? Don't you dare say it's not my problem. I'm here to help, ok? So don't act like some crazy dumb girl."

Signe was silent while Irma wiped off her skirt.

"You told Uncle Dirk, didn't you."

Irma stopped and looked at her.

"You told Uncle Dirk about the Bridgettines. About me going to Vadstena."

Irma resumed wiping. "He said he needed as much information as possible to make a good case. I told him because I wanted to get that guy punished. How was I to know you'd fallen in love with him?"

"I'm not in love with him." Signe retorted. "I was drunk and I didn't know what was happening."

"Si, I think from what you've told me you really fancy this guy, but you didn't understand that's what it was. You thought it was the music and the Passion, but I think that was only part of it. It's ok to fancy a man Si. You can't help it if it happens, it's not your fault."

"But how can I join the Bridgettines now, when I've kissed a man?"

"Oh Si, that's not a sin. You can still become a nun if you really want to."

Irma took the cloth back to the sink with Signe's cup which she wiped off and replenished from the machine.

"But I shouldn't have been tempted to look at a man when I'd decided to become a nun. I shouldn't have had those thoughts."

"You can't help being tempted, that's only natural. Look, if you weren't tempted how could you resist; I mean if you never felt tempted you'd never have the opportunity to resist."

Signe thought for a moment. "But Jesus was pure, He was sinless."

"If you want, but that doesn't mean he wasn't tempted. Anyway he **was** tempted, in the wilderness, wasn't he? Surely the point is that he knew temptation but he resisted it. You had the temptation and if you want you can now resist it and not go there again."

"But I didn't resist it. I wanted to kiss him."

"But you said you thought he was Jesus, so you were just embracing the Divine. Isn't that what you're supposed to do?" Irma was obviously pleased with this neat solution.

Signe sat disconsolately and pulled Caspar's ears. He'd suddenly come in and plonked himself next to her. She looked down at his wide head.

"I wish was a dog. It must be so much easier. All you've got to worry about is food and a walk and normally they're provided for you."

Caspar suddenly got up and trolled over to Irma, nudging her leg and wagging his tail madly.

"I don't think you should have mentioned the word 'walk', you've given him an idea. Actually I don't think he's been out today. Do you want to take him round the park with me?"

Caspar gave a sudden impatient bark. Signe laughed despite herself.

"Sure, why not."

They finished their coffees, picked up Caspar's lead and all went out into the weak sunshine.

Chapter 19

"Hi Mags." He grasped her hands across the table and she took the hint, transmitted by the arms-length grip in which he held her, that she couldn't lean across to kiss him.

"Oh Matt babe, I can't believe you're in here. Look at you."

They sat down across the table, she taking his hands again, he aware of the screws watching out for any transfer of anything between them. She caught his sideways look.

"What's it like babe? Is it...dreadful?" she said in a lowered voice.

Matt sighed, looking down at their hands and stroking her fingers with his.

"It's okay. It's boring as hell. There's nothing to do. That's what really gets you. It's such a waste of time. You know, you don't realise how much time there is until you're doing it, then there's hours and hours of it, doing nothing." He looked up at her, noticing the amount of lip gloss she'd applied and the trouble she'd taken with her make-up. For him. To show she cared. But it was tantalising. He wanted to snog her; those weird dreams he could only vaguely remember a flavour of – or had he imagined them? - had sharpened his sexual appetite and filled his waking hours with perverted thoughts of Maggie, amongst others, submitting to any and every kinky thought that entered his head. Now that she was here, concern wrapping her features, he felt a bit guilty at the resurgent urges but at the same time enjoyed the kick.

"What are we going to do Matt?"

"What d'you mean?"

"Well, you know," He wondered if this was her asking for a let out, to go her own way. Two years is a long time.

"It's okay Mags, I don't expect anything. You've got to get on with your life. You know, live. You can't wait for me."

Her eyes were brimming. "I still don't understand how it happened, how you ended up, you know, on top of her, if you didn't mean to.... And they said there was your semen on her clothes."

Matt took his hands away, and covered his face, rubbing his eyes and forehead. "Mags, I told you on the phone. I was pissed – you know what Champagne does. It was the situation, the build up, your email" (that was a bit far- fetched, implicating her, but he put it in for good measure. He was struggling here) "it all came to a head at the party, after everything. I don't know, I've gone over it again and again. I was carried away. It was like a different reality, parallel universe." He blew out, like when lifting weights, expelling the air through his mouth, tight-lipped, to relieve the tension.

"But Matt, you're not normally like that. That's me. It's like you suddenly became some kind of animal. I mean when we, you know, do it, that's consensual and it's usually me instigating it all, but suddenly you seem to have, I don't know, broken out and gone rampant or something."

"Oh Maggie, let's leave it shall we. I've said what happened. I'm not proud of it. I can't even explain it completely. What's done is done, so there's no point in going on about it."

She looked away, surveying the other tables of prisoners seeing visitors, talking in hushed voices, trying to keep the conversations private. Then they both spoke at once, which could have been funny.

"You go," he said.

"It was nothing. I was just going to ask what the food was like."

"It's okay," he shrugged, "like hospital food. Sometimes it's alright, sometimes it's a bit crap."

There was a pause.

"What were you going to say?"

"Oh, er, can't remember... oh yes, have my parents rung?"

"No, haven't heard anything."

"Beginning of the new term. They'll be busy. And dad's head of department now...."

"Yeah, more responsibility right?"

"Yeah right."

Again they fell silent. Maggie fiddled with a button on her coat and smiled awkwardly, not like her. He grimaced back.

"I still can't believe you came all the way to Gothenburg, found the courtroom and everything."

"Well, it's what people do, Matt. When they're together. When they're a couple."

She looked at the clock on the wall behind him and he realised she must have someone to see, something to do later, which perhaps explained the careful make-up. Why had he thought it was for him, in prison?

"Maggie, don't feel you have to stay. I'm fine. Get on with your life."

"It's okay, I said I'd meet Tommo and Pete for a catch up, and Tash is going to join us later. But we're not meeting til five'ish."

"That's great. But look, don't come. Don't come here. Let's just talk on the phone. It's a crap journey from Leyton to here and it'll be easier if I just ring you now and again. I mean, it's not like there's much going on in here." He forced a laugh.

She took his hands again. "Matt, whatever happened, you know I'm always your friend, right? The situation may have changed, but I'm not going to give up on you, okay? Just because you're in here, don't think I'm going to forget you and go off. I don't do that."

She looked him dead in the eyes, serious, intense. God, he wanted to fuck her. He loved it when she was serious and business like. It was a real turn on.

"Mags, I don't want you to stop your life for me. That's not natural. It's unrealistic. I wouldn't ask it of you and I'd feel uncomfortable if you....you know...sacrificed yourself for me. You've got to carry on living even tho' my life's on hold. Promise me you'll get on with your life, please."

There was a look in her eyes he couldn't interpret. Relief? Compassion? He couldn't tell.

"I promise Matt, but I've no intention of going anywhere. I said, I'm not giving up on you." She paused, apparently considering what to say. "I'm going to have to give up the flat though or else find someone to share with me. You know, it's a lot..."

"Yeah, I know, the rent's too much for you. I'm sorry Mags, it's a big fuck up. And it's affecting your life now. There's money in my account, you can use it. You might as well – I'm not going to be able to."

He then gave her all his bank codes which she wrote so she could do online transfers. They organised stopping life insurance, putting a hold on pension contributions, discussed whether she could do all this without him authorising it but realised most things could be done online using passwords and he directed her to the paperwork for each. It was amazing how much there was to be sorted now that he no longer had access to his business affairs. He was impressed with how organised she suddenly seemed to be and how capable, whereas he'd always thought her scatty and muddled. Maybe she was one of those people who could organise other people but not herself. Maybe when he was there she relied on him for the organisation and didn't feel she needed to, but now that he was here she was stepping up to the mark and taking responsibility which he hadn't allowed her.

"Matt, I don't know what to say to Katie. If you don't want your parents to know, is it the same for her? Doesn't seem right and I don't see it being possible really. I mean I don't see how you can keep it from everyone."

"I know, I just wanted a bit of time with my parents. I've got to work out how I want to tell them. You can tell Katie, god you know her well enough, she's one of your best friends, she's how we met, but swear her to secrecy from mum and dad. She'll have to lie to them, play along for now. I can't tell them yet, I don't know why. I just need some time. Huh, that's ironic!"

"Okay."

"What about everyone else. Has anyone called?"

"God, Matt, you've no idea. Your emails are full of questions asking why you're not responding to anyone. People are starting to get worried online, you know, saying has anyone heard from Matt? What's happened to him? What do I do?"

"Right. I don't know, Mags, I need to get my head round that. I've been so wrapped up in being in prison and dealing with all that. I haven't really thought about how to deal with all the other stuff."

He twisted the curl of flesh around the top of his right ear, which was a default gesture when he was thinking.

"So you'll tell my parents I'm abroad suddenly on a late-booked contract and I'm very busy learning a role and rehearsing, and in any case the internet's not good there, something like that yeah?"

"Where shall I say you are?"

"Oh God, I don't know, Argentina? Buenos Aires? Say there's a great opportunity to try out some new roles without being under the European spotlight or something like that. Say it was a last minute contract, some guy dropped out at very short notice. He was booked to do three roles or something and my agent put me forward to replace him. They'll never know whether I was there or not. Stuff there isn't really reviewed or listed except in the professional magazines and they don't read those. They'll have to know the truth eventually, but for now...."

Maggie wrote it all down in a notebook she had in her handbag.

"What about all the emails and messages, Facebook? They'll all know you're not in Buenos Aires?" She was sucking her biro, lip-sticked lips unintentionally pouting provocatively.

"I don't know" Matt blurted out, shaking himself to concentrate. "It's bloody difficult to think what to say." He forced himself to look down at the table, at his conjoined hands writhing their dance of dread, trying to wring a plausible solution from thin air. "Mags, I don't think I can cover it up from them. I'm going to have to say something and ask them to keep it quiet or...or else let the whole thing out. But that would be insane, like total suicide. I'd never work again. The whole bloody profession'll know about it. I'd be crucified. The press would have a field day: 'Royal Opera protégé rapes innocent Swedish sixteen year old' or 'Messiah messes with virgin in Passion'. I'm dead Mags."

"Couldn't you say, like, what actually happened. You were accused of rape by some neurotic girl, it was all blown out of proportion and the jury believed her story."

"Yeah, well, they're just going to say, aren't you going to appeal if you didn't do it?"

Couldn't you? I mean can't you? Why haven't we thought of that? That's the answer, you've got to appeal. You say you didn't rape her. It's just her word against yours. She's the one who's lying or was so pissed she can't remember."

Matt looked at her eager face, all hope and righteous indignation. Gently he said, "Mags, I know. It seems obvious but it won't work. The court's in Sweden, what evidence there is, although not absolute, points strongly in her favour. The lawyer who represented me there, you know, you met him, said we could try to appeal, but he said it was highly unlikely there'd be any change. It would have taken a couple of months to come to trial again and all that time I'd have been held in custody. It would have been like an extra two months if the sentence wasn't changed. I've been over it a hundred times in my head. All the hours I've spent locked up I've tried to think if it could be proved another way, but there's no evidence to the contrary, so they're always going to come down on her side as the vulnerable victim. It's just how it is."

"So you're just going to take it, waste two years of your life rotting in here under a false conviction. And all the time she's gadding about free as a bird doing whatever she wants. Is that fair? Is that what you're happy with?"

"Ssh Mags, keep your voice down."

"I don't care Matt, this is important. I can't believe you're going to sit here and not make any attempt to get released. You could get an English lawyer to fight your side. There's the European Court of Human Rights or whatever, you could make an appeal to them. We should write to your MP or, or the Foreign Office or something. That's what they're supposed to do, help people who've been wrongly accused abroad. Now I'm thinking about it, we should get up a petition for your release. You can do it online, you know, through Amnesty..."

"Mags, Mags, calm down." Matt looked around as other inmates and visitors were noticing Maggie's raised voice and the screws were visibly alert to the situation.

"Matt you gotta help yourself and get active. I'll get active if you don't. I'll get active anyway. I'll talk to Tommo and Pete this afternoon. They'll get things going..."

"Maggie you mustn't do anything. You're getting hysterical and you're not thinking straight."

"At least I'm thinking, Matt, which is more than you're doing. You're just wallowing in self-pity and giving up completely." Maggie's voice was rising all the time and she was getting animated. One of the screws came over and asked her to calm down and control herself.

"I'm perfectly in control, mate," she snapped, that fire burning in those coal black pupils.

"That's fine, young lady, if you could just keep the noise down."

"Don't fucking 'young lady' me, mate. Can't I have a discussion with my partner without you sticking your bloody noses in?"

"Right young lady, I think your time's up."

"Don't fucking touch me, you bastard, I've got every right to stay here and talk. Oi, let go of me you bloody bastard. That's assault. I'll have you prosecuted. Fucking let go of me...."

Matt watched, helpless, as Maggie was bodily removed from the room, various of the visitors looking horrified, some of the inmates smiling and cheering.

"Alright, alright. Show's over for the day. Let's all calm down or I'll have to end the session."

The remaining screws walked threateningly down the line of tables as the hubbub died down. Matt sat despondently, lost in thought til a screw stood over him.

"Time for bed, said Zebedee." Matt looked up at the supercilious smile on the screw's face and got up to return to the joys of Ricko.

Oh Maggie, Maggie. You and your bloody Italian temperament. Please God you don't go and do anything. ...God?

Chapter 20

It was a short walk down Stjernsköldsgatan, left onto Godhemsgatan, right onto Slottskogsgatan and then all the way down to Slottskogsparken, the huge park where they always went.

Caspar trotted along, stopping frequently to investigate the latest messages on lampposts and fences and cocking his leg to leave replies. They walked in silence for quite some time, each digesting what had been said. Eventually as they approached the entrance to the park Irma spoke.

"You still definitely want to go into the Bridgettines then?"

"Course. That's never changed. I can't think of anything else I'd rather do."

Irma let Caspar off the lead and he galloped off happily to meet a friend.

"Ok, but wanting to do something's different from actually doing it. I mean, lots of people have an idea they want to do something big in their lives, particularly when they're young and idealistic, but then they realise that actually that's not where they're at and they do something else."

"Irm, I've wanted to be a nun since I was about twelve ok? Nothing's changed, except that night. And the trial.... and everything that's happened after..."

"Which is quite a lot right? I mean, it's like it's affected you big time. You're not the same person you were a month ago, because of what happened. That's what life's like; things happen and they affect you and you change slightly, right?"

"I suppose." They walked on, not really thinking where they were going, just wandering along. "But right now," Signe continued, "I don't know what to do. Because he's been sent to prison and I think it's my fault and I don't know how to go about getting him out."

Irma stopped and turned to her. "You want to get him out now? Si, you may have wanted to kiss him, but then he tried to rape you..."

"That's just it, I don't think he did. I don't think he would have done. I think he thought I wanted him to make love to me because that's what it seemed like. Because I was kissing him like I wanted him to. Oh God it's so difficult to explain." She broke off and turned away hugging herself and looking across the open parkland. "Why did I do it? I just don't understand. I've never felt like I wanted to do that before, never had that feeling before, all I ever wanted to do was follow Christ's teachings. It was so simple and now I've gone and ruined it all."

"Si," Irma spoke very gently, "it's okay. You just fell in love with someone, that's all. It happens."

There was silence for maybe twenty seconds, broken only by the distant sounds of kids shouting, playing football.

"But what am I going to do?" Signe's voice was low now, calm.

"You mean about him? I don't know. Don't they sometimes have a retrial when they find new evidence? I'm sure I've seen that on TV."

"What, and have to go to court again? Can't I just tell someone and then they let him out, because it was all a mistake?"

"Well, I don't think it's that simple, Si. You know, they have to overturn a previous ruling and I think it has to be official and everything."

"I wish I'd never gone to that concert and then none of this would have happened."

They walked on, Irma linking arms with her friend and squeezing her elbow.

"You can't stop things happening by just not doing them. Whatever you do things will happen. That's what life's like, Si, things happening. It's how you deal with them that's important."

Signe looked sideways at Irma with a smile, "Oo, get you. Quite the philosopher these days. What's going on?"

She thought Irma coloured slightly. "I'm seeing Karl."

There was a pause as Signe stopped abruptly pulling her arm from Irma's.

"You're what? You mean you're...?" Irma smiled coyly. "Oh Irma," Signe's tone had changed from shock to annoyance. "But that's crazy. He's much older than you and...isn't he married?"

"Ya, got a baby."

"But his wife doesn't know right?"

"Course not. God, that would be.... weird."

"Irma, that's not right. You can't date a married man."

"I didn't mean to. What, you think I thought 'I really fancy going out with a married man' and then tried to find one?"

"Course not."

"It just happened. You know, we saw each other at rehearsals and then he gave me some coaching and we went for a coffee afterwards, and the next thing you know we're kissing. I didn't plan it."

They walked on separately now in silence, each appreciating that their experiences weren't so dissimilar although the circumstances and repercussions were very different. They came to some benches by a stand of trees and without consulting each other they sat and looked at each other. Casper was fussing about the tree trunks and giving an occasional yelp at a squirrel which was teasing him, hanging precariously from the bark halfway up and twitching its tail angrily.

"But you wanted it to happen. You really fancied him, right?" Signe said.

"Ya, I know, but I didn't kind of, you know, force it. He was just as keen. I don't think his relationship with his wife is very good right now."

"I'm not surprised."

"Si!"

Signe looked away. "It's not right Irma. He's cheating on her. And what about the kid?"

"Look, Si, I know it sounds bad, but it's like, as I said, things happen and you just have to deal with them. I think he really needs me at the moment. He says it's such a relief to see me because of the stress at home. He's struggling to do teaching, playing in the orchestra and spend time at home with a young kid who's very demanding and he's feeling a lot of pressure."

Signe felt herself digging in, determined to take the opposite view.

"I bet his wife feels under pressure too and she's not getting any relief from the stress of childcare. Ok we have to deal with what happens in life, but, like, you can't just do whatever you want in life; people get hurt."

Irma took a deep breath, held it briefly then puffed out. "I don't want to hurt anyone, but I'm not going to lie about my feelings. D'you think the first time Karl leant across to kiss me I should have stopped him, because he was married and it might hurt his wife? He wanted to and I wanted him to. I'd have been lying if I'd pretended I didn't want him to. You can't live other people's lives for them."

"No, but you can't just let yourself do anything you want. It's not right." Signe wasn't looking at her, but across the park.

"Isn't it? Why can't you? At least it's honest. That's the problem with people in this country, they're all so bloody screwed up. Everyone crapping themselves that they might do something that people won't like. Everyone's got to act normal like a whole lot of automatons. You know, I don't get it. You see all that stuff that went on in the sixties with the Beatles and the Rolling Stones, free love and breaking out of all that convention, and then you look at now and it's like it never happened. You can't do this, you can't do that! Oh My God.... Casper, come here boy. Here, stop making all that noise, come on, sit here. There's a good boy."

She got him to sit momentarily for a stroke and tickle, before he wandered off again into the undergrowth near the trees, snuffling in the leaves, but at least not barking anymore.

Signe felt unhappy now. Somehow the discussion that was supposed to have been about her predicament had been hijacked into one about Irma and Karl. It was like Irma's situation had taken precedence.

"Si, he's a really nice guy. We get on really well. I understand him. It's not just sex, right?"

"You're sleeping together?"

"Oh come on Si. What d'you think?" She felt her appeal didn't convince, Signe's expression remaining resolutely unforgiving. "I think the reason he doesn't get on so well with his wife is that she's not a musician. She's reserved, a librarian or something, although of course she's on maternity leave right now. But she doesn't understand the performance thing, you know, touring and concerts in the evening and coming home late. She just wants him to do a day job, but that's not who he is; he's an artist, he needs the freedom to express himself."

"Yeah, but he's got a baby now. Things happen, like you said, but it's how you deal with them. Seems he's dealing with it by having an affair."

"I hate it when you get on one of your moral crusades. You just don't see the other side of the story do you?"

"But Irm you're twisting it because you're in love with him. You're just making excuses to make yourself feel better about it. You can't change the facts."

"I know, but it's how you interpret them that's important. You're just ignoring the emotional side of it and being really harsh. It's not black and white Si."

They were both silent, watching Casper rootling about in the bushes. Signe was upset. She'd started the day so excited to see Irma and looking forward to spending time with her and now it had turned into this; arguing, bitching and blaming each other. She had no answers to her problem and now they seemed to be dealing with Irma's affair.

"Shall we go on?" Irma interrupted her thoughts.

"Sure."

They walked on in silence for some time. Pigeons strutted about on the path in front of them, puffing themselves up, the males pursuing the females, trying to impress them with their enlarged chests and insistent cooing. The females wandered about pretending to ignore them, pecking at bits of nothing as if they had far more important things to do. They waddled out of the way as the trio approached, continuing their cooing when they'd passed. Casper hardly looked at them. He wasn't interested in flappy birds. He was a squirreller and he trotted ahead, eyes alert for any movements in the leaves under the next group of trees.

They passed a kiddies' play area, the swings going back and forth, and saw a mother quite near the railings lifting a baby into the sandpit area. She stooped down and put the crawler on all fours where it started squidging the damp sand between its fingers, fascinated with the feeling, and then looking up and beaming with dribbling chops. Signe looked at Irma, then put her arm round her shoulder.

"I didn't mean to accuse you, Irm, I'm just feeling a bit crap at the moment."

"I know. I guess I'm being defensive. It's all so new and I'm really happy and I don't want to spoil it."

"Do your parents know?"

"No. I think they'd be really worried. You know what my dad's like. Mum would probably talk about it to all her friends and make a drama of it. Better see what happens and only tell them if I have to."

* * * * * * * * * * * *

When they got back they slobbed in front of the telly watching back numbers of 'The Big Bang Theory', which was 'wicked'. Irma's mum came home, fussed over Signe and then tactlessly launched into a monologue about youth drinking problems leading to teenage violence, rape and under-age pregnancies. She was completely oblivious of the effect she was having and only let up when the phone rang and she got into a long conversation about the curling club dinner. When the news came on they watched for a bit but gave up when a report came up about the cuts to social services and the effects this was having on single mothers. It seemed everything had a bearing on their situations when all they wanted to do was forget about them for now.

So they went upstairs to Irma's room and she logged onto Facebook to see what was happening. They chatted with various friends and Irma caught up with the latest parties which were being planned. Signe resorted to reading a magazine that was lying on Irma's bed. There was an article about contraception questioning some faith groups', and particularly the Catholic church's, continued stand against it. She read the whole article through feeling as always that society and her religion were at odds, and not knowing what she believed to be right. For her personally, she was in no doubt, because of her intentions, but for Catholics generally she felt confused. It seemed that people today were trying to make religion fit with their lifestyles as opposed to the other way round. But she was also keenly aware of problems of population increase and the tragedy of unwanted pregnancies. As Irma said, things never seemed to be black or white.

Later that night, after supper, they went back upstairs to escape from her mum. Irma's brother was away at uni so they decided to use his double bed and set up Irma's laptop. They had decided to watch 'The Hobbit, An Unexpected Journey' again, which was one of Signe's favourites with its age-old format of hope and resolution in the face of adversity and the few struggling against the massive odds of the unknown. It was almost biblical and for Signe was a metaphor for life which mirrored her religious belief and gave her strength.

"I wonder if you'll be able to watch this in the convent. I bet they don't get to watch movies and stuff there. Isn't it all praying and contemplation? And you aren't allowed to talk are you?"

"It's a different life," she replied quickly. "You get your pleasure in a different way, from devotion and spiritual fulfilment." She realised it didn't sound convincing to Irma.

"But Si are you really sure you want to give up everything you enjoy for the rest of your life? It seems so....extreme. Couldn't you just work in a convent school or something and that way you'd be teaching kids about God and stuff?"

Signe thought about it for a moment. "But that would seem like a betrayal, like I'm giving up before I've even tried it. If I really hate it I can come out again. It's not like prison you know. Oh Irm, what am I going to do?"

"About what?"

"You know, him, in prison. I've got to do something to get him out."

"But Si, he's not blameless. They looked at all the evidence and they found him guilty."

"I know, but as I said, it wasn't like that. He thought I wanted him to. It was all a mistake."

Irma was turning off the laptop, putting the DVD back in the box. "I think the only thing you can do is find out from someone at the court what you're supposed to do. I'm sure there must be an advice line or something. I'm tired now. We'll look it up tomorrow, okay?"

"Okay, thanks."

They brushed their teeth together, Irma noticing the sanitary towels in Signe's washbag. "I've just had a really bad one; went on for two weeks it seemed."

"I'm really late. Should have been on about a week ago but...."

"I bet that's the shock. I heard somewhere your period can go really weird if you've had a shock or if your body's under stress. Sometimes you can miss it completely."

"Sounds good. The last one I had was really painful. I'd be happy if I never had one again."

"Well, that would be fine if you never wanted kids."

"I don't want kids. Never want kids."

"Really? Well, I suppose if you're in a convent there's not much chance anyway." They laughed. "I want four kids, two boys, two girls. And a big dog, a Newfoundland."

"You'd better find yourself a rich husband. Better not go for a musician."

"Mmm, ya, that's a problem right now."

They snuggled up in the double bed.

"Actually the money's not important really. Nor are the kids or the dog. That's just me thinking what I'd like best, but it probably never works out like that. The most important thing is to be happy, isn't it?" Irma was talking low and slow, contemplatively. "I mean, surely the point of life is to be happy and make other people happy? That's why music's so wonderful. It's so uplifting and takes you out of yourself."

"That makes it sound like you want to avoid your life and get happiness by pretending you're somewhere else."

"Well, that's ok isn't it? That's what we did when we watched the film, we went to another place for a few hours. It made you happy, so that was ok wasn't it?"

Signe didn't reply and Irma couldn't see her face in the dark, could only sense her breathing softly close to her on the pillow. Signe was suddenly struck with the thought that she couldn't think of any moments in Christ's life or ministry when he appeared to be happy. There were moments when he was filled with the Holy Spirit and uplifted with the love of God, but mostly his demeanour was humility, sadness and an anticipation of his destiny on the cross. She couldn't think of any incident when Jesus relaxed and said 'Okay, we've all worked really hard, let's have a party'. Unless turning the water into wine could be seen as Jesus getting the party going. The bible seemed exclusively serious, there was nothing about enjoying yourself and letting your hair down, it only talked about finding eternal happiness and peace in heaven. Maybe, she thought, that's because at the time life was a living hell for the Jews under the Romans and they could only envisage happiness somewhere else.

As if echoing her thoughts Irma said, "I mean, we can't always be serious can we? You've got to be able to enjoy yourself sometimes."

Signe didn't reply, so after a pause Irma continued, "You know, Si, I don't want to be mean or anything and I know you've just been through a terrible experience but really I think sometimes you need to lighten up a bit. You take everything so seriously and sometimes you make me feel guilty for enjoying myself. I know you don't mean it, but it's difficult having a best friend who's so....strict and disciplined. You know?"

Signe still didn't reply.

"Si, you're not angry with me are you?" Irma put her hand out under the duvet to find her friend, to give her a reassuring squeeze. She found a shoulder and stroked it gently. Then she felt it begin to shake. "Oh Si, I'm sorry."

Signe rolled towards her and buried her head into Irma's neck, pouring forth a jumble of sentences which Irma couldn't understand at all. Irma managed to extricate her arm which had got trapped under Signe's body and held her close, shushing her and trying to calm her convulsing body. Signe clung onto her, wetting her shoulder with her tears and all the time explaining an anguish that Irma couldn't make out.

Eventually she calmed down and Irma flicked on the bedside light and found some tissues with which she helped Signe mop up.

"You ok now?"

"Ya." Signe snuffled back the involuntary cry shudders. "Ya, sorry Irm. I - can't control .... can't control it when ..... when it comes on ...."

"That's ok, you just let it out."

"It's ...... it's like...... a wave of ...... a wave that swamps me. A rush of sadness .... so strong. She blew her nose. "So strong, I can't control it and," she coughed, "it overwhelms me."

Irma searched her friend's face, aware that this was some strong emotion. Irma had hardly ever seen Signe cry. Although outwardly a fragile–looking person, she knew she was fairly stoical and she'd usually just walk away stony-faced if she was upset and would want to be on her own. So this outpouring of emotion was totally new to Irma.

"Hey, come here you." And she pulled Signe down onto her chest as she leaned back on the pillows so that her head lay under her chin. Signe was content to lie there listening to Irma's heart beat beneath her ample bosom. She snuffled occasionally and played with the little bow in the middle of Irma's pyjama top. Signe liked the smell of Irma's skin close to hers and Irma's chin on her forehead wasn't scratchy like her dad's. After a minute Irma spoke.

"So what's all this about, this rush of emotion? Is it something different from the... from, you know, what happened?"

Signe didn't reply immediately. "It's like, you know, I've tried so hard to follow His way, to be a good catholic and I'd set my heart on a life of devotion and....and then this happens and all my plans have been ruined. It's like it's been destroyed."

"What d'you mean, destroyed? What's been destroyed? You can still be a good catholic. You can still join the Bridgettines if you want. That hasn't changed."

"It seems like it has. It all seems different now. It's like something happened that night. I mean I know nothing really happened that changed anything, but I feel like I'm a different person now. I don't know how to explain it. It's like something changed inside me and now my life's different. Like I lost something I had before and therefore everything's going to be different now."

Irma stroked her hair. "I think you're still in shock, and ya, something like that's going to change you. But it doesn't mean you can't do the things you want to do. It may just not feel the same."

Signe was quiet, enjoying the soothing warmth of her friend's body.

"And you know Si, everything changes all the time. Life's like that. Sometimes we plan all sorts of things and they don't happen 'cos something else happens before we can do whatever it is. I never thought I'd meet someone like Karl before I left school. And I didn't mean to hitch up with a married man with a kid either. It's not exactly convenient and it makes it a big problem, but it's something that happened, we just met and that was it. It wasn't like we chose for it to happen. But when it happens you have to go with it. Or else I suppose you try to pretend it never happened and stick to your original plan, but it will always be different, just because it *did* happen." She was still stroking Signe's hair. She yawned. "But anyway, I suppose we ought to get some sleep. What d'you think?"

She stopped stroking and realised that Signe was fast asleep already. With difficulty she slid herself away from under her, switched off the light and lay thinking for a long time listening to the even suspirations of the body nestled by her side.

Chapter 21

Two days later Ricko was gone, transferred to another prison. No one knew why or where but apparently this is what happens inside. Someone's there one day, gone the next. Maybe it's to break up cliques, Matt thought, or to keep prisoners moving about to stop plots and insurrections. Anyway, he was on his own for now, Ricko having been moved out first thing in the morning, complaining and kicking up a fuss but eventually compelled to toe the line.

"Hey man, you look after dis place til I come back, you know wo'ameen? An keep owda way o' Stevie, okay? Dat's one crazy bastard." With this last piece of sage advice he disappeared behind the slammed cell door and Matt found himself sole occupant of his domain.

The last couple of days had been a steep learning curve. After solitary confinement in Sweden before the trial and similar isolation awaiting extradition after his committal, having to share a small space with someone else, particularly Ricko, had been a shock. Similarly social time at Wandsworth when the cell doors were unlocked was formidable; hundreds of prisoners wandering the galleries and corridors, hanging about, looking hostile and conspiratorial. On the surface many seemed nice enough, but Matt felt they all seemed to hold such an undercurrent of resentment that it bled through their conviviality. Now that Ricko was gone he felt a release from the pressure of conversation and the presence in the room. With no one else there and the door closed he felt a strange freedom. Ricko's presence in the room had been an additional restriction on his body language, his mood, his self expression. Now, with no one to see, he could sprawl on the bed or pace the narrow confines of the room or even squat on the floor John Cleese fashion with his hands over his head and hop around like some crazy eccentric if he wanted to.

But of course this wouldn't be for long; sometime soon the spare bed space would inevitably be taken up. They couldn't have an empty place at a UK prison for long; by all accounts they were totally oversubscribed. So he grabbed this opportunity and relished some time alone with his thoughts.

Dinner came and went. He switched on the TV and flicked through a few channels, nothing grabbing his attention. When the doors were unlocked for social time he took the opportunity to ask one of the screws about work opportunities. He would have to see the liaison officer who was around on Fridays at social time, but he could go and put his name down now at the opportunities desk. He went along where directed and gave his name to the recalcitrant clerk there who was totally unhelpful when asked what the jobs might be.

"Depends wot's available mate. I can't tell you wot it might be, cos it could be anything, so there's no point me telling you anything. I'm not being funny, but it'd be better to wait til Friday."

And that was that. So he wandered aimlessly along corridors just to get some exercise, skirting groups of inmates hanging around talking in low voices. He leant on a rail on an upper walkway and looked down on the levels beneath. He'd been there a few minutes, not thinking about anything really, letting his mind go blank, just being, when he was interrupted.

"Can't even do that anymore."

He looked round to where the voice had come from. A thin, raffish guy was standing leaning against the open door of a cell. He had long grey-streaked black hair which hung festooned around his shoulders like a mane. He had sharp quick eyes looking out of deep sockets in a crinkled leathery face. He must have been in his fifties but could have been much older. A face of experience, a face of life.

"I'm sorry?"

The face crinkled more, a broken smile.

"They used to try that a long time ago. Now they've put the net across, so no more misadventures."

Matt turned back to the drop beyond the rail and saw the mesh spanning the void and took the meaning.

"New?"

"Yes, just a few days ago."

"Thought so. Haven't seen you. George."

Matt, surprised, took the outstretched hand and shook it firmly in response to the grip offered. "Matt. Nice to meet you."

The eyes twinkled. "Really? Hmm. Best to reserve judgement in a place like this. Never know who you're talking to."

"Well, yes, I suppose." Matt immediately felt comfortable with this stranger. Something about his manner, his laconic style and laid back drawl. It was totally non-confrontational, which was so different from most of the others. His companion was looking him over gently whilst fiddling with some paper, folding it, turning it about, refolding it. He didn't seem to be giving it much attention, but it was obvious he was doing something particular with it, almost automatically.

"How long you waiting on her majesty's pleasure?"

"Uh? Oh, right, ha ha, yeah, two years."

He was looking intently at the paper now, twisting whatever it was inside out it seemed. Then he looked up. "Seems like a long time, doesn't it?"

Matt shrugged an agreement. George smiled loosely.

"It's just perception," he said slowly. "Time is of course a constant. Goes the same speed in here as outside. Just seems slower." He winked, folding the paper some more and then pulling one end out. "Fly envious time, till thou run out thy race, Call on the lazy leaden-stepping hours, Whose speed is but the plummet's pace."

He emphasised the weight in the words of the last two lines by way of explanation. He continued folding, occasionally looking up briefly at Matt as if to judge the effect his quote had evinced.

"I recognise that. Can't place it," Matt said. "Shelley? Keats?" he hazarded.

"John Milton, 'On Time'," he said succinctly. "Appropriate isn't it?"

"You just happen to know that?"

"All of it. Just read it a few times and really liked it. Never forgot it." George carried on folding, twisting the paper this way and that, a crease here, a tuck there. "Bit of a gift, a retentive memory. Just sticks in there."

"Right. What's a plummet?"

"Lead weight. Like plumb bob." He saw Matt didn't show signs of comprehension. "Refers to the weight on the pendulum in a clock, slowly ticking the time away."

"Right," Matt said again, intrigued by his new friend.

"Fascinating things, words. So much meaning hidden in them. How many people appreciate that the word plumber comes from that too, someone who worked in lead – old lead pipes, you know. And the word 'aplomb'. To do something with aplomb meaning with assurance and calmness, as if using a plumb line." He continued folding.

"Yeah," Matt said, "I don't know if I knew that, but now you say it, it certainly sounds familiar."

"It's right, right enough. Nothing sinister about it at all," he chuckled mischievously, those soft eyes searching Matt's face to be sure he took the reference.

"Ah yes, sinistra in Italian, left."

"Which came to mean evil or bad because it was opposite of right which was correct and good and honourable. The right hand of the Father. The devil was presumably on the left."

Matt had a great desire to know what George was in for, but knew better than to ask. It seemed improbable that this guy was in here for a sex offence, but then he had to remind himself that he was.

"How long have you got?" Matt ventured.

"Got a couple of months left now," George replied and with a small flourish presented a paper swan sitting on the palm of his hand. "Duh duh!"

Matt clapped quietly with genuine admiration. "You been doing that all the time you've been inside, making paper models I mean."

"Helps to pass the time, doing time. Origami. Very satisfying. You need to find some satisfaction in here. Small achievements, they count for a lot. Otherwise you feel like you're wasting time."

"Well, I suppose you are inevitably," Matt said. "You can't do the things you want to do, so all the time you can't is a waste of the time you could be."

"No time is a waste of time." George had moved to the rail beside Matt and was leaning over, looking down with him. Matt waited, anticipating more.

"You see them all down there? They're eating themselves up, resentful of their lack of liberty. They're punishing themselves on top of the punishment they've been given."

"How's that?"

"You have to rise above the moment, see beyond the now. What is liberty? We're none of us free really. We're all bounded by time. Our time here on earth. All our laws are based on time, our mortal time in this life. 'Thou shalt not kill.' Why? Because we value life. Our lives here on earth are considered the most valuable thing, because without them we apparently don't exist, so our time here is precious. It's the only time we have if you choose to believe that."

"But you don't?" Matt looked at him quizzically.

George returned his look, those brown eyes deep as truth.

"I don't have to believe, I know."

"Know what?" Matt was beginning to enjoy this discussion.

"There are more things in heaven and earth, Horatio,

Than are dreamt of in your philosophy" George said cryptically.

"Shakespeare."

"Hamlet."

"And?"

George took a deep breath. "It means there's a lot more than meets the eye. The technological advances that have been made in the last fifty years have perhaps taught us more about our world than we've learnt in the previous two thousand, but these layers of discovery have often just revealed further layers beneath and given rise to further questions. The more we learn, the more we learn how ignorant we are, how much more there is to learn. And we certainly have so much more to learn about how to use the information."

"Yes, I'd agree with that. But how does that make you know about time. Or what's beyond belief?"

George gave an indulgent smile. "Most of what we choose to believe these days is based on what scientists claim to be provable fact i.e. what has been proved as fact in the absence of anything disproving it. This doesn't allow for all the scientifically unproved theories, wisdoms – beliefs if you will. A belief is something unproven, but it doesn't mean it's not true."

George cleared his throat and adjusted his position, now leaning sideways against the rail to face Matt. "If you accept that scientific proof is only true in the absence of contrary evidence, then you could say you only believe it to be true, because there's always the possibility it could be disproved. Then where's your scientific truth? Well, it's just a belief based on a set of as yet irrefutable facts. It's no different from any belief you might choose to have, but perhaps backed up by fairly incontrovertible evidence; until something else is discovered."

"But you said you didn't need to believe, you knew."

At that moment the signal for end of social time blared out, disrupting their talk.

"I've seen beyond the curtain of our world, beyond the limit of our knowledge." He must have caught Matt's expression of incomprehension and misgiving. "Don't worry, it's all good." He smiled.

"Can we meet again and talk?"

"I'm not going anywhere." George said with a smile.

They shook hands, George turning and going back into his cell, Matt walking away to the stairs to get back to his, his mind spinning with the encounter. He felt buoyed up by this chance meeting; a kindred spirit, here in Wandsworth prison. What was the likelihood? He felt almost happy and his mind was already formulating questions to put to George at a future meeting. He whistled in time with his steps, only aware a minute later that it was one of Figaro's arias from The Marriage of Figaro, 'Non piu andrai', a jolly banter at the young Cherubino, teasing him about what he'll have to put up with now he's in the army.

He thrust his hands in his pockets and felt sharp paper scrunch beneath his fingers. He pulled out a crumpled white origami swan and chuckled with surprise. How the hell had that got in there? He'd last seen it on George's palm. He must have slipped it in his pocket, but when? He'd not been aware of him doing it and thought that most of the time he'd been watching George closely, intrigued by his every word. And what did he mean 'I've seen behind the curtain, beyond the limit of our knowledge'? That man was an enigma. He looked forward to seeing him again.

When he got back to his cell he found a new room- mate. Damon was different from Ricko in every respect except for his interest in football, which was probably his only one, but Matt was never likely to know, he soon discovered, as he hardly said anything. His method of communication was a series of grunts and incomprehensible monosyllables, so Matt soon gave up his initial attempt at interaction. Damon lay slothfully on his bunk, his bulk seeping out of the joints of his clothes and his breath wheezing through the gap in his face, which was the only noticeable feature in its doughy expanse.

The following day being Friday Matt went to register for work. The officer in charge was pleasant enough and gave him some options; textiles, woodwork, metalwork.

"Actually," he continued, "we could do with someone in charge of stores in the kitchen. You seem a bright bloke. Fancy running the stores?"

It sounded perfect; not cleaning toilets or some mundane repetitive job, but organising and accounting for supplies.

"Sounds good."

"Right, so you work mornings eight til ten thirty and afternoons two til four. You get paid for ten sessions a week but you can work more if you want to. If you come in early and work from seven every morning you don't get paid extra but you get a cooked breakfast on Sundays. That's the deal. You get one pound fifty per session, that's fifteen pounds a week. Can't do better than that, my final offer." The man looked up with a cheeky grin and questioning eyebrows.

"Yeah fine. It's better than lying in a cell all day. When do I start?"

"Bloke's leaving tomorrow. We'll see you at eight then."

Matt walked away, unable to stop himself comparing the weekly fee he'd just been offered with his concert fee or opera performance rate. It was ludicrous. What was that per hour? Something like thirty pence. He laughed. What would his agent say to that? Which reminded him, he had to sort that out.

He didn't see George for a few days, being caught up with the new job. Matt had to account for all supplies in and out and found his position gave him a certain kudos with the other prisoners. He soon learned whom he could trust and which screws to avoid, how to fiddle the system to take extra food and sell it on to other prisoners for extra money or as a bribe to borrow a mobile and make a clandestine call. In fact, prison taught him how to beat the system, how to be a criminal.

Because of the job he sometimes missed social time, or only caught part of it, so it was a while before he managed to catch George on the landing. He was leaning on the rail surveying the milling throng below.

"Hi George."

"Ah, the commissariat!" George said with a twinkle in his eyes. "How's it going?" They shook hands.

"Yeah, fine. It keeps me out of trouble and makes the day pass quicker."

"Ah yes, our old friend Time." George grinned and offered Matt the bag of nuts he was grazing from.

"Where d'you get those from?"

"Well you see Mr Chamberlain, you're not the only inmate with access to contraband supplies. Don't forget I've been here for a while. There's a healthy black market in here as I'm sure you've discovered."

"I can imagine," Matt said through a cashew, impressed with George's knowledge of him.

They stood silently chewing on nuts leaning on the rail as a scuffle broke out below them and shouts went up. Two inmates were grappling, others encouraging them and whooping before some screws intervened and broke it up. It was an insignificant outburst but there was the potential for a bigger event if the bystanders had chosen not to stand by.

"They missed the opportunity. It was there for a few seconds, but if you hesitate it's gone."

"What, you wanted them to riot?"

"They always want a riot. It's a diversion, a bit of fun. But you've got to seize the moment- carpe diem, – or you miss it."

"But you'd never riot George. You seem like a pacifist. Non-confrontational."

"You're right. But I'm not talking about me, I'm talking about them. I don't need diversion. I can divert myself easily enough just living in the moment."

Matt hesitated, but then pressed on with the question he was unsure whether to ask.

"George, I know it's not done to ask why people are inside, but I can't imagine how a guy as grounded and chilled as you ends up here."

George smiled and paused before replying."You know Matthew, life is a strange thing. We live in a wonderful society in the West where we celebrate the diversity of the human spirit. We love that everyone is different, with different talents, strengths, weaknesses, characters, personalities etc. But actually society only caters for people to be pretty much the same. When it comes to the law everyone is judged according to an accepted norm and, very often, the differences are perceived as faults which need to be punished, although the person being punished may not think what they've done is wrong."

Matt waited, wondering where this preamble was going. George was looking at him with those brown eyes, but they were less focused than usual, seeming to be looking past him, focused on a distant image.

"What do you think love is, Matthew?"

He was the only person apart from Caterina to call him Matthew. He hadn't asked him to, but he didn't mind, it felt comfortable. The question was so abrupt and huge that he struggled to find a succinct definition in response. "I don't know; it's difficult to say in a sentence. It depends what you mean; the circumstance."

Again Matt waited, used now to George's mode of delivery, who now looked into the middle distance, talking low.

"I knew a young girl. She was about twelve when I first met her, an only child. Her mum was a crack addict. Sometimes she was together and could cope, sometimes she was all over the place, or rather, wasn't there at all. They lived in the next door flat. I knew what the mum was going through. I'd been there, but it's really hard to help someone like that. They kind of have to get to a state where they can get themselves off it, otherwise it's only temporary. Sometimes she could control it for a bit, but then she'd have a relapse, normally brought on by the ex-lover who had a hold on her and occasionally turned up and screwed her over again.

"Anyway, when she couldn't cope I'd take over and look after Keira. I became like a kind of uncle. I'd take her into my flat and we'd play cards or watch TV. She loved X Factor and wanted to be a singer. She'd never have made it, but she liked to think she could, it was her dream.

"When she got a bit older, she'd knock on my door when things were bad and we'd talk about stuff; her relationship with her mum, why her mum did drugs, how it made her feel, you know, heavy psychological stuff. I suppose I was someone to let it all out to, but also I gave advice and supported her emotionally. Sometimes she'd break down and cry her heart out and I'd hold her, hold her shaking little body and she'd calm down. Then she'd sit and I'd make her a cup of tea, two sugars, and she'd get herself back together. She grew into a beautiful young woman, although her head was a bit screwed up and she'd harm herself.

"By the time she was fifteen she had a key to my flat so she could let herself in if things were really bad, escape from her mum's madness. She was seeing boys and she'd tell me about her relationships. She was messed up, going out with wild types who treated her rough. She'd come back with bruises sometimes and I'd comfort her. She said she didn't really like any of them much. She wished they could be like me, she said. Said she felt so safe and complete when she was with me. I told her we were soul mates, meaning we met on a similar emotional plane. She liked that. I think it gave her strength.

"Anyway, one day she came in and she was in a real state and once I'd calmed her down and we were sitting on the settee having a cuppa, she just leant across and kissed me. Now Matthew, I've kissed a lot of girls before, but believe me this was different. I said 'Keera, let's not change this lovely relationship we have. It's a bad idea.' She said, 'George, please make love to me. I've loved you for ages and it just doesn't seem right with other guys.'

"Now, you've gotta understand, I knew I'd loved her for about a year. Gradually I'd realised I was completely in love with her, but I wasn't going to do anything about it. She was fourteen/fifteen and I was forty odd, but that doesn't stop you loving someone. I knew it was against the law, of course, but Keira wasn't stupid, she wasn't out of control and although as I said she was a bit screwed up, she knew exactly what she was doing. I told her again I thought it was a bad idea but she took me, forced herself on me and well, there's a limit to a man's resistance when he already loves a girl.

"It was the most beautiful thing I've ever experienced. It was like finding the other part of me. It was like it was meant to be. We became lovers and Keera became a different person. She calmed down, she stopped self-harming. She seemed to be able to cope with her mum and suddenly found a purpose in her life. It was like she found her self-esteem and wasn't blaming herself for all the shit in her life. She knew she was valued and none of it was her fault. We were really happy, although it had to be a secret.

"Her mum was still in a state of course, sometimes clean sometimes on a bender, you know how it is, history repeats itself as they say. Anyway, one day Keera had left her keys at home and was with me when her mum burst in on us. She must have found the keys and worked out what was going on in a lucid moment. I don't know whether she was jealous or angry or just vindictive, but she called the police and reported me.

"Of course there was no defence. She was under age and I was branded a paedophile, but somehow it doesn't seem fair does it?"

George turned sad wet eyes to Matt, who felt that his weren't over dry.

"Rough justice."

"Yes, and the law only sees it as black and white. No account taken of how she was a psychologically far more stable person as a result of our relationship or the consequences of taking me away from her. How's she coping now? I really don't know, but I bet she's self-harming again, thinking that me being in here is her fault."

George looked away again, lost in thought.

Matt didn't know what to say. This story had tumbled out so quickly and unreservedly that he was slightly embarrassed to know all this information, particularly as he now couldn't think of anything to say in response.

"Has she visited you?" he ventured.

"I think she finds it too upsetting." He looked down at his hands. "So do I," he added. Matt too looked at George's hands, tanned and dextrous with the raised blood vessels and long fingernails, like a guitarist's right hand.

"But you'll be out soon, hey?"

"Yeah," George said with a sigh, "but I just don't know if it'll be the same. It's been a few years and we're both probably changed. Sorry, shouldn't have told you. Silly."

Matt detected George closing off, regretting opening up to him.

"Sorry Matthew, I think I'd like some time alone now," and he turned away into his cell leaving Matt standing by the rail, stunned that their conversation had been terminated so abruptly.

Chapter 22

"You got a visitor." The screw held the door open.

Matt felt a pang of adrenalin. A visitor? How could that be? He hadn't had any notice. You always got told the day before, or earlier, that a visitor was booked. No one except Mags knew he was here and it wasn't her, because they'd agreed she wouldn't come and anyway he'd only spoken to her the previous night and she'd said she was going to a class at the Actors' Centre this afternoon. A mixture of worry and excitement accompanied his thoughts as he followed the screw to the visiting room.

Ah, of course. He remembered. Katie knew. That's it. Mags had been going to tell his sister and swear her to secrecy. It would be Katie, come to check up on her little bro. Somehow they must have forgotten to tell him. She'd be full of indignation and talk about getting him out. She was so like Mags, which was why they got on so well, he and Mags, because she was so like his sister. As he walked the corridors and waited for the doors to be unlocked and re-locked, he felt excited to see her, but at the same time dreaded having to go over the whole thing again. He knew she'd want to hear every detail and then he'd have to find all the logical reasons why her fighting for justice wouldn't work. It would be emotionally draining and he knew he probably wouldn't get through to her. She was volatile and emotional, as well as being very bright, so it was never easy arguing with her, because although her ideas were often radical and impractical she'd back them up with uncompromising logic based on 'why not?'

Glancing quickly around the room he didn't see her and so looked more carefully at the singly occupied tables, those awaiting an inmate, and as his eyes moved from one to another he saw, *God, it can't be.* His body surged with a rush of conflicting emotions. *Looking, oh God, so beautiful.* He didn't think he could move, but did, un-really, reeling really across the room to the table and plonked himself down in the chair, feeling his nose tingle and his eyes smart.

"Hello Matthew."

He couldn't physically speak for a moment, but then managed to clear his throat.

"I can't believe you're here." His voice sounded weak and discordant to him. He sniffed sharply and blinked back emotion.

"I can't believe you're here either." She gazed at him levelly, seemingly fighting emotions too.

"Caterina, you look so beautiful." He wanted to take her roughly now and devour her beauty in a frenzy of lust; but also wanted to curl up in her lap and sob his heart out.

He looked at her faultless features framed by the carefully coiffured hair. No faux-fur collar today nestling against the smooth skin of her neck. Now an open-necked silk blouse with striking blues and greens on a cream background under a light grey jacket.

As always she looked effortlessly ravishing and he gazed into her welcoming face. She had that expression when she sang a sad phrase, a pained empathy, and he could hear her liquid voice cascading a run of golden notes.

His hands were lying limp on the table between them and as he felt the convulsions of stored up tension release through his shoulders, he noticed them shaking through his clouded vision as his head dropped. He couldn't control this sudden outpouring of grief. He had held it in, suppressed it through those hours alone and then in public, but now, here with Caterina, suddenly his vulnerability poured out of him. He would normally have been mortified to be seen like this, particularly in front of fellow prisoners, but he was beyond that controlling sensibility, lost in an unravelling of enormous stress.

He felt soft fingers on his, gently searching under his down-turned hands, feeling for the soft skin of his palm sides, slipping under, the thumb rubbing the upper skin. She slowly massaged his hands, sensually and silently while he wept, her finger pads stroking upwards, smoothing and soothing. He couldn't see, he was flooded and had to wipe and cover his face. He felt soft tissues pushed into his palms which he used to mop his eyes and wipe his drooling nose.

"It's just tissues, look. It's ok I'm not passing him anything." Caterina's voice was authoritative and roused him from his abandonment. He looked up to see a warder standing over them questioningly. He turned his palms showing the crumpled wet tissues and the screw nodded peremptorily and turned away with a grunt.

He blew, he choked, he breathed, he settled. He looked at her and tried to smile. He knew it didn't work.

She laid her hands on the table, palms up inviting his grasp. He laid his hands on hers and felt an electricity of desire. They were warm and tender, pink, small and delicate and he stroked their silky surfaces relishing the feel of skin on skin. She looked in his eyes and he saw no awkwardness or embarrassment that this fully grown man before her had just wept in front of everyone. She was totally focused on him and seemed oblivious to the room. He also saw deep concern, compassion and forgiveness.

Her voice was honey-soft. "What happened, Matthew?"

He took his gaze to the fingers he was slipping gently between his own, a delicate movement she didn't resist, offering just a hint of reciprocation. His fingers tingled with the friction and sent pulses of fire shooting up his arms and into his viscera, which leapt in response. He didn't know how he could talk; he just wanted to continue this delicious hand-fondling. They hadn't touched before, just her arm through his and her peck on his cheek. This intimacy she seemed to have intended was strange and unexpected. Well, her being here was totally unexpected, but now this sudden closeness took him aback. Was she absolving him, showing she didn't judge him or was she just flirting again? It was enough to deal with her being here, but dealing with this as well was rocking him. In his present state of mind he didn't have the perspicacity to comprehend her intentions, all he knew was she was here and giving him her full attention.

"D'you mean at the beginning, or since?"

"Tell me all of it Matthew. I want to understand."

Oh, how he longed to kiss her. He stopped caressing her hands, it was too distracting, and held them with an even pressure which she returned.

In a lowered voice he recounted the details of the concert, how he'd seen the girl, their interaction and then how he'd spotted her at the reception after. He tried to paint an honest picture and her calm serious look held him to that resolve. He knew he couldn't lie to her. He admitted how he had bent over and kissed the girl's upturned mouth when she was insensible, admitted his desire for her in his drunken state, but emphasised how when she came to her senses, she had proactively embraced him, kissed him passionately until....until she felt him mounting her, when she had screamed so irrationally, loudly and unremittingly.

All the time Caterina held his gaze with a look of seriousness and clear-eyed concentration. But as his story had become more involved he thought he had detected her becoming less calm, her fingers twitching minutely and her eyes blinking and losing that cool connection.

"And then you were there," Matt finished up, giving her fingers a little squeeze.

"Yes," she said, far away in thought, although still looking at him. "And so they took a statement and you had to go to the police station, right?"

"Yup. Pretty much in solitary until the trial."

Concern again, "That must have been hard, Matthew."

He realised he adored the way she used his full name. Most everyone else used the abbreviation, which he encouraged, enjoying the chummy familial sound of it. But her pronunciation of his whole name felt right and so sensual; something to do with the movement of her mouth and the quick flick of the pink tip of her tongue between perfect lips did it for him.

"Yes," he said heavily, "it has been hard. It's been, unreal. A kind of hell to be honest." His attempt at a smile was more successful this time and she squeezed his fingers.

"What happened at the trial? I guess they didn't believe you."

"I suppose not. They made out I was some kind of pervert taking advantage of an innocent girl and the jury swallowed it. The odds were stacked against me you could say."

"And then they transferred you to England. But you can appeal, find a British lawyer to fight for you. I mean, how long is the sentence?"

"Two years – well two years less a month now."

"Matthew, you've got to get out of here. You can't stay here for two years. What about your career? God!" She was squeezing him hard now.

"I know, I know. Believe me, I've gone over it a thousand times. I don't see a way out. Look, even if I got an English lawyer to appeal the sentence, there's no guarantee they'd change it. And how much would it cost? It would be a wild goose chase."

She smiled. "Sorry, 'wild goose chase', I haven't heard this before. It's funny. No I understand what you're saying but can you bear to be here and do nothing for two years?"

"I work in the kitchen, looking after the stores." She grimaced hopelessly. "It's something to do and can help my record – maybe get an earlier release."

"God Matthew, I can't bear you being in here. You're worth more than this. This is a tragedy for you, for your family. Your poor parents must be so worried."

"They don't know."

"You haven't told them even? But how can they not know?"

"They think I'm working abroad somewhere. I needed some time before telling them. I can't hold out much longer."

"What's happening with your work, your agent?"

"He thinks I've got some illness and has cancelled jobs short term. I've got to sort that out soon, it's not fair on him. But I was hoping for some chance, I don't know, some miracle I suppose. But it's not going to happen. I have to accept that and let everyone know. It's just so terrible having to tell everyone the truth."

Caterina pulled his hands toward her, as if to force his attention. Matthew, you are not a sex criminal. This is, how do you call it, yes, a miscarriage of justice. You are the scapegoat for this. It is easier for the jury to convict you than to think this girl is guilty. You should not be ashamed."

She must have seen that he wasn't convinced.

"Ok there is a grey area. What were you thinking of, getting involved with a young girl you didn't know? But, hey, these things will happen, especially when there is alcohol. People should accept that. You must claim your innocence of the rape and explain what really happened. Your friends will trust you to be honest with them. Others will believe you or not, that is their choice, but that is beyond your control."

She paused, holding his gaze. Then leaning towards him in a calmer voice, "I know you are an honest man, Matthew. I knew it the first time I heard you sing. I can hear it in your voice. It has a truth; there is no cover up. Some singers, you know, you can hear the artifice when they sing, they do it for the effect. But you are a true artist, close to your heart, close to truth. This is important."

Their hands rested content now in their togetherness. Matt looked down at them, noticing the pattern of tiny freckles on her skin, the perfectly applied subtle-toned nail varnish glinting its glossy patina. He lifted them up and kissed them slowly, holding them then against his cheek and searching her eyes before gently lowering them.

"Thank you," he said.

Her look was steady, wide-pupilled and unblinking, and he knew she desired him. He noticed the increase in her breathing and the colour suffusing her cheeks. Her lips seemed to glow and grow as the blood coursed into them and her fingers squirmed in his, then gripped with surprising strength. He thought this moment was eternal though it must have lasted a mere ten seconds before she released her hands and the passion had passed. She smiled and sighed and gathered herself, taking back her hands and rubbing the knuckles.

"How come you're in England? You didn't just come to see me!" He laughed self-consciously.

"I had a concert at the Festival Hall. Exultate Jubilate with L'Orchestre de l'Age Enlevée."

"Nice."

"Well, yes of course, I mustn't complain, but it would be good to do one of the other Mozart concert arias. You know, they always want to do the most popular one because people know it, but there are other lovely ones so seldom done."

Her mood had switched to international singer, efficient business woman. He liked it too, but the intimacy was broken.

"And so you're over for a few days; your daughter with your mum?"

"Yes, my dear mum. She's so good to me." She had now splayed her hands on the table, palms down, absent-mindedly stretching and contracting the fingers whilst she thought. "She adores Tanya though so it is a pleasure for her. They get on very well."

Matt had suddenly noticed, as he watched her moving fingers, the whiter mark where her wedding ring should have been. She caught his quick look to her face and knew his question.

"A lot has happened, not just to you Matthew," and he saw the pain in her eyes. "There was a reason my husband was so often away which was nothing to do with conferences. He had been having an affair for years. A much younger woman. A research chemist for one of the pharmaceutical companies he worked for. It explains lots of things."

She had to delve into her bag to find the tissues again, this time for herself.

"Caterina, I'm so sorry," Matt felt dreadful; all this time they'd been talking about him and his problems. But at the same time a wicked selfish glee flitted through him; *she's free!*

"How did you find out?"

She had collected herself. "I had to get some concert dresses dry-cleaned and thought a couple of his suits could do with going too, so I went through the pockets and discovered a note. You know, the usual thing. So of course I had to ask him about it. He admitted it immediately. It was like it was almost a relief for him. It's a whole lot of mess now of course, sorting out a divorce and for Tanya it's a big trauma. So I had to think carefully if I want to do this job, but you know, it's what I do and I have to maybe support her more by myself now. I can't rely on him for anything."

She was dabbing the corners of her eyes regularly, not allowing herself to flood over, keeping control of her emotions. Matt's mind was racing now. Was this why she was suddenly intimate with him? Why she'd come to see him? She needed to find out how she felt about him? But what was the point? She might be free now but he....

"So there's no hope for your relationship?"

"If it had been a quick affair, perhaps. But this has been a long term relationship. He wants to be with her, that's the heart of it. I couldn't trust him again when he cheated on me for so long. So, a new beginning." It was her turn to force a smile.

"I'm so, so sorry," he said again, now saddened that she seemed to have withdrawn from him. This unburdening of her sorrows had taken her back into herself, like she'd put up a barrier from him to keep strong. He somehow felt he couldn't intrude into her barricaded self.

"How did you know I was here? How did you manage to get an appointment? Apparently it's almost impossible from outside."

"Ah well," she smiled now, "I have contacts. I know a very successful businessman in London. He sponsored some performances I did a long time ago and he follows my career and always comes when I sing if he can. He came to the concert, so I asked him if he knew how I could make contact with you. He's amazing. He knows everyone. Anything you say he will know someone who is something to do with it. Somehow he knows the prison governor here and they make a special case for me to visit you."

"Wow, that's amazing."

"He's a very generous man actually. He takes me to The Ivy after shows if he's here, but often he's abroad, all round the world, you know. Very successful. He works very hard, but he likes to enjoy himself also."

Matt felt a leap of jealousy, which was obviously ridiculous, but couldn't stop himself saying.

"So you really like him."

She flashed her eyes at him sharply but immediately they softened and curled at the edges with the hint of a teasing smile.

"Yes Matthew, I like him very much. But not in the same way I like you very much." Once again she took his hands, this awkward and only way to physically interact in this restricted space when really she wanted to hug him. "I am frightened for you Matthew. I worry about you being here. And I worry for your career."

"Well, there's no help for that right now. I'll have to get through this period and pick up when I get out. Two years is not good, but it's not much different from a woman taking time out to have a baby."

"True. I suppose I took about eighteen months off, although I did a few concerts. But I wanted to spend time with Tanya."

"And what's happening with you now?"

"Well, now that all this has happened, I have to rethink my life. Obviously we are splitting everything up. I don't know what happens with the house yet. I think I need to keep it so we stay in the same area and Tanya can stay in the same school so she is disturbed as little as possible. To be honest, my husband was away so much it won't be a great shock to her, but keeping in the house will mean consistency. It depends how the settlement works out."

"Is it amicable?"

She smiled grimly. "Well, we are speaking, but I can't pretend I find it easy. When someone has cheated on you like that it's difficult to remain calm. I feel he has had a good time when I have sacrificed a lot of my career for Tanya. So he should pay for that. He doesn't see it in the same way. Surprise, surprise."

"So you want to be doing more singing than you have been doing?"

"Seems crazy doesn't it? I'm splitting up from my husband and thinking of spending more time away from my child when she needs me most. I don't know, it's so difficult. On one hand I feel I need to go to work to provide for her and on the other I feel guilty for leaving her. But to be honest she and my mum get on so well together that I don't worry leaving her. She's like a second mother, not a grandmother."

"Would you take on an opera contract again?"

Her eyes lit up, "Oh Matthew, I've been thinking so hard about this. I find myself saying 'Yes I must get back into opera. I could earn a lot of money which would be good for us as a family. My mum could move in with us to look after Tanya. This is the logical way to provide financial stability'. But then my guilt answers me saying 'You are just using this as an excuse to go and do what you love doing. Your responsibility is to be around for your daughter, so just go and do an occasional concert'. I fight myself all the time with this and it's driving me crazy right now, trying to work out what I should do."

Matt looked at her worried face, the beautiful features rippled with frown lines. She had separated her hands from his, clasping them together. He cupped one hand below and one on top of hers as if making a consecration.

"Maybe you should move your mum in if and when the time comes, and put yourself out there in the meantime and see what happens. If you get offered contracts then you can take them up or not depending how things are. It seems you're getting stressed about it way in advance of the situation when actually you've got to get there before you can make the decision, which will be based on all sorts of things – how much you want to do the part, where it is, how long the contract is, whether you can get back easily during it for visits etc."

Was this some of George's wisdom coming through?

Caterina's face relaxed. "You're right. I'm rushing ahead. I don't know how things will be in a month or two." She smiled with gratitude. "But you know, it's suddenly me who has to make all the decisions and there is so much to organise. I hate not knowing what is happening. I like everything to be sorted out, but at the moment it's all over the place."

"Sometimes we can't organise our lives. Sometimes we have to roll with whatever life throws at us. We're not always in charge." *It really is George! It's amazing how much easier it is to sort someone else's problems than your own.*

"You're quite the philosopher, Mr Chamberlain," she said with a taunting smile. The way she said Mr Chamberlain took him right back to the courtroom and the prosecutions sarcastic intonation of his name.

"Five minutes, ladies and gents." A warder was beginning to tidy up the kids play area in the corner and the cafe was closing up.

"Oh Matthew, I should have bought you a coffee or something. I completely forgot, we were talking so much."

"It doesn't matter, honestly. I didn't really want anything. How long are you here for?"

"I go back tonight, to the mess. I suppose it will sort itself out."

"Of course. I'm sure it will get easier. It's just all on top of you right now."

"I'll write to you Matthew. I suppose you don't get email."

"No, nothing like that. I can make phone calls to vetted numbers, but they're expensive and the money doesn't last long, and to Finland? huh...."

"I'll try to visit you if I'm over. Maybe I get a contract here somewhere, in London. Then I can see you again." They both knew that contracts were usually arranged years in advance. It was unlikely that anything would come up before the end of his term.   After a pause she continued, "Or maybe I just fly over and visit you when I've sorted myself out."

She tried to smile reassuringly, but he could see the doubt in her eyes. They both knew it was unlikely to happen.

"I'll be okay Caterina. You need to concentrate on yourself and Tanya right now. You've got enough to do without worrying about me too."

"I suppose I'm not allowed to kiss you goodbye?"

"It's just hands I'm afraid."

She kissed the palm of her hand and placed it against his cheek. He did likewise and they held each other's faces cupped in their hands as they held their other hands across the table. But as Matt stood and watched her escorted out he knew he wouldn't see her again until these walls were far behind him.

Chapter 23

Signe fell in and out of sleep in the half light of a gentle dawn. She was half aware of the creeping daylight permeating her bedroom but then fell back into oblivion again.

She remembered the promise she'd made the night before to sort out the legal and moral mess she felt she was in regarding the outcome of the trial. She had to right the wrong. She couldn't bear the thought that that man, however much she felt humiliated by what he'd attempted to do to her, was locked up when she was in part to blame.

With sudden clarity she decided to get up before everyone else, despite the usual sick feeling in the pit of her stomach, force some breakfast down and go to do her church job again. She hadn't told Father Stefan she'd be in, but she knew he'd be okay with it.

She had a shower, noticing that the rash she had had ages ago and which had recently reappeared, was still there, but not as angry as it had been. It had come back with a vengeance after the Easter weekend, a sure sign of stress, and had been itching her ever since. She had used E45 cream and stopped any dairy in her diet, like had been prescribed when she was young, so maybe this was having an effect. It was certainly much better and not nearly so aggravating. She towelled down and applied some cream, enjoying the cool smooth feeling on her skin, then dressed and went back to her room to sort her hair.

She made her favourite breakfast of a banana cut up with yogurt and honey poured over. Although her stomach was a twisted bag of nausea she forced herself to eat, thinking it might settle it. She put her bowl in the dishwasher, scribbled a note and managed to get out of the house just as she heard movement upstairs. She didn't want to see anyone, she just wanted to get out.

She walked quickly away across the grass which was wet with dew. It was a still day which seemed to be holding its breath, amazed at its own beauty and fearful of breaking the perfect moment with a breath of wind. The sun was bleeding through a thick mist which hung fragile and chaste in its gossamer whiteness, like an innocent bride veiled before her betrothed. After about fifty metres she stopped, brought up short by a wave of nausea which caused her to retch her breakfast. After coughing and spitting she expected the usual release, the payoff for the misery of throwing up. But the nausea was persistent, unmoving, and she continued across the grass, unable to enjoy her surroundings. It crossed her mind to go back home to bed, but she immediately rejected that idea; she'd spent so much time alone in her room after the trial, that this was preferable.

It was still early and being a Saturday in this residential part of Göteborg there were very few people about. Her usual shift at the church wasn't due to begin until nine so she had decided to go to confession first. Father Stefan she knew was always available from eight am for 'surgery' as he called it, which was really just a private chat and absolution before the weekend masses. She didn't know why she hadn't thought of going before when she was so guilt-ridden and raw after the event. Maybe she had been so shocked and traumatised she hadn't been able to think straight. Now it seemed such an obvious thing to do. It would make her feel better mentally, however sick she felt bodily.

The trees were dripping as she tramped across the springy new grass, weak sunlight now diffracting through the countless droplets clinging to the ends of freshly unfurled leaflets. Small birds, goldfinches she thought, were calling loudly in the still air and she stopped again to take a deep breath to cope with her cramp, and in that moment appreciated the suspended beauty around her which transcended her discomfort.

Arriving at the church she was still early for confession and ambled around the graveyard killing time. She read the names on the tombstones and wondered what these people were like who had died in 1876 or 1894 and had such evocative names like Hans-Erik Björklund, Theobald Sigmundsen and Wilhelmina Mårtensson.

What lives had they led? What children had they born? Whose ancestors were they? Hers? Might one of these be her great great grandfather or a far-distant maiden aunt? Who was she really, this girl without provenance, wandering amongst the history of others? The headstones told their brief bare facts – born, died, beloved father and grandfather, sorely missed, rest in peace – disconnected by time, connected only by lineage, but not hers. What was her lineage? Who were her parents? Ever since that discovery of her adoption this question was ever present lurking in the back of her mind. Often she just wanted to forget about it and pretend it didn't matter, after all God was her Father, but it still niggled and wriggled demanding attention.

A sudden flash of orange swooped across her vision and landed on one of the stones she'd been reading. A robin pranced its bobbing dance and gurgled its rich throaty song through a beak full of small writhing red worms, before ejecting a neat white-grey dropping and flying off. Life in death, she thought. So many dead who had given rise to so many lives. But who had given rise to hers, and why and how and where, and where were they now? Part of her was eager, but part terrified, to know a truth that might hurt and inaugurate a relationship she might regret. The unknown could be exciting but also held potential disappointment and unhappiness. Why did she need to know her parents? Would it change her, alter her life, her personality? Possibly to a certain extent, but without knowledge the question would always be there. Most people knew their parents, why shouldn't she? Why was she denied the right of daughterhood and a knowledge of her parents? Since the discovery of her adoption she had felt a disenfranchisement and to a certain extent a disconnection with the family she lived with. She knew it wasn't their fault, they had acted with the best of intentions, but it still hurt and she felt a lack in her life, of belonging, of history.

Her ruminations were interrupted by the church clock chiming eight and bringing her back to the immediate intention of her confession. She felt a certain excitement mixed with trepidation; excitement to be able to unburden herself of her feelings of guilt to her priest and receive forgiveness; trepidation in wondering whether he would guess the connection with the news reports. She would try to make it suitably obscure and imprecise.

She held back from entering the church immediately. She walked around the church three times slowly, noticing the robin flitting through some shrubs on the second circuit and then appearing on the branch of a sycamore tree and launching into a full–throated cascade of song which echoed off the church walls. He was so bold, only a few feet above her head, cocking an eye at her and unafraid to deliver this instinctive outpouring of his incantation of life. He gave her courage, this small bird, unashamedly and naturally responding to his inherent nature and embodying so completely his predestined role.

She completed her third circuit and entered the hushed church, enjoying again the subdued light and close easy comfort of incense and wood. Father Stefan's door was ajar and the slider on the door read 'vacant'. She knocked and entered.

"Good morning father." He was sitting at his desk reading on his laptop. Looking up his face beamed when he saw her.

"Signe, how good to see you. I hope you're better. We've missed you."

"Yes, sorry father, I hope you managed without me."

"Well fortunately it was a quiet time after Easter so, yes, we managed. Are you able to stay today? The website needs updating and we need some filing."

"Yes of course, I was hoping it was okay to start again. I'm sorry I should have rung you, but I only felt well enough this morning."

"Wonderful, I'll sort out a little list of things that need doing. But you're very early."

Signe felt a rush of embarrassment, but continued, "I wondered if I could talk to you Father, you know, in your surgery."

He gave the briefest of looks that she couldn't read. "Of course, of course. Sit down. I'll just shut the door," which he did after moving the slider across. "So what's up? Nothing serious I hope." His eyes twinkled encouragingly and he did that funny eyebrow raise of his which she always thought was really weird, but knew it was just his nervous way of being friendly. Now that it came to it she couldn't quite think of how to explain the situation without being specific.

"I didn't tell the truth father. Someone's being punished because of me."

He obviously expected her to say more. "Okay, well it's sometimes not easy to tell the truth if you think you might end up in trouble. We're none of us perfect and sometimes it's hard to do the right thing."

"But this person, father, they shouldn't be punished. It was a mistake and it was my fault."

"Well, you could go to this person and explain to them how badly you feel and ask them to forgive you. When you have received their forgiveness you will be able to forgive yourself and God will also forgive you."

"I can't father, I don't know where they are. They are still suffering the punishment."

Father Stefan paused, trying to see the way through this problem. "Well, then you must pray for them to forgive you, pray so fervently that they hear your prayers and God will forgive you."

Signe paused, frightened yet determined to go through with it. "I also lusted for a man father. I..." his image flashed into her mind, those soft eyes accusing by merely gazing at her, "... indulged my desires and tasted the forbidden fruit which I promised I would never touch." She felt tears coming.

"We are all tempted Signe, and we are all weak without Jesus' guiding strength. If you truly repent of your sins God will forgive you, for you are merely a frail mortal in His benevolent eyes."

I have seen those eyes and they accuse me now, though I adore them and want them to adore me in return. "Father, can God make me clean even though I am dirty with lust for a man?"

"God's capacity for forgiveness is endless, my child, as is our capacity for failure. But if you truly repent He will never deny you forgiveness. The purity of your thoughts purify your actions provided your intentions are guided by truth and love for Him."

"They are father, always. I was just...tempted and was confused and made a mistake."

"That's why we're here, my child, to make mistakes and learn from them. Jesus was faultless and didn't have the capacity to make mistakes. In trying to follow Him our imperfections will always lead us astray, but this only helps to show us His perfection and encourage us to try to follow His example."

But that's not what Irma said, and it doesn't seem to make so much sense. She was about to question this but then changed her mind. "Thank you father."

"May your sins be forgiven and the Blessing of the Father, the Son and the Holy Ghost be with you now and for ever, amen." He made the sign of the cross in front of her and smiled.

"Amen." Signe crossed herself and got up.

"Did you want to start now, Signe? It's early but you're welcome if you want."

"Yes father, I'll go and start up the computer."

There was no one around and she booted up the machine and went online. They didn't mind her doing what she wanted on it as long as she got all the church business done whilst she was there. This was useful because it meant she could go on lots of websites which she wouldn't necessarily want those at home to know about. Not illicit ones, but things she might want to research without questions from Gustav, who was computer savvy and sometimes checked the browsing history. Here at the church they were pretty useless and wouldn't know how to do that, so she saved those searches for here.

She logged into the government website which contained all the information about the court in Göteborg and scrolled through looking for any information on retrials and ways of going about them. Apparently these things were usually done through a lawyer; there didn't seem to be a facility to apply to the court directly. The only lawyer she knew was Uncle Dirk. Could she go to him now and ask him to re-open the case with this knowledge which would completely undermine his case and render his conviction worthless? Gustav would be furious, it would be such an insult to his old friend and embarrassing for the family. They'd never forgive her, but it was the truth and it had to come out. She'd have to put up with the recrimination but if she could explain it as memory loss they'd surely understand. What they wouldn't understand was her desire to kiss him, her desire for him. She, who was wanting to go into a cloistered order of nuns. It was something she didn't understand herself.

As she sat there looking blankly at the screen and wondering how she was going to approach Uncle Dirk, the image of the Christus hovered in front of the screen. Father Stefan's words echoed in her head 'ask their forgiveness', and those eyes held her to ransom. She must find out where he is, visit him and ask his pardon. She would tell him how sorry she was, how she'd been confused and explain her cowardice and shame at her actions. Yes, that's what she'd do.

But where was he, how would she find him? The court would be able to tell her where he was being held. She would go down there after school one day and enquire and then she'd be able to visit him and explain it all. He'd understand and forgive her and then she'd tell him there was going to be a re-trial and they would release him.

He'd look at her with those melting eyes, a look of tender forgiveness, and she wouldn't feel accused anymore. It was good to have made those decisions and she felt a cloud lift. She even felt some absolution even though nothing practical had been achieved.

'Further search or click to exit.' The screen stared back at her expectantly, waiting for her decision, hungry to help. She wrote down the number and address of the court office and logged out. It was a week since she had stayed at Irma's and a month since she'd worked at the church. Looking at the website she noticed nothing had been done to the rolling calendar and there were still notices up since before Easter. She scrolled through and saw there was quite a bit to do to bring it up to date. She went back into the diary and began removing notices, taking out links and returning the diary to its basic state.

'Notices for Holy Week: Palm Sunday, masses at 8 and 10. Consecration of palms. Children at 10am service carry palms to the altar. If you would like your child to participate please see Fröcken Hollander and meet her in the community room before the service. The children can join the Sunday worship class before the mass'

'Holy Week: meditation takes place every day from 12 -2, an opportunity to reflect on the meaning of Christ's ministry at this time and follow Our Lord's journey to the Cross. The Passion of Our Lord is studied and Father Stefan will lead vigils each day at 3pm, a time for prayer and contrition to acknowledge His suffering for us.'

As Signe read, Bach's music played in her mind again. And she heard the rich voice of the alto pouring out her soul 'Grief for sin, rends the guilty heart within. May my weeping and my mourning be a welcome sacrifice. Loving Saviour, hear in mercy.' And again that face hovered over the screen, his eyes boring into her, and her eyes sprang again with remorse.

A knock on the door threw her into a panic and she dabbed her cheeks with her sleeves and sniffed back emotion before seeing Father Stefan holding some sheets of paper.

"Sorry Signe, you okay?" She nodded. "I just brought these notices for the next few weeks and a couple of announcements and updates for the website. Are you sure you're fine? You know you don't have to…"

"No no I'm fine, thank you father. I just, um, you know, get upset about silly things sometimes."

He looked at her closely, gently. He was a nice man, a decent man, she thought.

"Signe, we have people you can talk to. Not me or anyone in the church, but lay people, ladies who are experienced in, in helping, talking. If you want I can give you a number. Sometimes it's easier talking to someone you don't know than your friends or family. Less pressure, hmm?"

She took the papers he was holding, not wanting to look him in the eye. "I'll be okay father, thank you. Really." She smiled awkwardly and glanced obliquely at his face for a fraction of a second before turning back to the computer. She heard him turn and leave and felt relief. But what did he mean by that, did he know?

'Good Friday: The Passion of Our Lord at 3pm. Candlelit reflection with the reading of the Passion and the progression through the stations of the Cross.

'And about the sixth hour there was darkness over all the land until the ninth hour. And about the ninth hour Jesus cried with a loud voice Eli eli, lama, sabachthani. And behold the veil of the temple was rent in twain, from the top unto the bottom, and the earth did quake and the rocks rent…'

And my world was shattered

'Low Saturday: the church is open for private contemplation and prayer. The Easter vigil begins at 6pm followed by mass.'

'Easter Sunday: The Easter candle is lit, the Light of Jesus.'

As she deleted entries she couldn't help thinking what she had been doing on Good Friday and the subsequent days, the events reel-playing through her mind in a fast forward return of that dark weekend. She had not sung hallelujah on Easter Sunday morning. She had been conspicuous in church by her absence, she who was usually always there, either with her parents, but more recently alone. She tried to dismiss the images flooding through her head, becoming increasingly aggressive with the delete button which had the desired effect on the screen but only seemed to sharpen the pictures in her memory. Feeling increasingly upset she went off to the toilet to freshen up.

When she got back ten minutes later there was a note on the desk with a name and telephone number. 'Signe I'm leaving you this lady's number in case you want to call her. She's a lovely person with lots of common sense and wisdom. I know she would love to help you.'

Signe involuntarily looked towards the door almost expecting to see Father Stephan there, which was ridiculous. She looked back at the name as if expecting to glean the character and physiognomy it represented, again a ridiculous thought. She put the paper in her pocket and returned to the entries. She'd think about it.

Chapter 24

"It was like there was this immediate attraction, so strong and powerful, like we knew each other already and had just met again after a long time."

They were standing in their usual place, George leaning on the rail looking down at the melee below, Matt standing sideways looking at him. He'd just related his experience in Gothenburg and had found it cathartic. He realised he hadn't ever just talked about it to someone without a vested interest, that is, someone impartial. Maggie and Caterina had been too close, the lawyer intent on the legal aspect. He hadn't had anyone to unburden to without judgement or emotional involvement. After George's candid revelation in their previous conversation he had felt encouraged to likewise explain his presence at Wandsworth.

"Have you heard of Twin Flames?" George asked, still looking down.

"No."

"Hmm. Well you know we sometimes come across people we call soul mates, people we seem to immediately have a rapport with, people we seem to know almost instinctively."

"Yes, sure."

"It's not uncommon. There's a belief that these are souls we've known before, in previous lives." George looked at Matt now, perhaps to gauge his reaction, but seeing a non-committal expression he continued. "You know about re-incarnation, well, this belief has it that we interact with some souls over many lifetimes. A soul might be your mother in one incarnation, your son in another. We work through problems and faults in our natures in each mortality, gaining wisdom in this plane until we are ready to progress to another dimension."

He searched Matt's face for signs of disbelief. "Twin flames is a visual description of the duality of souls. Your soul is only a part of your true entity. This entity is composed of two parts, the male and the female, the positive and negative, the yin and yang. They are inextricably connected and form the most powerful attractions when manifested and encountered in this plane.

"You may have encountered your twin flame, it sounds like this was such a powerful meeting. However, twin flames are not necessarily destined to co-exist in this plane. Sometimes they do and the experience is total fulfilment, a wholeness and completeness which is inevitable and extraordinary. Very often, however, the recognition of the special relationship manifests, but one or other of the pair does not see it for what it is, or is not ready to embrace that level of oneness. It takes trust, confidence and maturity to see beyond the temporal desires and commit to the ideal. It sounds to me like the recognition was there but there were, or rather, still are, obstacles to a present union in this plane. Many twin flames co-exist in this life without con-joining in a relationship. They can be friends who don't allow of more familiarity, or awkward acquaintances where neither can understand the enormous attraction nor act on it because they are not yet developed enough to appreciate the depth of the association."

Matt was feeling pretty uncomfortable with the conversation now. It had begun as slightly extreme, just touching on the nature of souls, but now was seemingly going into the realms of predestination and 'the great plan'. He felt it would be awkward now to say he thought that was a load of bollocks, so just said,

"Okay, well that's pretty heavy stuff."

George smiled. "You don't like that idea, Matthew."

"No, no, I didn't say that, it's just quite a lot to take in."

"You don't have to 'believe' it if you don't want to, obviously. I'm just saying it's a theory, a belief that many have, and a truth that some have experienced."

"Have you?"

"I feel Keera and I have that bond. But, although we have experienced each other in this life, I think our time together is limited. It may well be that I have to learn to let her go in this experience, to find her own way."

Matt turned and followed George's gaze to the levels below. This really sounded very dodgy. Maybe George was a member of some weird religious cult and was subtly trying to bring him in. It was one of those alternative new-age philosophies which were springing up everywhere, like crystal skulls, realms of angels, lost civilisation of Atlantis and so on. They all sounded wonderfully appealing to believe in but in reality were totally crazy. They didn't add up scientifically and as Richard Dawkins said in 'The God Delusion' (which he still hadn't finished of course) a religion or belief is just a convenient explanation if you haven't yet found the scientific answer to a question.

Matt had that feeling you get when a good friend reveals a liking for something you hate and suddenly you question your affection for them. He had liked George from the word go, but now he was showing signs of being a bit of a nutter.

"How d'you know this stuff?"

George's look told him he'd conveyed his scepticism in the tone of his voice and use of the word 'stuff'. He felt admonished in that look, but George replied gently.

"I've had many experiences, Matthew, and they all point in the same direction. I never accept anything I'm told without finding out if it's true for me, so I've made it my business to find out for myself what I believe. I could never accept a lot of things which society or tradition considers normal, because they didn't resonate with me, they didn't seem true. So I went to find truth for myself. I've travelled all over the world and met many different people; Buddhists in Tibet, Jaynes in India, a philosopher in China. I've been on silent retreats, I've meditated, I've taken Ayawaska many times with a Shaman in Mexico. I've experienced deep trance, out of body experience, near death experience and moved between this plane and the spiritual world.

"This may seem unreal and it's difficult to describe. We're compromised by a lack of language to describe what is really beyond language. When we use language to try to describe it the words seem overblown and extreme, but that's because the experience is so much bigger than language can accommodate. These metaphysical experiences are bigger than us and we can't comprehend them, but we can accept that they are there, are part of our lives and point to a larger picture. Just like Hamlet said," and he smiled and winked at Matt, that gesture alone absolving him, he thought, for his cynicism.

"So you reckon this girl, who I don't know at all, is my real soul mate, like the other part of my soul?"

"Well, I'm only suggesting it's a possibility. If the sense of recognition was that strong and there seemed to be such a level of unspoken understanding, it would seem likely, but she could just be a close soul mate of whom you might meet many in this life."

Matt felt very uncomfortable with this talk of 'this life', 'this plane' and 'this experience'. It sounded like so much new age rubbish, fortune-telling speak, everything he hated about the complementary therapy thing which seemed to be an endless rip-off using untested claims and labels worded 'may alleviate,' 'may reduce', 'can help'. But George's demeanour of calm, considered confidence was infectious and Matt felt himself wanting to believe it.

"Some kind of soul mate, landing me in prison for two years! I think I'd have preferred never to have met her."

"Yes, I can believe that. But we can't choose these things. Unfortunately for you she wasn't ready to recognise this bond, or maybe she was aware of it but was too frightened to accept it. This is obviously something she has to deal with and learn from. Maybe you have to learn how to deal with this rejection. I don't pretend to understand the higher purpose in your case, but I know there will be a reason. These reasons may be obscure and incomprehensible to us because we have limited knowledge of our soul's experience, but we have to listen to our inner nature and allow our subconscious to lead us. It knows what we should do, but it is usually drowned out by the clamour of our noisy conscious lives. We have to find a way to listen to our true natures and hear the still small voice of calm inside ourselves. But it's easier said than done."

Matt smiled, recognising the quote. "Ah, yes, the still small voice of calm – 'Breathe through the heats of our desires, Thy coolness and Thy balm' etc."

George smiled too. "So you know that hymn."

"I sang in church choirs a lot. Must have sung that hundreds of times. Are you a Christian?"

"I was brought up so, but as you can tell I've made different choices now. Doesn't mean to say I don't respect a lot of those teachings, but I feel they were for a place and time that is not ours. They are a metaphor for life which I think resonated more in other eras. We need new interpretations and explanations in our hectic world more appropriate to our particular lives."

The signal sounded for the end of social time and Matt felt annoyed that he didn't have longer to talk to George now that they had got onto this subject.

"Ah well, maybe we can carry on this discussion another time. I need to pick your brains about all this alternative philosophy. It's fascinating."

"It's essential," George replied with a smile.

They shook hands as usual and Matt wandered away back to his cell. When he got there he found an envelope on his bed with the prison stamp on it. Opening it he found it was a notification from the City Court in Gothenburg of a retrial of the case Larsson v Chamberlain to be held on 18th May via video-link with Wandsworth prison. He would be required to give evidence again at 9am on the said date and would be represented once again by the same defence lawyer Bergstrom.

He didn't understand and read it again. *What's going on? How come a retrial? Have they discovered some new evidence? But what? Someone has come forward to protest his innocence? But that doesn't make sense.*

His mind raced over the possibilities but failed to find a satisfactory explanation, yet the seed of hope was planted that there was a chance the sentence might be revoked and he might get out.

He thought back to the trial, so recently described to George, and he saw so clearly the details of that day; the prosecutor laying in to him, the girl giving him that agonised look but condemning him nonetheless, the jury giving their verdict. He hated the thought of going over all that ground again but if it meant getting off he was keen to get on with it. May 18th was only three days away. Was it possible he might be out in three days. He hardly dared hope and forced himself to be negative. It was a formality, a procedure they had to go through to discount some unaccounted-for evidence. It wasn't possible a retrial by video-link could end his sentence just like that. But the nugget of hope sat fatly in his every thought however he tried to suppress it.

The next few days were a trial in themselves. The harder he tried to ignore the upcoming trial the more it impressed itself on his mind. He couldn't stop projecting scenario after scenario and each time ending up with his release, which he knew was madness and a sure-fire recipe for exactly the opposite result. He was tempting fate, dicing with his future by daring to be optimistic, but it was impossible not to hope. Why did he want to build up his hopes so much, knowing they would probably be shattered? He couldn't help wondering what he would do the moment he was out. Would he head for the nearest pub and have a solitary drink to celebrate? Would he rush back to Leyton and hope that Maggie was in and fuck the arse off her? Would he ring all his friends and organise an impromptu party and get completely hammered? Maybe he'd do all three in that order and the second one again afterwards.

But he couldn't let himself think like that, because in all likelihood this would just be some proceeding which confirmed his guilt and he'd stay here in Wandsworth with Damon. Or what if there was some evidence which incriminated him further, made the case stronger against him and he got a longer sentence? It didn't bear thinking about. He went from one extreme to the other, tempting himself and torturing himself by turns and making himself sick with anticipation.

He tried to keep busy in the kitchen and forced himself to watch the drivel on the TV that Damon was watching when he returned to the cell, but he had the impression that if it had carried on much longer he'd have developed an ulcer. Fortunately time has the habit of continuing inexorably however we perceive it and Thursday came as ever it was surely going to and at 8.45 he was led from his cell down various corridors to the room used for video-links. As he walked he regretted he hadn't managed to see George, who had not been on the landing the one time he'd managed to snatch some social time after work. He'd have to see him after, whatever the outcome.

He was shown into a smallish room with a video camera and monitor screen which showed the courtroom in Gothenburg. There were two people standing talking and what looked like a court official putting out papers and arranging things. He sat in the chair nervously watching the screen, feeling his heart beating out the seconds til he'd know if this crazy miracle he hoped for was just so much wild dreaming. *But there must be substantial grounds for a change of verdict if they're holding a complete retrial.* It seemed to take ages for anything to happen.

At last there was some activity and a distant sound of voices. The prison official moved to the monitor and turned up the volume. A grey-haired man took the judge's seat and thumbed through some papers before beginning to speak. A couple of seconds later a female voice with a Swedish accent came over the monitor translating, which Matt found initially so confusing.

The judge convened the proceedings, named the case to be tried and the lawyers representing. He began by saying that this was an unusual situation, that a plaintiff should ask to re-open a case. He briefly explained the circumstances of the trial two months ago which had resulted in Matthew Chamberlain being convicted of attempting to rape Signe Larsson on the strength of the testimonies and the medical and witness evidence provided.

"The Gothenburg City Court has been instructed by the Court of Appeal to hold a retrial of this case as the plaintiff has now come forward asking for new evidence to be taken into consideration. I would ask the jury to refer to the transcript of the trial which you'll find in front of you, particularly pages five to seven and ten and eleven which are the testimonies of the plaintiff and the defendant. I will give you five minutes to read these through so that you are acquainted with the case as tried."

When they had read through the material the judge invited the lawyer for the plaintiff to open the case. He appeared and called the plaintiff to the witness stand. As she stood there, a small figure on the monitor but her expression and appearance recognisable enough, Matt was hit by conflicting emotions. On the one hand he felt a rush of anger at the person who had locked him up and screwed his life over, but on the other such a strong desire to fold himself round her. Images of her in the concert, at the reception and on the deck tangled with images of the statue, invoking a tenderness which counteracted his aggression. He tried to concentrate on the proceeding being relayed from Gothenburg and focus on the simultaneous translation but it seemed like a sound that was echoing from miles away down a resonant corridor.

Her lawyer was asking her why she had approached the court to ask for a retrial. She hesitantly explained that at the trial she hadn't been able to remember things very clearly and had agreed with what her lawyer had suggested had happened, but now she had remembered what had really happened. He asked her to relate in her own words what had happened.

"At the reception I felt dizzy and needed to get outside, into the fresh air. I went on deck and there was a beautiful moon over the water. I remember I was very happy. It was such a beautiful scene and the music was still going round in my head and I felt like it was all perfect. Then I heard a noise behind me, someone said something. I turned round and he was there."

She was swaying, seemed to be drunk.

"Who was there?"

"Jesus. Well, the singer from the concert who was Jesus. I was confused. He was standing there in the moonlight with his arms stretched out like he was...."

Offering to help you...thinking you were going to fall over...

She stopped, at a loss and looked helplessly around the room, embarrassed.

"Like he was?" the lawyer prompted.

"It sounds stupid now, but at the time I thought he looked like a crucifix, like Jesus on the cross, but talking to me. In English. Asking if he could help me." *Wanting to kiss you.* She dabbed her eyes with a tissue and blew her nose briefly.

"And what happened then?"

"The next thing I remember is being somewhere else, lying down and looking up into his face. I didn't know where I was. It seemed like I was..." embarrassed again, shifting her eyes down and colouring.

In heaven

"Like you were?"

"Like I was in Heaven."

"Can you explain what you mean by that?"

In paradise

"Like I was the bride and had just been laid down by my husband. I....I was so happy. I just wanted to love him, to show him how much I cared." She paused, struggling to force the words out, and suddenly looked straight at Matt, at the camera where, he realised, she could see the monitor relay of him. She was looking right at him, at his image on that screen all those miles away in Gothenburg, appealing with those eyes, braving herself. He was motionless, held in the spell of the video-linked moment, not daring to breathe.

"I kissed him. I wanted to kiss him, and he kissed me, and it seemed right and perfect. I couldn't stop kissing him. I wanted him to be a part of me. I felt we were one..." Those eyes now welled and brimmed and sent streams sliding down her cheeks.

In that moment we were one.

The lawyer let her again wipe her eyes and collect herself before asking

"So he didn't force himself on you?"

"No."

"You encouraged him and enjoyed him kissing you?"

"Yes."

"Did you say you wanted to have sex?"

She hesitated, her face screwed up with anguish as if tortured by this suggestion, then mouthed an answer which carried no sound but a whisper.

"No."

"I'm sorry, again for the court please."

"No." She gasped out and broke into sobs.

"Did you say anything?"

It's you!

"Yesu."

"As in Jesú, Jesus?"

"Yes."

Jesu, oh God, of course. Sounded like...

"I'm sorry, Miss Larsson, but I have to ask you. Did he ask you if you wanted to have sex?"

"No.," she said decisively, then quieter, "it wasn't like that. It was... *beautiful*...we didn't say anything."

"And what happened next?"

He had to wait a moment whilst she managed to control herself again. Matt found himself gripping the chair, wanting her to get the story out.

"I got lost. I was lost in him... *drowning in her, urgent...* I don't know how to describe it, but it was like I was dreaming, but it was real... *deep, desperate embraces*...I'd never felt anything like it before. It was almost like... *dying*...like I died a little..." She stopped abruptly.

"But you came to your senses. You suddenly didn't like the experience."

"I....he started doing something... *urgent*...reaching, down... *soaring*... I suddenly knew what it was. I panicked, I...*fumbling, unbuttoning*..it was a shock. I hadn't expected it...*silk*...That... *bursting*. It wasn't what I meant when I...*kissing, urging*.. It was a misunderstanding...*standing, understanding*"

"And you shouted 'No' and pushed him off."

She was shaking now. "I don't remember...*coming*..Yes, I pushed him off... *coming*. I realised what he was trying to do. It was horrible. I...*falling, shrinking*." She couldn't continue. She was crying fully now, falling apart.

The lawyer raised his hands and appealed to the judge, who nodded and gestured to wait. A court official brought her a plastic beaker of water. The prosecutor walked slowly back and forth and then stopped in front of her again whilst she wiped her nose and straightened herself out again.

"It's okay Miss Larsson, you're doing really well. We're nearly done. Just a couple more questions." She nodded. "When you pushed him off, did he try to kiss you again, or force himself on you?"

In a very quiet voice she now replied, "No, I don't think so. I was screaming I think. I can't remember."

"Miss Larsson, I just have to be very clear that as soon as you showed him you didn't want to have sex, he stopped, he didn't continue."

"He didn't, no."

"And you realise by giving this evidence you are taking equal responsibility for what happened that night?" She nodded. "You have to answer please."

"Yes."

"I have no more questions, Mr Chairman."

The judge looked down at his papers. "Thank you Mr Fosberg. Mr Bergstrom do you have any questions?"

"Yes, Mr Chairman."

Matt saw his council appear from the corner of the screen and go towards the witness stand.

"Miss Larsson you have changed your evidence quite substantially. One might almost say completely. It now appears that my client has been falsely accused as the sole protagonist in this case, as you now admit to having an equal involvement in the interaction. It appears that my client didn't in fact impose himself on you or force you to do anything you didn't want to do and stopped as soon as you showed you didn't want to go further."

He paused. Matt didn't know whether he was expecting her to respond, but she just stood there with her head slightly lowered, avoiding his look.

"You are asking us to accept that the reason my client has been in prison for two months is on account of you not remembering any of the events you have just related. Did you really not remember any of this at the trial? Has all this evidence only come back to you since the trial?"

The girl turned her head towards where her lawyer had gone. Obviously she was confused as to what to say. She looked back to Bergstrom, then down at her hands.

"I wasn't sure what I remembered, what was real and what I thought I'd dreamed."

"So, you testified that he had tried to rape you even though there was doubt in your mind as to what exactly had happened and whether that was in fact true?"

She didn't respond, just kept looking down at her hands.

"Miss Larsson, I would suggest that by the time of the trial you had a fairly good idea of what had happened. I think you remembered most of the events that took place that night, but having accused my client and come to court you felt pressured to continue with the accusation even though by then you knew it was untrue. I think when it came to it you were too frightened to admit your part in the events and so continued with the accusation to save face. And since the trial you have been tormented with guilt such that you felt compelled to own up to your lie and admit the truth, which is that you knew all along that he wasn't guilty."

The translator didn't need to explain the helpless whimpering that Matt could hear distantly through the speaker as the blond head began shaking and then collapsed slowly over the clasped hands. Her torso was overtaken by sobs which, now amplified by the close proximity of the microphone, seemed to echo around the court.

"Thank you Mr Bergstrom, I think that's enough."

In spite of his elation that he was now exonerated Matt felt a wave of compassion that surprised him. He felt her grief keenly, realised the depth of her shame and, although part of him welcomed her suffering for having ripped is life apart, the other wept with her in her remorse.

Matt watched her being helped from the witness stand and move out of view. Who was she? Who was this girl whom he'd thought about so many times and who had influenced his life so much over the past two months? He knew nothing about her, except that she was a devout Catholic and fifteen. What was her family like, her interests, her life? He knew none of this, yet on a deeper level he felt he knew her, knew her core, her essence, her passion.

"Ladies and Gentlemen of the jury, you do not need to consider the possibilities suggested by Mr Bergstrom, whether Miss Larsson in her confusion knew for sure at the time of the trial the true circumstances of the events. I am satisfied from her testimony today that the evidence she gave originally she gave in good faith, although possibly, due to emotional pressure, she was persuaded against her better judgement. You should take account of how much courage it might take for someone of her age to go through the original trial and then two months later, reapply as she has now done to have the case reviewed.

"You should consider the case now in respect of the new evidence put before you and decide whether the sentence for the accused should stand. Is he now guilty of rape or was the involvement consensual and he should be acquitted? I should add that the Court of Appeal finds no evidence of coercion on Miss Larsson in bringing this appeal. She has approached the court freely and of her own will."

The judge left the court and the jury of three conferred.

"D'you wanna cuppa tea?"

Matt started. He'd forgotten the screw standing in the room behind him.

"Yeah, that'd be great. Thanks. No sugar." Matt got up and walked about the room, occasionally glancing at the monitor to check for any developments. *They haven't asked me anything. I didn't need to be here. And now are they going to me let off and I needn't have been stuck in this shithole at all?*

"'Ere you go." The warder passed him the tea. "Looks like you might be outa here, mate."

"Well, I can't say I'd be sad to leave."

"Too right. Need to get on with yer life. Young lad like you." They hung around for about ten minutes, Matt pacing the room in anticipation sipping his tea, before, " Ooh, 'ere we go." The warder pointed towards the monitor. Matt went and sat down again and saw the judge returning to his seat.

"Ladies and gentlemen of the court have you reached a decision?"

"We have Mr Chairman."

"Do you find the accused guilty or not guilty?"

"Not guilty, Mr Chairman."

"I concur."

A spasm of exhilaration shot through Matt's stomach. He didn't hear the rest of the proceedings in the court. The minder was congratulating him and his head was filled with thoughts of release, his family, Maggie and flashes of the last few months all jumbled together.

"So what happens now? Is that it?"

"Should all happen fairly quickly. Depen's 'ow efficient they are in Sweden, but usually they can get an email over with the release papers attached. Then they just need to process it all 'ere and you can go."

As it turned out Matt had a frustrating wait of about four hours before the paperwork was completed and they could discharge him. During this time he was given back his personal possessions so had money to buy a coffee. He made a couple of phone calls, to Maggie but got no reply, and to his agent but got a new member of staff whom he didn't know. Peter was at a first night at Glyndebourne, could she take a message? He said he'd ring in the morning. He spent three cups of coffee going through hundreds of messages, group chats and notifications. He was eventually released at 3.15.

Chapter 25

It was a soft May afternoon with a light breeze, gentle sun filtering through a haze, sparrows chirruping and pigeons cooing in the trees along the road. He wondered what was the best way to get home from here. Overground to Waterloo, northern line, central line? Bus? None of that appealed, he wanted to be outside feeling the air on his skin, the sun in his face. He decided to walk. This was probably madness he quickly realised, but he felt like a madman. His joints ached for the exercise and he welcomed the challenge. He set off towards Clapham Junction his legs feeling pumped with adrenalin at being out and free.

Life was good. He took deep breaths of the blossom-scented air, honey-ceanothus and pungent honeysuckle, which wafted from green-dripping gardens. The puffing breeze fluffed his hair and breathed a coolness on his already moist neck. He felt like singing for the first time in weeks and realised in fact he hadn't sung a note since that fateful performance. He began to hum in time with his steps, a random tune, anything, experiencing again the vibration in his throat that was his life. He was only mucking about but could tell his voice was all over the place, unfocussed, spread, weak, without its customary ease. It was hardly surprising. It would be like a runner doing the hundred metres having not done any training for two months; unlikely to impress.

Two teenage girls were walking towards him, pretty, in short skirts and clinging vests, aware of their effect. They were chatting and laughing, shaking their hair, tossing it with their hands the way girls do. One of them caught his eye as they passed, a confident, sassy look, challenging, knowing. Then they were gone. They were attractive, possibly a bit tarty, but on a sunny afternoon with the sap rising they ticked boxes.

Matt wondered how old they were. Fifteen? Sixteen? What was his status now? He hadn't asked. Was he still on record as a sex offender? Presumably the retrial exonerated him, but did it wipe the slate clean? Every time he saw a teenage girl he found attractive would he now be reminded of his experience, of the girl in Gothenburg? And what did he feel about her now? What did she mean to him? He was unsure. George's words ran through his mind, the twin flames, not necessarily to co-exist in this life but aware of each other, aware of each other's beings, each other's souls.

Matt quickened his stride, irritated by this thought and the accompanying thought that it was probably a load of rubbish. But he regretted he hadn't seen George to say goodbye. He'd undoubtedly never see him again and he'd liked the guy, even if he was a bit crazy.

But he didn't need to think about that anymore. He was walking through London on a fabulous sunny afternoon and he was free. Free to do what he wanted, pick up his life, go home and give Maggie a good seeing to. He didn't care what she wanted to use, how she wanted to be used or abused. He'd indulge her, do whatever she wanted as long as he got his end away. He got quite carried away with an imagined scenario. He hadn't been able to try calling again as his phone was dead. Maybe he'd ring her from a phone box if he saw one, to gee her up with anticipation. Or maybe he'd just surprise her, pounce on her from behind, throw her over the back of the settee. She'd like that. She liked a bit of rough. He'd tie her up with her clothes, hobble her with his belt and force her to beg him to 'treat her nice'. She loved that, being forced to beg. It really turned her on.

He found himself chuckling and grimacing, when he saw a bloke looking at him strangely, and had to look away and quicken his pace. He was elated with excitement, imagining having a curry afterwards and then lying in bed watching a movie and tickling Maggie until they had a romp and did it again. Then they'd lie there exhausted and find they'd missed most of the film and laugh about it and Maggie would roll a joint and they'd drift off into a cosy sleep clothed with the smell of sex and weed.

These thoughts spurred his steps and he hardly noticed the effort of walking up to Vauxhall Cross, along the embankment and round Lambeth Palace. By the river the breeze was cooler coming off the water and was ruffling the surface of the flood tide. A tug boat was towing two huge container barges upriver with the tide, as a clipper chopped downstream diagonally across the Thames from one landing stage to another. The sun was dazzling on the gilt-work of Westminster and there were MPs taking tea on the terrace. The Millennium wheel was turning slowly, the ant-like bodies in the capsules just visible, pointing and clicking cameras.

He crossed over on Waterloo Bridge and took Fleet Street down towards St Paul's. The sun by this time was at his back and Wren's great structure loomed up white and imposing.

He remembered he'd thought of having a pint as soon as he got out. Somehow he'd forgotten about it, but right now he was really thirsty and longed for an ice-cold coke. He went into a newsagent's and bought two cans. He couldn't believe how good it tasted. Whether it was not having had one for ages, being hot and thirsty or just the sudden craving for one he didn't know, but he sank the first one very quickly and then spent the next minute belching uncontrollably.

He walked on sipping the second one and realised he was a bit knackered. By the time he got to Aldwych he worked out he had been walking fast for an hour and a half and thought 'sod it' and caught a number twenty five, fighting his way upstairs and luckily finding a recently vacated seat near the back. His calves were tense and his feet hurt and it was a relief to sit down. The bus was hot and soon he found himself nodding off, embarrassing himself by collapsing against the person next to him, a large black lady who was talking endlessly on her mobile phone with bags of shopping at her feet and on her lap. Apologising he then found himself swooning the other way, jolting awake and only just catching himself before falling into the aisle. The fight to remain vertical while cat-napping continued until he got off at Stratford where he couldn't be bothered to change, opting to walk the fifteen minutes home from there in a bid to wake up.

"Mags?" His voice echoed up the stairs and through the flat. "Mags, are you home?" Stupid question, he thought; she's hardly going to say 'No. I'm out' and anyway he thought he heard movements upstairs.

The place was in a bit of a mess. Clothes were heaped in various places; unwashed dishes and evidence of meals having been cooked or re-heated; a book of audition speeches open on the table together with some loose photocopied scripts; a full laundry bin with various garments on the floor next to it in the bathroom. He went into the bedroom and stopped short, staring at the bed. He felt his heart beating and a panic in his throat. What was going on? What was she up to? Okay she wasn't expecting him, so that explains the mess, but? Someone else must have been here, with her. She couldn't have done it by herself. He saw the open window, the means of escape.

She didn't know he was here. She couldn't see or hear properly because of the leather hood tightly encasing her head. She was moaning slightly through the gag strapped across her mouth, the bite-ball clamped into her jaw. The restraint suit she'd sent him a picture of was tight over her body, her nipples erect through the cutaway holes. She was hobbled at the ankles, another thong attached from there to a halter around her neck pulling her head back. She was kneeling on the bed, her bare buttocks offered up for the disciplining she obviously desired from the leather riding crop lying beside her on the sheets.

Matt couldn't move for a few moments. During that time he realised she became aware something wasn't right and her body language changed to one of insecurity and panic. He was suddenly furious with her and snatched up the whip and gave her several cruel lashes across her buttocks, much harder than he imagined she'd been expecting. She yelled through the gag, which resulted in a muffled moan. He threw down the whip, suddenly realising he didn't want to pleasure her, rather punish her by not punishing her. He felt like walking out, but he couldn't leave her trussed up, she'd never free herself. Her hands were tied in strait-jacket sleeves and buckled behind her back. He undid the buckle and released her arms. She quickly but hesitantly undid the hood straps and mouth gag. Her shock at seeing him was monumental. He saw the panic, the thoughts racing through her head, the incomprehension of the situation, the total disbelief at his presence. She was speechless.

"I'm going to make some tea," he said at last, and walked away to the kitchen. He filled the kettle, not knowing what he was doing. The mechanics of tea-making took him over physically although his mind was teeming with contradictory thoughts. *She came all the way to Gothenburg to help me and now she's fucking around with someone else. Some home-coming!* The kettle rumbled to its conclusion. He found a tea bag and a mug, poured the water, stood looking at the tea bag gently circling round the mug, the bubbles from the pouring gradually dispersing.

He didn't want tea. He didn't know what he wanted. Something to fill this void in his stomach, this emptiness after the exhilaration of release and the anticipation of coming home. He stood there stupidly looking at the mug, waiting. Inevitably he sensed her behind him. He didn't want to turn to face her. He wished he could avoid all this, this mess, this dirt. He felt defiled, hurt, injured. In prison on a false charge, and what was she doing?

"How come you're out Matt?" Her voice was low, conciliatory, apprehensive.

"Who is he?"

"No one. Just someone. It doesn't matter."

"Doesn't it?"

"Matt, I can't believe..."

"It doesn't matter that while I'm fucking banged up in prison on some shit charge, you're fucking around here in our house, screwing around with some other fucking pervert, kinking about and getting off on your filthy porno shit." He spun round. "You're bloody obsessed aren't you! Can't control your fucking desires. You've got to indulge yourself haven't you, like some, some addict. You just can't leave it alone. You're some kind of sex-maniac desperate for an orgasm."

She moved towards him her hands held out, supplicating, appealing, a look of intense pain on her face. It was the grimace of a smile crumbled by unsuppressable anguish.

"Matt..."

"Don't touch me, Maggie, just....Jesus," he back-handed her arms away. "And you even had to send bloody pictures on the internet, in a fucking email, and implicate me in your bloody shit perversion. That was brilliant in court."

She was standing, rebuffed, a few feet from him, hugging herself with one arm, the other hand lifted to her face to wipe away the tears and cover her mouth to stop herself breaking down.

"Matt that's not fair..."

"Too right it's not fair. It's not fair I've spent two months in jail with a whole lot of fucking perverts, ruined my career and been through all that shit, and my partner's shagging some other pervert in my bed." He turned and threw the tea in the sink, rinsed the mug furiously in cold water and slammed it in the drainer.

"No Matt, I agree that's not fair. But it's not fair you're shouting at me. I didn't put you away."

"Well, what d'you expect me to do? Say 'Oh sorry, am I interrupting something? Sorry I just happened to be released from prison. Sorry I came home, I should have gone to a hotel til you'd sorted yourself out, got rid of the evidence.'? I'm so sorry I presumed it was okay to let myself into my home."

"Matt, how was I supposed to know you were just going to turn up when you were supposed to be there for two years?"

"I phoned but you didn't answer, it went straight to ansaphone. Then my phone went dead."

"Yeah, my phone's not working. It fell down the bog."

"What?"

"It was in my back pocket when I went to the bog. I pulled my jeans down and it slipped out. Fell in the water. Hasn't worked since."

Matt suddenly laughed. Only Maggie could do that. It was typical of her. It was always dramatic with Maggie. Not falling on the floor, but down the bog.

"Come on Matt, that's not funny. It's an iPhone five."

"Have you got insurance?"

"You must be kidding. I can hardly afford the bloody phone. But look, how come you're out?"

His anger had subsided a bit, but he wasn't going to make it easy for her, he wasn't going to forgive her. In fact maybe he'd leave her. He didn't know what he felt, what he'd do.

"There was a re-trial. It all happened very quickly."

"How, when? What happened? You didn't go there again?"

"No, it was done by video-link." He began to explain the details, cagily at first, but in more detail the more she pressed him. She had a knack of wheedling, coaxing answers out of him in spite of himself.

"So what's been going on? You seeing someone?" He blurted out after he'd finished telling her all about the retrial and release.

She looked at him levelly, candidly. "Matt, you know me. I've got needs. I can't do things alone. I'm no saint, Matt, you know that. I didn't do it to hurt you. I did it because I needed to, because I have to be able to function. Maybe I need to see someone, a specialist, I dunno, sort it out, but right now I need to have it. This guy's been at the club. He's been kind of hot for me and... Come on, Matt, you were going to be inside for two years, what did you expect me to do? You said when I visited you in prison you'd understand if I couldn't wait. Did you not mean that?"

He remembered now, and he'd meant it at the time, in his misery inside, but now it had happened it was difficult and he wished he hadn't said it, wished he'd implored her to wait for him, make a sacrifice for their union. "Yeah."

"I mean you can't have it both ways, Matt. You can't try to screw a girl in Sweden and then expect me to be 'Holier than Thou' here. Where's the fairness in that? What, because I'm a woman I'm supposed to be faithful? Come on Matt, fucking hell, I know you don't sign up to that."

"It's just a shock, Maggie, right? I come home, I'm all excited to see you, I've just been let out and then... it's all fucked up." He shrugged, moved away from the sink, went and leant against the fridge, arms crossed, hands in his armpits.

Maggie was perched on the kitchen table, her hands now shoved between her thighs, palm to palm, shoulders raised, leaning forward and rocking slightly.

"It was just sex, Matt, nothing more. I needed a fuck okay? You weren't here, what was I to do? Yeah, yeah I know, well I don't do that; I need help. And he was up for it, so. I saw him at the club last night and, well, there you go. Oh shit, what time is it? I'm going to be late."

"You got work?"

"Shit shit shit, and I was going to have a shower and wash my hair."

"Can't you ring in and say you can't make it?"

"No, no, Marcel's ill and Chelsea's on holiday. The new girl's only been in a couple of days and she can't do it on her own. No, I'll have to try and get there as soon as I can. Shit."

She rushed around grabbing things, changed into tight jeans and a top. Raked her hairbrush through her hair and stuck it up in an elastic. "I can't even fucking ring them because of my phone."

"Use mine? Oh no, it's dead."

"Never mind, got to go."

"When will you be back?"

"Late. Thursday night crowd. They normally stay."

"Right, I'll see you later."

Maggie stopped rushing suddenly. "It shouldn't have been like this Matt. I'm so happy you're out. We'll sort all this out, okay?"

"Yeah."

"Sorry about the mess. Don't clear up. I'll deal with it tomorrow."

She hesitated by the table, unsure how to leave.

"Bye then."

"Bye."

He watched her turn and go out into the hall, heard her pull on the leather jacket and grab the helmet and then clatter down the stairs and slam the door. The distant sound of a motorbike roaring off.

The fridge motor kicked in, shuddering the frame as he leant on it. He moved to the table and sat down on a chair. There were crumbs on the table and occasional sugar crystals. He pressed his finger down on them, collecting them with the pressure, then rubbed them off into a pile. It took him about a minute and a half to clear them all into the pile. He stared at the pile for some time with his chin in his hand.

So, back to reality.

Chapter 26

Signe felt empty. The school term over and the summer holidays upon her, there seemed to be nothing. The events of the Passion and trial having subsided, followed by the adjustment again to school, she now found herself in a void, uninvolved, listless.

She'd hardly seen Irma, who seemed wrapped up in music now, and Karl. She could never get hold of her, to talk, to see her. She was always busy rehearsing, performing, practicing, mixing with another group, but Signe needed her advice, her friendship, so had made a concerted effort to tie Irma down now that term had ended. But she'd texted back to say she was really busy with a summer music course that Karl had asked her to help him run. He'd even asked her to teach some of the younger ones – "I mean, imagine, he thinks I'm good enough to teach!" she'd bubbled down the phone excitedly when Signe eventually got through to her.

"That's great Irm, you should be really proud," Signe had said, seeing the truth behind the invitation. "Irm, when can we meet up? I really need to see you, you know 'best friends' time.'" This was a euphemism for a weekend together which had been a regular thing.

"Oh Si, I'm really wiped at the moment with this summer course."

"Don't you have any time off?"

"Well, not really. Oh actually, what are you doing for Midsummer?"

"Well we usually go to the Thorsteinsson's cottage. It's a kind of tradition. Gustav gets the boat out and we all pile over there with tons of food Melissa's spent days preparing, and Gustav and Mr Thorsteinsson get drunk and Melissa gets mad."

"Who?"

"Melissa, you know, Lars' mum."

"Right." Irma still couldn't get her head round Signe referring to her mum and dad as Gustav and Melissa. It was really weird.

"But I'm not going to lie to you, I'm out of it. What are you doing?"

"Well, it wouldn't really be 'best friends' time', but Karl's going to be doing stuff with his kid, taking him to see his parents or something, so we could get together then."

"Cool, what like?"

"Oh I don't know, do our own picnic and go somewhere?"

"Hmm."

"Tell you what, we could go to the Liseberg."

"The amusement park?"

"Yeah, why not? It would be a laugh."

"I haven't been there for years, since we were little. Remember? We used to go there practically every weekend in the summer?"

"Yeah! What d'you reckon?"

"Well, I won't be going on Balder, I'm no good at rollercoasters. In fact I probably won't go on any rides. My tummy's not too good these days."

"Really? You didn't tell me."

"I haven't seen you."

"Okay! Sorreee! What's wrong?"

"I'll tell you when I see you."

"So we're going?"

"Sure."

"We don't have to go on any rides, we'll just hang out."

"Okay, that sounds nice."

"I'll do some food and stuff. What time shall we meet?"

"Ten o'clock, my place?"

"Okay, it's a date, Si. See you Friday."

"Sure. Love you."

"Love you."

Midsummer Eve had threatened to be a washout. The weather reports during the days leading up to it had predicted heavy rain showers with strong winds, the last in a succession of low pressure weather systems ploughing up from the south west and causing unseasonable wet weather, even for this notoriously wet coastline of Sweden. Pessimists, or realists as they preferred to call themselves, were putting it down to man-made climate change; bullish industrialists were claiming natural cyclical weather patterns.

Mrs Larsson wasn't particularly concerned who was right as the result was the same anyway and meant she was fretting as to whether it would have been better to have prepared soup, as it would undoubtedly be cold and wet after a boat crossing to the little island and carrying all their provisions. Her husband had tried to reassure her before leaving for work the day before, that she was over-reacting and they'd be fine. Art Thorsteinsson had a log burner in the cottage, it would soon warm up and they would make a large pot of coffee and be snug as anything. But of course, as he'd anticipated, his words had had no effect and she'd continued to worry and no doubt did for the rest of the day despite anyone's reassurances. So he'd pecked her on the cheek and gladly slipped off to the office. Her next port of worry had been Signe whom, when she came downstairs, she accosted again for abandoning them for Midsummer celebrations. Why didn't she want to come? Was this how it was going to be now, the family disintegrating, her children going off and doing their own things?

"I haven't seen Irma for ages properly. We haven't spent any time together and this is the only day she can manage." Signe explained for the fifth time.

"But she could come with us, there's plenty of room. Why d'you have to go off by yourselves?"

"We just need some time together." Signe couldn't be bothered to argue the point and was just going to say 'no' from now on or ignore her. She went to heat a waffle and warm some milk for hot chocolate.

"But it's Midsummer, it's supposed to be a family day. Your father will be so upset if you don't come."

Well, he's not my father for a start off, and after the first schnapps he won't care anyway. They'll either be holding a post-mortem on the last season's hockey championship or predicting the result of next year's. Or else discussing their next hunting trip which always seems to involve a huge amount of planning even though they end up doing the same thing each time.

"I've made the arrangement now, I can't change it," she said bluntly. She whisked up the chocolate, squidged nutella onto the waffles and took them across to the table where this morning's Sudoku beckoned.

As it turned out the day was beautiful with clear skies, no cloud and hardly any wind. A storm had raged all night and blown itself out by morning, the weather system having arrived and tracked through far quicker than expected. Signe was up and out in good time, wanting to avoid the usual kerfuffle of the family packing up for the day and the usual petty bickering. She took her contributions for the picnic – chocolate, nuts and raisins, a couple of Gwendolyn cakes Melissa had made, a bottle of sparkling red grape juice and a couple of granola bars. She texted Irma to say she'd meet her at the gate rather than at her house and decided to walk instead of catching the bus as she had so much time. It wasn't so far from her house to the Liseberg, in fact nowhere in Gothenburg was, but you just got into the habit of catching a bus or tram. She was pleased she'd decided to walk. The pavements were still wet from all the rain but were drying fast in the bright sunshine and the beginning of a gentle breeze from the sea.

She passed the park at the end of her road and noticed a covering of daisies and suddenly had the idea to make a daisy chain, a Midsummer garland, like they had always done as kids.

She smiled as she set about the task, gathering and linking more and more and then deciding to make one for Irma too. By the time she'd finished there was barely enough time for her to get to the Liseberg for ten thirty. She gathered up both garlands and carried them carefully, her backpack slapping with the day's provisions.

"Hey," she said, out of breath when she saw Irma waiting. "Sorry I'm late. I made you a garland."

"Hey. Oh that's so cool, thanks Si, it's sweet."

They put them on and admired each other, taking selfies and generally, Signe admitted, being a bit silly.

"D'you want to go straight in?" she said.

"Sure. It's so good it's not raining anymore."

"Ya, would've been grim."

They paid and went in, the lad on the gate giving them an events sheet for the day.

"Look at all the flowers, wow, I never realised all this was here. I don't remember that when we were kids."

"No, me neither. They must have put all this in since then. Mind you, I shouldn't think we'd have noticed then, we just wanted to get to the rides."

They walked on a bit, looking about at the gardens. A group in traditional costume passed them chatting and joking loudly. The men were in mustard-coloured breeches and brightly coloured waistcoats over blousy shirts. Some of the women wore the blue and yellow of the Swedish flag, others rich reds and greens in long skirts and bodices with beautifully braided hair and flower garlands in place of the men's felt hats.

"I had a black velvet bodice and a bright blue skirt when I was little," Signe said. "I loved that outfit so much, I remember I cried when I couldn't fit into it anymore."

"I remember you in that. We've got a photo somewhere on the computer when we all went to some castle. We were really young."

"Gunebo castle."

"Yeah that's right. D'you remember?"

"Seems like ages ago."

"It was. We must have been about six. It was ten years ago Sig!"

"Wow." Signe smiled at Irma, trying to picture her all those years ago, but their knowledge of each other since and the young woman standing before her prevented that young image from taking shape.

"Where shall we go?" Irma said looking at the Liseberg Midsummer programme. "They're doing the maypole at twelve up over there in the middle of the gardens. We could go there and wait if you want to see that. Or we could walk about a bit first?"

"Yeah let's do that," Signe said.

They wandered off along the first path that presented itself between lush gardens planted with nodding annuals – cornflowers, cosmos, and marguerites – still shaking off droplets of rain in the light breeze. When they rounded a corner and found themselves in a protected garden, it was suddenly hot and humid, the lack of air movement concentrating the sun's rays and making the atmosphere heady with smells of rich vegetation and exuding oxygen. It felt almost tropical.

There was a bench close by and Signe suggested they sit and sun themselves. She got out the grape juice and they took swigs of the still-cool fizz.

"So tell me, what's up. How's it going Si?"

"I'm fine. Not sure what I'm doing this holidays. I had it all planned out but it doesn't seem it's going to happen."

"How's that?"

"Well, I applied to go and work at the convent in Vardstena, in the guest house they have there. They take volunteers to help run it and you stay there, like you're kind of part of it. I thought it would be really good to be there and see what it was like for the summer, but I haven't heard anything back from them."

"Oh, that's too bad. 'Cos that sounds like it would have been great for you."

"Yeah, I mean you don't get paid or anything but I wouldn't mind that. I'd just like to be there. But you know it's really annoying; you can't take orders there til you're twenty-five. I thought I could go as soon as I left school."

"Well that's quite good, means you can see a bit of life before you shut yourself away for the rest of your days!"

"Hey, don't sound like my dad, I mean like Gustav. He and Melissa have been on my back so much since it all came out at the trial, no thanks to you."

"Hey that's unfair."

"Okay, you're forgiven, but you'd think religious people would be glad their daughter, that I wanted to take Holy Orders. But they go on about it as if it's the end of the world."

Irma bit her lip, reining in what she wanted to say. "Well I suppose it seems to be extreme to them. You can still serve God and stay in the community, you don't have to cut yourself off completely."

"You're not cut off completely. Family and friends can visit and people stay at the guest house."

Irma knew better than to pursue this topic. "So, what are you going to do now?"

"I don't know. I could get a summer job in a restaurant maybe, but most of those will have gone already."

"No, I meant now you can't go to Vardstena til you're twenty five."

"Yeah, well, that's the thing. I'll have to go to university anyway. Try to use up the time. They say they like you to have work experience and qualifications because it can help with life in the convent. Did you know, they do all their own stuff there as much as they can, plumbing, carpentry, decorating. They try not to get anyone in if it's not necessary because they don't have any money. I was thinking I could go on lots of courses before I go so I could do tons of things."

"That sounds useful. But I don't really see you as a plumber! To be honest Si, you're not very practical. You know you find it difficult making an omelette, and that's just breaking eggs!"

"Alright, but I can learn." Signe took a swig of fizz and looked hurt.

"Oh Si, I'm only kidding, but you know you should really be concentrating on your strengths not your weaknesses."

"That's easy for you to say. You've just got a natural talent, so it's easy for you to know what to do. It's like it's all laid out for you; practice hard, get into a conservatoire, do some auditions, get into an orchestra and there you are."

"Says who? It's not that easy you know. There are some seriously good musicians out there and there aren't that many opportunities in Sweden."

"Oh come on, Irm, you're doing really well. All these semi-pro groups you're working with. You're going to walk into the profession."

"Well. I dunno, you say that, but…" But Irma couldn't really deny it, she was well on her way already. "Anyway what would you study?"

"Theology of course. But what then? I'd have about four years to wait."

"VSO? You'd learn practical skills there."

"S'pose."

They stopped talking as an elderly lady using a Zimmer frame was being helped along by a middle-aged lady.

"Why are we going up here?"

"We're going to the café remember mamma?"

"Why are we going to the café?"

"Because you said you wanted a coffee."

"Did I? But why is it all the way up here?"

"Well, that's where the café is you see."

"Well, why didn't you tell me?"

"I did but I expect you've forgotten." The lady smiled at them as she helped her past and said "Happy Midsummer."

"What's for supper?"

"No mamma, I was just saying Happy Midsummer to these ladies here."

"Why?"

"Because it's Midsummer's Eve."

"Well I know that!"

The lady smiled at them and mouthed 'she's got dementia' and they smiled back. "It's just up here mamma."

"What is?"

"The café."

"And do they sell coffee?"

"Yes mamma, they sell coffee. That's what cafes do?"

"Well I know that. So why are we going up here?"

"You'll see mamma, you'll see."

"But what I really want is a coffee."

"I know mamma, I know. Aren't the gardens lovely?"

"Oh it's so hot. I really need to sit down."

"Well we can sit when we get to the café."

"What café?"

"The one where we're going to get you a coffee."

"But what I really want is to sit down. Can't we sit on that bench there?"

"Of course, but I thought you wanted a coffee."

"In this heat? Of course not. Some water maybe."

They had gone past and were sat on a bench about ten metres away.

"Or care in the community?" Irma said smiling and raising her eyebrows.

"I don't think I'm that patient," Signe replied, still looking at the ladies now seated on the bench. "Poor woman, that's really hard."

"My gran got a bit like that before she died. She had short term memory loss, couldn't remember anything from one minute ago. It was really sad because she used to love reading books, but she had to stop because she couldn't remember what she'd just read in the previous paragraph so none of it made sense."

"Brutal." They sat for a minute in silence.

"Anyway, Si, what's this about your tummy not being right?"

"Oh it's probably nothing. Me being paranoid I expect. Just feels weird and I've got a lump there."

"Really? What kind of lump?"

"Well, not a lump exactly, like it's swollen."

"Let's see?"

"I can't show you here. I mean it's not very noticeable except when I've got my clothes off and stand sideways in the mirror. Then it's really obvious."

"But when you say it feels weird?"

"Well, you know for ages I felt sick all the time, after the trial and everything?"

"But I think that was just nerves Si. You were really stressed. Oh my god, I wonder if it's an ulcer. You get that with stress."

"Do you?"

"Of course. That's one of the main causes."

"But do you get a swelling?"

"I don't know."

"I was really worried it might be cancer."

"Cancer? Why?"

"Melissa's sister died of bowel cancer about three years ago. I just worry it might be something similar."

"So why haven't you been to the doctor to get it looked at?"

"I'm scared in case it is."

"God, Si, you'll be a hell of a lot more scared if it is and you've left it too late to get it treated."

"But they might not be able to treat it."

"But what if they can? Honestly Si, you've got to go to the doctor as soon as possible. If it's cancer the sooner they see you the better."

"I s'pose."

"But look, it probably isn't anyway. There's no point getting really upset when you don't even know what it is. That's why you need to find out."

"I haven't had a period since the trial either."

"Yeah, well I know why that is, because you've been so stressed. You hear that all the time, girls missing periods when they've got exams coming up and things. Did you know often athletes and dancers don't have periods at all. It's because their bodies are under so much stress from training that the body automatically decides it can't cope with periods as well. Isn't that amazing?"

"So they don't have periods at all?"

"Well I'm not sure, but they often miss them for quite a long time."

"Wow."

"Hey, what time did it say the maypole was?" Irma looked through the leaflet. "Oh yes, it's in ten minutes. We'd better get up there."

They walked past the lady with her aged mother and nodded sympathetically. She returned a resigned, tired smile. They found the site where there was a large crowd gathered around a central flat area with the long maypole lying in the middle. Preparations were being made for the lifting of it, ropes attached at one end and lying the length of it ready to be hauled on and men walking about with poles of various lengths with crooks at their ends. A woman's voice over the Tannoy was explaining how the tradition of the maypole had come about, what they were going to do and how everyone was going to help the intrepid crew to lift it by shouting in unison 'Heave' whenever it was lifted in stages.

There was a great deal of to-ing and fro-ing, checking of ropes, discussions of who was going where, until it appeared all preparations had been made and everyone was in position. The woman on the Tannoy then gave a 'one, two, three' and everyone shouted 'Heave' and the pole was raised about half a metre off the ground, in which split second a man at the head slid what looked like a little bench under the end. Some re-positioning and excited directing by the leader ensued before another 'one, two, three, heave' and the pole came up about two metres whereupon a couple of men jammed equivalent length poles with cradles at one end under to support it. More repositioning and the ritual was repeated continually with longer poles to support it at various height stages until it reached near vertical. With a final heave it was raised to its upright and slipped into the prepared hole at its base and was chocked in firmly with sledge hammers to a great cheer from the crowd.

Signe and Irma had joined in and now clapped and cheered with the rest.

"I haven't been to a big maypole raising for so long," said Signe, "for as long as I can remember we've gone off to an island or someone's cabin for the day."

"Ya, me too."

Just then the folk band started up, playing a traditional Swedish song with violins tripping and an accordion rattling an infectious, jaunty melody which some of the crowd took up, nodding and swaying in time and looking up at the high crossbar on the maypole with the traditional hoops at each end, the whole thing covered in leaves, branches and flowers.

A cordon had been quickly set up some distance from the base of the maypole to create a large square around it and a group of people in traditional costumes, just like the ones they'd seen earlier, were assembling inside. When the music stopped the announcer informed them they were in for a treat now, watching some folk dancing by the local folk dance club. They were going to do some traditional Midsummer dances which represented fertilising the ground, sowing, reaping and making bread.

Irma and Signe happily watched the display, applauding at the end of each number and joining in clapping in time for mixing and kneading the bread. It was simple stuff but heart-warmingly nostalgic.

"Right, now it's your turn," the announcer cried as the applause died after the last dance and they took away the cordon. They were invited to make a circle, or rather a number of concentric circles as there were so many of them, around the maypole. "Now of course we have to sing Små Grodona, because no Midsummer is complete without it," and she proceeded to explain the steps and gestures. Irma started laughing when she saw Signe raise her eyes to the skies saying "Not Små Grodona!"

"Come on Si, it'll be fun," and grabbed her hand as the music began and pulled her to the left singing "Små grodona, små grodona" and Signe had no option but to go along with singing "Little frogs, little frogs" too.

Then they put their hands on their heads like everyone else, singing about and imitating ears, which of course frogs don't have, and then waggling hands on their behinds representing tails, which they don't have either. By this time they were both laughing as they went hopping like frogs and could hardly join in on the oowacaca, oowacaca to imitate them croaking. When they'd done that, before they could catch their breaths and stop laughing they were being pigs, going through the same routine but now singing durf durf durf to imitate grunting. By this time they were screaming and hanging onto each other, and were completely unprepared for becoming elephants on the next round, with enormous ears, little tails and excessive trumpeting. At the end they collapsed on the grass, hugging each other in complete hysterics and gasping for breath.

This was probably the silliest of the songs, but there were others that came near, where you had to play violins of different sizes and flutes and trumpets, going around in a circle and then inevitably hopping and skipping about. They joined in most of them, crying with laughter until they were exhausted and went and sat down under a tree still giggling and shrieking.

"Oh Irm, I haven't laughed like that for years. My ribs are hurting," and Signe laughed again.

"It's good for you. You need to do it more often, it relieves tension."

"Yes, doctor."

Suddenly Irma was serious. "You will go won't you Si. Promise me."

"I promise."

"Friends' honour?"

"Friends' honour," and they clasped arms in that way they used to all those years ago.

Irma's phone bleeped a message through and she looked it out to read it. "Sorry Si, d'you mind if I phone Karl quickly?"

"Course, go ahead." Signe got hers out to check it and found a message from Melissa, 'Sorry we didn't see you to say Happy Midsummer. Didn't know you were leaving so early. Hope you're having a nice time.' Signe felt there was a touch of reproof there and could hear her tone of voice saying it. There was an uninteresting group chat, her friend Katya posting a selfie of herself in an exceptionally over-the-top, obviously bought, garland, which was so like Katya – she always had to look better than everyone else. And an email from Sister Teresa at Vardstena.

Signe was shaking by the time she finished reading and couldn't wait for Irma to finish her call.

"Irm I just got a reply from the convent. They want me to come for the summer."

"Oh Si, that's awesome. Come here," and she gave Signe a big squeeze. Signe was crying.

"I'm so happy. That's all I wanted right now."

" Wow, Happy Midsummer."

Chapter 27

"Hey, Chris, good to see you man. It's been ages. How the hell are you?" said Matt, giving his old mate a bloke-hug.

"Fine, fine. Yeah, good. How about you?"

"Yeah, I'm great. What are you drinking, beer? Lager?"

"Beer. What they got on?"

"Er, looks like Doom Bar, Young's, Adnams, well there's about eight. Oh they've got Sambrooks. You tried that?"

"No, is it good?"

"Yeah, I really like it. Battersea brewery. Really tasty."

"Okay I'll try one."

"Two Sambrooks please. Yeah, God, it's been too long Chris. What you been up to?"

"Just finished that tour with The Academy of Early Music doing Schütz, Scheidt and Schein."

"Ha ha, yeah, I heard about that. Christ. Who thought that one up? Someone said it sounded like polishing turds!"

"Yeah right. Ha ha. Well it was a bit like that; Simon was there."

"Bloody hell. Did he do any concert sober?"

"Well actually he wasn't too bad. He's going out with one of the mezzos, Sally Becton, d'you know her? No, well, she's fairly new, but she's been keeping him under control, so he was quite well behaved most of the time, except when we had a reception sponsored by Mumm champagne. Well you can imagine."

"Can't I just."

"Cheers, good to see you again. Shall we find a table upstairs? It's quieter."

They squeezed their way through the packed crowd in the cramped corridor-like bar and went up the steep narrow steps to the comparative calm and opulence of the lounge.

"I love it up here. It's always heaving down there but you can usually find a couple of chairs up here. A lot of people go to The Marquis or the Lemon Tree but I prefer The Harp. Beer's bloody brilliant."

"Very nice. So I heard you were ill back at Easter time, some dangerous infection or something. You look alright now."

Matt hesitated, then, "Chris, you're one of my oldest mates. I'm not going to lie to you, but keep it to yourself okay? It wasn't an infection."

He then told Chris all the details of the concert and the two months after it. Chris whistled and nodded, sipping his beer and rolling his eyes. When Matt had finished he exhaled through pursed lips.

"That's pretty tough. I can't believe you managed to keep a lid on it. Everyone I've talked to thinks you were very ill. Impressive." He winked knowingly.

"Well, I couldn't afford that getting round the profession. I mean, now I've been released and the sentence is revoked it's not so bad, but even so, people jump to conclusions."

"So how's it all now? How's Maggie with it?"

"Well, that's another story. Not too good really. To be honest it's a bit difficult. She was very supportive to start with but it's kind of gone a bit sour now. I dunno, something's changed. It's not like it was."

"She doesn't trust you now?"

"Yeah, probably. I think she's hurt or something. I don't know what it is, but it's not going very well. We're going on holiday in a couple of weeks, get away, try and work it out. So we'll see what happens. How's Hattie?"

"Oh she's fine. Bit full-on with the second one, but she loves it really."

"Does she miss the singing?"

"Yeah, I suppose so, but she says she'll get back to it when they're older, but for the moment she's just loving being a mum. Same again?"

"Sure, hang on I'll just finish this."

Chris shuffled off downstairs to do the honours. Matt looked out of the window at the traffic and the pedestrians adeptly avoiding it. *Two kids now. What a responsibility.* Matt thought of himself and Maggie and how free they were, how they could just decide to go and see a film or catch a show on a whim, no planning, no babysitters. He couldn't imagine it, that amount of organisation and compromise, that complete disruption to a way of living. The idea of having kids was attractive but the reality was daunting. He somehow doubted ever going down that road. Particularly with Maggie. Particularly the way things were right now.

"Here we go. Sorry it took so long, it's rammed down there."

"Yeah, it'd be better if there was more space, but that's part of the charm. Cheers."

"Cheers."

"So how's the little one doing? She must be, God, it was months ago when I came to see her in hospital."

"She's five months next Tuesday. Eighteenth of March."

Yes, I remember. It was about a week before Easter – just before I went to Gothenburg. Time flies." He took a long swig from his pint.

"Matt, we were wondering, would you be Godfather? Hattie'd like it. You're one of our oldest mates and, well, we'd be really chuffed."

Matt felt a lump in his throat. He was shocked, touched. "That's...well, I'm honoured, but, you know Chris, I'm not exactly religious. I don't go to church or anything. In fact I'm a bit the other way."

"It doesn't matter about that. You don't have to prove your faith or anything."

"No, but don't you have to undertake to help teach the child the Christian faith or something?"

"Matt, it's fairly laid back. You just agree to help to bring the child up as a Christian. You don't have to make any big commitment. It's more an honorary title than anything else."

"Wouldn't it be better to have someone who was religious?"

"Well, ideally I suppose, but Hattie really wants you to be Phoebe's godfather. She's very fond of you Matt."

"Oh well, now you put it like that, how can I refuse?" He laughed, embarrassed and moved. He adored Hattie. She was a gem and she and Chris were very special to him.

"Fantastic." Chris beamed, that childish enthusiasm breaking through his older-than-his-years face. "She'll be delighted."

They clinked glasses and drew on their pints. "So what are you up to next?"

"I've got this Bohème at the Garden starting in September. Thank god I didn't lose that."

"Did you miss out on work because of..?"

"Yeah of course. My agent had to cancel stuff. I lost a few grand."

"That's tough. Puts a hole in your bank balance."

"I actually got some compensation from the court. Not a lot, but something, a bit of a bonus."

"But Covent Garden will be brilliant. That's your first substantial role there isn't it?"

"Yeah, a bit nerve-wracking. Can't muck it up. Actually, between you and me, I'm shitting myself."

"Really? But you'll be great."

Matt paused, thinking, looked around the room briefly, but then went ahead. "Since the thing in Gothenburg and being in Wandsworth I've really been having problems. Vocally I mean. It's like the top's gone."

"Really?"

"Yup. I mean, not really gone, but it's kind of cracky and unreliable. It's like it's an effort whereas before it was easy. I dunno, maybe it's tension with Maggie or something, but I'm scared it may just crack when I'm at the Garden. I mean, Colline's not high, but I can't risk fucking up, you know?"

"Maybe you've got an underlying infection or something. Sometimes you can have a bug that hangs around and you're not really aware of it."

"I went and saw a throat specialist a few weeks ago because I was really worried. Well actually my teacher Tom suggested it. They put a camera down my neck. Said there wasn't much wrong they could see. One of the chords a bit dried out and red. Just said to drink more water, which wasn't helpful. So, I don't know what's going on, but it's a bit hairy."

"And it's pretty much the same all the time?"

"Yup, doesn't change as far as I can tell." Matt forced a smile and took a pull of his pint.

"Right. Worrying." Chris drank thoughtfully. "Look, Matt, you may not want to do this, but have you thought of going to someone alternative? No wait, let me explain, it may sound whacky but honestly there's a woman we've been to, well Hattie really, and she's, well, she's amazing."

"Reflexology or some new wave stuff is it?"

"Matt, just listen. I know you're a bloody confirmed sceptic but for once open your narrow scientific brain to another possibility."

"Oh god, well I'm going to need another drink if that's the case. You on for another?"

"Go on then."

Matt took his glass and left Chris still nursing half a pint. Somehow he'd sunk his pretty quickly. As he negotiated his way to the bar he felt Chris was going to go on one of his preachy alternative-living crusades. He loved Chris and Hattie dearly, but they really were a bit up themselves with organic food, homeopathic remedies and a puritanical avoidance of anything potentially containing toxins. The fact that they lived in London where the nitrogen –dioxide levels were one of the highest in the world didn't seem to bother them. He'd have to just grin and bear it and let Chris have his say.

"They ran out of Sambrooks so I got Fiddler's Elbow. It's a bit pokey but they gave me a taste and I thought it was pretty brilliant."

"I'll finish this first, thanks."

"Go on then, persuade me I've got to go to some crank who'll charge me a fortune for rubbing some plant juice on my larynx and chanting incantations."

"Bugger off Matt, you know I'm only trying to help. I'll shut up and you can fuck off if you want."

"Nah, go on, I'm only kidding. I'll give it a whirl. I might as well try anything, I'm getting a bit desperate."

Chris finished the Sambrooks. "You know Hattie's had that psoriasis for, well, as long as I've known her, which is ages? Well, after Alfie was born it got better for a bit, almost disappeared. Then when she stopped breast-feeding it came back again, but worse. Then she got asthma as well and ended up on an inhaler. We didn't want to go down that route, you know, but honestly she was struggling and I tell you she eventually relied on that thing. Anyway, when she got pregnant with Phoebe we thought she'd improve like before with the hormones flying around and everything, but she didn't. If anything the asthma was worse with the extra weight and being out of breath. She'd done everything, cut out lactose, gluten, all that kind of stuff. She had remedies from the homeopath, but nothing touched it. Anyway, someone suggested this woman; she's a kinesiologist."

"A what?"

"Kinesiologist."

"What the fuck's that? Sounds like a bloody geography thing or astro-physics or something."

"Shut up and listen. You might learn something."

"Oh, certainly Professor Thomash, pardon me for interrupting your letcher."

"Look Matt, stop taking the piss. If you're really not interested, forget it."

"No no no, come on, I'm only kidding; so she's a kinologist."

"Kinesiologist. It's body balancing. Anyway, Hattie went to her and after a couple of sessions it had completely gone. Like a bloody miracle. No psoriasis, no asthma. She didn't even need the inhaler anymore."

"Really? Brilliant. And what does she do, massage? Acupuncture stuff?"

"No it's body-balancing. Balancing the energy in your body. Like the Qi, you know, in Chinese medicine they talk about the Qi? The energy flowing round your body in the meridians."

"Like yoga stuff."

"Yeah, it's like freeing the energy to flow properly. Apparently very often the energy gets trapped, won't flow, and when that happens it has a knock on effect on other things. She said that the reason Hattie had developed psoriasis in the first place was when she had been doing her GCSEs. She'd been in a very competitive academic school, very high achieving, and although Hattie's not stupid she's not, you know, Oxbridge material. But there were tons of kids there getting straight A stars and that was kind of what was expected. Hattie was into the arts – music, painting, you know, practical stuff – but she was expected to get all these A star grades. It stressed her out and the energy got stuck and the body developed psoriasis."

"Really?"

"And Hattie's had this GCSE stress all this time, until now? That's a bit unbelievable isn't it?"

"I know. It sounds crazy doesn't it. But apparently if you never get over a trauma thing it can stay with you, then whenever you have a stress situation again it feeds into the unresolved trauma situation and compounds it. So Hat's been carrying this trauma, like low-level, permanently and then it pops up whenever she gets stressed. Of course, having two kids is pretty stressful and when I'm away it's all down to her."

"But she hasn't got it anymore? It's just gone?"

"Yeah, like a kind of purging."

"Christ! That's a bit medieval isn't it? A bit shit, shite and shine! Oh no, it'd be earlier, Praetorius or someone."

"You should try it, Matt. Sounds like your energy might be blocked. Could be the stress with Maggie, or the court case. Or just being generally stressed. You know, what you do is stressful, up there singing solo stuff. Why d'you think I stuck to consort work? Less stressful, more relaxing, not so much pressure."

"Yeah, well you always were a lazy bastard."

"Hey!"

"Yes you were. Voice like yours, you should be singing lyric tenor roles all over the place. Bloody waste."

"Wouldn't have suited me Matt. Couldn't have hacked the pressure. No I'm happier with a quieter life. I really like the choir work. God, trying to sing all that Rossini stuff. You've got to be top of your game all the time, particularly as a tenor."

"You'd have been brilliant, voice like yours. Look, are you having another?"

"I shouldn't. What's the time? Bloody hell, Hat'll kill me."

"Oh, go on, we haven't been out for ages. She won't mind. She's very fond of me remember?"

"Not fond of you leading me astray."

"I'll take that as a yes."

Two hours later they were both pissed as farts. Matt was telling Chris he really loved him. Chris was telling Matt he was the most beautiful man he knew. Matt said only a beautiful man would say that. Chris insisted Matt was his brother, and he'd always be his brother and no one could take that away from him. Matt asserted that he'd kill anyone who came between them because their friendship was....was eternal and everlasting and...and...

"Impregnable." Chris hazarded.

"Indistru'tible." Matt emphasised.

"Incredible."

"Indiscribal."

"Hey, Matt, you bootifal man, I fuckin' love you. You take care, ri'? An' I'll test you tha' number termora."

"The Kino whateversheis."

"Yeah yeah, Kineishologisht. Honis', 'sbrilliant, really."

"Okay, You ta'care. Bye."

They wobbled away in different directions, Matt vaguely in the direction of Holborn, Chris to Charing Cross. It was only when he got on the central line that Matt realised how drunk he was. The carriage was swaying somewhat more than the usual rolling of the tracks dictated. He only just managed to get out at Leyton having been rocked into a fitful slumber and woken with a jolt just before the doors closed.

God he hadn't been this drunk since Chris's stag night, when he'd woken up in bed with...Chris!

****

Matt sat in the reception of the beauty parlour sipping a complimentary coffee and looking across at the various ladies with bits of silver foil in their hair, plastic bags over their heads with goo underneath or rubber swim caps with holes in and tufts of hair sticking through. *God, what they go through to get a look.* Another lady was at the nail bar in deep conversation with the beautician who was buffing and polishing. It was a female domain and he felt distinctly out of place and wondered what the hell he was doing there.

He'd had second thoughts that morning about whether to cancel the session, which had come up so unexpectedly soon on a cancelation when he had rung the afternoon after his drunken evening with Chris. In a rash moment he'd thought 'Oh well, what the hell, might as well give it a try' and had been booked in for the next day. Now he was thinking it was a very bad idea and was feeling very uncomfortable in this emporium to female beauty.

What was he doing allowing himself to be taken in by this voodoo stuff? It just showed how freaked out he'd got about his voice that he was prepared to go against his reason and waste money on some crank therapy. But it was too late now, a tall, athletic woman in a short white medic's jacket and black trousers had appeared from the back of the room and was showing out a man who looked in his late fifties.

"I'll see you in a month Mr Jefferson. You take care." After conferring with the receptionist briefly she came across to Matt with an extended hand. "Hello Mr Chamberlain."

"Matt please."

"Hello Matt, I'm Jackie. Let's go upstairs."

They went through the door at the back of the salon and up some steep stairs to a small room with a treatment table diagonally across the cramped space.

"Right, first we have to do some house-keeping I'm afraid. I need you to fill in this form so that I have all your information and medical history. It's useful to me and also a requirement of the Association of Complementary Practitioners."

Matt took a cursory look around the room whilst she found the form and a biro, noticing the drawings of the human body with strange lines dissecting it, symbols of yin and yang, a representation of the Buddha and various crystals and rocks on a shelf. *This is such a bad idea.* He duly filled out the form.

"So why have you come to see me? Is it a specific problem?"

"Well, to be honest I'm not much of a believer in alternative therapies, but a friend persuaded me to come because I'm having problems with my voice. I'm a classical singer and just lately my voice hasn't been acting normally, the range is limited and it feels tight and constricted. I've been to a throat specialist who looked down and said the chords were a bit dried out and red, but didn't have any answers to the problem. Said it might be good to have some speech therapy. Huh!"

"Okay, well let's have a look. If you'd take your shoes off and jump up on the table."

Whilst he complied she lit a candle and switched on some soft background music - classical orchestral, nothing loud or fast (was it Vivaldi?), probably from a collection of 'Classics to relax to'. It was getting worse and Matt could feel his resistance mounting, but he was here now, lying on a table with a rolled towel beneath his knees staring at the ceiling.

Jackie then described the rather weird therapy she was going to do and reassured him not to be alarmed if she did some rather strange gestures. She told him she was going to test the flow of energy in his body by using a muscle in his shoulder. She would hold his arm up out straight and he had to push up and against her whenever she said. They did this a few time; sometimes his arm felt strong and he could push against her, other times his arm inexplicably collapsed at the elbow and he couldn't push. It was like he suddenly had no strength.

"God that's weird, how does it do that?"

"I'm asking your body questions and depending on whether your arm remains strong or not I get my answer."

After a bit she put his arm down and placed it under the thin blanket she'd draped over him. Then she did some hand and arm movements over his body, not touching him, but circling around and pointing. She then placed her hand on his shoulder standing on one leg sideways to the bed, her other leg raised and bent at the knee which she seemed to push with her other hand. She did this a few times, nodding and gesturing, before turning the other way and apparently repeating the process.

"Well, your energy is badly blocked in places." She gestured some more, nodding and pointing to different parts of his torso.

Matt felt himself getting frustrated now. This really was a load of bollocks. How could she possibly know his energy was blocked by doing all this totally bizarre stuff, pointing and nodding. What had he paid for this? Sixty quid? Bloody waste of money.

"Don't resist me Matt. You're putting up barriers."

Shit, that's freaky. Does she know what I'm thinking?

"You had a severe trauma four months ago. You haven't got over this yet, you haven't resolved this."

Four months ago? That was the concert, the arrest, the police cell.

"You've been under a lot of stress because of that trauma. You were in a bad place for a long time. You're better now, but you're still carrying this trauma with you. You haven't resolved it in your mind, so you can't let go of it and it's blocking your energy."

God this is just so weird. How can she know all this?

"I'm going to work on this trauma and see if we can shift it." She moved around and sat down behind his head so he couldn't see her. "I'm going to go into your sub-conscious *–what? –* I just want you to think of a peaceful scene, like you're sitting in the park on a beautiful sunny day, completely relaxed. Just let your mind forget everything else and focus on the scene. I'm just going to place this crystal above your third eye, *– my what? God this is crazy –* the space between your eyebrows. So just relax and concentrate on that picture in your head."

Her voice was soporific and he almost felt himself nodding off. He envisaged Victoria Park, sitting on a bench and looking at a bank of tulips nodding in a gentle breeze backed by dense shrubs and low branched trees just unfurling in leaf. He felt calm and collected, content.

"Now think of the event four months ago, what happened, how you felt afterwards..." He felt a sudden surge of anxiety, anger, panic. "Whoa, that's it alright. Now, hang on to that. Focus on how

 you felt. What was your overriding concern, can you remember? What was the most important thing you felt afterwards, your biggest fear maybe?"

Fear? Getting found out. That I'd kissed her. The shame? The embarrassment? I don't know. Oh yes "My career, I was terrified my career would be over. That would be it, finished."

"Okay I want you to focus on that fear, bring it down to the front of your mind, think of exactly how terrible you felt, how anxious, how frightened. Now move yourself away from it, imagine it's fading so that it doesn't affect you anymore."

That's really weird. I can't concentrate on it anymore, it's fading, disappearing.

"Good. Take a deep breath and exhale. Good. Feel better?"

"Like a weight lifted off me. Really weird – like I feel lighter, not weighted down." His voice purred in his throat, the pitch had dropped and it felt free and loose.

"Yes, I think we've subdued that a bit now." She came back beside him now and did more pointing and waving, more knee-jerks and nodding. Matt lay there trying not to smile. "Yes, that's much better, much better." She was silent for some moments, pointing and nodding all the time. "You're a singer now because you need to express yourself through your voice. Previously you worked with your hands."

"I'm sorry?" Matt didn't know if he'd heard her correctly.

"This life you need to sing. This is your bliss. In your last life it was different, you constructed physically, expressed yourself through your hands. You made things. This is what I'm getting."

"You mean, you can read my past life?"

"No, I feel an echo of your experience, an outline if you like which suggests ideas to me. It can help to analyze conditions in your present life. We sometimes are affected by experiences from a past life, they can colour our present experience. Your experience in your previous life wasn't resolved, you didn't have time. The experience was cut short I think, so, if you like, there is unfinished business."

By this time Matt didn't know what to think. It sounded completely outrageous and like so much charlatanism, but at the same time he was feeling so much better.

"Right," he said.

"But..." she was still, eyes closed, concentrating, "this time you will be rewarded. It's already happening."

Despite himself he said "What is?"

"Your life ended abruptly before. I think you will find completion in this experience."

Sounds like George – 'this experience, this plane'. I can't believe I'm hearing this, let alone listening to it.

Jackie moved back to sit behind his head again. "I'm going to try to clear a bit more of this trauma. Just relax, let your mind go blank if you can, or think of the park."

She remained still, cupping his head with one hand and holding the crystal above his forehead for a long time with the other. He felt increasingly light-headed and became aware of a tingling feeling as if static electricity was concentrated on his forehead and the hairs there were magnetised upwards. He closed his eyes. He tried to relax his mind but found himself prompted by the recurring thought that this was totally ridiculous and so much mumbo-jumbo which he didn't believe in. It was against every scientific principle and he felt ashamed he'd allowed himself to be drawn in. Science didn't allow for this. His mind wandered over chemical properties, physics lessons on force and gravity, the motions of the stars and planets, Hubble and beyond. He felt himself moving through space, skirting the moon and out across the solar system. The Milky Way opened towards him as he accelerated past Saturn in one of those filmic space sequences. Other solar systems sped towards him, colossal suns flashing by, gas giants bearing down on him so enormous until they disappeared in an instant. The Crab Nebula's gaseous web magnified exponentially, engulfing him for the few seconds that his increasing velocity allowed, before he had seared through it and was shooting with increasing velocity inexorably faster and faster. And the faster his passage the more stars filled his view until his vision was whited out with the brightness and he broke through a blinding white barrier.

He was travelling so fast that he was stationary. There was suddenly no point of reference. No light, no stars, no anything. It was impossibly dark. He couldn't detect anything but what he was in was full and dense with matter. It was a void teeming with the essence and intensity of everything. He was being compressed by a vast pressure but inside him there was an equally enormous force pushing outwards so that he was suspended in a state of stasis, balanced in an equal continuum, in a force field so great it didn't exist.

Everything was there, but there was nothing; all light, all darkness; all knowledge and absolute ignorance; all power and all fragility; all matter and anti-matter. It was totally terrifying and sublimely comforting. All opposites combined to form the completeness of everything in its totality. He comprehended it yet was completely ignorant of it. It stilled him.

He opened his eyes with a start, the light in the room blinding him.

"My goodness, you were fast asleep."

He wrestled with reality, visual cues booting up his memory banks as he dragged his consciousness back to the now. He felt exhausted and strangely renewed, his skin tingling with electricity.

"I feel I've been asleep for hours."

"About five minutes, that's all." Jackie went and wrote at the small desk by the window. "You will likely feel very tired for the rest of the day. This kind of treatment, going into the sub-conscious, is very tiring. You should try to rest if possible."

"I don't think that will be difficult. I feel absolutely wrecked."

She smiled. "Yes, we went quite deep."

Matt got off the table and put on his shoes. He was wobbly, light-headed. It was only with care that he negotiated the steep stairs and emerged into the salon. He thanked Jackie and paid at the front desk.

Outside on the pavement he felt strangely lost, like when you come back from a holiday and can hardly relate to normal life again. He watched, zombie-like, as people went about their business, vehicles passed in different directions, a dog fussed on a lead, and none of it seemed relevant or joined up. All this activity seemed superfluous, unnecessary, like so much irrelevance.

The next day there was a letter.

Dear Mr Chamberlain,

You do not know how badly I feel about the trial and how you have been in prison all this time. I cannot hope you will ever forgive me because I said you attack me and you probably never understand the reason. Please let me explain.

I could not remember what happen to me that night. My friends give me alcohol and I believe I am drunk when I saw you on the deck of the boat. I don't know why, but after I fainted and I woke up again I thought you were somebody else and I am very confused and don't know what is happening. When I understand, I push you and I have the hysterics because of the shock.

Then my friend asks me if you attack me and I say yes because I am ashamed and confused. After this I still can't remember what happened and then they make a case for the law court and I have to answer what they say to me.

It was only in the trial I begin to remember and then it is too late and I cannot say what I think I remember because it is not all of it. A long time after the trial I remember everything and I know you did not force me. I know I was guilty to kiss you too, and I think you are believing I want more than this. I think you mistake me and so it's not your fault only.

I went to the court again and I told them what I remember now and of course they see that it is not your fault. I ask you please to forgive me and want you to know I have been so unhappy about all this since the trial. I know I have done you a great wrong and this has been an awful experience for you. I pray for you and pray you can find it in your heart to forgive me and you can go back into your life and forget this bad time.

Please know I never mean to hurt you, but I was confused and not strong enough to stop what happened.

With good wishes,
Signe Larsson

Matt turned the letter over to see if there was anything written on the back which, as he knew there wasn't, made him wonder why he had. He looked at the writing again, soft curving letters, rather childish, naïve.

"Who's it from?" Maggie called from the kitchen.

Matt wished she hadn't been here when the post had arrived as she wouldn't have needed to know about it. "It's from Signe Larsson, you know, the girl in Gothenburg."

There was a pause before Maggie said "What does she want?"

"You can read it; she's just apologising."

"Apologising? Huh!" Maggie came into the room with buttered toast and her coffee. She plonked herself down with a sharp look at Matt. He offered her the letter which she didn't take, so he let it fall on the table. "How does she know your address?"

"It was forwarded by Peter. She must have Googled my name and the agency came up. It's easy enough to do. He's forwarded mail from people before."

"What you gonna do? Reply?"

"Course not. I don't want anything to do with her." Matt sensed a small shift in the cold front across the table.

"Don't think she feels the same. Sounds like she's wanting to get involved again."

"Mags, we weren't involved. You still don't get it do you. There was nothing, it was a moment of madness, okay? We were out of our heads, intoxicated."

"Well, never heard of anyone apologising after a court case before." She was immediately busy on her phone, reading messages or scrolling through Facebook.

Conversation over, Matt thought, and cleared his plate and mug to the sink. Why was all conversation with Maggie barbed these days? It made the flat claustrophobic. And there wasn't even the satisfaction of sex to compensate. He wished he had another 'away job' imminent as opposed to this holiday. And actually, yes, he did feel like replying to the letter. Its honesty and humility touched him. After everything that had happened and despite how he'd hated her for what she had caused, he was still extremely attracted to the girl in the audience.

But it was stupid even to consider, and pushing the letter and the girl away in his mind, he concentrated on organising his day.

Chapter 28

"So when did you begin to notice this swelling?" Doctor Wikstrom was taking notes on her computer.

"Well just the past couple of weeks I suppose. But I had the sickness feeling for a long time before that."

"But you don't feel sick now?"

"No, not really. It just feels funny sometimes. Like it's different."

"Okay, apart from this are you feeling alright, no other symptoms?"

"No."

"Periods normal?"

Signe stopped as a sudden premonition presented itself. *But no it's impossible.* "Well I…I haven't had a period recently."

"Really?"

"No. not since…it happened."

"The attack, now let me see, when was that? Ah yes back in March. Right."

"My friend said that's probably because of shock. Some people have a shock and they miss a period." Signe was agitated.

"Well yes, that can happen, but I'd have thought you'd be menstruating normally again by now. This was three months ago. Have you done a pregnancy test?"

Signe reeled. "No. That would be impossible. I don't have a boyfriend….I don't…" she struggled to find the words, then confidently and with some pride "I'm still a virgin."

"Yes I can see the report here, no penetration, but I think it might be good to rule that out completely before we think about other things. Let's have a look at you. If you just take your skirt off and hop up on the couch I'll have a feel."

She rubbed her hands together briskly then prodded and pushed deeply into Signe's abdomen, who was shocked how hard she pressed and had to stop herself gasping.

"Well that feels pretty much like a baby to me. Have your breasts been sensitive?"

Signe couldn't grasp what she was saying. "Sorry?"

"Have you noticed your breasts are sensitive, maybe a bit swollen?"

"I don't know, maybe," she whispered; she was hardly hearing this, there was so much white noise in her head.

"Well I think that really confirms it Signe, but we'll just do a quick urine test which will settle it for sure." She went over to a drawer and pulled out a packet. "If you go to the loo at the end of the corridor and pee on this tester we'll know for certain. It only takes a drop to register."

Signe was panicked. It was ridiculous, she knew she wasn't pregnant because that was proved when she was investigated after it happened.

Trembling she took the packet down to the toilet and locked herself in. She opened the envelope and put the length of paper under her but although she knew there was pee there it refused to come. She tried pushing but elicited merely a small fart. She felt like crying. She took a deep breath and blew out a juddering breath. She had to relax. That's the problem with relaxing, she thought, you can't force yourself to; it's like people saying 'don't worry'.

She sat there for what seemed like ages and at last felt a thin trickle seep out and hastily moved the paper to catch it. Thankful that she'd managed it, but now terrified of the result, she returned to Dr Wikstrom's surgery.

"Yes, you're pregnant." Dr Wikstrom said immediately.

Signe couldn't speak. It was impossible and obviously the test was wrong, but still she was shocked. "But that's impossible," she managed.

"Well, these things don't lie I'm afraid. This registers something called HCG, that's Human Chorionic Gonadotrophin, which is the pregnancy hormone in your urine. Naturally this is only present if you are pregnant so I'm afraid there's no doubt."

"But maybe that particular test strip is faulty or something, I mean I can't be pregnant. I haven't been with anyone."

"Yes, well I agree it would seem to be impossible, but you are definitely pregnant. You have all the symptoms and the HCG test doesn't lie. Here are some tissues. Now look there's nothing to worry about. We can deal with this and sort you out."

Signe was trying to sort herself out right now and it was a few seconds before she could blurt out "But I don't understand, how is it possible? I haven't slept with anyone."

"Well, tell me about the rape. I see from the report he didn't penetrate you. I'm sorry I know it's probably painful to bring all this up again, but we need to find an explanation for you. Did he ejaculate even though he didn't enter you?"

Signe was trying so hard not to cry, squeezing the sodden tissue in her hands which she clasped together.

"They said there was semen, on my clothes, yes."

"And was this in the vicinity of the vagina?"

Signe shrugged "I don't know, they didn't say exactly. He was, on top of me, about to….I felt him…"

"What did you do immediately afterwards?"

"I was screaming."

"Yes, I'm sure, it was such a shock. But did you wipe yourself, try to wipe away the semen?"

Signe struggled to think. "No, I don't think so…Irma said I was protecting myself. That's right, she said my hand was 'clamped' so tightly on my…on me, that she could hardly move it. I was hysterical."

The doctor's face displayed comprehension, her lips pressed together and her head nodding.

"I'm afraid that sounds like the explanation. You see, I think he must have ejaculated very close to the vagina and then you grasped yourself and held on tight to protect yourself. There have been cases, very rare admittedly, where sperm has travelled into the vagina from the outside and across the hymen. Unfortunately by holding your hand tight over your vagina you must have inadvertently helped this process, possibly pushing the sperm into the entrance."

Now the tears came.

"I'm so sorry Signe, I just wanted us to have a logical explanation for how this happened. It's important that you know the mechanics so you don't think this is some kind of magic. It's an unfortunate series of events and you were really unlucky that it resulted in pregnancy."

"But when I was examined they didn't say this might happen. They said I was intact," Signe wailed.

"I know, well, again, it's a very rare occurrence. It's extremely unlikely to happen and I imagine the investigating doctor never thought of that possibility. Honestly Signe, I've never come across it, I only remember reading of such cases when I was at medical school."

"What am I going to do?"

"Look, there's nothing to worry about. We have teenage girls, unfortunately, getting pregnant all the time when they don't mean to. The abortion service is very efficient and discreet. No one needs to know, just you and me. And as you know, there is complete patient confidentiality, your family never needs to know unless you want to tell them. You're young and healthy and you'll recover in no time at all, you'll hardly notice it."

Signe was shocked at the speed of this presumption and immediately wanted to resist it. She hated the thought of her body being violated in this way. But the alternative…

"Look Signe, I don't want to force you to make a decision, but we need to get this sorted quickly before the pregnancy proceeds any further."

"I'm catholic."

Dr Wikstrom's manner changed abruptly. "Of course, you'll need a little time to consider. But there are lots of support networks for young mums too, so you'll never be on your own. Look, we've gone over time and I have other patients waiting. Here's my direct line if you want to talk, and here's the number for the abortion clinic, which I suggest you ring as soon as possible if you decide to go ahead. Also here's the number for the family support group. They don't just support you when you have a family they offer general friendly support and advice if you need to talk about anything."

"Thank you."

"Now look, this is a big decision. Please talk to friends and family if you can. You don't want to be making these decisions on your own. Depending on your decision we can get a scan done very soon to see if everything's okay or so you can know the sex if you want. It's up to you. And as I said, I'm always here. Goodbye."

Signe didn't know where to go, what to do. For a few minutes she stood outside the clinic completely stunned and unable to make any decision. The world looked the same as it had half an hour ago when she had entered the building, but it was totally different. The her who had walked in had been worried about possibly having cancer, a tumour, a fibroid, some weird medical complication. The her standing here now was carrying a baby, a child. She was a mother.

She put her hands to her belly and gently cupped it, as if by physicalising the idea it would help her mentally grasp the concept. It was incredible, magical. Dr Wikstrom had said that explaining it mechanically, as she'd put it, would stop it being a mystery. But it **was** a mystery, a miracle. A miracle which totally ruined her life, all her plans, her invitation from Vardstena, her taking of Holy Orders.

Why? Why should this happen now, just when everything seemed to be sorting itself out? The summer had been looking terrible until that email, when all her dreams had been fulfilled and she'd been to church and thanked God for this gift, this dream job at the convent. And now this. How could He let this happen? How could He play with her like that? It was brutal.

She was still standing there she realised and started walking to avoid appearing weird and attracting attention. It didn't matter where she walked, she had to move on, somewhere. As she walked she felt calmer. It was doing something that helped to ease the tension, the regular rhythm of her legs releasing held muscles.

"Why?" she asked herself again, out loud this time. After all her devotion, her prayers, her focus on a life of service and contemplation, why had God thrown this back at her? What had she done wrong? Where had she fallen short of His expectations?

It was all too hard, this life she'd wanted. She obviously wasn't good enough for this task. Otherwise what was the message He was sending her? Showing her the way, encouraging her to take it, rewarding her with the email but then immediately smashing her dreams. Pregnant! What did He mean her to understand?

It must be a punishment, for that transgression. That was it. When she had wanted him, when she had encouraged him and given in to that overwhelming urge, that exquisite physical pleasure that had swarmed over her body and engulfed her with such passion. That was her weakness which God was punishing now. Punishing with a child which she must now decide what to do with. To either destroy or bring into the world, as a single mother, an adopted parentless mother of sixteen. *Oh God, how cruel a cross you give me and me so weak and unprepared to bear it.*

She turned absent-mindedly down another road, unaware of where she was going, not seeing her surroundings, just walking.

A mother at sixteen. She couldn't bear the thought. What would her family say, how could it work if she kept it? She obviously couldn't, but this was a life she was talking about. Life that God had placed in her womb, literally. Because, yes, she was still a virgin.

And then it hit her. The enormous realisation, the bare undeniable truth struck her. But was this complete fantasy or was this God's true purpose? Was this what He was trying to tell her? She started to go over the facts.

He revealed Himself to her in the perfection of the Passion on Good Friday. Through that sublime interaction with Him as the singer in the concert, when it was like she had seen into his very soul and His Passion had been revealed to her. When she'd met him on the deck and she'd felt such overpowering passion. When she had caused him such grief by committing him to prison and then knowing she had to fight for his release.

And the other signs He had shown her, the dreams. When she had been picked out by the angel to do God's work; when she'd had the nightmare but then been shown God's purpose for her in finding the church which had appeared out of the forest. Her duty to resist the snake, which she had done again on the deck, but God had still impregnated her with His Holy Spirit, in a miracle, an almost impossible occurrence that showed His purpose. They were all signs. And the email also, showing her that her way was with God, He was welcoming her to serve in His church, but then revealed her true destiny, to bear His child again for His second coming.

The truth was almost crushing when she truly grasped the enormity of it. She, Signe Larsson, of all the possible women in the world, had been chosen by God for this honour, the highest possible honour any woman could dream of. To bear His Blessed child through a virgin birth. It was the final sign, a summation of the signs He had sent her. How slow she had been to read them, but now that she had she was filled with wonder and gratitude and humility. *Behold the handmaid of the Lord.*

She stopped abruptly and crossed herself, falling to her knees and praising God for His mercy and begging forgiveness for her unworthiness. How could she have doubted His intention, not have understood His purpose?

Abortion! The very thought gave her a panic that God might take away this gift because of her temptation even to consider such a thing. Abortion?

No one, but no one, was going to take this baby away from her.

Chapter 29

The acoustics of the Opéra Comique in Paris reverberated to the brilliant clear harmonics of her burnished soprano. The honed tones carried Matt back to that Passion seven or so months before when he'd first witnessed that thrilling sound and been drugged by its siren allure. The subject matter then was tragic, whereas now it was flippant, but again that voice captured his heart and quickened his pulse.

She was magnificent, born for the stage and it for her. Matt was lost in that simple delight of being in a theatre and being transported out of yourself by a witty production and irresistibly chirpy music. The frisson for him was knowing the leading lady and wondering whether the complementary ticket she'd left him for the opening night of Offenbach's 'La Belle Hélène' promised more entertainment than just the performance indicated. He couldn't help hoping so, especially now, watching her neat, petite torso twisting effortlessly across the stage, then stopping as she flashed her eyes provocatively at the audience. Were those looks for him? Did that coquettish tilt of the head presage an intimacy he'd long desired? It was so tempting to believe so. Although rationally he admitted she was performing for the whole audience, she would be aware of his presence and know he'd be watching her every move, so he indulged his fantasy.

Oh Caterina, what is it about you that I desire so much? You press all the right buttons.

Afterwards, waiting at the stage door, Matt couldn't believe how ridiculously excited he was. His heart was pounding with anticipation and his palms were sweaty. He felt like a teenager about to meet his pop idol. There was quite a crowd and he forced his way through saying 'Excusez moi s'il vous plait, excusez moi' and informed the stage doorman that Mlle Jokela was expecting him. This paean to the social graces spoke on the phone for a few seconds then without looking at Matt, announced "Mlle Jokela vous attends. Chambre deux, premier étage."

When he reached the top of the stairs there was a throng spilling out of a dressing room with loud laughs, hugging, air-kisses and general sycophancy. Matt stood back, taking in the scene. She was dressed in a navy negligee presumably between taking off her costume and dressing in her usual clothes. Although it was obvious the stocking she'd had on her head under her wig had only just been removed, her hair managed to look elegant behind the Alice band. She had removed her stage make-up and must have been in the process of applying moisturiser when she was interrupted, but as opposed to looking washed out her skin was radiant, flushed with the excitement and euphoria of a triumph and in doing what she loved best. At that moment Matt would have given good money to have all these people de-materialised.

After a few minutes what looked to Matt like the business end of the admirers – agents, director, coaches, producer etc – left having heaped their laudations on their star, leaving a mix of hangers-on.

"Matthew, come in, come in. How lovely to see you." She gave him a huge hug on tip toes and he buried his head into the intense perfume of her neck. That scent hit his senses again, flooding his nerves with tingling passion on top of the adrenalin, and his body responded with that well-known desire.

"You were magnificent Caterina, truly amazing. You're just so right for the stage. I understand what you said in Gothenburg; this is who you are."

She beamed a smile so ravishing, eyes brimming with happiness, that if it hadn't been for the small audience in the room, he would have kissed her unashamedly.

"I'm so happy to be back, Matthew. You can't know what it means to me. This is my friend Matthew who's a wonderful singer. These are my special Paris fan-club," and she laughed a bell arpeggio of sheer joy. They all laughed and cheered.

There followed introductions and small talk with her fans. In halting French Matt summoned up his limited vocabulary and strung sentences together with desperate grammar and worse conjugation. *Why are we Brits so terrible at languages?*

It soon became obvious that Caterina needed to dress and the fans began taking their leave, Matt holding back deliberately. When they'd gone Caterina took his hands.

"Matthew, it's so good to see you. You're at The Bastille?"

"Yes, Tosca. We've just started rehearsals."

"That's wonderful. We can see lots of each other." Her eyes searched his. *Does she mean what I'm thinking?*

"That would be brilliant."

"I'd have suggested dinner tonight, but I have to go for a meal with everyone. It's all been booked, the sponsors there, you know, the usual thing."

"Of course," he hoped his voice didn't betray his disappointment, but her next words suggested she'd detected it.

"Don't worry, what about tomorrow night? My next show's not til two day's time."

"That would be fantastic. I'd love to."

"Where are you staying?"

"Oh it's just an apartment in Montmartre, not far from the Moulin Rouge."

"Ah, you can catch a show after your performance." She winked mischievously. "Look, I'll text you tomorrow and we'll go for dinner." She gave his hands another squeeze and then reached up and kissed him briefly full on the lips and pulled away. He immediately grabbed her shoulders and drew her to him with muscular intensity and kissed her passionately. She didn't resist but, responded with kittenish coyness.

"Matthew!" she said with mock severity, "what **are** you doing?"

"Just thanking you for a wonderful evening and making sure you don't forget you have a date tomorrow."

"Well, you never know, I might change my mind," she teased.

"Ciao bella."

"Tschüss." She blew a kiss with beautifully pouted lips.

There's a romantic notion that people who fall in love don't feel the ground beneath their feet; they walk on air. Matt wasn't aware that this happened to him after he left Caterina; on the contrary, he wasn't aware of anything. In fact, when he reached his apartment he was aware that he had no recollection of his journey from the Opéra Comique to Montmartre. It was a blur. His initial deflation on learning that Caterina was engaged that evening had been immediately banished by the overpowering anticipation of the promised rendezvous the following evening.

****

Matt arrived at the restaurant far too early. He hadn't wanted to be late and this combined with his excitement had led him to leave a ridiculous amount of time to take the few stops in the Metro from Pigalle to change lines to get to the Madeleine. The restaurant was up a back street, a venue only Parisians knew and guarded jealously, Caterina had said. It was her favourite restaurant introduced to her by a French conductor and she insisted on treating him – her invitation, her night. How could he refuse?

Having located the restaurant, which looked a bit shoddy he thought - run-down paintwork and smoked windows which didn't promise an attractive interior - he walked into the square where a Grecian temple loomed before him. It was totally incongruous, perfect lines of Corinthian columns running the length and width of a pediment-fronted roof, an Athenian archetype if ever there was, plonked in the middle of nineteenth century Paris and illuminated on all sides by an impressive array of floodlights. He walked round to one end, the front as it transpired, and read 'L'Eglise de la Madeleine' on a placard on the railing. So, the church of Mary Magdalene, the whore whom Jesus saved. Or was she a whore?

What was that he'd read somewhere about that being a slur that the later church had added for some reason to discredit her? Which didn't make much sense when she had been canonised as one of His disciples? But then that was after she had been 'saved' by her Lord. And then there was that theory that she had been His wife, and even that they'd had children; the blood line of Christ, the Merovingian dynasty, the supposed secret blood line through the French throne. It was all so wonderfully fanciful and conspiratorially attractive in its potential to topple the pillars of traditional belief.

Matt perambulated the square, watching Paris go about its evening business; waiters wiping down outside tables under the glow of overhead heaters, people window shopping in the halo of shop lights, a man walking a Pomeranian which insisted on stopping at every bollard, couples wandering idly arm in arm. Yes, there was no denying it, Paris was a quintessentially romantic city. Or was it just the mood he was in, on tenterhooks with the imminent delight of Caterina all to himself?

At last the bright digits on his phone declared it was nearly eight o'clock, so he made his way back along the now familiar streets and arrived outside the restaurant at three minutes to. He wondered whether she had arrived punctually and was already inside or whether he preceded her. He decided to go in.

"Er, bon soir, est Mlle Jokela arrivé? Elle a réservé une table à huit heures." *Was that right?*

"S'il vous plait, m'sieur." The waiter indicated for Matt to follow him without the hint of a smile or greeting.

Caterina wasn't there. He was placed at a table at the far end of the modest room, which was understated in its decor, which is to say there wasn't really any statement at all, or rather, there wasn't any one style which could have been said to have been understated. It was, Matt thought, out of time. There might have been a design about a hundred years ago or so, but this had been worn away by various upgrades, additions, changes of furniture, revamps, and the effect now was of an indeterminate age and a taste which was so diverse that all it said was 'old'.

"Un aperitif, m'sieur?"

"Non, merci. J'attends."

The waiter moved off smoothly, his black waistcoat appearing to cut a furrow through the sea of tables above the bow-wave of his long starched apron. There weren't too many diners, two couples, a table of three and a party of six. All conversation was muted and the whole place had an air of old world sophistication with no quarter for contemporary trends. He was aware of the subtlest of background music, a string quartet, possibly Haydn? He began looking at the menu the waiter had left and had just clocked the steep prices when she was before him.

"Matthew, I'm so sorry I'm late. The taxi got stuck in this Paris traffic."

The waiter was slipping off her black wool coat to reveal a cream cashmere high necked top with half-length sleeves above a russet-brown, flared, below-the-knee, tweed skirt with tan boots. Released from the coat she hugged him warmly as he stood, kissing him on both cheeks and then standing back and holding his arms as if inspecting him.

"You look fabulous Caterina, but you always do."

She smiled knowingly. "You don't have to say that Matthew, but thank you."

"I wouldn't say it if I didn't mean it."

"Come on, let's sit down or you're going to distract me."

They sat opposite each other, Matt feeling that tingling rush of excitement in his stomach. *Does she mean what I think she means?*

Caterina spoke briefly to the waiter, who responded with a respectful nod Matt noticed. Was it because she was a woman or that she spoke excellent French?

"I've ordered us my favourite aperitif. You'll love it."

"What's that?"

"Pousse Rapière. It was supposed to be the drink of Les Trois Mousquetaires, so this explains the name. Crème de Limoux with Armagnac and Grand Marnier."

"Sounds wonderful." He didn't need a drink; he was drunk already, her eyes having already worked their wonder. It was going to be a tantalizing evening. "You really were fantastic last night. You were made for the part."

"The stage is where my home is. I love singing the concerts, but on stage my heart truly sings."

"I know, I can see that."

"Let's choose what we're going to eat. I have so many questions to ask you and I don't want to be interrupted. Now, everything here is very good, but I recommend the fillet be boeuf. The magrêt is delicious too, oh yes and the pintade is excellent. You know this? I don't know how you say this in English."

"What kind of meat is it?"

"This is a bird, like a chicken, but grey feathers and a bald head. They are very strange and make a funny sound."

"Oh, I know, um, guinea fowl."

"Yes, this is it. They do it in a fabulous sauce."

"It all looks quite expensive." Matt hesitated.

"Don't worry about that. My treat, remember? We're celebrating. Ah, the Pousse Rapière."

The waiter ceremoniously placed the tall flutes on the table together with some choice olives and morsels of foie gras on tiny toasts.

"To La Belle Hélène," Matt said.

"To a beautiful friendship," she replied, clinking his raised glass and giving him what he took to be a loaded look.

It was sublime; refreshingly clean fizz with an undercurrent of rich alcohol fruit. No doubt lethal, Matt thought.

"Mmm." She smacked her lips and the pink tongue tip flicked across their satin-sheen. "Now, what are we going to have?"

Matt was almost past caring, which was a shame in such a place, but he had food enough already. "I'll go for the beef. Are we having a starter?"

"Of course. We have to do this properly."

Caterina made the order, deciding on the pintade for herself preceded by salade de chevre chaud and seafood platter for Matt. She plumped for a bottle of Margaux as complementing both meals.

"Now Matthew, bring me up to date." She took a sip of her drink and gave him a searching look over the top of the flute.

He told her all about the video-link trial, how he had been released and gone home. He told her how things weren't very good between Maggie and him despite the holiday they'd taken in Corfu, where it had been almost too hot and they'd spent most of the time reading books, flopping into the sea and trying to work out why they didn't seem to communicate anymore. He told her how he had had vocal problems and ended up going to the kinesiologist after which it had miraculously sorted itself out. He told her about the Bohème at Covent Garden and how it had been such a great success and he'd had good reviews, and now here he was in Paris. She never interrupted, but the expressive changes of light and shade on her face told him her changing reaction to these events.

"So Tosca," she said, "and Angelotti's a very good part for you."

"Absolutely. Not much pressure, off after the first act, early shower!"

They'd finished their starters, accompanied by another Pousse Rapière each and were now into the entrée which, as Caterina had promised, was delicious. Matt's mignons melted in the mouth, the taste swiftly suffused with the soft tannins of the exemplary Margaux; velvet on satin.

"So how did you get this job at such a late stage?" he said.

"My agent had rung me about it ages ago, last year actually, saying the conductor really wanted me to do it, but I had turned it down, thinking I couldn't commit to this long time away. They had asked someone else, but then this person had cancelled late on just at the time all this happened and I had decided to accept opera work again, so it all worked out for the best. Sometimes fate smiles on us."

"And what's happened with your husband and your daughter?"

"Well, everything happened very quickly. My husband is going to make a good settlement and has made the house over to me."

"Really, I thought he was going to be difficult."

"He was, until the lawyer my friend recommended got him in the corner. He pretty much showed him that the case against him was so big he didn't have a chance, you know, a young child, how I'd given up my career almost to look after her, how he'd cheated on me for so long. And he would have been all over the papers. He opted for the quiet life. So, a new beginning." She lifted her glass which Matt matched before quaffing a mouthful of rich, dense Bordeaux.

They were both fairly replete after the entrée so decided to skip the cheese, Matt opting for Isles flottants and Caterina going for a mango sorbet.

"So is your mum living with you now?" Matt resumed.

"Yes, it's worked out very well. She's got her own sitting room which I converted from Alban's study, and most of the time we get on okay. You know, it's always difficult living with your parents again and we have a few disagreements in the kitchen, but she's wonderful with Tanya so I'm happy to put up with a bit of quarrelling."

"So, here you are."

"Yes, here we are, in this most romantic city. I'm so full after that wonderful food, I feel like walking it off. Would you walk me back to my hotel?"

"How could I refuse after you've bought me such a wonderful meal."

Caterina paid the bill and they issued out into the cool air of the empty street under a cloudless sky speckled with stars. She took his arm in that familiar way and guided him along the route. It felt so natural, almost like he was being chaperoned, and he thrilled at having this elegant beauty on his arm, chatting calmly about music and art, singing and performing, about love and life. He felt they were on the same wavelength. He didn't always agree with her, but they understood the same language, read off the same score. As they walked he became aware that he was really quite drunk, the cold air increasing that feeling rather than the purported opposite.

When they got to the Seine she wanted to sit on a bench and look at the river. She leant into him and he put his arm around her shoulder. They watched a barge chugging upstream on the dark water with the embankment lights reflecting in the disturbed wake. She turned her face up to him and he accepted her offered lips in a kiss that was at once forbidden and sweet, tasting hot and honeyed with mango. She nestled again against him and he rested his hand on her thigh and felt the tell-tale button suspended there. The Eiffel Tower rose before him, backlit by a harvest moon, huge and suffused with blood.

They wandered on in silence not wanting to talk, stopping instinctively at intervals to admire the view and turning in to each other in embraces that became increasingly trusting and intimate. Her mouth was delicate and soft but held an erotic urgency. Her kisses were loaded with emotional charge, a searching and yearning which reminded him of her singing.

They crossed over a bridge, stopping in the middle and leaning over the balustrade. He thought of that similar moment after the concert in Gothenburg since when so much had happened to them both. They continued onto the south bank, turning down streets she deftly navigated. He had no idea where they were, being intoxicated with drink, perfume, Paris and her. When they reached the hotel and came under the light of the entrance canopy, Matt expected her to look a bit dishevelled, but her face was radiant, flushed and glowing, her lips full and expectant.

He was about to say something about going or thanking or seeing her tomorrow, when she said "I think you deserve a nightcap Mr Chamberlain, for walking me all the way home," and linking her arm through his again, she propelled him gently through the revolving door and to the lift. He suddenly got the impression that all of this had been planned. He didn't know whether he felt flattered by this or used, but hadn't time to ponder this dichotomy as he was engulfed by her in the lift, flattened against the wall by surprising force as she clung to him, each of them gasping for air between the intensity of their kissing. The interruption of the stop lasted only as long as it took them to hasten down the corridor and into her suite where he found himself pinned to the back of the door with an unbelievable force for someone so small.

But although her arms gripped him like a vice her mouth melted in his in a tenderness that defied the passion in her body. Any thoughts of holding back had by now left him and he stooped and lifted her easily off the ground and walked slowly across the room. He didn't know where he was going but instinct found a sofa where he placed her gently down, she still cupping his head in her arms and seeking the depth of him with her soft tongue.

He wanted to free himself from his clothes but the hunger for her mouth was intolerable and he felt he couldn't forego one moment of the sweet soft mouth slipping in his and their licking their love against each other. Eventually he managed to quell his desire sufficiently to struggle out of his clothes and stood straining before her as she swiftly slipped her skirt from her legs and unsheathed her torso from the clinging cashmere to display a perfectly proportioned physic swathed in peach-coloured silk camisole and French knickers with suspenders peeping provocatively from beneath.

For a second he stood incredulous, hardly believing that this was for him, but her expression assured him that this heaven was his in this moment and he entered her with a shudder that she reciprocated with a muscularity which took his breath away. Soft waves of incredible force rocked them in synchronicity. They were lost in a passion so deep and intense that it transcended the moment, transcended time and space and took them beyond themselves, until the tides of their passions broke over the shores of desire and the tumult subsided.

Whether he slept for a while Matt couldn't tell, but he eventually found himself rolling off her and slipping beside the slumbering silk form. She had an expression of ineffable calm, a serenity of stillness as she slept softly beside him. He looked at the beautiful profile of her nose and chin, the perfectly shaped eyebrows above heavily lashed lids. There was a drift of dew on her temple below the fair hairs flicking upwards from the hairline. Faint freckles speckled her cheeks now suffused with a rosy glow. Had she planned all this? Was all this an elaborate ruse to bed him, to get what she wanted? Well, he'd wanted it too, so what matter? Only that it had been taken out of his hands, like he hardly had a say in it.

He leant forward and nuzzled her cheek. She sighed, languidly opened her eyes, turned her head and opened her mouth to him again. How deep was it possible to feel? It seemed, possibly, infinitely. She rolled away and got up amazingly elegantly he thought. In a haze he saw a vision of extreme eroticism waft across the room to what must be the bedroom. He lay reeling in the aftermath of heightened stimulation, mentally pinching himself to know if it was real. Shortly he heard the cistern flush and a minute later Caterina reappeared with a large towel wrapped around her.

"Have I exhausted you?" she teased. "I was just thinking of champagne?" She went to the fridge and pulled out a half bottle of Veuve Cliquot and found two glasses. "Are you coming to bed?"

Matt gulped, hardly believing she was serious. "I'll just use the bathroom," he said brushing past her with a wry smile.

When he entered the bedroom having freshened up, she was lying in the large bed with the sheet pulled up and music flowing from a large iPod dock on the bedside table. It was baroque, oboe and string orchestra. He stood unashamedly with nothing on, enjoying the risqué novelty with this sophisticated woman he hardly knew, but now knew so well.

"What's that?"

"Albinoni. Oboe concerto. It's sublime."

It was the slow movement, the oboe arching a long plaintive phrase above violins.

"I could die listening to this," she said. "Come."

He slid into the generous bed beside her. She handed him a glass and tapped hers to his before drinking. They lay still, letting the melody flow over them, the oboe searching out their emotions, sighing and soaring over the changing, stepping harmonies, yearning and teasing out feelings within. The slow, walking bass was a heartbeat, off which the rest of the string orchestra harmonised a cushion of velvet sound punctuated by the upward arpeggios of the first violins. The oboe crept in again, almost imperceptibly, repeating the opening phrase with a long held note, the intensity deepening with the crescendo and increasing vibrato, until it was constrained to move up to the fourth above before, returning again to the original note and unwinding the tension in a falling phrase to a trilling cadence. It was so simple, so pure, so perfect. You couldn't fault it or argue with it. It was a statement of utter beauty.

Matt let a trickle of effervescence tingle over his tongue as the oboe warmed to its theme, expounding on its original idea, developing the argument, expressing all the aspects of the subject. It questioned with rising suspensions, suggested different keys, different tonalities. It answered itself with falling phrases and possible explanations, hunted around all the alternatives, searched for hidden meanings, but ultimately it came back to its original statement and again, in the simplest fashion, reiterated that long, arching, opening phrase of unquestionable beauty.

The third movement burst in playfully, the strings chasing each other in a fugue-like theme, daring the oboe to join in, which it gamely did eventually.

Matt turned to Caterina and saw the tell-tale moisture at the corners of her eyes. She smiled at him, "It does it every time," she said by way of explanation and found a tissue.

Matt took another mouthful of fizz. "What does? What is it that speaks to us and destroys us like that? Why are we moved by certain sequences of chords?"

"How do you mean, Matthew?"

"Well, that slow movement. It got you, didn't it. It made me sad too, but elated. It was sheer beauty. I mean, what is beauty, or rather, why is beauty? What makes something beautiful as opposed to not so beautiful? What makes something move you? I mean, I'm not just saying this, but there's a quality in your voice, a frequency which just gets me. There's a pathos in the quality of the sound which gives me goose-bumps."

"There, you're on about the goose again, wild goose chase, goose bumps! What is it with the goose for you?" She smiled mischievously, covering up her self-consciousness at his comment, and took another sip from her glass.

"No, but seriously, I really want to know. Why do certain things affect us, deeply, at a very basic level, almost at a sub-conscious level? It's like they resonate at some level we can't otherwise get to."

"It's what makes us human, Matthew. It is our divinity." He looked at her questioningly, unsure whether she was being serious as she still had a teasing smile on her face. "Anyway, it's too late for these kind of discussions."

"I can't believe you opened champagne."

"It's an aphrodisiac," she said with a wink and took another swig.

"You don't behave like this usually do you?"

"No, only in extreme circumstances."

"And these are extreme circumstances?" he said, taking a gulp which frizzed his nose.

"Yes, very extreme, if that's not, how do you say it, repeating yourself?"

"Tautology?"

"Yes, maybe."

"Why extreme?"

She paused, looking down at her glass in her lap. "Because I feel this is the beginning of a whole new phase of my life, and I'm in bed with an incredibly handsome man who makes me feel like a million dollars, as the saying is."

"The feeling is mutual, I assure you," he said, tipping another rivulet of frothing biscuit-dry champagne down his throat.

"Do you think I'm wicked?" she cooed.

"Yes," he said, pretending sobriety through the intended provocation.

"Good. Because I've been good for so long for someone who didn't appreciate it, and now I want to indulge myself."

"I noticed," he said smiling.

"And I want to be so wicked with you," she looked at him with eyes that challenged him to respond.

To his surprise he found he was already recovered, and gulping the last draft from the glass he ripped away the flimsy sheet and threw it down the bed. She lay completely naked, unashamed, appearing to relish his sudden ferocity, with dilated pupils black as obsidian. She obviously noticed his excitement and finished off her bubbly too with a flourish. He leant across her and grabbed the bottle.

"I think you need some more champagne."

"Oh yes, I do," she purred and held her glass out expectantly.

He poured some in her glass and then deliberately tipped the rest over her supine body. She gasped with shock and delight.

"What are you doing to me?"

"I didn't say where," he replied, and leant over to lap the golden liquid from her navel, licking and kissing the champagne sprinkled skin. She shivered, the hair follicles risen with the cold and excitement. He nuzzled his way up her body, investigating all her curves and crevices with his tongue's tip, responding to her reactions with more attentions. He slid his tongue up her neck as she writhed beneath him and again found her mouth. His body slipped seal-like against her glistening skin, mouth on mouth. The music had changed to Monteverdi, The Coronation of Poppea, the rising and falling answering phrases of the final love duet matching their bodies' rhythm.

'Pur ti miro, I adore you, Pur ti godo, I desire you, Pur ti stringo, I embrace you, Pur t'annodo, I enchain you, Piu non peno, No more pain, Piu non moro, No more sorrow

O mia vita, O mi tesoro, Io son tua, Tuo son io,

Her skin consumed him. He drowned himself in her. Their sliding shared skins coalesced. Velvet, deep velvet,

Folding, deep on deep.
Immersing sense,
Scents leap and leap.
Clear eyes, bright pained
With joy-lust fire,
Hold hovering
Breathless expectation,
Brink-teetering
With desire.
Urge surges, urgent,
Urge on urge,
Swift scything
Hot ferocious rush,
Locked soft
In vice-clamped,
Skin-seared,
Breathless hush.
****

Matt became gradually aware of his breath, of the air flowing gently in and out through his nostrils, the inhalation drawing cool, sweet, scent-laden wafts through his nasal chambers, the exhalation puffing warmed sighs of satisfaction from his somnolent body. His ears became aware of a wash of harmony, dense, hypnotic and loaded with claustrophobic tension. It was Rosenkavalier, Act 3.

There was a clink of china. He opened his jaw, clicked open skin-suctioned lips, un-sticking saliva-stuck cheek linings, and swept his tongue across chalk teeth to rehydrate dry membranes. Light seeped through his cracking eyelids and squinting to sharp shards of sunlight stinging pupils, his aching head intensified with the light. He groaned.

"I brought you coffee."

With an effort he focused under a shading hand, and made out an elfin vision of silken skin; of silk and skin; of silk on skin.

She was standing by the bed pouring a dark stream of steaming liquid velvet from the cafetière, the sun cascading through the window and evanescing the edges of her ivory silk pyjamas, shorts and short sleeves sheening and scintillating in the bright light.

With an effort he dragged himself up to sit against the headboard and watched her move softly around the bed to place the cup beside him and then lean to place her mouth gently on his. He kissed her lips in return, inhaling a mixture of mint and sandalwood. She must have showered and brushed her teeth.

"How long have you been up?" he croaked.

"Oh about an hour."

"I feel dreadful. Well, pretty hung over. God those rapier things are lethal."

He gratefully swallowed a couple of mouthfuls of coffee and welcomed the rich bitterness cleansing his mouth and clearing his head. The three soprano voices soared in the emotion-loaded opening of the trio. It seemed to Matt that the pain and joy were intertwined and he was suddenly overcome with a foreboding that this beautiful moment might be taken from him. He abandoned his coffee and took Caterina in his arms, enveloping her in a passion he couldn't explain. She must have reached the same pitch of emotional intensity, the music overpowering them both, for she immediately responded, slipping him deftly up a leg of the silk shorts and drawing him into her with a gasp.

The harmonies deepened, dissonances promising to resolve but complicating and soaring to higher suspensions. Matt's muscles strained, incited by her pain/joy face. The frequencies increased as layers of vocal lines entangled, laid and overlaid each other above the urging orchestra beneath. He wanted to subsume himself inside her, wanted her to melt into him, wanted their bodies to meld in this ecstatic fervour, beyond physical restriction.

The harmony released, the tension spilled. The orchestra's rich density of sound unwound in falling phrases, softening, sighing, folding down. Matt lay beside her, deep inside her, cherishing the last convulsive phrases as the texture thinned.

Caterina smiled sadly. "I haven't been this happy for a long time." She smoothed his cheek. He turned and kissed her palm. His headache had gone.

"After what you've been through you deserve it."

He slipped out and went to the bathroom, realising immediately from his difficulty in holding a direct course that he was still wondrously drunk. When he came back to the bed she was fast asleep, heavily peaceful.

He slunk under the sheet and watched her breathe for a minute, then drank the rest of the coffee, savouring the full flavour and the sunshine flooding the bed.

He thought of Maggie.

Chapter 30

Signe rolled onto her back and placed her hands on the soft skin of her tummy. She wasn't imagining things, it had definitely grown. Only slightly, and not so that anyone else would notice, but it had. She could feel it, feel that slight plumpness swelling under her ribs. And it would get bigger and become more obvious, but how big and how soon? How would she hide it, keep it secret? It would be impossible, living at home. Melissa would be sure to guess, sometime.

So far, Signe felt, she was in the clear; no-one knew, not even Irma. And it hadn't been difficult so far, apart from the nausea, which hadn't lasted long. Now it was going to begin to get difficult.

She needed to make a plan, find a way of keeping it secret. Because it had to be secret, she reminded herself, otherwise they'd all interfere. Giving birth in Göteborg just wasn't an option. She imagined the shame of her family, in the church and the community; Melissa tight-lipped, biting back the indignity whilst attempting to show support; Gustav confused, probably excited, concerned for her but trying to steer a judicious course in regards to his wife; Lars bragging to his friends about becoming an uncle. It just wasn't an option. It would be suffocating. She couldn't imagine coping with all the attention, with Melissa fussing, with Facebook probably going crazy with excitement, both positive and negative.

It had to be like the first birth, inconspicuous, humble, without publicity. Once the baby was here then everyone could know. Then there would be time for celebration when His Divinity would be apparent. Because that is how she envisaged it, like in all the paintings and pictures of the nativity where the baby's holiness is so unmistakeable. He rests in the Virgin's lap or sits on Her knee, calmly exuding love and compassion, a model baby come to save the world. And she knew that God would send the signs again so that everyone would know that He had arrived, that this was the time. Then her family and friends would be rewarded, then they'd understand why she had had to deceive them and have the baby secretly. Because this was what God had led her to do, to protect His Son from the publicity that would have resulted.

She had to avoid the possibility of it hitting the news and becoming a reality TV moment. What if a newspaper or magazine heard of it and created a big splash which would be taken up by every religious and non-religious faction, fighting over the truth of the report, swarming around her to get the facts, the background, create some media hype. It would be all over the internet. She rolled her head away from this thought on the pillow, trying to avoid it. There was the possibility she would become an immediate celebrity, like royalty. Well she would, wouldn't she? The Mother of Christ! How much bigger does it get? The thought was terrifying and she knew it was her duty to protect against that, to keep everything low key, modest, just like before.

Lying there, with her hands still on her stomach, she couldn't believe that all this could happen, would happen, in just a few months. It was terrifying yet at the same time exciting, that surge of adrenalin flitting through her body feeling almost like the Holy Spirit. It made her feel so alive and full of purpose, this secret that now she held under her hands. But was she strong enough to bear it, to bear Him, and not fail this honour?

Suddenly she felt a fleeting feathering under the skin, a tickling movement so slight she might have missed it if she hadn't been lying so still with her hands cupped there. It was Him. She had felt Him for the first time. A gentle stroking inside her womb had told her physically of His presence. She was swept with an enormous emotion, a love so deep and raw that a sob caught in her throat. Then she smiled, laughing through the tears with the relief of knowledge. She would do this thing, would bear this Child, whatever it took, because her Lord would lead her, would guide her in His way.

Signe found a tissue and dried her eyes, feeling renewed, invigorated. She slipped from the bed and knelt beside it, lost in thanks and praise. She wanted to tell someone she'd felt Him, wanted to share this miracle of creation. But who? Who would understand and keep her secret? The obvious person was Irma. But she wasn't confident of her silence now. She'd secretly told Uncle Dirk about the Bridgettines. And anyway, she hardly saw anything
of her these days as she seemed to be so tied up with Karl.

Signe sighed, her joy at having felt Him tempered by sadness that she couldn't share this joy. How would she contain this secret for so long? Alone. In silence.

She got up and sat on the bed, smoothing the duvet with the flat of her hand, feeling its clean, white crispness. She needed a plan, she told herself. She needed to organise herself for this birth. She obviously must get away somewhere to avoid the attention, leaving it as late in her term as possible, but so that it still wouldn't notice. But where? She thought of Vadstena, the convent where she'd spent the summer and where she'd felt so welcome and secure. But there was no facility there for her. She couldn't stay in the guest house where she'd worked; she couldn't just turn up and impose herself, with child, on their silent community, intent on devotion. Could she? Was that part of God's plan? Was that why he had led her there in the first place? Would they understand?

She thought it would seem like a kind of blackmail, knowing they wouldn't be able to turn her away and therefore would be forced to take her in. She would feel bad putting them in that position, compromising their devotions with the sudden upheaval of a birth. But was that the Intention?

She didn't know. It was so difficult to read the signs sometimes. With hindsight she'd recognised others for what they were, had been able to explain them later, from a distance. Sometimes, she admitted, when she was in the midst of it, the signs escaped her, she didn't see them. Sometimes she thought there was a sign and it was perhaps her imagination. But they'd been stacking up recently as she'd uncovered more, so there was no doubt about them any longer, it was just a case of making sure she recognised them and interpreted them correctly.

She hadn't really worked out a good way of knowing which ones were true and which ones weren't. She usually just waited to see if it seemed right and made sense. Looking back she thought she'd recognised the important ones. The dream when she was chosen by the angel to do God's work. Her nightmare when she was quite young, which had so terrified her, showing that she was destined to run away from the sins of the flesh, to take root in the church of God with the saints and His Son on the cross and resist the temptations of the devil, the snake. She so wanted to believe the old priest showing her the Via Crucis in his study and confirming that she was indeed pure and spotless was a sign, but now had to admit he was a pervert, which changed the whole thing. He had left the parish shortly after that when Father Stefan had taken over.

And other things too, which she had been working out, although they were more hidden. When she had been overwhelmed by science and it was conspiring to undermine her belief and He had shown her the Fibonacci sequence, revealing His plan to her. When she'd been doing genetics and she'd got upset about evolution and He'd sent her the dove to show her His meaning, and that it was building a nest, another symbol of her destiny, to bear His child. The robin in the graveyard symbolising rebirth, 'out of death shall come life', which echoed her situation; out of the story of Jesus' death in the Passion at Easter had come the life in her womb which was to repeat His birth again at the time of His Mass, Christ's Mass.

Even her shock and pain at finding she was adopted now seemed to hold a hidden meaning. Her birth, like Jesus's, involved a mystery. Her parents apparently couldn't cope, they needed help. Maybe they also weren't religious, but God had chosen her and then saw to it that she was brought up in a religious family to learn His Word and become a true disciple. And now, all that had been fulfilled and through the telling of His Son's Passion she was fruitful with His second coming. 'Behold the hand maid of the Lord'.

These thoughts warmed her, reassured her that she was following His way. But now she felt she needed another sign to guide her forward in this difficult decision of how to handle the birth, how to prepare for it. She must be patient; it would come, sometime, somehow, if only she could see it.

She got up and went over to the dressing table and picked up her hairbrush. She noticed it was choked with hair and she had to free the tangle in the bristles. It reminded her of how Aunt Agi's hair had fallen out after the chemotherapy. But no, she didn't have cancer, she was pregnant and these changes happen. It was the hormones.

Uncle Mats, and Elizabetta and Marta! She could perhaps go to them in Stockholm, explain the situation and ask them to hide her. It would be good to be far away from Göteborg, from everyone who knew her. But they'd immediately ring Melissa to say where she was. She'd never manage to swear them to silence.

She paused in her brushing, gazing out of the window as if trying to find an answer to her problem there. A nuthatch, striking in his grey and pink plumage, shuffled up the birch tree opposite, probing the bark for insects. Yes, that's it, she could go to Stockholm and stay at a cheap hotel or hostel and only get in touch with them if she had to, if it was an emergency. That could be her security, just in case. But she wouldn't tell them she was coming, it would be a last resort.

She brushed vigorously now, turning back to the mirror and stroking her hair into place, smoothing its glossy sheen, her blond hair.

His was brown, rich and dark. What colour would the baby's be? Brown, long and curly like in the pictures of Jesus in Melissa's bible? Or blond like hers? Is the brown hair allele dominant, like with eyes? Because there was a part of him inside her now, mixed with her body, with her genes, **in** her body. God had impregnated her through the Christus, using his body to re-create His son. But she was unviolated, still a virgin, undefiled. Hers was also an immaculate conception.

She went to the wardrobe to get out some trousers and noticed her travel bag sitting there. Yes, she would use this, pack clothes and have everything organised and ready for when she left. It would have to be quick, before anyone was up, out the door and away to the station. They'd only know when she'd gone, when she didn't reappear after school. They'd check her room and only then....

But they'd notice the bag was gone. They'd know she'd packed and gone away somewhere.

They'd tell the police who would start a nationwide search. They'd be bound to look in Stockholm. Well, they'd check the station, they'd trace her bank card when she bought the ticket.

Signe sank down on the bed. This was going to take some real planning.

She'd need money in Stockholm, but she mustn't use her card there; they'd trace it. She'd have to take money out a bit at a time before she went. She'd have to use cash. She'd have to buy her train ticket with cash too, even though it would undoubtedly cost more than booking online. But she couldn't take that risk, couldn't leave a trail which could lead to her.

She would have to buy another bag and another set of clothes so that when they looked in her room, in her wardrobe, everything looked normal. They wouldn't suspect she'd left Göteborg, they'd just think she was somewhere in the city.

She'd go to the church today and look things up on their computer. That way she'd be safe. That way no-one would know.

Chapter 31

The thrust of the full throttle engaging always gave Matt a thrill, although he'd flown countless times now. That surge of power driving into his back and the rush of the plane bowling down the runway, the mown grass and the runway lights flashing past at increasing velocity, before the tip and lift of take off, was inevitably exhilarating.

But the rush was short-lived this time, tempered by an anticipation and regret. It had been an extraordinary time, an unreal time, a time out of time. The rehearsals had been obligatory interludes between time with Caterina. They had floated beyond time in an affair that had consumed them; consumed their sense of reality, suspended it in time. Their only reality was their work, Matt's rehearsals and Caterina's performances. These proved enemies of their time, because Matt would have rehearsals in the day and Caterina performances at night. Of course these latter weren't every night, but sometimes Matt had evening rehearsals on the nights Caterina had off. So they would grab time late at night after either was ended, loving long into the night, and he'd have to drag himself away in the morning to another rehearsal, leaving her somnolent form in satisfied sleep.

Then she was gone. Gone back to be with her daughter, the run of shows finished.

Paris had become empty, unromantic, a husk that had once contained the most blissful time he could have imagined, but now a hollow, meaningless shell. He'd had stage and piano rehearsals, sitzproben, stage and orchestra rehearsals, piano dress rehearsals, orchestral dress rehearsals and finally the Dress Rehearsal. It hadn't seemed to mean anything. Of course the production was good, Bryn was fabulous and he'd been moved sometimes, but the rest of the time, time had dragged since she'd left. The first night over, he was now going home. The next performance was in four days' time, so time to go home. Back to real time. Back to reality. Back to Maggie.

He spent the journey reflecting, holding a mirror up to himself and trying to read who this person was who was him. Trying to understand what he wanted. He was obviously in love with Caterina. He was obviously going back to Maggie but quite why apart from habit he couldn't answer, except that's what he did, he went back to Maggie.

He'd hardly heard from Caterina. A few texts to say she missed him but she was busy sorting stuff out at home and how lovely it was to see Tanya. She had a few weeks at home before another contract and needed to get on top of the music, so was having some coaching locally. Another text had said that he was a very special person to her and he'd always have a special place in her heart. This had sounded strangely distant although expressing great intimacy. He had felt cut off. It seemed like it had never been, like it was out of time. From a different time.

He'd texted back of course, telling her how Paris was intolerable without her, how he didn't know what to do, how he longed to love her again. She'd said not to be silly, in that motherly tone of hers. He needed to attend to his work etc etc. How could she be so detached, so business-like? It had rocked him, this separation. He had felt like he was suffocating, like he was being denied oxygen. All he'd seemed to be able to think about was her and the more he thought of her the less anything else had seemed to mean.

He realised he'd felt this way before, back in Gothenburg, when time had warped and he'd been bereft except when in the presence of the statue, when time had stood still and he'd seemed to be in a perfect unity. Then seeing the girl in the concert, when a bolt of electricity had struck him and he'd become obsessed with that pure desire, that bright, clean lust to purge himself through her. His lust for Caterina was different he felt, more indulgent, immersing, hedonistic even, but supremely beautiful and almost transcendental. Which of these was more right, more true? And then there was Maggie, what did he feel about her?

Going home after a month in Paris was always going to be difficult he knew, after the awkwardness of the previous month, but now, after Caterina, he had no idea where he was, how he felt. It was therefore with a feeling of dread that he exited the tube station at Leyton and walked to the flat. He wasn't sure whether she'd be home, as when he'd phoned from Heathrow to say he'd landed, she'd said she had a few things to do and didn't know when she'd be back. He thought of the other time he'd come back, from prison, and caught her 'inflagrante delicto'. Or rather 'in flagellante delicto'! Oh Maggie.

"Hi Mags, I'm back."

The hall had a strangely tidy look and he heard a movement and a couple of bangs from the kitchen.

"Hi babe." Maggie appeared out of the kitchen. Matt couldn't believe his eyes, but they didn't lie. She was dripping with latex – black, shiny, sexy latex above knee-high, stiletto, pvc boots. "I was just preparing some lunch, but it's not quite ready yet," she said with mock servitude and put a long black latex-gloved finger between glossy red lips.

Matt felt the spasm in his loins and taking the cue replied "But I said I'd be back by one. It's now one thirty."

He saw her gasp and shudder with delight, "I know, I'm sorry."

"Sorry? I'll make you sorry," and he lunged at her, grabbing a latex wrist and tried to swipe her backside, but the bouffant latex mini skirt with the red latex frills prevented contact. Feigning increased anger he dragged her into the bedroom and flung her over the base board, noticing the bed all prepared. He grabbed the restraints at each bottom corner and lashed her wrists, pulling these tight so she was prostrate bending over, her rubber-frilled buttocks sticking up pertly.

By this time Matt was bursting with excitement and revelling in the role-play, high on the adrenalin of sudden physical aggression. Having restrained her he now moved to the next stage of the game and ripped off his jacket and shirt. She could just manage to turn her head enough to see the huge lump in his jeans and he knew she was well on her way, as she moaned with delight.

"You know what happens to servants who don't do what they're told."

"Oh, please, not the paddle. It's so painful."

"You've only yourself to blame. You've been disobedient, lazy, wicked. And now I'm going to deal with you."

She gurgled something incomprehensible as he went behind her, grabbed the convenient paddle, lifted up the heavy red frills and thwacked her a few times on the bare buttocks. Very quickly they gained a pleasing red glow divided by the string of the black rubber thong. Maggie was moaning with satisfaction. Then he walloped her really hard and she cried out with real pain followed by small pants of delight.

He dropped the paddle, ripped open his trousers, tore down his pants and rammed himself deep into her hot wet cunt, the rubber thong rubbing him and threatening an early climax. After a few thrusts he withdrew, untied her and threw her on the bed, the latex squealing against the rubber sheet, and re-tied her by the ankles and wrists face up, spatch-cocked at his mercy. Her face showed an agony of desire and frustration at his teasing, short-lived penetration. Now he could really tease her

He clocked the pierced nipples peeping over the top of the tight rubber corset, longing for attention. He saw her watching his look and the anticipation on her face. He kicked off the rest of his clothes, jumped on the bed and sat astride her chest, his cock riding high between the mounds of her tightly enclosed breasts. She was in an ecstasy of anticipation. He gently stroked the hard nuts of her breasts, squeezing and tantalising her so that he could feel her squirming beneath him, the rubber stretching and squeaking. He took hold of the nipple bars and twisted and pulled them gently but suggested impending rougher treatment with a sadistic smile. She responded with tempered fear laced with a degree of real concern; she was helpless, under his control.

Her eyes were fixed on his huge erection pulsing and glistening just out of her reach. He knew she longed to suck him, swallow his enormous sex, engorge that delicious throbbing hunk of flesh and suffocate herself with its thrusting power. He leant forward and teased her, wiping it across her hungry mouth, letting her licking tongue snatch tastes of its lactating head. She moaned with frustration, raising her body muscularly trying to throw him into her. He drew back reprimanding her with his eyes and threatening her verbally, calling her a filthy bitch, a dirty whore and any other delightful epithets that made her writhe with a sudden orgasm.

Now there would be no stopping her. She would be insatiable.

He let her have her way, turning and thrusting himself into her ready mouth and reciprocating with avid lingual attention to her labia and clitoris. The rubber thong rolled mischievously under the probing of his tongue, slipping this way and that over her burning clit. He was always amazed how long she could hold her breath and control her gag reflex and was sometimes worried he might accidentally asphyxiate her, but her heaving body told him she was very much alive and riding high to another orgasm.

He pulled away, leaving her gasping, whimpering even. He couldn't hold himself off for long, but found time to attend once more to the erect lanced nipples before shafting her roughly, brutally almost, heaping thrust on thrust, deeper and faster as she screamed and he erupted in an explosion which arched his back and sent his senses soaring.

He collapsed panting on top of her squirming, drenched body, the rubber seething with sweat and sex.

"You're the only one who really knows how to do it for me Matt."

He didn't reply. They'd showered and were cleaning up the gear.

"I'd saved myself for you, you know," she continued. "I decided it was only fair, you being away working, so I didn't... you know."

Matt couldn't look at her. "So you were a bit desperate. That's why you dressed up."

"It was for you as well, Matt. I know what you like too."

He felt sick. All those nights, days with Caterina; and she'd been waiting for him.

"It was certainly a home-coming I won't forget!"

"You are pleased to see me, aren't you Matt?"

"Of course, Mags. I'm just a bit stunned. And you know, it always takes me a bit of time to adjust, coming home. I'll be fine." He paused, unsure how to deal with the bed. "Anyway, look, I'm starving. Did you actually do some lunch?"

"Just a meze. Usual stuff we like, hummus, tara, olives, Turkish bread."

"Yum. Come on, we can finish this later."

Something about cleaning up the gear revolted him. He wanted to get away from the bedroom and eating seemed the easiest excuse.

They set about the meal, opening pots, tearing bread, setting plates and knives. When they were seated she suddenly said "I'm sorry about the summer Matt. I think it was my fault. All that stuff in Sweden, I thought I'd handled it, but maybe I hadn't. I think I didn't really understand what it was all about. Well, I still don't, but I think I've got over it now."

He looked at her, saw the truth in her eyes and felt worse. "It's okay Mags. It's not just your fault. Well, it's all my fault really, right?"

She smiled. "Well, yes, I suppose it is. What was Paris like?"

"Oh, you know, lots of rehearsals. Lots of hanging around."

"Did it go well, the first night?"

"Yeah, really good. Production was a bit weird in places, but musically fantastic."

"Can I come and see it?"

He was taken aback. She wasn't into opera.

"Of course, yes. You must. It's a brilliant piece, Puccini at his best. Really dramatic. I'll get you a seat. When d'you want to come?"

They discussed dates and possibilities, he finding her unusually interested now in coming to an opera. Normally she was a bit distant about it and certainly wouldn't have suggested going to Paris. They decided she'd come for the third performance and stay the three days until the fourth, they'd make a break of it. She had nothing particular booked then and Matt thought he might be able to arrange an audition with a conductor who wanted to hear him sing some Handel. It was a departure. She had never accompanied him on a foreign gig before. It had never occurred to them, maybe because she was always worried about missing an audition or casting, and that she felt she should be working at the bar.

It felt weird travelling to a performance with Maggie. He never usually had anyone 'in tow'. On rare occasions Katie had come along in the early days, and of course his parents used to come to everything, but they'd just turn up at the performance. Having someone with you permanently was a bit restricting. He couldn't do things on a whim, like go for a sleep for a couple of hours before the performance, eat a meal at a strange time in the day to last him through til after the show, but not too near it.

He felt responsible, that she needed entertaining, that this was a holiday for her, but at the same time it would be fun, showing her how his life was, knowing that she'd be there after the show and he wouldn't be going for a lonely drink somewhere feeling the post-performance let down.

They went for a meal after the show, nothing like the one he'd had with Caterina. She fancied Italian, a bit odd in Paris he thought, but didn't object, and they ended up at a very pleasant Trattoria where the pizzas were from a wood oven and the garlic bread very garlicky.

Maggie had loved Tosca. She said she never realised that opera done well could be so dramatically believable. For her, the singing had always got in the way, been too unreal to engage her fully. That's why she hated musicals. How could you have a serious dramatic situation in dialogue and then, believably, have someone burst into song? It was ridiculous. But tonight, she said, had opened her eyes. The fact that it was all sung, she said, had set a precedent and you accepted the genre, and the music was so dramatic it kind of emphasised the emotion rather than taking away from the realism.

Matt felt a door had been opened. When they were first together they'd argued endlessly about the difference between straight theatre and opera, she vehemently asserting that opera was a bourgeois conceit where historically the audience went to be seen, didn't pay much attention most of the time and just tuned in for the big numbers. She always maintained that singers couldn't act, the whole thing was totally unbelievable and it no longer had any relevance.

"The operas of today are films" she'd say. He'd agree to a certain extent. Films certainly had taken their place as a dramatic alternative – epic subjects in epic situations backed up by epic musical scores, he'd concede – but he always championed music's ability to take emotions to places straight theatre couldn't go, touching emotional strings that pure theatre never reached. They had always ended up agreeing to disagree but he'd always felt hurt that she obviously didn't value what he did as highly as her art, although she loved to hear him sing.

"Bloody hell, Mags, I never thought I'd hear you say you liked an opera. Cheers." They clinked glasses and he winked at her and swallowed down the nutty house Chianti which was surprisingly good.

"You've never taken me to one as good as this. They've all seemed silly. Either comedies that weren't believable so weren't funny or costume dramas where people say the same thing over and over again. I mean, once you've heard it you've got the message right? She loves him, but he's gone off with someone else, but then she goes on about it for ten minutes, and then she goes right back to the beginning and starts all over again."

"It's called a 'da capo' aria."

"Whatever. But you don't get Shakespeare writing 'To be or not to be, that is the question' going through the whole soliloquy and at the end writing 'Hamlet then repeats the first lines but embellishing them with more emotion and pathos'. The audience would be shouting 'Alright mate, we get the picture. You've said all that once. What d'you think we are, stupid? Get on with it.'"

Maggie's voice was rising as she got more drunk and animated, but Matt hardly noticed as he was concentrating on not choking on a mouthful of pizza whilst laughing. Maggie was in full swing.

"I mean, can you imagine it? 'To be or not to be...Oh...to be, to be...or...or not...to be or not to be...aah, that is the question. The question....the question is to be...aah...to be or not to be. That is...that is...that is the question. ....aah ...the question. The. Question. The question is to be... Aah... Is to be, the question is....oooh... to be or not to be'. You see what I'm saying?"

Matt couldn't reply. Whether it was the wine or Maggie's cod-serious face as she performed this little improvisation with accompanying gestures he didn't know, but he was wasted in a fit of giggles which had tears streaming down his face. Maggie suddenly burst out laughing loudly. "Well, that's how it would be, isn't it?"

They had hysterics for what seemed like ten minutes but was probably two, and caused the rest of the restaurant to fall silent and turn and stare. A waiter came over to ask if everything was alright. Maggie buried her face in the ample napkin, stuffing some of it in her mouth, her eyes bulging at him over the top, til he was doing the same and shrieking noiselessly into his. She nodded to the waiter and he withdrew smiling indulgently, whilst they pulled themselves together, panting and taking draughts of San Pellegrino.

"Oh Mags, you're killing me. I haven't laughed like that for ages." He laughed again, wiping his eyes with the napkin. "Oh my god, my ribs ache."

She was smiling at him, her face flushed with wine and laughter. "Well Mr Chamberlain, you shouldn't be so serious all the time. You're supposed to enjoy life you know."

Another pang of guilt shot his stomach. Isn't that exactly what he'd been doing the last time he was in Paris? She must never know. Despite her apparent nineteen sixties hippie outlook, embracing alternative culture and broadmindedness, he instinctively realised that she had insecurities that couldn't take these ideas to their logical conclusions. She relied upon him being there to be the rock round which her wild emotions broke and their energies coalesced, effervescing but subsiding against the solidity of his more stable and grounded character. Little did she know the emotional turmoil he'd been through and not just with the girl in Gothenburg. It had shocked him how much she'd been affected by the rape case and he'd had to adjust to this side of Maggie he'd been unaware of; her insecurity and reliance on him. Seeing her grinning there in front of him, he was even more aware of her rather schizophrenic character, one minute loud and brassy, confident and outrageous, and the next insecure, unsure and needing constant reassurance. Typical actor.

"I am. What are you talking about," he replied.

"Well, you know Matt, sometimes you're a bit serious. You need to lighten up a bit. It's like you keep yourself on a tight leash all the time and don't relax."

Matt raised an eyebrow, "Well, I know someone who likes to be on a tight leash – the tighter the better."

"Ssh, Matt. Not in public," she replied, eyes burning suddenly at the thought.

"Mags we're in an Italian restaurant in Paris. No one's going to understand what we're saying."

She giggled dirtily as her phone bleeped a text message from the depth of her bag.

"Have you got anything with you?" Matt asked, suddenly feeling amazingly horny, seeing her responding so swiftly to his innuendo.

"Never travel without," she responded, challenging his look with greater insinuation, and responding to the second bleep from her bag searching for the phone. "It's from Pete." She began reading while Matt poured more of the increasingly acceptable Chianti and took a mouth-rinsing swig.

When he looked back at Maggie her face was a wreck.

"God, no, no." Tears started immediately in her eyes. "Oh my god I can't believe it."

"What's up? Mags?"

"It's not possible. I need to talk to Pete. Oh my god."

"Mags what is it? What's happened?"

"A friend." She was crying fully now. "An old friend. He's dead. I don't understand. I need to talk to Pete....find out what happened.... I can't believe it, oh my god..."

"Mags, Mags. Ssh ssh. Who? Who is it?"

"You... you wouldn't know him. He helped me....so much. When I was..... lost. When I was fifteen, sixteen, I don't know. Oh my god I can't believe it."

"Mags, don't phone on your mobile. It'll cost a fortune. Look, wait a minute." He looked at the menu, at the cards on the table. "Look, look there's free Wi-Fi here. Skype him, it'll be free."

He grabbed her phone and went into the menu to get logged on to the local net.

"This is dreadful. I haven't seen him for ages. Oh god."

Matt gave it back to her after pressing Skype on Pete's number. He didn't know what to say, he obviously didn't know the guy. Someone from before they met.

"Hi Pete. What the hell happened?"

"Mags, oh god, I don't know exactly. It was some kind of domestic thing. I got a mixed up message from Don, you know his old friend on the estate. Something about he'd been friendly with this teenager next door which is why he'd been in prison. Some bitch had set him up and squawked to the pigs. Anyway he hadn't been out long and some guy comes round and sticks him for messing with his step-daughter. Turns out he's some crackhead, out of his skull most of the time."

"I never knew he was inside. I hadn't been in touch for a long while."

"Well, you know George, never one to back down. Apparently tried to reason with the guy, tried to talk him down, but this guy was too far gone. Smacked up and shit faced. Just pulled a knife and stuck him, no discussion."

"Oh god Pete." Maggie was crying. Matt was fitting the story together with the facts in his head – a teenager, a mother and violent ex-lover, George, prison.

"Mags, I've got to go. There are all sorts of people ringing me, you know, all the old gang. Let's meet up soon. Well, there'll be the funeral anyway."

"Pete, I can't believe it."

"I know, babe, he was the best. An inspiration. I'll let you know the arrangements. Ta ta, look after yourself."

"Bye." Maggie's last attempts at holding it together gave way and she let the tears flow.

"Oh Mags I'm so sorry." Matt moved around the table and knelt at her side and held her.

"Matt, he was a wonderful guy, like a teacher.... a guru."

"I know, I know Mags. I think I met him. George right? I met him in prison."

"You what?" The shock stopped her crying.

"I met him at Wandsworth. Thin, long hair, deep brown eyes. Talked about philosophy, belief, poetry."

"Yeah, that's right, that's George. He was on the marches, on the demonstrations. He was like a father-figure. He helped everyone, he was like our spiritual leader. Oh Matt, I'm so sad I haven't seen him all this time. He just....he kind of disappeared from my life, but I knew he was there, somewhere. And now he's not."

Matt held her tight, held the shaking body. "I know, he helped me too. He was a solitary light in that dark place, a sane voice in that mad chatter."

"Why didn't you tell me?"

"I didn't know you knew him. I forgot about it."

After a few minutes they paid and left, the waiters looking bemused. They walked slowly, sadly back to the apartment where they went soberly to bed and held each other gently, quietly talking about George, his message, his wisdom.

Maggie wept silently. Matt kissed away her tears, trying to offer some consolation, but failing. The truth was he missed George too, knowing that he wasn't of this world anymore.

"He's still with us Mags, just behind the curtain, beyond the limit of our knowledge."

"I know, I know..." she said, and slept.

* * * * * * * *

When Matt woke he was aware he'd been dreaming he was having a shower, but the shower still seemed to be on, the sound of the water still filling his ears. He quickly realised that torrential rain was hitting the windows of the apartment and Maggie wasn't beside him.

Pulling himself from sleep he glanced around and blearily made out her silhouetted form hunched on a chair by the window. She was hugging herself wrapped in a bath towel gazing through the droplet-spangled pane. Although she must have heard him getting out of the bed and clumping across the floor towards her, she didn't move. He put his hand on her shoulder.

"Mags?"

She didn't respond. There was a half empty mug of black coffee on the floor by the chair. She had her knees up by her chest and her arms wrapped around them, her mouth kissing a knee-cap.

"Are you okay?"

She nodded imperceptibly. "I can't believe he's gone, Matt," she said in a tiny voice. "Just can't believe it."

"Oh Mags." He stooped to the side of her and awkwardly hugged her sideways, straightening up almost immediately because it was so uncomfortable. "D'you want more coffee?"

"Sure."

He took the mug and busied himself with the kettle in the kitchenette. This wasn't what he'd planned. He'd wanted to show her around, take her to the Louvre, the Eiffel Tower, all the sights. Treat her, spoil her, to assuage his guilt. But now she was upset, grieving for George, and the excitement wouldn't be there. The trip was overshadowed by George's violent murder and Paris for her would now be forever associated with this event. Not that he wasn't upset too, but George, for him, was a more fleeting acquaintance.

Returning with the coffees he coaxed her away from the window to sit with him on the bed.

"Tell me about George, Mags. When did you meet him?"

She blew her nose on a tissue and sipped some coffee. "It was on the anti war march, Iraq, WMD. We all met, Pete, Tommo, Tash, the whole gang. And George. He was like, like, our dad, but on our level." She paused and took another mouthful of coffee, shook her mane of curls out and cleared her throat. "Some of us were very militant, wanted to do more than march. We wanted to storm Downing Street or cause trouble in Parliament Square, but George always calmed things down, talked sense, told us that wasn't the way. He talked about Ghandi rising above the moment, showing strength through restraint, all that stuff. At first we argued with him, told him he was soft and we needed to be more pro-active, but eventually, quietly, he talked us round."

"Yeah, that sounds like George."

The rain had almost stopped now and the sky was lighter; maybe they'd be able to get out in an hour or so and not get soaked, Matt thought.

"I was going through a bad time with my dad back then. Well, you know things are never that good with him. It all started about that time."

"Why was that?"

"It was when Gabriella started getting straight As for everything. Dad thought that was it. At last he'd got a daughter who was achieving at school as opposed to one that was always in trouble and in detention. After that it was always 'Gabriella this, Gabriella that. Why can't you be like Gabriella' etc. That really pissed me off, having a younger sister who was better than me. It made me want to rebel even more and dad hated me for it. George was what I wanted a father to be. He kind of became my dad for a bit. For me."

Matt thought of what George had told him about the other teenager which had sounded so plausible and innocent. Was that really the case, or was George, or rather, had George been a serial paedophile? He'd probably never know. But had he had relations with Maggie? He looked at her drinking her coffee, peering into the mug lost in thought.

"So you saw a lot of him?"

She considered for a moment. "Yes, I suppose I did. We hung out a bit. I used to tell him about my dad, how we didn't get on. George always managed to get things in perspective, see the wider picture. He made me feel valued. Like I wasn't worthless just because I wasn't good academically. He encouraged me to do drama when I told him that's what interested me."

"Did you go round to his place?" Matt couldn't help asking the question and hoped he'd made it sound off hand.

"Sometimes, but mostly we'd meet up in Soho. He'd buy drinks at The French House. He liked cocktails. I thought it really exotic and sophisticated. That was before cocktails got popular again. We'd talk for hours. Then sometimes he'd take me to a film at the art cinema off Leicester Square, or we'd go for a meal in Chinatown. He was really good at oriental food, knew the best things to get."

Matt couldn't ask the next question that was on his lips. He didn't know what to think now or quite how he felt, not knowing the answer to that question. He'd instinctively trusted George when he'd met him, but now he didn't know if that initial feeling was correct. A seed of doubt, of suspicion, had been planted in his mind and niggled him, growing by the minute from a floating suggestion to a rooted idea. 'All you need is a little doubt'. Could George really have been a serial sex-offender? Maybe, as he'd said, it depended what you chose to believe.

It was late morning by the time they eventually left the apartment after more cups of coffee and croissants Matt had fetched from the boulangerie downstairs. A weak sun was struggling through the post-rain haze as they walked through the city making for the Louvre. Matt had persuaded Maggie that since she was in Paris she had to visit it if only to say she had. Uncharacteristically she'd readily agreed, her usual independent assertiveness giving way to a willingness to be led in this instance. More surprisingly Matt now found her holding his hand as they walked the Paris streets. She seemed suddenly to need physical contact and he noticed she appeared to have shrunk somehow. Her more usual confidant, strutting gait had been replaced by something more apologetic, less assured and vulnerable. That spark wasn't there.

They stopped by the Seine and leant on the substantial balustrade. The river moved heavily on its inevitable journey, eddies and vortexes in places mere adjuncts to its un-opposable will, this liquid leviathan silently sliding between its banks.

She leant her head on his shoulder, an unknown gesture. "It's beautiful," she said, her voice cracking, and he knew she was crying. He let her be, not wanting to break the stillness, then when she sobbed he put his arms round her and folded her into his chest. He felt protective, paternal. He stood shielding her, his lips pressed into the thick mat of curls on the top of her head, inhaling the smell of her hair.

The Louvre is vast and they only touched a small part of it. Despite the time of year there were crowds, particularly around the iconic pieces – the Mona Lisa, the Venus de Milo – and they found they tired quickly sauntering the wide galleries and endless art. There's only so much you can take in at a time Matt told her, so they decided not to make a misery of it and went in search of food.

Ultimately they found it more convivial to their mood to roam around the city, going into public buildings they came across if they took their fancy. The Sainte Chapelle was just such a sight they happened upon and Maggie loved the amazing blues of the stained glass.

So they passed the few days they'd booked, quietly in each other's company. They hugged and held hands. They didn't have sex. Matt did his audition, which passed off well enough, the conductor non-committally appreciative. He managed to raise Maggie's spirits a few times with a joke or the trip up the Eiffel Tower, but generally she was unimpressionable, George's death permanently colouring her mood and opening up memories she'd kept locked away for so long.

She talked of her teenage years over dinners, her resentment of her dad's treatment of her and lack of understanding. Then she blamed herself for failing at school in a confused vindication of her dad; Why would he have been proud of her? She was a loser! Of course Gabriella was his favourite, she had achieved something. By the time they were half way through a meal and she'd had half a bottle of wine she'd become maudlin, blaming herself for everything and again beating herself up for not having kept in touch with George.

Pete had texted to say the funeral would be in ten day's time and that 'date in the diary' concentrated her mind. A visit to Sacré Coeur was a high point. She loved the cocooned dark stillness inside, lit only by candles, an occasional window and the light spill from the entrance doors. Having climbed up to its elevated position looking out over Paris and been blinded by the bright white of the exterior, the contrasting close womb-like interior was welcoming and reassuring. They sat in the pews in the centre of the church looking at the sanctuary covered by the huge domed mosaic of Christ with outstretched arms. Although the inside of the church was generally dark this mosaic was lit by up-lighters and the blue background and gold illuminations glowed in the gloom.

Maggie felt for his hand. They sat in silence, broken only by the shuffle of visitors and the echoing plunk of pews being knocked.

"What are we doing here, Matt?" she abruptly whispered.

Matt was a bit confused. *In Sacré Coeur? In Paris?* "What do you mean?"

"Here. On earth."

"Phew, that's a big question. A bit unexpected Mags."

"When things like this happen it kind of makes you wonder, doesn't it? I mean, religion, war, birth, death, it's all random stuff right. You're born, you kind of go through life and shit happens sometimes and some people have a great time and some people have a crap time. And some people believe in stuff and some don't and everyone's fighting about something or other, grabbing this and fucking up that..."

"Sssh Mags, we're in a church."

"We're in France, no one'll know what I'm saying. Anyway I'm whispering! And then all these people die and nothing's changed. Everyone's just as fucked up as the previous generation. And what does it all mean? It's all so depressing."

"Mags, I think you're upset. You're sad about George and it's making you depressed. Honestly, you'll feel so much better when all this is out of the way, after the funeral."

"What, so I can forget about it? So that I can pretend everything's okay? What am I doing with my life Matt? What the hell am I doing trying to be an actress and working in a shitty pervy joint? Where's the meaning in that?"

Matt knew there was probably no answering this kind of interrogation but had to find something to say in return, preferably something positive, and instinctively chose to agree obliquely.

"I often think things like that Mags, you know, what am I doing singing a role in some opera house to filthy rich people when others are starving in Africa and refugees are drowning trying to get away from a living hell that used to be their home? But we've all got to do our thing, follow our different destinies, try to help others where possible, but ultimately we can't change the world, we can only change little things in our immediate lives and hope that helps the situation."

"But that's such a load of shit. That's just a cop out. That's tokenism. You might as well do nothing at all." Maggie's voice was rising as she warmed to her theme.

"Mags shall we go. I need a cup of coffee."

"Oh," she inflected, "I like it here. Let's stay a bit longer?"

"Well, let's not have an argument. You know?"

"I'm not arguing Matt, I'm just saying you can't pay lip service to it. You've got to do more than that."

He thought of replying and trying to rationalise the point, but changed his mind. "Maybe."

They sat in silence once more, he holding her hand in his.

Time yawned in the cavernous space.

"It's so beautiful it makes you want to believe," she said.

Chapter 32

"Oh god that's all I need. Now Richard's pissed off with me."

"Why's that?"

"He wants me to audition for this West Side Story thing and I've told him all along I don't want to do musicals."

They'd been back from Paris a few weeks now. Matt's contract was over, and they had slipped into a temporary 'home routine' before his next engagements.

"But Mags, he's going to be pissed off if he's trying to find you work and you refuse even to audition for things. And why won't you anyway? It's a brilliant piece, fantastic music and amazing dance numbers which you'll be really good in."

"Yeah, but I don't want to get known for doing musicals. You know once you go down that route, you don't get any respect as a serious actor."

"Mags, this is one of the best musicals ever written, a really tight script, lyrics by Sondheim, and Bernstein writing phenomenal music. You know the story right?"

"Not really. It's got that Maria song hasn't it?"

"Yes, but you know it's Romeo and Juliet updated to twentieth century America?"

"Oh right, because it's based on Shakespeare that makes it different."

"Mags, come on, give it a chance." Matt went to the kitchen to get some coffee. Maggie was still looking at the computer screen. "Why not look it up? Go on YouTube and watch some clips. Honestly I'm sure you'll love it," he shouted. "D'you want coffee?"

"Sure."

When it was made he came and stood behind her sipping his coffee as she found the site and began scrolling through the offerings. "Don't watch the Carreras/ Te Kanawa version; that'll put you right off. Go for an American company, a Broadway production or something. Yeah that looks good."

She clicked on a New York off-Broadway production done with minimal sets and costume. It was edgy, pacey, looked the part. From her silence, as the footage rolled, Matt knew she was interested. After watching a bit of the overture she skipped forward to the Jets music. Who couldn't be excited by the tension in that finger-clicking, percussion tingling routine? He noticed her ankle twitching in time with the beat. It was hard not to get involved.

"Is Richard putting you forward for a part?"

"It's ensemble and maybe cover Anita."

"Well you'd certainly look the part."

"That's just it Matt, they're interested more for what I look like than my acting ability."

"Well, Mags, that's the way it is. Most casting's done as much on the way you look as anything else. Then they sift out those who can act, sing, dance etc."

"I know, I know..."

"So they're obviously going to try to find people who look Puerto Rican."

"Oh wow, look at that."

Even to Matt's untrained eye there was clearly some pretty spectacular dancing going on, with acrobatic leaps and slides thrown in. She was getting into it and by the time she'd got to the finale he was fairly sure she was convinced.

"So what d'you think?"

"I don't know. I mean it's a really good show, I can see that. But it's only chorus and a cover. I was doing that kind of thing in rep theatres ages ago – bit parts and covers. I've been making a stand to get something decent. And this is going out on tour for weeks before a 'possible' West End transfer."

Matt's heart sank. "But Mags, without being cruel, you haven't had much work recently and is it really worth holding out for parts endlessly? Isn't it at least better to be working in the profession?"

She sighed, tapping her fingers absent-mindedly on the computer. "It means going out of London, living in some shitty digs probably, sharing with people I don't know, all that stuff. I don't know I want to do that enough just to do chorus. And I'll probably be older than most of them, you know, young hopefuls just out of college all expecting to be the next, I don't know, Hugh Jackman or Anne Hathaway."

Matt was determined not to give up so soon. "But come on Mags, wouldn't it be better than what you're doing now? Turning up for castings and hardly getting anything and working at the club. I mean in Paris you said what the hell am I doing working there or something like that. I know, you said 'Where's the meaning in that?'"

"Well, it's fairly good money with the tips."

"I know but.." *How to put it?* "Wouldn't you prefer to do something you could be proud of, working as a team to make a quality show which would move audiences, maybe change their lives in some way, than just tarting around in a pervy bar just to earn good tips."

"Oh thanks, tarting around in a pervy bar, that's what you think I do."

"Well, you said it yourself."

"But you're making it sound really sordid, like some prostitute's joint."

"Well it is, kind of; a kinky sex bar where people go to get off on S and M and probably pick up a screw."

"Fuck off Matt. What's the difference between that and kids going to a nightclub hoping to pick up? People who go to an S&M bar are just going to meet like-minded people in a consenting environment. We all get kicks different ways, Matt, don't be so bloody purist."

"Yeah, but you've got to admit that dressing in all that gear and turning up with a whole lot of other people who are just trying to get off on S&M is a bit different from normal people going to a bar."

"It's still trying to get off Matt. They're trying to get off too, they're just not into S&M."

"But you must admit it's different. It's not so natural, you know, it's more extreme."

"It may be extreme but it's just being honest about what turns you on. I mean are you suggesting that I'm perverted just because that's how I get my kicks?"

"No, of course not. That's up to you, but...." *Can't she see it's different?* "Look it's not the kind of thing you'd let a six year old see, right?"

"You wouldn't let a six year old see an X- rated straight film either."

"No, but if a six year old happened to catch her parents having sex normally it would be much easier to explain and less damaging than if they were whipping the shit out of each other dressed like Nazis."

Maggie didn't say anything immediately. He thought maybe he'd got through. "It would be better if she didn't see either."

"Okay, maybe, but don't you see the difference? One is pure lust, sex for its own sake and the other's...making love."

"What are you trying to say Matt? We don't know how to make love?"

"I don't know. No. I'm just saying it's different."

They were both silent, digesting the impasse and its implications. A can of worms had possibly been opened and neither knew if this signalled a complete showdown or whether it would pass and they'd carry on as before.

"All I was saying was..."

"It's okay Matt, you don't have to."

"No, listen, I didn't want to get into an argument about that, I was just suggesting wouldn't it be nicer to be involved in a show, in an artistic enterprise, than carrying on with what you've been doing."

"I don't know."

"Well at least go to the audition and see if you get offered it and then you can decide. It's a bit theoretical at the moment. Promise me you'll do the audition at least."

Her silence, Matt thought, suggested a possibility, it was just a question of how much what she'd seen on YouTube had tempted her.

"I bet George would have encouraged you to do it, to use your talent, to give people joy." Matt realised as soon as he said it that this was an unfair and manipulative way to urge his case, emotively invoking a dead friend's memory, but he'd said it now, and went back to his score.

Twenty minutes later he heard her humming along with Anita's song playing on the computer. She had a husky voice, sexy and jazzy, and Matt had never understood why she didn't work on it.

A few days later she burst into the flat flushed and out of breath.

"Well, how was it?" he asked after she had flung herself into his embrace.

"Great, they want me to go back and sing some of Anita." She was ripping off her coat and scarf. "They were really nice. The choreographer was fantastic; god, I tell you Matt, that routine was hard." She kicked off her shoes and went to fill the kettle.

Matt turned off the recording of the Arsenal-Wolves match he'd been watching, knowing she'd need to unload the day's events which she duly proceeded to do, telling him in detail about the audition, the other people involved, demonstrating bits of the routine, what the audition panel were like. It was obvious she was fired up by the whole experience and he was infected by her enthusiasm. He hadn't seen her so animated for ages, George's death, followed by the funeral, having depressed her for weeks. It was wonderful she was so inspired.

"So when d'you have to go back?"

"Friday, three twenty. It's only four days away. And I've got to learn that song by then."

"Well, you've got some work to do. Are you going to go for some coaching?"

"Don't know. It's a bit late notice. I haven't been to David for over a year."

"Give him a ring, see if he can fit you in. I'm sure he'll manage something if you explain the situation."

Maggie's original reluctance to be in a musical tour seemed to have disappeared in the excitement of the audition process and Matt could tell she now desperately wanted to be offered the job. He knew the feeling himself, sometimes it wasn't that you wanted the job so much as being offered it; you didn't want anyone else being offered it over you. That competitive instinct drove you to want to be picked above everyone else to reinforce your worth and massage the ever-present ego. That was the cruelty of auditions, the inevitable rejections which, though doubtless objective, nonetheless hurt your self-esteem every time because it felt so personal. We all want to be loved, Matt thought.

Arsenal thankfully beat Wolves three one, but as so often their unpredictable form and lack of cohesion gave Matt some minor heart attacks, as they so nearly let Wolves through on countless occasions.

Two days later Matt had to go to Ireland for a series of four Messiahs in five days, a traditional pre-Christmas fixture of one of the leading Dublin choral societies. The fee pro rata wasn't wonderful but the four concerts together provided a satisfactory pay packet for the week so his agent had booked him in. He hadn't been to Dublin before so was looking forward to seeing the city and judging for himself whether the renowned 'genius' pint was really so much superior to the licensed variety everywhere else.

Maggie's recall fell on Matt's second performance day and she texted shortly before the concert to say she'd got the job. As he had anticipated she then proceeded to wonder whether she really wanted it. Her agent was mad keen she should do it and Matt again warned her that he would undoubtedly be hacked off if she now turned it down. After all, he continued, if it did transfer and was a hit with the critics it could be a good run and she would be bound to get on as Anita. He texted he thought she should do it, but didn't get any response before he had to turn off the phone to get ready for the performance.

During the opening Sinfonia he found himself thinking of Maggie. Would she do the tour? Or would she throw it away stubbornly to satisfy her pride? She really was impossible sometimes in her expectations.

The tenor began his recitative 'Comfort Ye', repeating the opening phrase several times so that Matt found it difficult to refrain from smiling as he remembered her in the Paris restaurant doing her Hamlet soliloquy. And then in the aria that followed, 'Ev'ry valley shall be exalted', when the constant repetition of 'Ev'ry valley' additionally brought to mind an imaginary energetic Male Voice Choir eulogising the ascendancy of the Rhondda! He found it difficult to stop himself from smiling. Maggie! 'To be or not to be.. to be…to be or not…' He was shrieking again inside, seeing her cod-face across the table, remembering their helpless hilarity. The stabilising influence of the uplifting chorus 'And the Glory of the Lord' settled him somewhat before his prophetic proclamation, 'Thus saith the Lord'.

Matt proclaimed the prophet's words of his next utterance with Old Testament vehemence, threatening to 'shake all nations, the earth, the sea, the dry land' with ever increasing intensity of coloratura in the alliterative runs.

He was still vaguely thinking about Maggie and whether she'd do the tour when the alto announced 'Behold, a virgin shall conceive, and bear a son, and shall call his name Emmanuel, GOD WITH US.'

Matt was struck by the bare cold import of the prophecy in the next number, set to Handel's lean accompaniment, and the peremptory finality of the last chords, as if saying 'That's it'. He couldn't help thinking back to that concert nine months or so before when he might have got a virgin pregnant and what kind of finality that might have had on his life; paying maintenance for a child in another country! Despite his term in prison, he thanked his lucky stars that the girl in Sweden had fought him off and avoided such a possible outcome. On reflection, how mad had he been to even think of screwing her without protection? God what would it be like to be a father, to actually have a child? The responsibility, the compromise!

Yet, there was a part of him, he realised, that envied Chris's uncomplicated existence, the roundness of it, the completeness of that circle of love. With a start, he came back to the concert to sing his next recitative about darkness covering the earth, and the aria describing the people of the earth walking in darkness until they discover the light.

Sitting, he thought back to Phoebe's christening a few weeks ago and what it would be like to have a child. He'd really enjoyed holding her and there was something primordial that had come over him, an overpowering instinct to protect this tiny helpless thing in his arms, almost a genetic compunction to preserve this embodiment of his species. Was this a mid-life crisis? Was Dawkins' 'Selfish Gene' asserting itself? Was his mid-life genetic make-up urging him to project his characteristics forward in time in his progeny? And this feeling wasn't just sexual desire; there was the beginning of a different yearning here, a need for nurturing and emotional investment.

It had surprised him, that feeling, as hitherto he'd felt no desire for a family, for pro-creation. Now he wondered. Somehow it didn't seem much of a possibility at the moment. Maggie and he weren't exactly thriving sexually, a subject not mentioned since George had died. And he was still unsure how he felt about her. It was like they were together from habit and too apathetic or scared to change the situation.

He thought back to his days and nights with Caterina in Paris and he suddenly longed for that fulfilment, for that complete immersion in divine union. He wanted to escape again to that neverland of blistering romance, secret sex and lavish living. An immoral hedonist's delight. He could almost taste the joy on his tongue.

But, he'd heard nothing from her. Not an email. Not a text.

Chapter 33

The train at last pulled to a halt in the covered station of Stockholm Centrallen where the reduced light turned the window glass into a mirror bringing Signe's reflection eerily before her staring eyes. She saw a teenage girl gripped by a panic she hadn't foreseen, arrived in a city she hardly knew with virtually no luggage and a couple of thousand krona in her purse.

She got up with a start, realising that everyone else was leaving and not wanting to appear weird staring at the window, fetched her trolley bag and exited the carriage. She followed the other passengers trying to give the impression she knew where she was going. In the main concourse of the station she picked up a map of the city from the tourist information stand and stuffed it in her bag then made for the main exit.

Coming out onto the street the damp cold hit her and she buttoned up her coat and put on her gloves. She had no idea where she was going or what she was going to do. She'd not really thought further than the train journey. On the way she'd been reflecting on what she'd left behind, not looking forward to what lay ahead. Once on the train she couldn't help feeling that what she was doing was crazy, reckless, but it was too late. She'd done it, there was no going back. She had felt guilty for putting her 'parents' through the agony of not knowing where she was, but she hadn't seen a way around it. They just couldn't know, because if they did they'd just come and find her and take her home. And that wasn't an option; this was her time, her choice, her baby.

Now she was here in Stockholm, alone, knowing no one. Everything was grey. She looked up and down the street and although she could see some colours in windows and cars hissing by on the wet road the whole impression was grey. It was drizzling and calm, low clouds hugging the tops of the buildings and wetting every surface. Signe walked right and under a concrete bridge to a large intersection. She waited as the pedestrian crossing bell clanged out its dull seconds telling you to wait, and crossed when it suddenly went into machine-gun mode. She had to wait again at another crossing as the intersection was large. Reaching the other side she was startled by a train rumbling across the bridge to her right. There was open water in front of her and she walked to the quay and looked into the dark depths. It was totally black and forbidding, steely-still, just puckered by the falling drizzle. The opposite bank was hazy, all definition lost in the spectrum of infinitesimal water droplets between her and it.

She looked to the right and saw a huge dark tower at the left end of a tall imposing building which had long narrow windows like giant arrow slits along its length. On top of the tower was a circular stone canopy with a gold orb above. It was obviously a church right by the water, just over another bridge. Signe suddenly felt the need to pray, to humble herself before God and ask his forgiveness and for His help now in her loneliness. She made her way over the bridge and came to where she imagined the entrance should be, but it wasn't there, it was further along a wall which linked with this end of the building. She walked to the entrance and saw the large sign - Stadtshusset.

How stupid. Of course, she recognised it now. She'd seen pictures of Stockholm town hall so many times before, but from a different angle. She felt silly as she trudged back across the bridge with no more idea where to go. But she now had it in her head to find a church and struck out across another bridge parallel to the railway bridge towards a black steeple above a tower. This must be a church. At the end of the bridge she followed a cobbled street round a corner and up a small rise, then turning left saw the church standing tall and lean across the square in front of her. Encouraged, she walked down the slope and across the road to the entrance. It was Riddarholms kyrken she discovered, but also read that it was now a museum housing armour and weaponry.

She turned away, walking around the museum and wandered across another bridge onto Gamla Stan. Ahead of her was another church up an incline. By now she was tired of walking and dragging the case which was awkward when there were cobbles, the small wheels resisting and bumping behind her. She was also very wet. Although for most of the pregnancy she had remained small and had easily hidden the bulge in her stomach by gradually acquiring a new wardrobe of full loose sloppy tops over baggy trousers mostly in black and grey – very 'emo' – the last few weeks had proved difficult, her bump suddenly catching up with the gestation period and swelling her to an uncomfortable size. At home she'd contrived to adopt a penchant for uncharacteristic fattening foods under the guise of appearing a bit depressed and comfort eating. Her family had initially been surprised, given her usual faddy habits, but had got used to the change, Lars enjoying an accomplice in the greed stakes. Melissa had made a few comments about her appearing to be putting on weight, but she'd played the emotional teenager role to perfection, going off in a strop when it was mentioned, but being sweetness and light when she was indulged, so that they preferred the rather overweight teenager 'going through a phase' than the thwarted, moody youth she became when they challenged her.

But now she was uncomfortable and had to stop, set the trolley bag upright and stretch her back, taking a few deep breaths to ease the pain in her lumbar. She felt a bit weak and faint from the sudden exertion after the four hour train journey and seeing a clock noticed it was in fact lunchtime. She knew she'd have to eat as she'd only had fruit and yogurt on the train. She crossed the wide road and started up the cobbled street to the church, but then saw an inviting coffee shop with warm lights glowing and a tempting display of cakes and pastries in the window. The drizzle was persistent and she was now cold as well as wet so the decision to go inside was easily made and within a couple of minutes she was sitting at a table with a steaming mug of hot chocolate, awaiting a baked potato. She was very aware that she wouldn't be able to do this often on her limited amount of cash, but she had to eat right now and her resistance was low. The enormity of what she had chosen to do was now hitting home. What had seemed a noble endeavour to fulfil this duty to her ideal now began to feel foolhardy and reckless and she was frightened of failing.

How had Mary managed it, had the strength to go through with it, in those days, without modern conveniences? Well she'd had Joseph, she conceded, who had 'hidden her away privily'. She had travelled on a donkey to the census, not wandered around alone in the rain dragging a suitcase. The hot chocolate was comforting and the warmth of it and the shop began to lift her spirits. When the potato arrived she realised she was ravenous and it didn't take her long to get through it, the tuna and cheese filling tasting particularly delicious. The warmth of the coffee shop was appealing and she was loath to leave it and brave the miserable streets again but the desire to reach the church inspired her, so after visiting the ladies' she paid and walked the short distance to the church.

When she came up to it she realised it was the Storkyrken which she knew of because that's where all the official religious ceremonies were held and the royalty married and buried. Inside it was warm and bright, the space lit by three, tiered electric candelabras suspended on long chains from the tall archways of the nave. The church was made of toffee-coloured bricks, the tall columns breaking into high arches of brickwork flanked by cream plastered walls and ceilings. Signe knelt for some time in the back row of the ivory painted pews, soaking up the atmosphere.

"I'm so sorry, could I ask you to move into a different pew. We have to replace some light bulbs." Signe was shocked by a man leaning towards her.

"Of course." In her confusion she dropped the gloves that she was holding between her palms and had to scrabble on the floor to find them. When she got up she knocked over her case which was propped in the pew beside her and it was awkward to pick up as it had fallen away from her, the handle beyond her reach.

"Don't worry I'll get it," the young man said and went around into the next pew to retrieve it for her. "I'm really so sorry to disturb you but we have to get this maintenance done before the services today." He smiled at her reassuringly. "Gosh, this is heavy, are you moving house?" he said with a small laugh.

Signe smiled shyly, caught off guard and embarrassed to know what to say. "No," she said, too hurriedly and earnestly, "no, just on my way. To see someone. To stay with a friend, yes."

"Oh, for Christmas?"

"Yes, that's it, for Christmas."

"Well, you'll have a wonderful long holiday." He was looking at her strangely holding the handle of her case in the aisle as she shuffled to get out of the pew. Her mind raced. *How long is it til Christmas? What's the date today? Of course, the fifteenth..*

" I'm..I'm not going to her immediately. My friend. I'm just going to spend a bit of time in Stockholm. You know, shopping, looking round the Christmas markets. Thank you." She took charge of her case once more. His expression was of concern. She felt she was blushing in her confusion. *Why can't I be more confidant? I'm acting like a naughty kid.*

"Have you got somewhere to stay?"

"Oh yes, I'm fine thanks." She realised she sounded unconvincing. As she turned to leave she noticed the large ladder another man was holding and which her new acquaintance went to help him erect under one of the large candelabras above the pew she'd been sitting in. He spoke briefly to the man before disappearing quickly across the church. The other man climbed the ladder and began replacing occasional bulbs in the array.

Signe turned towards the exit but her attention was caught by the incongruity of a model boat hanging in mid air in the side aisle. It was old-fashioned with gun turrets and masts and she couldn't think why it would be hanging in a church. She went over to it but there was nothing nearby to explain it. As she walked to the exit she saw a plaque of the Last Supper on the wall to the right of the west door and went to look at its heavily embossed brass relief work. There were the eleven disciples around the long table with Jesus in the middle and a female figure leaning, swooning almost, against His chest. Mary Magdalene. Signe felt a prick of pique. She wished she could have been in that position, so close, so intimate with the Lord.

But she was chosen now. She had been chosen above the Magdalene to carry the Lord for His second coming. The signs had all been there; the annunciation, His manifestation in the concert, the Immaculate Conception. As she thought this, as if in confirmation the baby moved awkwardly and she had to shift her position to ease the abrupt pain in her side.

"Here is an address if you need it," the man from before was at her side proffering a card, slightly red faced, "just in case you need a place to stay at short notice."

Signe didn't quite know what to do on the spur of the moment. Accepting might suggest more than she wanted to reveal of her circumstances, but refusing would cut off a possible refuge.

"Oh thank you. I'm sure I won't need it, but it's very kind of you to think of it." She took the card, shoved it in her pocket, nodded an apologetic smile at him and headed for the door. *He seems to have guessed my circumstances. How did he know? Of course, my case. But lots of people have cases and are travelling. It must be because I look young and should be in school. I need to be careful.*

Outside the church the cold was immediate and she buttoned her coat again, turned to her right and walked as briskly as she could in the grey light. It was only about two-thirty but the afternoon was even now beginning to fade in the gloom of the overcast day. She again didn't know where she was going but found herself walking across an open space with a huge building to her left. Of course, now she realised, the royal palace with the state rooms. She had a vague memory of going there ages ago when they had stayed with Uncle Mats and Aunt Agi. She remembered they had got really bored going around all the rooms and hearing the history, but it had been worth it because they'd got huge ice creams afterwards on the quay.

She walked down to that very spot by the water, dragging the case over the uneven cobbles, and stood looking across the water at the taxi boats nosing to the various landing stages on the other bank where grand buildings lined the road. Then she saw it and panicked. The boat, the Viking Barking ship, and all the memories flooded back – the concert, the meeting on the deck, the trial, the agony. But then she saw it wasn't, of course. It was another ship, but so similar, with masts and spars, an old-fashioned sailing boat just like in Göteborg. She relaxed and was even able to be amused at her mistake.

And then she thought, that's why I'm here and seeing this boat, because it all started then, at the concert, with him looking at me, signalling that the time had come which had been foretold. She marvelled again. "God moves in mysterious ways," she said out loud and smiled, warmed by the revelation and aware again of her divinity. She, Signe, had been chosen by God, of all the millions of women in the world, to bear again His manifestation on earth. It was so humbling, so incredible, so unspeakably amazing that tears started to her eyes and she knelt in the instant on the cold stones to offer a prayer, no a confession, an apology for not being worthy in spite of God's superior knowledge. She had to beg His forgiveness for not being worthy enough, but also thanking Him, beseeching Him to accept her thanks for His undeserved trust and faith in her, this unworthy human who now begged for His strength to carry through His will, to carry His most precious Son to heal the world again.

"Thank you Lord. I'm sorry I'm not good enough, forgive me in my weakness, I can only try to do better…" Her tears prevented further prayer and a sudden shooting pain in her knee on account of the cobbles caused her to stand, which she did with difficulty and with the aid of the case beside her. She brushed away her tears, rubbed her knees and noticed an elderly couple observing her nearby. She made a sign of the cross, nodded to them and smiled. They nodded back, seemingly reassured. Then suddenly, not two metres in front of her, a seagull landed on one of the posts that boats tie up to, landed and looked at her with its grey eye. It turned its head and looked with the other eye, then lifted its wings, stretching them back, arching upwards exactly like the Angel Gabriel's wings in the picture in her mum's, in Melissa's, bible, while lowering its head as if bowing to her. Signe stood motionless as it slowly lowered its wings, ruffled them into its back, gave her a sideways look again and threw its head back emitting a deafening repeated call which was immediately taken up by hundreds of other gulls which miraculously materialised above her head, wheeling and swooping til the din was almost unbearable. The gull on the post then flapped its wings, lifting off and hovering about ten feet from the ground looking at her, before elevating vertically amongst the tumultuous host of wings and they all peeled away noisily across the water.

It was an extraordinary moment which left her stunned, her head ringing with the noise. The way the gull had bowed to her and looked at her so knowingly and then hovered as if suspended from the sky amongst those beating wings, was so unbelievable.

Unnatural, she thought, and then thought that too must be a sign, of course. Like the dreams she'd had, when she'd been chosen by the angel to serve God. She was beginning to work it all out. Just now she had prayed to God to help her and now this bird had bowed to her, arched its wings like an angel to show God had heard her, sent his angel to acknowledge her and all the other angels in the form of birds rose up and saluted her as the chosen one.

Now it all made sense. As she had always been told and read, the signs were always there if you could only read them. And now she could. And the boat was a sign too, the boat suspended in the church and the one she was now looking at across the water were symbols of her conception, of the vessel that she was for this precious treasure.

She was elated, these revelations emanating as they did from her confusion and doubt, now reaffirming her duty, her role in God's plan, a role she now felt even more inspired to fulfil. It had been so difficult recently and she'd felt so alone, planning her flight from Göteborg in the train. The secrecy, the need for complete invisibility then and now until the day of her delivery, had been a huge burden and she'd wondered whether she'd been correct. She'd prayed but had felt alone as if God had abandoned her. But now these signs showed her so clearly that all was well and that her decisions were correct. Here in Stockholm God was speaking to her, allowing her to see his messages to her and helping her piece together the tapestry of His design, all the threads coming together to complete the perfect picture.

These thoughts were wonderful and filled her with a glow. She felt it was the Holy Spirit and at that moment the baby moved inside her as if confirming all these things. It was too much and she wept again in her gratitude, her hands on her belly, smoothing the restless movement inside.

Recovering herself, she was aware that the afternoon was fading away and it was beginning to get dark. She'd have to find somewhere for the night soon. Putting her hand in her pocket to replace her tissue she felt the card the man had given her in the church. She read the details; it was a hostel for homeless people, an ecumenical foundation. It seemed safe enough as long as she didn't have to answer all sorts of questions and provide ID. It seemed the sensible option despite her misgivings. She went over to a street lamp and got the map out to find the street, which she soon located on Södermalm island, just south of where she was. Feeling like everything had fallen into place, she set off along Skeppsbron.

When she reached the address she found the hostel was closed. A notice on the door said it would reopen at 1700. Signe groaned, now really tired after walking about for so long and the baby was paining her and her back ached. She wanted to be rid of the case and sit down. In addition she was hungry again. It was four o'clock. An hour to kill.

She toiled back up towards the centre and found a café in Götgarten and bought another hot chocolate and a cheese and ham Panini which they warmed up for her. The food was welcome, but she realised how alone she felt. Here in Stockholm, away from family and friends, not that she had many, was hard.

But she now imagined how they might react at home, their adopted daughter disappearing just before Christmas, probably thinking she'd been abducted by some lunatic, locked up in a basement to become a slave to some weirdo's sexual fantasies. She'd heard of that, people being locked away for years, eventually becoming completely dependent on their abuser and even, bizarrely, becoming emotionally attached to them. It was called Stockholm Syndrome, which was weird. It seemed crazy. How could anyone subject themselves like that? How could they want to be ruled by someone dictating to them, demanding obedience, insisting they blindly obey their rules and almost, like, worship them? She didn't get it. She couldn't imagine ending up like that.

She looked at her watch, it was twenty to five. There was a queue of about a dozen people already waiting for the hostel to open when she got there. One or two acknowledged her with a nod, the majority avoided eye contact. She shuffled forwards with the rest when the doors opened. It was 230SK a night the guy on reception told her. Just one night? She was so tired and the thought of traipsing around with the case in the drizzle tomorrow weakened her resolve. What if the baby took a few days to come? She needed some rest to be strong for the birth. "Two nights please." Four hundred and sixty krona, nearly a quarter of her money gone, what with food and drink as well. But it wouldn't be long now, a couple of days.

She was given a wrist band, one of those ones that tighten and you can only get off by cutting. It had a blank square on which the guy had written 15/16 with a sharpie pen, then she was through to the lobby area. It was cleaned but grubby. There was no dirt on the floor but the walls were scuffed and marked, bits of paint flaked off here and there. It seemed like a mixture of school and hospital she thought, as there was a smell of institution overlaid with sanitation.

There were some tired notices on a cork wallboard informing lodgers of the house rules, opening hours, washing facilities and responsibilities. She noticed the hostel closed at nine in the morning. It seemed to be merely a place to sleep, but you could get breakfast. Another section had services that were available; advice, legal aid, government benefits, back to work schemes, therapies. There was the Stadmission offering advice, training, rehabilitation.

She found the women's sleeping area, about twenty beds in a room, no privacy. A simple frame bed with duvet and pillow. She looked around, noting what other people were doing with their possessions, arranging them by or under their beds, making some semblance of ownership and individuality. One had a teddy bear on the pillow, another a Koran. She chose a bed and set her case beside it, smiling shyly to a woman next to her who didn't smile back but continued sorting her things.

She was tired now, really tired, and just wanted to lie down which she did, fully clothed but without her coat and boots. She pulled the duvet around her, welcoming the horizontal, and closed her eyes. It was bliss, the weight of the baby now supported, her back curled relieving that ache of uprightness. *Thank you Lord for helping me find this place of rest, this sanctuary for the night. Forgive me for my weakness and give me strength to complete your will.*

She woke with a start, hot and disorientated, disturbed by raised voices close by. The woman next to her was arguing with another woman, accusing her of putting her bags in her space. The altercation didn't last long, a few traded insults ending the matter, but leaving an edgy atmosphere.

Signe checked her coat pocket for her purse and felt relief. She found her toilet bag and went to the washroom she'd passed in the corridor on the way in to brush her teeth and again use the toilet. The baby moved, pressing down on her pelvic bone. Would it come soon? Would this be where he'd be born, with all these people he didn't know in a hostel? It would certainly be humble, but more public than she'd have liked. But God would decide, she merely had to submit to His will.

Back in the dormitory she got ready for bed even though it was only 7pm. The hour or so she'd slept meant she wasn't exactly sleepy anymore although her body was still tired, but she didn't know what else to do. And it was then, lying in the impersonal dormitory, with the movements and noises of the unknown occupants of the hostel shifting around her that, despite her size, she felt very small. Why had she not anticipated it would be like this? She had been so wrapped up in the excitement of organising her disappearance from Göteborg and keeping her pregnancy a secret for so long, that she'd never envisaged what the reality would be like. She'd put off any such thoughts and left them for the future. She'd had some vague idea about the birth being in a bright white room, bare and clean with a minimum of fuss. Some lady in a white medical coat assisting her, maybe it was a natural birthing unit in a hospital she didn't know, but it was straight forward, simple, uncomplicated. She realised she hadn't considered the practical reality of passing the time before the birth, being here in Stockholm with nothing to do and nowhere to go just waiting for it to happen. Somehow she'd deceived herself into thinking it would happen as soon as she'd got here in some miraculous way.

She turned onto her other side, the weight making this an effortful manoeuvre, and wondered what was happening at home. Her family would be worried now, wondering where she was and why she hadn't come home or contacted them. They'd have been into her room, checked and seen that all her things were there and been assured that she hadn't done exactly what she had done. They'd have rung Irma to see if she was with her and then perhaps tried another couple of friends. But Melissa wouldn't have wanted to make a noise about it, she'd have wanted to keep it quiet until they knew what had happened. She wouldn't want everyone talking about it. She'd have told Gustav not to ring the police or raise the alarm yet, which he undoubtedly would have suggested, she'd want to keep a lid on it for as long as possible to avoid embarrassment.

She thought of the Christmas preparations which had been planned for the weekend, bringing the tree in, decorating it and making the house ready for guests. The presents that had been bought and the cooking that Melissa would always do in preparation for the big day would all be thrown into chaos as the hours ticked by and she didn't show. How could she do this to them and put them through such anxiety? But they'd understand after the event when it was all revealed. They'd appreciate the importance of the secrecy and deception. That was a comfort at least, and the feeling of aloneness was tempered by the warmth of anticipating their joy at the revelation of her delivery of God's Son, of the honour that was bestowed on her and her family.

Chapter 34

Unfamiliar noises woke her. It took her moments to realise where she was, micro-seconds for her mind to process information particles from yesterday, stored in elusive chemical pathways, which had to stimulate the tender endings of nerves. Eventually a meaningful memory sequence presented to her awareness and seconds later she was sensible of her surroundings. She must have slept deeply, as one side of her body was numb. People were moving about, trudging to showers and back, wet hair, wet skin, towels moving through her vision. What time was it? She managed to find her watch in her sleeve. Seven-thirty. She must have slept for twelve hours but she felt exhausted.

What would she do today? The baby was due to come today or tomorrow so she wouldn't have long to wait. She wanted to find the Catholic church and see a priest. Where would she have the baby? She was waiting for a sign, some guidance. Everything had led here, but where to now? Time in the church praying would tell her she was sure, and feeling confident she went to shower and dress.

There was a simple breakfast downstairs in the one public room, so she followed the example of others and loaded a tray, finding herself hungry again. Over breakfast she studied the tourist map and located the Catholic Cathedral. Around the edge of the map there were adverts for restaurants, jewellery stores and clothes shops. Amongst them she noticed a young persons' 'drop-in' centre, the Ungarstation.

Back in the dormitory Signe stowed her bag under the bed and then set out in search of the cathedral. The drizzle had cleared leaving a colder, clearer day with a weak sun struggling to raise the temperature and hanging ineffectually above the horizon. Signe orientated herself to the main street and walked south to Medborgarplatzen which was bustling with people browsing the Christmas markets. Brightly coloured lights festooned from the canopies reflected off cellophane-wrapped multi-coloured sweets and chocolates, fruits and nuts, crafts and collectables. Cafés and restaurants were laying up tables under interlinked square umbrellas complete with space heaters and cushioned chairs. There was a huge Christmas tree in the middle of the square with a kiddies' merry-go-round next to it. She wandered between the stalls, distracted from her mission by the wealth of things for sale, things she remembered from when she was very young, things that reminded her of Christmases past.

There was a stall laden with smoked fish, herrings and soused mackerel, another covered in cheeses, fresh yogurt and butter. Next to this was an array of wild animals jointed and hung; boar, reindeer, elk;

pheasant, duck and goose. Wooden ornaments, carvings and wooden children's toys in bright colours, competed with sculptures made from glass, metal and enamel. A large bearded man was hanging a delicate wooden mobile from the canopy of a stall, looking incongruously like a giant from a fairy story in an Aladdin's cave.

She eventually dragged herself away from this cornucopia of colour and texture and found her way out of the square to Folkungagaten where she found the Cathedral. It was not what she'd expected at all; it looked more like a small church. She thought it looked sweet, orange brickwork set between stone pillars, decorative but modest, with twin domes either side of the central façade, but not a Cathedral! She went through the iron gateway, pushed open the wooden door, crossed the vestibule and entered the church.

She felt robbed. Well, cheated at least, but now she understood. It was a tardis. The inside was what she had expected except the middle of the east wall wasn't there. Where the altar should have been there was a gaping hole, the arch which formed the sanctuary roof had no back to it. Signe looked through this emptiness to another church, completely different in appearance. A gold geometric ceiling took the eye to a distant altar wall on which hung a large crucifix. The design was contemporary and made no concession to the design of the original church which she was standing in. Obviously this modern addition had been simply clamped onto the older building. She looked around the horizontally striped walls in brown and cream, the pillars on the walls supporting similarly striped arches. She looked up at the blue and brown painted wooden panels between the roof beams matching the blue inlay on the walls. Wooden stations of the cross flanked the arched window recesses as two large statues flanked what would have been the sanctuary; the Virgin Mary and, presumably, Sankt Erik. It was a church like she knew it, with the shiny brown wooden pews, the stone pulpit with its suspended canopy and the large iron candelabra hanging above the nave.

For Signe, old churches supported her faith. The knowledge that the church had been there for ages and hundreds of people had worshipped there before her gave it authenticity. A modern church didn't have that gravitas and provenance. A modern building for her failed to resonate with the bible stories, with the pictures in her mum's, Melissa's, bible. She couldn't relate to abstract designs and stylised iconography. For her the symbolism had to reach back in time and link with the days of Christ's divinity or it ceased to have meaning.

Out of curiosity rather than desire she walked down the nave and up the steps into the new part of the church, or rather, the Cathedral which it had become, and found her impressions confirmed as she looked at the cold impersonal modern interior which had been forced onto the back of the dear old church. Black wooden pews on concrete bases curved in an arc to the right, the whole building expanded sideways away from the altar in a wing built out to accommodate an increased seating area. There were tall oblong windows without ornament or relief illuminating dark brown brick walls. The congregation were orientated towards the unadorned sparse wall with the spot-lit crucifix, grim in its solitude. The plain altar below more resembled an operating table than a ceremonial place of worship, as if the body of Christ's teaching was to be clinically dissected leaving its truths laid bare. There was no room for wonder or mystery. This was brute belief, hard truth.

Too hard for Signe. Despite her firm faith she needed softness and curved edges. She went back to the old part of the Cathedral and found a pew near the back to say her prayers and commune with her God in the sanctuary of sympathetic architecture. It was a relief to sit down again and she couldn't believe how tired she was now getting, just half an hour walking about killed her back. She found she couldn't kneel for long and prayed for God to forgive her for addressing Him from a sitting position.

What should she do now? She hadn't foreseen this abundance of time. She longed for Irma, for a familiar face, for a hug. This Blessing was an onerous privilege, a hard honour for her to undertake. Now, in her final stages, she felt like she almost wouldn't be strong enough to go through with it.

After an hour of sitting on the hard pew she decided she needed a change and after genuflecting with difficulty, left the cathedral. Outside the sun had been forestalled in its attempt to warm the day by a darkening sky which was just beginning to deliver wisps of sleet. The temperature had fallen and a rawness bit her skin and pinched her nose. Signe was tempted to go straight back inside but she'd exhausted that space and wanted somewhere more comfortable to hang out. Cafés were inviting but she would inevitably spend money and she needed to save that resource. Maybe a library where she could read, but she didn't feel like reading right now. A film? Money again. Normally she'd have gone on her phone and looked things up, logged into certain sites and downloaded interesting articles. But she daren't. Not here in Stockholm.

She remembered the Ungarstation Youth centre on the map, got it out and saw it wasn't far, so with a sense of purpose she followed the route and ten minutes later found herself outside a modern block.

"Good morning, how are you?" a cheery lady greeted her.

"Fine thanks." Signe replied.

"Come on in. Cold outside now isn't it?"

"Ya."

"Have you been before? I don't remember seeing you."

"No. I'm just here for the day. You know, passing through."

"Of course, that's fine. I'm Sandi, just come and find me if there's anything you want. I'm normally around the reception here or in one of the offices."

"Okay, thanks."

"I'll take you through to the social room. There are a few girls here who come in quite often. There's some lunch served at twelve-thirty and we're open til five. You can make tea and coffee if you want. There's a television room through there you're welcome to use. Most people seem to like to chat in the social room though."

They had come into a lounge area where some teenagers were sitting talking.

"Hi girls, this is, oh sorry I didn't get your name."

"Maria, I'm Maria. Hi."

"Maria. She's not been here before. I'm sure you'll show her around. So, see you later."

"Thank you." Signe was suddenly really nervous.

"Hi. You wanna drink of something? I'm Red by the way."

"Hi, Maria."

"Cool."

"No, I'm fine thanks."

"Okay, well, sit down if you want. This is Tula, B and Josie."

"Hi how you doin'"

"We're just hangin' out here so feel free to join in."

"Thanks, don't worry about me I'm fine."

Signe curled into a chair as best she could. She tried to cover her condition. It would be simpler. The girls were talking about jobs, trying to find them, trying to get government support whilst looking for them. Signe was happy to sit and listen.

It turns out it was difficult. Particularly if you have no experience and no qualifications. But sometimes that's better than too many qualifications. Sure, you can be too qualified. The trouble is that once you find a job, if you find a job, it needs to pay enough money that it's worth having the job after tax and stuff. Because otherwise you're better off not having a job, particularly if you have a kid. Then you really can get some good handouts. Sure, you can even get a place, they give you a place to live. No shit! Could be worth getting pregnant. Try not getting pregnant. Laughs. Signe smiled not wanting to look out of it.

"So, looks like you'll be okay Maria."

"Yeah, you'll be okay!"

Laughs. Signe was uncomfortable now, the focus, the attention. They had known immediately of course. How did she think anyone didn't notice anymore?

"So where are you having your baby?" Red asked.

Signe knew she must be bright scarlet by now. "I'm going to family. I'm on my way there."

"Cool."

"Nice."

"I gotta get a baby. It'd sort me out. Get a place of my own." B said.

"Sure, I shouldn't've got rid of mine, but it was kinda the wrong time. I was fucked up," said Josie

"Yeah well, we was all fucked up back then."

And so the conversation went on, reminding Signe at times of Pro Green in a rap it seemed to machine-gun so quickly from one sentence to another, which allowed her to retreat to the shadows again. Lunchtime came and she gladly partook of the subsidised meal offered for a few krona. More people had arrived so by the time lunch was served there were about a dozen takers. Signe happily sat on the periphery listening more than taking part, which she did reluctantly if asked a question, but tried to block anything that might turn into a conversation. Fortunately most kids knew each other and were more interested in their own chat than involving her. A while after lunch she went and sat in the telly room and fell asleep in front of a docu-drama.

She was woken abruptly by someone shaking her shoulder. "Hi, I'm sorry but we close in fifteen minutes. I wanted to give you long enough to wake up."

"Thank you," she mumbled searching for her watch in her sleeve. Four forty-five. How long had she slept? Most of the afternoon it seemed. It was an effort getting up and when she did the baby started turning somersaults. She must have woken Him too. She got herself together and left the Ungarstation. There was no-one else there.

Again she found she was hungry and on the way to the hostel passed a pizza takeaway. She was ravenous for spicy pepperoni, why she had no idea. Normally she didn't care much for spicy food, but now she had to have it. She went in and ordered a regular with a coke, something else she didn't normally crave. Having made the order she remembered having heard somewhere that hot spicy food can bring on labour. Was this true or just a myth? Well she'd done it now and besides the baby was due.

When she woke in the morning her first thought was that the baby still hadn't come. Again she had slept deeply, remembering strange dreams but not their details. She was dying for a pee and as she sat there enjoying the relief and holding the large lump in front of her she realised how naïve she'd been to imagine the baby would come on the due date. It was only rough anyway, she'd worked it out using the online calculator at the church. But somehow she'd been sure that because it was this birth, His birth, it would be exact, a perfect pregnancy, a textbook birth.

Well, apart from the sickness in the beginning it had been uncomplicated. She hadn't seen a doctor or midwife of course, except for the initial confirmation. It had been her treasured secret. It was uncomfortable now, but that was to be expected. Even Mary must have been uncomfortable with this big lump, but Her birth was without pain. Signe couldn't expect that. She wasn't pure like The Virgin, she hadn't led that spotless life. She'd tried, but she knew she'd fallen short of that perfection. But God trusted her, had honoured her with this duty, so she would do her utmost not to fail Him.

As she packed her trolley bag she regretted leaving the hostel. It was a security she'd been glad of, but she felt she couldn't stay longer. She only had a thousand krona left. She needed to move on. A hostel would be such an obvious place to look. She'd have to go to plan B. As she had breakfast she planned her day. She would go to the Domkyrka to pray and then go to the youth centre and hang out til lunch which would be a cheap meal. Then she'd go to her cousins' apartment. She would wait til after school and hopefully one of the girls would answer and their dad wouldn't be home yet. If she was lucky he would be away. She had heard Melissa say recently that Uncle Mats was really busy with work and away from home a lot, but as the girls were old enough to take care of themselves – Elisabetta being eighteen – they were quite capable of looking after themselves. And in fact, she'd added, they'd been running the house pretty much since Aunty Agi died.

She would explain her situation and swear them to secrecy and ask if she could stay. Once they understood her situation they'd have to help her, they'd want to help her. She hadn't wanted to use this plan, it was too risky, but what options did she have?

Chapter 35

Signe had looked up the address online at the church ages ago and had noted that it was close to Näckrosen station on the tunnelbana, and had made a little map of the route from the station. She vaguely remembered taking the tunnelbana on that visit all those years ago. The underground station still seemed vast now as she went down into its cavernous depths, made all the more so by the hunks of granite projecting from the walls and ceilings of the escalator shaft where the rock had been blasted and hewn out.

She was nervous, wondering if this was a big mistake. Maybe this is where she'd blow her cover, but she didn't know what else to do. She'd prayed for guidance but there hadn't been any signs. As she changed at T Centrallen and found her way to the T11 platform, checking that she was on the correct branch of the line, she convinced herself that she didn't have any option and maybe this was God's intention, that she stay with her family. Although of course they weren't her family really, she had no family, except for this burgeoning in her womb.

When the train came she was glad to sit down again as when she stood for long the baby pressed down on her pubic bone. She needed the toilet, which was becoming an increasingly regular occurrence. Näckrosen station was bright and light whereas some they'd passed through had been dark colours, reds and browns. There were displays on the walls, photographs of babies and models of costumes and something about a film studio. She didn't have the time or inclination to stop and look properly, she needed the toilet. She did however notice the beautifully decorated ceiling by the escalator covered with water lilies, like a pond upside-down or like you were under water.

She came out of the exit onto a pavement bathed in bright sunlight. It was a beautiful day, the damp weather from yesterday having condensed and crystallized into a crisp, fresh, dry coldness.

She plucked up the courage to ask to use the facilities at a café and felt huge relief even though she passed little. That was the problem now, she thought, you could be desperate to go but virtually nothing comes out. The baby must be restricting the bladder or something.

Orientating herself at the bus stop where there was a local map as well as her hand written one, she set off towards the street where the apartment block was. Näckrosvägen was a long curving road which skirted a park for some of its length, but she started down the part that was nearest to the tunnelbana not knowing whereabouts she needed to be. It was soon apparent that she needed the other end of the road, if the numbers were to go by, but she decided to keep walking along the road as opposed to trying to cut across the park with the case.

After ten minutes walking she regretted her decision as it seemed the road went on forever and she hadn't even come to the right angle in the road she'd seen on the map, before the curvy bit started. In spite of the cold she soon found she was sweating from tramping along the ice encrusted pavement, the case bumping over the rutted frozen sleet. She had to stop a few times to get her breath and undo her coat. When she reached the right fork she saw the road went slightly uphill from this point which, as she doggedly pushed up, made the case feel heavier to pull and her breathing more laboured. After another ten minutes or so she saw the park ahead and the buildings gave way to trees. The last building on the right she found was the one she was looking for.

She had to stop for a few minutes to catch her breath and allow her heart to slow. The breath smoked from her mouth and she welcomed the cold on her face in contrast to the hot sweat she felt trickling down her back. She reminded herself of the number of the apartment and looked it up on the entry phone system. Yes, there it was, Nilström, at the top.

Would she ring now or wait? She felt herself shaking, either from the exertion or nerves, or both. She had to do it. What was the point of coming if she wasn't going to ring? She'd already decided that if Mats answered she'd scoot. She pressed the button and received a loud buzzing from the intercom. Heart pounding she waited breathlessly. The seconds ticked by. Nothing. Should she buzz again? She looked at her watch. It was early, she realised, for the girls to be out of school. She'd leave it half an hour, but she didn't want to wait here. It was too public.

Turning back towards the park she saw a path leading up among the trees which looked inviting, the sun dappling through the branches of the firs. She'd go and find a boulder to sit on and wait out of view. The path led up a small incline into the trees and a bit further on opened out to reveal a pond. It was roughly circular with a boggy-looking bit at the near side, but the opposite bank had a path which branched off the one she was on, with some benches. There was no one there; it seemed an ideal spot to sit and wait. She deeked off onto the side path skirting the pond and found that the nearest bench was free of iced sleet, there being tree branches overhanging which protected it.

With relief she sat down and stood the trolley bag beside her. There were a couple of ducks dabbling at the far side by the boggy bit.

They seemed unconcerned by her presence and took no notice of her. The part of the pond that was nearest to her was still and clear, only the very edges where the water was shallowest had a thin veneer of ice begun to form. She could see the bottom, the low sun illuminating the muddy depths and highlighting wisps of weed and submerged leaves. Signe imagined Ophelia floating there, her hair fanned out as in that picture she'd seen online. They'd had to study Hamlet at school, comparing how the English playwright Shakespeare had used and adapted the story from the original Norse legend of Amleth. She'd been shocked at Hamlet's treatment of Ophelia, the way he'd insulted her, his anger towards her and she'd felt her anguish and could understand how she'd gone mad. It hadn't seemed unnatural to her that she should have killed herself in her grief. And the image she'd found online by Millais was so beautiful, her hair flowing in the water and that beautiful dress spread out and dotted with flowers. She had loved that image, the white faced girl, chaste and pure in the icy water.

Sitting here beside this pond she felt again that desire to slip into the water and let it drown those fears she'd had sometimes. It had seemed an option occasionally when she'd been down and the thought had been exciting, a tragic death in which she would take all her secrets undefiled to her grave. It had crossed her mind when she'd found she was adopted, and again after 'it' had happened. But of course it wasn't really an option, her faith didn't allow of it.

There was a movement, the ducks were alerted and paddled quickly away from the far bank. There were sounds of footsteps on loose gravel and a figure appeared up the further slope, looming larger as it breasted the hill. Signe was immediately alert, aware of her vulnerability alone in this secluded place.

It was a man, a great ox of a man with wild hair and a beard who, when he saw her, faltered as if suddenly embarrassed to have imposed on her space. He smiled nervously and, as if explaining his presence, took a bag from his pocket and lobbed a couple of handfuls of breadcrumbs into the water. The ducks pushed across and began gobbling up the bobbing pieces greedily. The man smiled at her apologetically, nodded and then shuffled round the edge of the pond to sit on the bench furthest away from her, nodding and smiling again as he did so. He watched the ducks feeding and seemed to be rewarded.

Signe realised she'd seen him before, in the market. He had been the man hanging the mobile. He had nodded at her then in that shy apologetic way and she'd thought he was like a big bear. Maybe he recognised her too and was embarrassed as she might think he'd meant to bump into her deliberately. But no, he was just watching the ducks.

It was peaceful sitting there and opposed to her initial concern there was now something reassuring about his detached presence. She wasn't alone. She was aware of him looking at her occasionally, not intrusively but just acknowledging her and one time she caught his eye and he smiled awkwardly and grunted something. She nodded, not saying anything, not wanting to get involved in case he was a weirdo. But he seemed satisfied with this distance and continued to watch the ducks which had consumed the bread and were preening themselves in the now weak sunlight.

"Oof," Signe suddenly crumpled over holding her side and panting. The pain was intense just under her ribs and she tried to move to relieve it but it just stuck in there.

"Are you alright?"

Shocked she opened her eyes in spite of the pain. He was standing right beside her, consternation on his face his arms flapping by his legs like paddles. She was panting still, trying to ride the pain and managed to gasp "It's okay, I'm fine, it's just a bad pain."

She turned to her left and pushed on the protruding leg or arm or whatever it was and shortly it moved and the pain passed. Signe gave a big sigh. "That's better. It was just the baby moving," she said, surprising herself at her candour with this stranger.

"The baby, ah yes, I understand. Beautiful."

Beautiful. The word was totally unexpected and caught her off guard. The baby moving was beautiful.

His face was serious again, frowning, as if trying to understand her situation and at the same time his eyes seeming to extend great sympathy. She found she didn't mind him knowing about it. Her female instinct told her he was no threat and wouldn't judge her.

"The baby's going to come soon and then I won't have the pain," she said, almost as if explaining to a child.

His face relaxed into a grin. "That will be wonderful, hee hee, a little baby," and he nodded, still chuckling and grinning. Signe suddenly felt overwhelmed, she didn't know why, but possibly the enormity of the imminent birth and not knowing where she was going to be, and found herself crying.

"Oh, I'm so sorry, I didn't mean to upset you," he was backing away, looking mortified. Through her tears she assured him it was okay, she was fine. She was just tired. He looked relieved and sat on a neighbouring bench, not too close so as to crowd her but close enough to be friendly.

"Thank you," he said unexpectedly, and she didn't know quite what he was thanking her for. Being fine maybe.

It was just then that Signe realised she was desperate for the toilet again. It was ridiculous and it probably wouldn't yield much but it felt urgent and uncomfortable. She wondered how far it was to that café if she struck out through the park, or maybe there was a public toilet here in the park. Maybe he would know.

"I wonder, d'you know if there's a toilet near here, in the park maybe?"

He frowned and looked serious again, worried even. "Ah, a toilet, yes," he seemed to be struggling with this question as if it had completely confused him. "Hmm, hmm," he didn't look at her, his eyes were flitting here and there unable to settle on anything as if he were having an anxiety attack. "Well, you see, I live quite close, hmm hmm, you could use… if you wanted to… if you didn't mind…" He was very perturbed now, turning his hands out in a hopeless gesture.

Signe saw a possibility of relief. "Well if you're sure, that's very kind."

"Thank you," he said, standing and beaming, "Thank you, please, let me…" and he grabbed the trolley bag, lifting it as if it was weightless and backed away from her, gesturing for her to come with him. He was making little noises in his throat like the beginnings of laughter but which didn't materialize. Signe sensed that he was delighted that she would make use of his toilet and that he was able to help her. She followed him at the pace she could manage against his shuffling excited backward walk. They went round the corner from the pond and there was a service road which led almost to it but which Signe quickly saw was for a small modern church sitting on a knoll to the left of them.

He led her along the service road to where after a hundred metres or so it joined the public road. They crossed this road and started along the opposite pavement which gave views through the trees right over Stockholm. Signe prayed it wouldn't be too far, but the houses here looked really expensive and not the kind of house she'd imagine he would live in.

"Huh, it's not too far for you I hope, hmm hmm, just down this hill."

After a short way the road curved sharply to the right but another branched off it to the left going steeply down the hill. He indicated this as the route and started down it, sure-footed, her bag clamped under one arm, not seeming at all concerned about the slippery surface. Signe felt silly to be feeling nervous about the incline, seeing him go down with such ease and confidence and so ignored her instincts. She tried to pick the least slippery-looking parts of the pavement, taking small steps and teetering in places, the baby pressing painfully on her pelvic bone all the time. He waited for her occasionally, but didn't offer to help with an arm or hand and she was too shy to ask.

Suddenly her foot skidded from under her, kicking her forwards. She struck out with her left foot to save herself but this hit a tuft of grass and twisted her ankle over as her weight landed on it. Collapsing in pain she pitched straight over onto her left side into the edge of a garden. She cried out as she fell and simultaneously felt a hot release in her groin. Fortunately her fall had been more like a roll which had broken the impact and miraculously she hadn't hit her stomach, but the immediate pain in her ankle was excruciating.

He was with her in seconds, making anxious little humming noises. "I'm so sorry, so sorry. Hmm hmm. Are you hurt? Hmm hmm." He fussed helplessly, his arms flapping in front of him attempting some sort of assistance but not achieving anything.

"It's my ankle," she whimpered, panting also, "I think it's twisted."

"How can I? …. can I help you?"

"Yes, yes," Signe reached an arm towards him, "if you can help me up I..."

"Yes, thank you, thank you," he blurted out and took her arm and with his other under her shoulder bodily lifted her up, whereupon she gave a sharp cry as the pain shot up her leg when she applied pressure on it.

"I'm sorry, I'm sorry," he cried, letting go of her as if he'd stabbed her and causing her to topple towards him now the support was gone. In a flash he realised his mistake and caught her in his arms and lifted her up with one sweep like a little girl. Signe was amazed at his strength, but he didn't even seem to register her weight.

"I will carry you. Is this okay?"

"Yes, if you can."

"Thank you, thank you," he said, a deep frown of concern on his face, and started down the hill with no hesitation. His breathing was the only thing which gave any intimation of the effort involved and Signe felt surprisingly safe in his arms even though she knew how slippery the pavement was. However this didn't seem to bother him, his strides solid and purposeful as they progressed down the hill and around to the left along a track or footpath which led from the road.

"I hope this will be okay for you. It's not far now."

"What about my case?" Signe suddenly remembered.

"Please don't worry, I will go back. But I must make you safe first." He trudged on, humming occasionally, still with a look of profound worry on his face. Signe bumped in his arms, noticing now his particular smell. It seemed to be a mixture of smoke and forest, a musty, sappy, woody smell overlaid with ash. He turned off the path and onto a narrow track towards the huge granite undercliff which supported the sheer rock face of the hill they'd just come down from. There, surrounded by fir trees and birch, was a large wooden shed sheltered beneath the thousands of tons of rock.

"Here," he said, seemingly relieved to have arrived, "this will be safe for you." He pushed the door open with a twist of his hand and they were in the dark interior.

"I'm sorry, it's my mess. I don't have visitors usually." He put her down in a big armchair and then reached to get an upright chair to rest her wounded leg on. "Please, let me find some light." He moved around nimbly for his size, finding candles from a shelf and then lighting an old oil lamp on the table. Fiddling briefly with the wick he had a nice glow in a minute and then turned back to her, wiping sweat from his forehead.

"I'm sorry, such a mess, hmm hmm, how is your…is it hurting now?"

Signe couldn't really move, half lying in this spacious armchair and feeling like a beached whale. "It's okay like this. I think just when I stand on it it's painful."

"Yes, thank you. I must get your case. Please, I won't be long, thank you," and he rushed out of the door making sure to close it carefully after him.

Signe looked around the room now that her eyes had adjusted to it and the oil lamp glowed brighter. She didn't know quite what to make of it. There was a wooden table with the lamp and a chest of drawers at this end together with the chairs. It was strange, the inside seemed so much smaller than the outside. When she'd first seen it amongst the trees it had appeared to be huge, but this was a very small cosy space. It was warm and she now understood the smell of smoke; there was a stove with a flue by the wall with an old fashioned kettle on it. She could see low embers through the glass in the door.

She shuffled in the chair, anxious to investigate the wet in her groin. Had her waters broken? Was she bleeding? An effort at getting her fingers there and feeling told her it wasn't excessive and the lack of blood and smell of urine told its own tale. She needed to change but this was going to be difficult. What was she going to do now? She couldn't walk, and who was this weird guy who was so nervous and awkward. He seemed harmless though, like he couldn't hurt anyone in spite of his size. Maybe she could rest here for a bit. But what was the time? She could see through the window the light was fading. Would she go and try at the apartment again? But she'd need help to get there now, and in the dark?

The door opened and a waft of cold air preceded the bear like figure carrying her case. He shut the door quickly and grunting nervously took his coat off and hung it on the wall. He went to the stove, opened the door and rattled the embers with a poker before chucking on a couple of small logs. He turned and faced her, his hands clasped in front of him.

"Hmm, how are you now?"

Signe felt a confidence she hadn't expected, something to do with his humility and nervousness; she felt she wanted to make it easier for him.

"I'm fine, really, it's just my ankle hurts." She smiled encouragingly. He cleared his throat and hummed again but in a more relaxed, thinking way it seemed.

"Yes, I think you twisted it, hmm. Nasty fall. Painful. Yes, what to do? Hmm, I'm not sure. I could make coffee?" He looked so worried initially, but then there was such an endearing 'light-bulb' moment when he thought of coffee, that Signe couldn't help beaming at him and saying yes, even though she didn't drink coffee. She was cold despite the warmth of the place, maybe because of the fall or the pain, and the thought of a hot drink was irresistible.

He seemed delighted to be able to do something and quickly made up a pot from the kettle on the stove which must have been simmering gently all the while, and found mugs from the shelf. He then disappeared through a curtain she hadn't noticed at one side of the farther wall, returning moments later with milk.

"I keep it in the cooler out there," he said by way of explanation, and she understood why the cabin looked bigger from the outside, it was divided. "Would you like sugar?"

"Yes please," she said, wanting to hug him. He was like a big teddy bear, the hums punctuating his sentences seeming like gentle growls. "Just one spoon."

When he'd prepared it he brought it to her almost like a chalice in church, cupping it with both hands and presenting it like a gift.

"There, that should warm you."

"Thank you so much you're very kind."

Suddenly he shot his hand out "I'm Joe."

Signe put her hand in his enormous rough paw and they shook solemnly.

"I'm Maria."

His face took on a strange look, like a miracle had appeared before his eyes. He turned quickly, "Hee hee, hmm, wait," and he took something off a shelf, fiddling with it and peering at it intently to an accompaniment of grunts and growls. "Ah yes, here it is." She saw he was holding an ancient iPod which he connected to a speaker that was also on the shelf. Shortly music was spilling across the room, a man's voice singing.

'The   most   beautiful   sound   I   ever   heard,
Maria, Maria, Maria, Maria'

His face was creased in an enraptured smile which spoke of intimacy with the piece and anticipation. He was watching her intently, waiting for her reaction.

..'All the beautiful sounds of the world in a single word, Maria, Maria, Maria, Maria. Maria, Maria, Mariaah…'

The orchestra swelled and the voice lifted from its quiet beginning pouring from the little speaker,

'Maria,   I've   just   met   a   girl   named   Maria,
And suddenly that name will never be the same to me'

"It's beautiful, yes?" He was beaming at her again, raising his eyebrows, encouraging a positive response. She nodded, listening to the words. "Like you," he added quietly, then looked down, embarrassed maybe. She observed him, his immense bulk, like an overgrown little boy before an inquisitive teacher. The music repeated the tune and then soared higher before lilting down again on the word Maria,

'Say it loud and there's music playing, Say it soft and it's almost like praying.'

It was very beautiful, and she indeed felt like praying, praying to thank God for sending this gentle man to look after her. Was this His plan? But surely not a twisted ankle, which was even now pulsing with pain. Was she meant to stay here, was that the need for the injury so that she had no choice? Otherwise she would undoubtedly have rung the bell again at the apartment.

A plaintive high 'Mareeeeah' ended the song and he looked up to see her reaction. She smiled. "It's lovely."

"It's from West Side Story. You like music?"

She didn't have much experience of music, it wasn't something that had grabbed her attention. Words resonated more. But the Passion, and now this. They had grabbed her.

"Yes."

"Me too. Hmm. It feeds me, hee hee."

Signe giggled accidentally, infected by his chuckle. Suddenly his face was serious again, "How is your leg?"

She wanted to say it was fine, her usual default response which discouraged further discussion, but his soft honest eyes she couldn't lie to.

"It hurts a lot."

His concerned expression made her regret her honesty.

"Where do you need to get to tonight?"

The direct question which she immediately realised was inevitable panicked her. "Well, the thing is I was hoping to stay with my cousins who live in the apartment near the pond, but when I rang there was no reply. If I couldn't stay there I was going to go back to the hostel in the centre."

His expression was serious and worried. He seemed to be struggling with some problem, his hums coming thick and fast. He got up and went through the curtain into the other part of the cabin. She could hear him humming constantly interrupted by abrupt scrapings of furniture and bangs. She wondered what was going on as she finished the coffee. Maybe she did like it after all. She felt her bump, a pang of anxiety questioning whether the baby was okay. She wasn't sure if it had moved since her fall and now she was worried. It would be her fault if the baby was traumatized, dead even. Could a baby die in the womb from a fall? Miscarriages yes, but so late in pregnancy? Again she didn't know. She couldn't feel any movement; the bump was just a lump.

The noises next door had stopped, leaving only the hums. They sounded less insistent, less frequent, more satisfied. The curtain twitched and Joe lumbered through breathing heavily and switched off a torch in his hand. He knelt awkwardly beside her and gave her an apologetic smile before putting on his serious face.

"Please, if you would like to, you can stay here. Hmm hmm. It will be quite comfortable for you. You see there is a bed here folded against the wall. Hmm. And I will be next door in there. It will be for the best because, then you can rest and get better. Hmm hmm."

His face was anxious, eager to know whether she approved of this idea. Her logical mind told her this was a dangerous situation, heavily pregnant and now unable to walk, staying at the mercy of this stranger. But what else could she do? There was something about him that made her female instinct override this initial precaution. She intuited that he wouldn't harm her, that he was meant to look after her, that maybe this was The Plan.

"But I can't take your bed," she said, knowing even as she said it that she would as he would insist. His look of chagrin at this

objection made her quickly add "but that's so kind of you and I really appreciate it."

"Please, it would be a great honour for me. I don't have much company, hee hee." He got up and with a broad smile continued, "So, you must be hungry. I can make some food for us." Signe nodded and he began making preparations for cooking, finding ingredients and cooking implements.

Signe lay back in the huge chair enjoying watching his obvious pleasure and the speed he darted about assembling things.

"I'm making some pasta, is that alright for you?"

"Lovely, thank you. Actually, Joe, I'm sorry but I kind of need the toilet and I don't know how I'd manage."

He stopped chopping onions and immediately started thinking through this problem, putting down the knife and wiping his hands on a cloth. "Can I lift you up, see how your ankle is?"

He came round and with her holding his massive shoulders lifted her forward onto her good leg. She gingerly put the other down and winced as soon as she applied pressure.

"No, no it's okay, I will carry you if you're happy. It's the only way, hee hee."

"If you're sure. I must be so heavy."

"Not as heavy as a reindeer, hee hee. I used to help with the cull. They are really heavy. Wait a second."

He went to the curtain and flung it up, hooking the swag on a nail. Then he came and lifted her up with an ease which again surprised her. She hung on around his neck breathing again the musty smell of smoke and resin as he stooped through the doorway. The adjacent room was a workshop, a bench crowded with tools of various kinds to one side of the room, the walls hung with other tools she had no idea about. There were candles softly illuminating this rustic scene and Joe moved across the space to a curtained enclosure at one corner where he put her down.

"I'm afraid it's a bit basic, hee hee. Just sprinkle some saw dust from the box when you've finished. It's not modern, but it works, hee hee. Call me when you've finished."

He went off humming and Signe was left to negotiate the procedure without putting her foot down which although tricky was helped by the proximity of the walls and the surprising height of the throne which made it easier than expected. She realised she should have got a change of knickers from her bag but he'd whisked her off so quickly she'd forgotten. They were right at the top where she'd left them deliberately for emergencies. Could she ask him to get them for her? It would be so embarrassing, but the alternative was to stay in urine damp knickers.

"Hello, Joe? I'm sorry."

" Yes," he growled from behind the curtain.

"This is really awkward. I forgot to get some clean knickers from my bag. I'm so sorry but could you get them for me? They're just inside the top compartment."

She heard a flurry of hums and him shuffling through to the other room. In a few seconds her case appeared under the curtain. "Here, this is easier, hee hee."

She smiled as she thanked him and with difficulty exchanged underwear and felt a deal more comfortable. He came and collected her when she called and installed her back in the chair with her bag beside her.

There was as pan of water on the woodstove with a frying pan bubbling beside it. Joe bustled about, bringing in more wood, clearing things from the table and humming all the while. He seemed to be really enjoying himself.

"Do you live here all the time?"

Joe stopped, apparently non-plussed by the question, but then looking around appeared to understand why she asked.

"Yes, this is my home. It's not much, but I like it."

"Did you build this cabin?"

"Well, no and yes. The building was here already but I've done lots of work on it. Hmm. You see, this was a big shed belonging to the lady who lived over there" he indicated through one of the walls, "and I worked for her for a long time, hmm, doing the garden and odd jobs around the house. This was my workshop and garden shed. Well, this lady, Mrs Wallin, she got very old and I spent more and more time helping her out. She paid me of course, but often she forgot. She was a very nice lady. Anyway, when she became ill she said one day, 'Joe, I know you love doing your woodwork and making things, so I want you to have the shed so that you can carry on and have somewhere to keep your tools. I'm going to have an advocate draw up a document making the shed and some of the land over to you.' Well, I never thought she would do it, hee hee. I thought it was just a nice idea she had, but when she died I had a letter with the deeds to the land and the shed on it. Hmm, she kept her word. She was a nice lady."

He got up suddenly and went to attend to the cooking. Signe watched his large frame dancing between stove and chopping board, his movements appearing to be those of a person half his size.

"Do you like mushrooms, peppers and garlic in tomato sauce?"

"Yes thank you," Signe said, although to be truthful she wasn't keen on mushrooms, but she wanted to please him. There didn't seem any need for conversation, she was happy to recline there and watch him and listen to his humming. Just then the baby moved and Signe put her hands on it, comforted to feel the flexing movements flitting under her skin. "Thank you Father for letting no harm come to the baby."

She awoke suddenly, disorientated and uncomprehending. It took her five seconds to remember where she was and why and, moving her foot, was immediately and painfully reminded of the accident. Her sudden intake of breath alerted Joe that she was awake.

"Hello, are you okay?" He loomed out of the shadows by the wall.

"Yes thank you. I just caught my ankle."

"Ah yes, it is very painful for you," his frown suggested he was threatening the offending injury for hurting her.

"I'm sorry I must have fallen asleep."

"Yes, you've been sleeping for some time. It's good that you rest."

"But what about the food? Did you eat already?"

"No, it's quite alright. The sauce is stewing nicely. It's always better for it to cook for a long time, hee hee."

Joe put the meal together and pulled the table next to her. He fetched a box from the other room for himself and served the simple meal up into bowls. As usual Signe found she was hungry and surprised herself by not minding the pasta mixed with the sauce. Joe ate slowly observing her from under his thick dark eyebrows, initially anxious that she liked the food, but quickly relaxed at her obvious enjoyment.

"When is the baby coming?" he growled.

Signe paused in eating, wondering how much to say, how much to divulge, but she couldn't lie to this gentle grizzly bear, this other Hagrid.

"Well, he should be born about now. It's difficult to know an exact date." How could you second-guess the will of God? And in a rush the enormity of the situation swamped her, the responsibility of this delivery, the needs of the world resting on her to fulfil this long-awaited promise. She hadn't the strength, and now with her ankle in agony...

She wiped her eyes and he looked distressed and hummed low. "I didn't mean to upset you."

"It's not you. It's me. I'm sorry, it's just, you don't know." She hesitated as those deep brown eyes shyly gazed at her. "Joe, this is a very special baby."

"All babies are special," he said gently.

"No but....well, yes, they're all special, but this is a very special baby because... You know about Jesus. He said He would come again. This is His second coming."

Joe had stopped eating and was still, looking at her. She couldn't gauge his reaction. Did he believe her? The words she had just spoken had filled her with sudden joy, an exhilaration that quelled that panic of a few moments ago. She didn't know where she was; it was frightening but also wonderfully exciting, and she felt the blood rush to her face. As if in response there was a slow gliding ripple across her abdomen like He was stretching, waking up, reassuring her He was ready.

A smile spread across Joe's face. "This would be truly beautiful. Hmm. And how do you know this?"

Between mouthfuls Signe related her dreams and all the signs she'd interpreted which pointed so unequivocally to the only explanation. The more she went into it, the more she realised how obvious it had all been, but it was only when she put it into words that she saw the immaculate logic of it all and, as she said to Joe, she was amazed how long it had taken her to read the signs. As she talked she found herself filled with a new confidence, a surety that dispelled that momentary doubt and the words flooded out of her. It was like a sudden fire burned in her and indeed the baby was moving more and inspiring her by His physical presence. And this is what she'd lacked over the past few days, despite the signs which had temporarily encouraged her, she hadn't found that inner strength. But now, now she felt it, strong and certain, the Holy Spirit moving within her.

And she cried with joy, smiling, the tears spilling into her mouth as she ate. And Joe looked on in wonder, smiling too, this vision of euphoric motherhood, emanating an electricity of infectious happiness. Joe fetched her a cloth to wipe her face, but she hardly paused, unable to stem the flow of this unburdening, and now he had tears in his eyes too. They finished the meal, but still she talked, needing to get the whole story out, the trial, her talks with Irma, her family, the difficulties keeping it all a secret. Joe's eyes responded and reflected each addition to the tale with surprise, sympathy, satisfaction.

"And then I met you and twisted my ankle, and somehow that seems to be a sign too, that I'm meant to stay here and not contact my cousins. I had always been worried about that and then God showed me the way."

Signe had to move. The baby was in an awkward position now and she needed to find relief. Joe was beside her in an instant helping her, plumping the cushion for her back and anxious for her comfort. Then standing back, pleased at her relief. He was humming gently under his breath, a tuneless personal reassurance.

"I am so happy to have you here," he said, and immediately turned to deal with the dishes.

Chapter 36

Signe had begun to panic. It was now days since she'd arrived at Joe's shack and the Holy Baby had made no sign of making His entry into the world. It should have happened by now. The doctor had predicted early to mid-December according to her last period and the date of the concert. It was remarkable that the date should be so close to Christmas as if.... Signe stopped. Of course, how had she not realised? That was the point. He would come at Christ's Mass, symbolically reappearing, re-birthing on His natal day. It was obvious now that she thought about it. And His conception had been at the time of His death. 'Out of death shall come life.' The symbolism was inescapable.

She tried to think what the date was. She'd travelled on the fifteenth then spent two nights in the hostel before landing at Joe's. It must be about the nineteenth or twentieth. Would it be another five days? She was very uncomfortable now most of the time. Although Joe's place was warm it was hardly comfortable or convenient. As for Joe he was out a lot, taking his wooden things to sell in the market – bird feeders, bird boxes and painted Christmas decorations – but he always came bustling back with some bargain he'd picked up at the supermarket and would concoct an ingenious dish from disparate ingredients. Signe's palette had been assailed by weird combinations which she had strangely accepted.

Joe fussed about the place, always trying to make her comfortable and assist where he could. Now that her ankle was better she didn't need the same help getting around, but she kind of missed that rough embrace when he lifted her up. He kept a discreet distance these days, but she rather longed for a grizzly bear hug and the close smell of the resin and coffee and smoke.

"Joe, I really feel so badly that you're having to look after me..." The irritated humming interrupting this weak objection warned her not to proceed and she trailed off, reassured when the hums returned to their usual level.

"What are you doing for Christmas?" The humming stopped. "I mean, are you going to see your family?"

Joe had his back to her, leaning over the table. His head was lowered and he didn't move for a couple of seconds. She wondered if she'd said something wrong. He carried on with what he was doing as suddenly as he'd stopped and the humming resumed, followed by "I thought I'd do omelette tonight. Is that okay?"

"Of course."

Much of the time she spent on her own, she tormented herself with questions which never found satisfactory answers. She felt badly about Irma, not telling her; but she hadn't been able to rely on her confidence ever since she'd divulged her plan to join the Bridgettines. Now with Joe, she'd let the whole thing out and he'd listened and done everything practical to support her, but she felt very alone. She'd confided everything in him but had got nothing back. Not in the way of emotional support, understanding or empathy. Irma would have helped. They would have discussed it, maybe argued, but at least they'd have talked it through. Joe was lovely to her, but he never questioned anything or gave a different opinion. He just accepted what she said and hummed and smiled.

She missed Irma, more than her family, her household. She was on her own now with God and the Baby. And Joe.

He had put some music on whilst he was cooking and Signe thought she recognised some of it but had no idea what it was. There was a lot of singing, it seemed to be a musical again. Joe seemed to like musicals. A young-sounding girl was singing a plaintive song which began very softly, as if she was crying.

'On my own, pretending he's beside me.
All alone, I walk with him til morning.
Without him, I feel his arms around me,
And when I lose my way, I close my eyes
And he has found me.'

The melody poured out, rising and twisting with pathos, echoing her emptiness. That face, his face, His face rose in front of her. He was the one she wanted to tell, the one she wanted to share this journey with, the one she craved to hold her and assure her that she was worthy. But wasn't that wrong? She shouldn't need anyone but her Lord. But he was her lord. She longed for his embrace, to feel the strength in his arms, to feel his breath on her lips.

'And I know it's only in my mind
And I'm talking to myself and not to him.
And although I know that he is blind,
Still I say, there's a way for us.'

It was all she could do to stop herself from crying out and she was thankful Joe was facing away from her and unable to see the calamity in her face. She sleeved her cheeks dry and endeavoured to control herself, but the music yearned and cried out its heartbreaking sacrificial message.

'I love him, but every day I'm learning
All my life, I've only been pretending.
I love him, but only on my own.'

The angels passed back and forth, their long-sleeved cloaks wafting sweet incense in her face. She knew this dream so well, she'd experienced it so many times before, either for real or re-living it afterwards. It was nice to slip back into it either when it happened upon her or willingly whilst awake. She wasn't sure which it was just now, whether she was asleep or daydreaming, but it didn't matter, she could enjoy it as much either way. She knew what would happen next. It was like a recording replaying a well-known event in which one almost invokes the next event from one's subconscious. The familiar scenes played out and as she knew the inevitable outcome – the Angel Gabriel choosing her – it was all the more pleasurable, her present condition fulfilling that sign she'd had so many years before.

In her dream she never lost that feeling of joy and wonder when the Angel said 'Hail, Signe, the Lord is with thee, blessed art thou among women.' And whenever it happened again her anticipation was exquisite, overwhelming her with that closeness to God and humbling her with His trust and honour. It would happen any moment, just when all the angels had knelt and given praise. Here it comes. Signe closed her eyes in her dream to feel the full effect of that Holy Hand on her head. The anticipation was rapture, suspense so delicious in the knowledge that all this love and divine spirit was about to enter her body again like liquid gold, honey-unction pouring through her head and saturating her whole body with its manna.

"Hail Mary, the Lord is with thee...."

Signe opened her eyes and saw the angel approach another girl, blessing her and raising her up in her place. A stab of unbearable pain sliced through her back. She let out a cry, curling her body in response.

"Maria, are you alright?"

Is that an angel? The dream has gone. Where is she? It wasn't supposed to end like that. It never did. But she's crying out again, another wave of pain surging through her back and crippling her. What pain is this? It's unbelievable, unbearable.

"Maria, let me help you, hmm hmm."

The wave passed. *Why did it happen? It never happens like that. Who is she?*

Strong arms lifted her, raised her a little and helped her up.

"Why not me? Why her now?" Signe cried out again as another agonising bolt of pain punched her lower back. She was panting, gasping to bear it.

Hot liquid cascaded across her thighs, drenching her and dripping onto the floor. She was kneeling on the chair, collapsing, heaving with the effort of the contraction. She saw the walls, the lights. They flashed past as she turned and fell against the back of the chair, clasping it with fingers like talons.

Sweet Jesus, help me. Forgive me all my sins. I'm sorry for my weakness…panting, gripping.

"Breathe deeply Maria, slowly, deeply, hmm hmm."

It's my punishment, I knew it would come, for wanting him, for allowing myself to love him. Dear God forgive me I beg you…"

She leant over the back of the chair, the action eased the pain on her back but pushed on her distended belly. She couldn't find a position of ease. The pain built each time after each release. And she was vaguely aware that this was only the beginning.

She could hear grunting and water sloshing. Jo was cleaning up the floor with a sponge and bucket of water, wiping down the chair behind her, humming intensely.

Grunt, grunt, the snake in the grass, slime-shiny, pulsing. That face, eyes dilated, excited, breasts heaving. Sweat streaming, bodies steaming, and panting, panting.

Signe retched over the back of the chair, the violent contraction simultaneously voiding her bowel. She let out a wail of despair.

Not this, dear God, not this. Our Lady never had this. A birth without pain, without sin.

Signe struggled to move from the chair to deal with her ordure. Joe fetched more water to clean the chair. She tried to remove her underwear before the next contraction. She was revolted by herself, her smell, her mess. She was so wobbly on her feet she couldn't balance, couldn't control herself. She was shaking with the pain and effort. She couldn't manage herself, she was disabled, stumbling, tripping, ungainly.

Joe rescued her, hefted her to the bed before she fell. She curled onto her side hoping to ease the pain, uncaring of her appearance, uncovered, covered in muck. He hesitated, caught between propriety and concern, wanting to clean her but anxious to save her further embarrassment. She moaned a self-admonishment of blame, unaware of his indecision, aware only of pain, of panic, of an overwhelming realisation.

This is my fate. I have failed. I'm not the one. This child is not He and I am punished for my arrogance.

"Please Maria. I have a towel for you."

How could I ever have imagined that it could be me, after what I have done?

Another bar of metal slammed into her back and continued to drive its brute weight against her frame, bending itself around her waist and clamping her with its vice-like grip. *This must crush the baby. But it isn't Him now, it doesn't matter. Oh let it end.*

"Maria, please, let me help you, hmm hmm."

She was vaguely aware of rubbing, of soft damp sponging as the bar unclamped and released her from its grasp. The action was soothing, reassuring. She would have liked it higher, on her back where the permanent fierce ache dwelt. Joe was wiping her naked buttocks. She didn't care. It didn't matter anymore. She was so shamed that this indignity didn't touch her. She was beyond shame.

Her mind was gripped by two thoughts, the anticipation of the next contraction and the nature of the baby in her womb. What was it now, this child? A thing of her making, a product of her lust, of that moment of animal passion. What kind of delusion had she been under to think God would excuse that transgression and instead reward her with His Son? She was crazy.

And now, what would she do? What could she do?

Another contraction gripped her, squeezed a long groan from the depths of her lungs. *Yes, Lord, bring it on. I'm ready to pay the price.*

"Maria, drink this, hmm, you must drink."

She swallowed, unaware of what it was she drank, but glad to relieve the dry-coated sourness of her mouth. She changed her position, rolling this way and that to find relief, and finally lifted herself onto all fours and leaned forward onto her forearms. She vaguely heard noises, metal hitting metal, a squeak of a hinge, water running, humming. She began to lose sense of time, her mind overburdened with pain-coping mechanisms and relentless recriminations. Survival mode had kicked in, where oblivion was interspersed with searing pain, heart-ache and back-ache.

In a few moments of lucidity she conjectured that she must be delivered soon of this baby; it felt like these contractions had been going on for ages, but in truth she had no idea. It was dark. Was it dark when she had started? Another wave, breath deep and shuddering, the gradual release of tension, the crowding foreboding.

Time stretched, contracted, ceased to be something she was conscious of. At times it was endless, a moment of eternity; at others it was fleeting, transcended. The rhythm of contractions became her timepiece, controlling her thought, dictating her response, ruling her every moment. Nothing existed but the next wave, the grinding involuntary pressure followed by the gasp and release before the long-drawn anticipation of the next cycle.

She was vaguely aware that Joe was there, attending in some way, humming, concerned but ineffectual. She got used to the rhythm. The pain became almost continuous and she was drunk to the highs and lows of it, its inevitability. Her mind wandered during that time, imagining it was a dream, a nightmare. Reality mixed with dreams and skipped in and out, eventually seeming like a dream itself. Sometimes it was so dark she forgot if her eyes were open or not. Even if she detected the light in the room her eyes were so unfocused it appeared dark in her mind until she focused back to reality. But then, eventually, she realised the night was not so dark. It had changed. The night was lighter and was in fact day, hollow, bland, insipid.

Everything ached. Her mind ached, bruised now by too many questions which attacked her reason, her faith, her sanity.

"Maria, hmm, I'm very worried for you. I think you should be in hospital."

"No, nooo." The wail dissolved into a groan of contraction. "Not hospital. They'll find me and then..." *Then what? If it wasn't He it didn't matter. But what would she do? Her family?* "No, please no, not hospital."

The pain eased off, the contractions not so intense and further apart. She was able to stand up and move around. She was weak, light-headed. Joe made sweet tea which she found welcome. She ate something, bread possibly. She wasn't aware. The pain changed, still in her back but also beginning deep down at the gates of the uterus. It began almost imperceptibly, sharp, spiky, eventually taking her legs from under her. This pain was so different. You couldn't breathe through it like the back pain. It was so painful she could only whimper til it passed. But it didn't come in waves, it was more or less there all the time, ebbing and flowing, screwing deeper into her nerves each time, as if her bones had developed nerves and were being crushed in a vice.

Now she struggled about the space, holding onto a chair, squatting by the bed, prostrating herself on the floor to try to find some relief. And then the contractions came again harder deeper and longer. It was impossible to bear, it couldn't go on. It was at times so intense she swooned and almost fell if it weren't for Joe. He hummed madly, dumb for words, helpless to help her.

She was deathly white, glistening with sweat although she was cold. The pain had chilled her to the core and she shivered.

"Maria…"

She was blowing through a contraction, the veins in her neck bulbous, her eyes pinched shut, her mouth twisted against gripped jaws, teeth clenched, lips pale and wrinkled. She moaned as the pain didn't release but continued to build. She squatted, but the agony in her opening only intensified. She couldn't get up, Joe lifted her but then had no idea where or what she wanted more than she did. She hung on him, crying, a hoarse rattle in her throat, a guttural animal gurgle which continued even as she breathed in. It sounded other-worldly, even to her, like a continuous occult cry of despair.

She suddenly collapsed her whole weight on him, which, even with his strength, because of the angle and the difference in their heights, he found difficult to support. He managed her onto the bed and then turned for his phone.

She slipped in and out of consciousness. Voices, fast and urgent, hands gripping her wrist, her hands. "Maria, it's okay my darling, you're doing fine." Hands lifting, pushing, spreading legs, fingers probing. "We're going to take care of you darling…"

Pain buckles, vice-clamping, muscles tight- strapped, groan-gargling pain, pushing blood headwards, straining, bursting, breath release breath release, moan, whimper, fade.

Jolting, rocking, jarring. Metal sliding, clicking. Engine, wailing, lights flashing. Pain, pain, intense pain. Pant, mouth dry, teeth clenched, endless endless agony.

Eli, Eli, lama, lama asabthami. My God, My God, why hast Thou forsaken me?
****

It was the smell she was first aware of, or lack of it. Not smoke or resin but fresh, clean, with a faint smell of antiseptic. It was quiet, distant, sub-nimbusly muffled. Her eyes flicked open, retinas reflexing down to pin holes under the shock of the bright white.

Her eyeballs turned up into her closing lids, the fatigue and impact of the light combining to make them withdraw before, a few seconds later, she tried again and this time flickering in a long attempt to conquer the stinging brightness and control her vision. Through half shuttered lids she saw white upon white, a halo of white above and all around her. Was she…dead?

As her eyes adjusted she was able to make out certain details and appreciate that it wasn't unremitting white. There were lights and shades, surfaces and edges which became clearer and more meaningful as she scanned tentatively the reaches of her vision. White plane intersecting white plane, white shadow, deeper shadow. At last white ceiling and white walls appeared from the depths of her visual cortex, unscrambling the previously incomprehensible jabbering nerve impulses from her retina. Her mental library now recognised the images for what they were and interpreted all the reference points for a room, just as her creeping limbs informed her of sheet and bed and her body of dead weight.

No pain. Peace. It felt like a miracle. How long had she been here? She didn't care, it was paradise. Soft, comforting, safe, clean. She drifted away again into a half sleep, cocooned in the pristine sheets and pure white light, happy to float without pain in an oblivion of sleep... 'and by a sleep to say we end The heartache and the thousand natural shocks that flesh is heir to. 'Tis a consummation devoutly to be wished'.

Devout. Dear Lord thank you for delivering me from that..

A short high noise, a squeak, interrupted her thought which had then suddenly crystallized to an idea which surged adrenalin around her numb body. 'Delivery'. Or had that word come before the squeak? She couldn't tell. "Squeak", again. Signe forced open her eyelids and turned her head. A transparent box by the bed with a bundled blanket. Another squeak and it moved. Signe went to raise herself up in the bed, but winced as a sharp pain warned her off that move. She had to roll onto one side and lift herself sideways, a manoeuvre complicated by the tube attached to her arm. Just as she succeeded a nurse entered the room.

"Ah, Maria, you're awake. And so is this little fellow it seems. Here we go. Come and see Mamma. There we are," and she laid this bundle in her lap.

"Squeak," it said.

Signe gazed down at it unbelieving. A small face with perfect features, tiny nose, closed eyes with long lashes; a little mouth with pouted lips which were moving slightly with the jaw. It was so small, so vulnerable lying there in its innocence. The skin was almost translucent with a downy velvet covering. She stroked a cheek and found it to be softer than rabbit fur. The mouth curled open, the bottom lip drawing down as another squeak startled her.

"I think he's probably a bit hungry. D'you want to feed him?"

She didn't. She just wanted to keep looking at him, soaking up that perfect image. How could anything so beautiful have come out of her body? It was difficult to understand. She felt she could hold him like this forever, but was pressured by the nurse standing there, obviously waiting for her to take up the suggestion.

The nurse helped her to manoeuvre him into position and explained how he was supposed to latch on, take the whole aura of the nipple into his mouth. Signe went through the motions, nodding and responding but hardly able to concentrate on what the nurse was saying. She was bewildered by the magical being in her arms. She wished the nurse would go away. She wanted to be alone with the miracle she was holding. At last the position seemed to be correct and the nurse left her to suckle her baby.

It was peculiar, this suction on her breast, like she was being drained of energy. But at the same time she felt life flowing back, a tingling starting in her skin which gradually penetrated deeper into her tissues and spread a glow through her whole body. Each flurry of gulping mouthfuls dragged from her, followed by the jaw-twitching pauses, flooded her with an electricity which touched deep into her being. This baby was beautiful beyond her imaginings and it was hers. She'd made it, this gentle infant suckling at her breast. She longed for it, felt all her love swarming over it. She cherished it in this moment more than anything she could imagine. How could anything surpass this feeling of joy and fulfilment? Her body stretched out from itself with an intensity of universal love.

Drops of water splashed on the baby's face and she panicked to staunch the flow. She was smiling idiotically, she realised, but she couldn't help herself. She wanted this moment to last forever, her and her baby. But memories crept back, pain, and foreboding. What baby was this? Was it Him? He was so beautiful He must be. But the pain, the agony of labour. The Virgin Mary had never known pain, not in birth. Later, of course; a lifetime of pain knowing the final outcome for Her Son, but not the physical pain of labour. Why had she?

The small weight of the tiny baby was nonetheless pressing on her abdomen and she was aware of an insistent pain. She felt so weak, but she had to move position. The baby intensified its gorging, instinctively fearing being parted from this security, then relaxed back to a comfortable regular rhythm after she stopped.

"Hello Maria. Happy Christmas, and what a lovely Christmas present you have there."

A young doctor was standing by the bed. She hadn't even noticed her come in. She was accompanied by the nurse who had helped her. Signe smiled, lost for words.

"How are you feeling?" she continued, "looks like you're doing well with the feeding."

"I, yes, he's so beautiful." Signe said.

"Yes, he's a handsome boy." The doctor was looking at some papers, at the various machines by the bed. Then she took her pulse. "That seems fine, so are you feeling okay?"

"I feel really weak. And my stomach hurts a lot."

"Yes, I'm sure, I'm sure. You've had a bit of a bad time. And a C section is a big operation, you'll have to take it easy for a bit."

"A what section?"

"Caesarean. We had to do an emergency procedure to get him out quick. He was in distress and quite honestly we worried about losing you too."

"I don't understand."

"When you came in you were hyper-ventilating, you were unconscious. There were other complications, anaemia and things which I won't worry you with, but the main thing is your baby is fine and healthy and it won't be long before you're back on your feet."

Signe looked down at the baby in her arms and when she looked up her eyes were frowning. "But why did you have to operate? Why didn't he come out naturally?"

The doctor sat down on the bed. "Sometimes it's not possible for the delivery to progress naturally. In your case your channel was too narrow and the baby was in danger. It was safest to get him out quickly and make sure you were both alright. The pain in your stomach is because of the section. We can give you more pain relief if you like."

Signe relaxed back against the pillows with the baby cupped in the crook of her neck. A wave of exhaustion hit her, like all the energy had been sucked out of her.

"Good, well, I'll leave you with nurse Krista here and see you later." She picked up her clipboard, gave her a friendly smile and let herself out.

Signe felt herself drifting away.

"Here, let me take the baby Maria, I think you need to rest." Signe made a feeble attempt to keep holding him, but with the nurse's assurance that she was just going to put him in the cot next to her and that that would be best for him, she gave in to this crowding somnolence.

She woke, startled by the panic in her dream. They'd taken him. She'd been trying to reach him but her legs were wading through thick mud until she couldn't move. Her legs had become roots spreading out in the forest temple with St Sebastian and St Jerome, and she'd tried to scream as she'd seen him being taken further and further away, but nothing would come out.

White on white and light on white. Panting in the sweat of her panic she turned her head and saw the cot and saw him there and the panic released in a rush of relief. She sobbed slightly with joy and lay gazing at him until her eyes again drifted closed.

Signe woke and slept, woke and fed the baby and slept, and sometimes it was light and white and sometimes it was dim with a low glow spilling from the central light. She had no idea of time, her world dictated by exhaustion and the needs of the baby. He became more precious to her with each nestling feed, with the way his tiny hand seemed to hold her breast.

The pain in her abdomen hampered her but she began to learn around it, negotiating raising herself, lifting him. It was new and strange and there was so much to occupy her that between it and her constant tiredness she hadn't time to dwell on her circumstances. She found later that she'd even forgotten to pray. But she gave thanks practically every waking moment, stroking his soft cheek and gazing endlessly at his moon face.

It might have been the next day or the day after she wasn't sure, but she woke to find a towering presence by the cot. At first she was startled but then recognised Joe beaming down on the baby. He took a step back seeing her stirring, as if not sure if he was welcome. She gave a reassuring smile and his face relaxed.

"Beautiful," he said and hummed contentedly.

"Hi Joe. You alright?"

He nodded, still staring at the baby and "beautiful" he repeated.

She smelt his woody, smoky smell which seemed so out of place in this pristine place. He had tiny bits of woodchips in his beard and hair, a bear just come from his lair. A nurse came in with some food for her.

"Ah, you have a visitor."

"My uncle," Signe said quickly, surprising herself with the readiness of this explanation. Joe looked at her with an uncomprehending smile. She smiled back at him, pressing her lips together. He seemed to accept his role.

"The doctor will be round to see you after you've eaten. Your uncle's very welcome to stay and then we'll be able to see about getting you home." She busied herself, straightening out Signe's bed and arranging the tray on the hospital table and checking the baby was alright. "Okay, I'll leave you to your visit. Would you like a coffee?" Joe hastily declined.

Signe was glad of the meal and offered Joe some too but he shook his head releasing a little snow of dust. He was humming happily and drew up a chair and stared at the cot.

"You can pick him up if you like," she felt she had to make this offer although she dreaded an accident.

"No, no, I might drop him," a look of tragedy on his face.

Signe smiled with relief and amusement that he'd taken the thought out of her head. "Well, he **is** sleeping and it would be a shame to wake him."

She ate in silence, Joe seemingly content to look at the baby and occasionally take in the room. When their eyes met he smiled simply but said nothing. It was nice to have him there, humming quietly, some company at least. It felt right that she should have a visitor even if he didn't ask her how she was, how she was coping.

The baby squawked eventually and she had to feed him, Joe at first offering to leave, but after reassurance staying where he was. He had a permanent expression of wonder and incomprehension and seemed lost for words. When Signe again encouraged him to hold the baby he humphed and fidgeted in awkward confusion so that she was sorry she'd suggested it.

The doctor came to check Signe and the baby and she again referred to Joe as her uncle. The doctor then tried to include him in the conversation, but he shied into a corner.

"Well, I think you're both good to leave tomorrow," the doctor announced. "The baby's doing fine and your scar is beginning to heal. Any questions? No? Well, I'll come and see you in the morning to discharge you. You have someone to collect you, your uncle?"

"Yes," Joe was suddenly involved, "yes, a friend of mine will come with a car. I'll come too."

"Excellent, well til tomorrow then."

Signe looked at Joe for some time after the Doctor had left. "Where are we going?"

"To my house. I've prepared everything for you. I hope you like it. My friends helped."

"Your friends?"

"Yes, my friends from the market, from the craft college. They came. They helped me."

"At Christmas?"

Joe smiled indulgently. "We're always together at Christmas. It's our tradition. We've done it for some years now. Don't worry, they like helping. We all help each other." He was smiling and nodding, then suddenly frowned. "That was right wasn't it? You did need somewhere to stay?"

"Yes, yes I do. Thank you, for a bit certainly. 'Til I sort myself out, you know."

The expression on Joe's face melted her. His wide cheeks plumed with rubicund joy and he hee hee'd his chortling giggle. "A baby in my house, who would have thought it, hee hee." As quickly again his faced changed to his serious expression. "But I must go know, there are still things to do. Is there anything you need for the baby?"

Signe thought quickly, but found her brain was mush and she hadn't a clue. "Well, nappies I suppose. New born size, that's the most important thing."

"Nappies," he said uncertainly. "Of course. Hmm. See you in the morning," and with a backward shuffle he bustled off leaving a musty smell.

It was then that the realisation of the difficulties involved with her situation hit her. A baby in that ramshackle set up he called home. It was all organised here, nurses to help, it was clean and tidy. How would she cope in that weird place of his? She thought of Melissa, efficient and organised, and a part of her regretted that loss.

It was a beaten up old Volvo, maroon paintwork scarred and dinted in places and making a noise like a tank, which was sitting outside the entrance. Signe was holding the baby, Joe had everything else.

"Haven't you got a baby seat?" the nurse exclaimed looking shocked. Signe and Joe looked at each other with similar confusion.

"We haven't got one yet," Signe stammered, "it all happened so quickly."

"We can hire you one. It would be safer for the baby."

"It's alright I'll hold him in the back. It'll be fine," Signe said defensively.

"But we don't like to let you leave if the baby isn't going to be safe," the nurse insisted. "I can call a porter to fetch a seat."

"No," Signe flared, then caught herself. "No, thank you, it's fine. It's a very short journey," and quickly got herself into the back of the car. Joe had already dumped the cases in the boot and bundled himself into the front seat. They thundered away leaving the nurse standing motionless on the kerb, a flat expression on her face as if she'd been slapped.

Joe's stress levels were high she realised, as he was worrying a tune in his hum that was anxious and fast. "This is Mia," he said shortly.

"Hi," Signe said, "thanks for this."

"No problem," Mia said in a low husky voice, "glad to help."

She drove fast but efficiently, ramming the gear shift which appeared reluctant. Signe clasped the baby to her, this precious part of her that lay helplessly in her arms, angelic in his perfect features. Golden curling eyelashes glistened around his eyes which, open now, gazed uncomprehending at light and shape. She searched their blue depths hoping for a glimmer of recognition, knowing that wasn't possible yet. His mental processes were only still coming to terms with the cause and effect of eye movement and altering image. The lenses wouldn't even be focussing, his perception merely an unfathomable blur. But she imagined her smiling and nodding communicated, her rationale brooked by the maternal need to love and be loved in return. This was her love, her life, her devotion.

Joe bustled with bags, shoving them into the dwelling, then rushed back and hovered by the car in an attempt to help Signe with the baby but didn't in fact help at all. Mia was standing a few feet off, bum perched on the bonnet of the car, smoking a roll up. She was watching distractedly but obviously didn't feel the need to help. Signe struggled to get out of the car, twisting to negotiate the door holding the baby, the weakness of her stomach muscles after the caesarean combining to make this a surprisingly awkward manoeuvre. Joe managed only to grab her arm and give her an apologetic tug to help her up.

The sun was shining brightly, the air hanging crisply and sucking plumes of vapour from their mouths. Signe could smell the earthy tang of Mia's cigarette which lingered hazily, suspended long after their breath-smoke had disappeared. It was very still. Signe squinted in the sharp light reflecting off every snowy surface and smiled at the fairy-tale picture, everything white and brightly brittle. Joe's place looked cosy, snuggled in close to the heaving buttress of the solid granite outcrop overhanging it and surrounded by snow-laden pines. A trail of smoke lazily lifted from the chimney and she caught the smell of wood smoke singeing the air.

She took a couple of dry-crunching steps then stopped, feeling she needed to say something more to Mia. She was awed by her presence and a little intimidated by her appearance. She had dark cropped hair and an angular abrupt face with an expression that was intelligent, defiant and argumentative. It was like she seemed to be about to challenge any opinion, but Signe was intrigued by the power and strength which emanated from her. Mia watched her closely and Signe felt excited and frightened by the attention. "Are you staying, coming in?" she offered.

"No," Mia pushed away from the car and scrunched the butt into the snow with the heel of her Doc Martin, "no I've got to get back. Hope it goes okay. Catch yer later Joe."

"Thanks for your help," Signe called, but the engine thudded to life and suddenly the car lurched backwards down the track and onto the road. Without a glance Mia was gone, leaving the two of them standing awkwardly in the collecting silence.

"Squeak". Signe was relieved by the deflecting interjection from the bundle in her arms. "I'd better feed him," she said. Joe ushered her towards the door and then squeezed past her on the narrow path to open it.

The room had completely changed. The bed was no longer behind the door against the wall, it was on the other side under the window with a rustic table beside it. There was new linen and a soft duvet and plump pillow. It looked warm and inviting. Signe gasped, "Wow, this is different."

Joe was humming with pleasure. "There's a curtain you can pull across here," and he demonstrated, drawing a think brown swag of material around the space where the bed was. "So you can be private but still in the warm room, hee hee."

Signe was touched. "Squeak."

"Thank you so much Joe, it's lovely." She sat on the bed in the curtained space and set about feeding. She could hear Joe moving about the room, loading the stove and knocking pans, accompanied by a merry hum.

She looked around. There was a pile of nappies on a shelf under the table, a towel folded on it and, what was that at the foot of the bed? She shuffled down the bed without detaching the baby and peered around the corner of it. A wooden rocking cradle. Had Joe done this? She felt a rush of affection. She felt similar feelings when she suckled the baby, but this was more a surge deep within her of gratitude and humility. Why would he do this for her? He hardly knew her. Surely she was disrupting his life. The hums were relaxed and contented. God moves in mysterious ways. How lucky she was to have found Joe, this kind man who simply enjoyed helping her.

Chapter 37

On Christmas morning Matt woke up with the most unbelievable pain in his stomach. It was like nothing he'd ever felt before, neither like food poisoning nor bad indigestion. Waves of agonising cramps bore into his guts and went right through to his back causing him to pant to try to deal with the pain. Maggie suggested kneeling on the floor with one heel pressing up against his anal sphincter, a yoga reflex point to relieve indigestion, but this had no effect and sitting in that position was excruciating. She was convinced it was on account of the meal they'd had with friends the previous evening involving kidneys flamed in brandy followed by roast duck with all the trimmings washed down by a substantial amount of Rioja. Matt said it was nothing like that; he felt hot and cold, like he had a fever, but his muscles were spasming, as if he had leg cramp in his stomach and back but couldn't, as with leg cramp, relieve it.

They hoped it would pass, but eventually began to panic. What if it was an ulcer or appendicitis? Maggie suggested it might be gall stones and they ought to go to A&E. He said that would be crazy on Christmas day, it would be full of drunks from Christmas Eve. So what were they to do, Maggie retorted, just sit there with it getting worse and worse? She decided to ring NHS direct. It took ages to get through, but after about ten minutes of holding she managed to explain the symptoms to what sounded like a very young doctor. Meanwhile Matt was still rolling around on the bed unable to find any relief. Eventually he was hardly aware of what was happening as no sooner had one wave passed than his anxious anticipation of the next overtook his presence of mind.

Maggie returned from the living room to say that the doctor suggested that if it didn't pass in the next fifteen minutes they should go to A&E. While they waited they discussed the feasibility of this. They didn't have a car and Matt said there was no way he was going pillion on her bike. A taxi? On Christmas morning? It would cost a fortune and how long would you have to wait? Maggie said there were tons of Muslim taxi drivers who would have no interest in Christmas, it would be easy. By this time Matt was past caring and agreed to whatever she wanted. She rang a local number when the fifteen minutes was up and there was no change in Matt's condition. She came back saying it would be half to three quarters of an hour; they were short staffed this morning as most of their drivers had been out all night dealing with Christmas Eve revellers. Matt groaned as another spasm hit him. Maggie tried another couple of firms but the response was similar.

"I can't take much more of this Mags. Oh God!" He felt tears shoot from his eyes as it seemed his back would break. "Christ Almighty" he screamed, gasped and suddenly lay still on the bed with his eyes closed, his body completely limp and covered in sweat.

"Matt!" It was Maggie's turn to scream. She grasped his shoulders. "Matt, speak to me. Matt!"

"It's gone," he whispered. "I think it's gone."

"Really?" Maggie's voice was high-pitched, disbelieving.

"I don't know, but suddenly there's no pain. It's like it just vanished from my body." He tried moving tentatively, expecting another attack, but got into a sitting position without any recurrence of the pain. "I can't believe it. It's simply gone."

"That's totally weird. I mean a few seconds ago you were in agony. Are you sure you feel fine?"

"I think so."

"I'll get you some water."

Matt sipped gratefully, Maggie sitting on the bed beside him unsure of what to do. "That was absolutely unbelievable," he said.

"And it's completely gone?"

"Yes, completely gone."

He looked into her eyes and saw real concern still there. "I was really scared then Matt. That really freaked me out. I thought something terrible was going to happen." She leant into him with an arm around his back.

"Yeah, well, me too."

"What shall we do about the taxi? Shall I cancel it?"

"I suppose."

"But d'you think you should be checked out?"

"It could take ages, we'd have to wait in a queue. I'd prefer to just stay here and see what happens. I'm fine now, apart from feeling like I've been kicked in the back by a horse."

Maggie laughed nervously. "But d'you think you'll be okay going to your parents as planned?"

"I don't know. I think I'm fine."

"You'd better have a shower; freshen up and see how you are then."

The shower was certainly refreshing and by the time he'd dressed, Maggie had completed some last-minute present wrapping and was more or less ready for the day.

"Well?" she questioned as he came in.

"Agh," Matt doubled over and fell to one knee, "Agh" he groaned again.

"Matt," she rushed to him "Oh God Matt." She fell to her knees beside him whereupon he rolled her over onto her back and lay on top of her. "Aah! Matt, you bastard! I was really worried."

He laughed, pinning her to the floor and kissing her angry frown.

"See, I told you I was fine."

"Are you sure, Matt, it could be something serious?"

"Honestly, I'm fine. Look, if it happens again I'll just have to go and lie down. My mum will fuss and sort me out I'm sure." He got up and pulled a small packet from his pocket. "Anyway, Happy Christmas."

"Oh Matt, sorry, Happy Christmas." She got up and they hugged and he kissed her on the mouth. It felt quaintly awkward. She took the present quizzically and he knew she feared it might be some conventional jewellery which he knew wasn't her style, and he enjoyed her attempt at concealing her misgivings.

"Thanks Matt."

"Well, you don't know what it is yet. You may hate it," he said, deliberately adding to her potential disappointment.

She opened the box and gradually unrolled the purple tissue paper inside. A length of silver chain fell into her palm and at first he could tell she didn't comprehend what it was until she lifted the tell-tale earring loop and the chain straightened to reveal the single drop amethyst suspended dangling at the end.

"Oh Matt, it's really beautiful. My birthstone?"

"Of course."

She kissed him coyly. "Put it in for me?"

"Which ear?"

"Um, well I think I'll keep the jade stud in the left ear, so the right."

He swept the thick tresses of glossy curls away from her face and took out the single gold hoop and replaced it with the silver loop of the single six inch long chain. She went to the mirror and her sparkling eyes told him all he needed to know before she turned and said "I love it" and gave him a huge smacker.

"I'm afraid mine's more practical than personal." She went to a cupboard and pulled out a thin A4 sized parcel, brown wrapping-paper she'd decorated with African-type geometric designs and tied with zany multi-coloured ribbon. He undid it and revealed a black leather folder which had two leather bands running down each inside flap.

"It's for your score when you're doing a concert. I had it made by that guy in the leather shop in the market. It's got your initials stamped on it, see?"

He was really touched that she had gone to such trouble. "I think it's very personal. That's really nice Mags, really smart. Thanks." He went to kiss her but she forestalled him, flinging herself into his chest with a cry of "I love you Matt" and holding onto him as if her life depended on it. Pulling herself back enough to look at him she then hungrily launched herself into his mouth, kissing him with unknown desperation. He responded more in shock than with volition, but abandoned himself to the warmth of her ready mouth.

"Make love to me Matt," she begged and began unbuttoning him as he stood stunned by this onslaught.

On the bed where he'd so recently writhed in agony they writhed in the unfettered freedom of a newfound loving. It was sweet in its shortness and tender in its gentle novelty. Their consummation was modest by either's standard, but each was aware of a nugget of purity in their fulfilment and wondered what that augured.

"Are you still alright?" Maggie smiled up at him, unused to this conventional missionary position."

"Absolutely. Feeling fantastic." He smiled back and snogged her shining mouth.

"I thought so. What's the time?"

"Eleven thirty."

"Shit! We're going to be late. What time did you say you'd turn up?"

"Twelve."

"Oh well, they'll have to wait. Shower?"

"I've only just had one."

"Come and scrub me down."

They washed each other off in the tight shower cubicle and kissed and licked each other in the jetting water, such that Matt found himself hard again, lifted her up and gently slipped inside her for an exquisite short second orgasm.

"Wow, life in the old dog yet," she quipped.

"It's been a long time, Mags."

Half an hour later she revved up the Yamaha and zoomed off to Canning Town to spend the day with her mum and her sister and her family. Matt looked out the presents for his family and realised he hadn't got a card for his dad's sweater. He went to the desk where they kept stationary and, rootling in the drawer, he chanced on the letter from the girl in Sweden and stopped short, holding it in his hand.

A sudden rush of remembrance of those feelings he'd had back in Gothenburg shocked him, coming hard on the heels of this newfound intimacy with Maggie, and he couldn't help comparing them and finding them not dissimilar. But his feelings for the statue and the girl in Gothenburg were of a different order. They were unalterably pristine whereas the new joy with Maggie was a novelty coloured with reference to a physicality which could never be forgotten, maybe never forsaken. Who knew where it would go, but holding this letter he was now overcome with an extreme tenderness and regret for the unfulfilled encounter with that embodiment of perfection which had filled his senses all those months ago. It haunted him and he felt there was a lack in his life, a story that was hanging in time, unresolved and questioning.

He felt remorse that he had waited so long before answering her abject letter with that brief Christmas card, sent as a salve to his conscience in a moment of emotional weakness only a couple of weeks ago. Maybe she never got it and would think he hated her still. Well, he didn't. He felt only sorrow for her lack of courage and his time in prison, but he supposed he'd forgiven her. There was no point in bearing a grudge.

He put the letter back, found a suitable present tag, addressed it, picked up the bag of presents and slammed the door of the flat to catch the bus up to Walthamstow.

Chapter 38

January found Matt rehearsing for a new production of Faust in Barcelona. He'd never done the role of Mephistopheles and rather fancied the idea of playing the devil. Most roles he'd done had been sympathetic parts, so to do a basically evil one would be fun and he anticipated a chance to investigate the Mr Hyde side of his persona. When it came to it he wasn't disappointed, rather, on the contrary, he found it a bit too psychologically analytical. The director was obsessed with thoroughly investigating the moral implications of abandoning oneself to lust as Faust in effect does, selling his soul to the devil for the opportunity of indulging his desire for Marguerite. Matt found himself asking similar questions in his relationship with Maggie and desire for Caterina.

Out of the blue in early January she emailed him saying she missed him, this after so much silence before Christmas when she had obviously been busy rehearsing the show she'd done in December. She said she needed to see him, desperately wanted some time with him to relive that Paris experience. She was learning, or rather re-learning, Despina in Mozart's 'Cosi fan Tutte' for a production in Rome rehearsing in early February. Did he fancy a couple of nights in Italy? She'd buy him a meal and, you never know, there might be a bottle of champagne in her room!

Who could resist that thought? It all came flooding back, that desire, that exquisite physical fulfilment. He'd gone to Barcelona without replying, having been hesitant in the home environment with Maggie getting excited about beginning rehearsals and their uncertainty about where they were emotionally. Once in Spain the distance had diluted the feeling of duty and it was easy to say yes, it was just a case of finding a suitable two or three days. He of course felt guilty, but that was all part of the wicked delight in doing something you know you shouldn't and besides he was tripping just imagining the delicious pleasures awaiting him in Rome. He told himself it was wrong two-timing Maggie, again, and he hated the thought of hurting her, but it was easy to make a justification that he needed to see Caterina again to know how he really felt about her. He remembered something his dad had once said – 'It's always possible to find a justification if you're desperate for something, however immoral'- which didn't make him feel good, but didn't persuade him to change his mind.

Rehearsals dragged and Matt began to find the subject matter too close to home, feeling he was Faust and Mephistopheles combined. He found that playing a less than moral person coloured his personality and helped him in his justification of his immoral liaison. He emailed Caterina and enjoyed titillating himself by making suggestive references and using euphemistic phrases which he knew she picked up by her responses.

After rehearsals that night, back in his apartment, he tried to analyse his feelings. Was he just sex-mad? Did anyone else love three women? Well, he didn't think he loved the girl in Sweden, but there was some strong attraction still which he didn't understand. Was it what George had said, the twin flames thing? And then he thought, why not? Why not love three women? Who said you couldn't? Religion? Social convention based on religion? But without a religious imperative where was the moral transgression? Deceit? But only when convention dictates monogamy as a norm.

Or was this Mr Hyde playing devil's advocate and twisting his thinking to accommodate his desires? And what were these desires? Were they merely animal instincts, genetic yearnings, which he couldn't govern or chose to indulge out of selfishness? Or did they constitute true feelings of love and intimacy? He felt drawn to all three women on different levels and for different needs. How could he satisfy his desires and appease his conventional conscience?

A text pinged through from Maggie. With only two weeks to go before the beginning of rehearsals the girl playing Anita had dropped out having discovered she was pregnant, and they'd asked Maggie to take over the role. She was euphoric, so excited. He immediately texted back congratulating her, telling her she deserved it and she'd be fantastic. After a few texts back and forth she had to get back to work and signed off.

Why did he feel uncomfortable? It didn't affect her what he was doing in Spain, what he was going to do in Rome. She wouldn't need to know. It was his life. He'd never promised her he wouldn't have an affair, but there was an unspoken assumption, a social convention that dictated that because they lived together they practised fidelity. Why? What difference would it make to her? It was only sex. It was only physical need and fulfilment. And love, what was that? Just a need, of something or someone.

A couple of weeks later Maggie was into rehearsals in London and Matt was running up to the first night. They'd agreed that if he had a free weekend he'd nip back and see her before she went up to Manchester. It had been easy enough to lie and say he had a rehearsal on the Saturday and book a flight to Rome on the Friday afternoon. His anticipation and excitement for the trip was not unwarranted, Caterina was sublime. More than sublime, divine. She was a goddess of delights, demanding, insatiable, generous and extraordinary. He found he plunged to the depths of lustful desire and rose to the heights of exquisite sensitisation.

The weekend was one long sensual indulgence of tastes, touch and torrid love-making. He returned to Barcelona exhausted and his fulfilled lust informed his performance of Mephistopheles for the premier, the critics saying he personified temptation of the flesh in just the way Gounod would have intended.

On the flight back to England he found himself analysing the euphoric weekend with Caterina and realised, as previously, she had somehow commanded the whole thing. She'd made all the arrangements, all the decisions had been hers, it had all been on her terms. And there was something galling about that, as if he was her poodle. Again it had seemed, although only on subsequent reflection, that he had had no say in any of it, she had orchestrated it all.

During the next few weeks he travelled back and forth from Barcelona, fulfilling his performance obligations there whilst fitting in rehearsals for a couple of semi-staged performances of Berlioz's L'Enfance du Christ and preparing for a Matthew Passion at the Barbican Hall for Good Friday with the Academy of Early Music. This time he was singing the arias and not having done them for a while he was having to get his cords round the baroque again.

Easter was unusually early this year and fell mid-March, whereas he remembered in Gothenburg it had been practically at the end. Strange how Easter was dependant on the phases of the moon, he thought. As he went over the music for the Passion, the events of the previous year inevitably flooded back and that image of the girl in the audience insisted its way into his mind.

On the Tuesday of Holy Week Matt went up to Manchester for Maggie's first night. He was excited to see the show as Maggie had sent him updates of the production and cast. She promised he'd enjoy it, of which he had no doubt, as he'd adored the piece since his teens and it had always made him regret that he hadn't a dancing bone in his body.

From the first notes of the prologue he knew he was in for a great evening. The tight rhythms, sharp accents and crazy syncopations of Bernstein's score swept you into a world of risk, excitement and danger, and unlike the nineteen sixty one film which he knew so well with its beautiful choreography but rather naive gang portrayal, this production got to the heart of gang culture, taking out any prettiness and exposing a ruthless underground where the knife ruled, drugs were currency and loyalty valued above friendship. It had unavoidable resonances with recent problems in the sub-culture of London and the tragic, pointless killings of teenagers there which, Matt felt, made it particularly pertinent.

Maggie was fantastic. He'd forgotten what a great mover she was. As Matt sat there watching her effortlessly execute what to him would have been completely impossible combinations of complicated steps, he couldn't understand why she hadn't gone for work in musicals as opposed to obstinately insisting on trying for straight-acting roles, for which she had little track record. But there you go, he thought, you couldn't tell some people.

Putting his frustration aside, he relaxed back into his chair, if that were possible in this high-octane performance, and enjoyed watching her triumph as the more mature, worldly-wise Anita to the impressionable young lead Maria. Her fiery Italian temperament exploded in the confrontation scenes and her voice was strong and assured in the main numbers, 'America' and 'A Boy like that'. She really was very good, Matt thought, and just wished she would have that confidence in her daily life. Maybe this break would change that.

By the end of the performance he felt wrung out, particularly after clapping them back again and again for more curtain calls. Maggie had told him there would be first night drinks in the circle bar afterwards and he should meet her in the foyer. When he got there it was full of people, all under the same instructions Matt presumed, and all talking loudly and excitedly. Eventually he saw Maggie come through flanked by a handsome guy who he immediately recognised as Bernardo the leader of the Sharks, and one of the ensemble girls. They were arms around shoulders chatting animatedly, then broke up as they looked for friends. Maggie saw him and skipped across with a cry of "Matt."

They gripped each other tight, Matt burying his face into her hair.

"You were fantastic Mags really fantastic," he reported into the depths of her curls.

"Did you enjoy it?"

"Oh God, it was brilliant. Totally brilliant." He could tell she was so happy. "What a production," he continued, holding her away from him and looking into her smiling open face. "Just so strong and, and amazing." He kissed her again.

"I'm so glad you enjoyed it."

Everyone began moving upstairs and she rattled away as they followed, telling him how the final preview had nearly gone wrong because one of the trucks had got jammed and they'd had to improvise without that bit of scenery. Everyone was so great, it felt like a huge family and they all got on so well. Oh, and did he see that Annie fell on her arse right at the end of America? No? Well it was probably in the black out, but they all had hysterics. Didn't he hear laughing? No? God it was so funny.

There was a crush of bodies trying to get drinks, but as it was on the house it didn't take long with no payments to be made. Maggie kept introducing him to members of the cast whose names he immediately forgot of course, and then she'd be chatting with them about things that had happened in the show and how they'd had hysterics. There were endless inside jokes and references which he didn't understand, often to do with things that had happened in the rehearsal period and been carried into the production. They were all high on adrenalin and knocking down bottles of Becks and Corona which hardly touched the sides. The guy who played Bernardo came up.

"Hey Mags, Josh says you've got to do a complete flip tomorrow, no hands right?"

"Oh yeah, sure," she replied. "Sam, this is Matt."

"Hey man," Sam shook hands familiarly, "how you doin'?"

"Fine thanks. Congratulations, great show."

"Sure, well you know, it's gotta be a winner if Mags is in it."

"Shut up," Maggie hit him gently on the arm and he pretended to fight her off.

Matt noticed the look in her eyes as she continued to pummel him and his enjoyment of teasing her. He didn't like the way he called her Mags. He found there wasn't much way into the conversation as they were all jabbering about the show and he felt peripheral.

After about an hour and an impressive number of beers downed by the cast (Matt wasn't really drinking much, having a concert in a few days), he reckoned they'd be able to leave, but suddenly there was talk of going for a meal and everyone seemed up for it. Matt wasn't on their post-performance high and was longing for a bed.

"Oh but Matt, come on, I really want to go," Maggie pleaded when he mentioned this to her. "We're only going for a quick pizza. Please. Don't spoil the evening."

What could he do but acquiesce?

The quick pizza turned into an extended meal, with bottles of wine ordered repeatedly until everyone except Matt was extremely well lubricated. He became more annoyed the more tired he became and the more frustrated he got at having to stay. There was the inevitable mess with the bill, trying to sort out who'd had what, who hadn't had a starter, who had ordered a liqueur, such that it was decided it was easiest to divide the bill twelve ways. Then of course various people had no cash and offered to pay by debit card, but there was a minimum charge so then it had to be worked out who would pay for a group, who would then pay cash etc.

Ultimately the bill was paid, but as always, in Matt's experience of these things, the people who had been modest in their orders ended up paying far more than their fair share, and those who had been most drunk and most indulgent, pro rata, seemed to end up paying very little. They spilled out onto the pavement, laughing and shushing each other in drunken attempts at keeping the peace.

After elaborate 'good nights' and injunctions to rest up, followed by adoration-heaped embraces and excitement-laced expectations of seeing each other tomorrow, they went their separate ways. Maggie was by this time needing assistance in negotiating the one foot in front of the other routine and it was fortunate the hotel was very central.

"Oh God, that was sucha laugh, wasn't'it'?" Maggie slurred.

"Sure."

"No, but they'ra great crowd aren't they? I mean they're really lovely, don't ya think?"

"Yeah, sure."

"Did you enjoy it Matt? I mean it was fun wasn't it? Did you enjoy yourself Matt? I mean be honest. It was a laugh wasn't it?"

With difficulty Matt got her to the hotel and managed to steer her through the entrance to the lift. Once in the room there wasn't much more he could do than try to get some of her clothes off and bundle her into bed, as by this time she had all but passed out. He got her to drink a bit of water before she burbled herself into a heavy sleep.

He brushed his teeth, checked his phone for messages and got into bed. He lay there listening to Maggie puffing away beside him and waited in vain for sleep. He was so tired he was past it and gazed at the faint orange glow seeping through the curtains from the street.

They passed an unsatisfactory morning the next day with Maggie nursing a hangover and fretting about the performance that night. Matt found it impossible to be sympathetic but assured her she'd be fine come seven o'clock. He found he was upset with her but wasn't sure why and suspected it wasn't justified. Was it the familiarity she had shown to the Bernardo guy? Was it that he was jealous of the close-knit family atmosphere of the cast? Or was it that he was hurt she was having a great time in spite of him? These questions remained unanswered, but accompanied him on the train south after he had said a rather peremptory goodbye to her.

When he got home he was able to distance himself from these concerns, having to deal with emails from his agent, arrangements re costume and wig fittings for an up-coming show and the need to get some new publicity photos done, which his agent had been on about for some time but he had never addressed. He'd booked a photographer for the following day so needed to get a haircut and generally sort himself out before the concert on Friday. In the late afternoon Maggie texted to say she was feeling much better and apologised if she'd spoilt his visit. Did her forgive her? He decided not to answer for the moment.

The Matthew Passion on Good Friday was a big concert, the tickets all but sold out for the 4pm kick off. He couldn't help making comparison with the performance in Sweden just under a year ago in that intimate church with the few hundred in the audience. Here the seats of the Barbican Hall lifted before him in the enormous space and they seemed a very small ensemble on the extensive stage. The audience here was lost in the mass of faces ranged before him so that it was difficult to pick out anyone individually. He couldn't make out his parents. He'd left their tickets at the box office and couldn't now remember where the seats were. He'd catch up with them on Sunday when he went over for Easter lunch; they would have to shoot off immediately after the concert to get back for his grandmother who was living with them now.

Again the image of the girl intruded his mind and her rapt expression contorted with emotion as the Passion proceeded. Where was she now? What was she doing? Was she at a similar performance of another Passion, her eyes fixed on a crucifix?

He had a perverse desire to see her again, perverse because of what had happened not because of the desire itself, which felt pure.

The performance was good, very good; high quality soloists at the top of their game with a first division baroque band and choir. It was everything that the original instrument movement had come to represent; scholarship, finesse, detail, subtlety, but somehow, for Matt, there was something missing. Throughout the performance he couldn't put a finger on it but comparing it to the experience in Gothenburg he found it wanting. Possibly, he acknowledged, he had been on some kind of emotional high at the time which now coloured his appreciation of the work, but now it somehow seemed soulless. It was strange how the same piece could appear so dissimilar. It was certainly the St Matthew, but without the Passion.

Going for drinks after at the pub on the corner across the road from the hall, the few lagers he had were wonderfully refreshing and the company jolly. Chris had been singing in the choir and managed to stay for a quick one and the conversation flowed with the usual anecdotes of recent performance highs and lows, but he felt empty, short-changed, like he'd performed this amazing piece of music but it hadn't touched him. On the way back in the tube from Liverpool Street he felt incredibly alone, bereft, and he tasted again those feelings he'd had when he was inside. Feelings of being cut off from reality, disconnected from life in a wilderness of emotional lostness.

He got a chirpy text from Maggie when the train surfaced from the tunnel at Stratford and the signal reconnected. He didn't feel like answering. Ironically although feeling alone he didn't want to connect with anyone, preferring rather to indulge his solitude in a weird, illogical, masochistic self-pity. He wanted to feel hurt and hurt himself more in the process, but didn't understand why. It was perhaps a pessimism which fed off a dissatisfaction with his present situation and the immediate effect of the unfulfilling performance, but he didn't even want to find a rationale for his mood, he just wanted to wallow in it.

Once in the flat he dumped his suit carrier in the hall, went to the fridge and found a couple of lagers and turned on the TV. He clicked through various channels and found nothing that interested him. He didn't feel that tired. He finished one of the lagers and looked at his phone feeling he ought to reply to Maggie. He sent a short text saying the concert was fine and hoping she was okay. Their texts had become prosaic these days, no mischievous innuendo, mere affirmations of association. They seemed to be in different worlds. As expected he didn't receive one back. She'd be out now whooping it up in some bar probably.

He went into his computer and logged into a porn site. He wanted to see filth and perversion. He wanted to dirty himself with immorality of the lowest sort, indulgent, nihilistic, gratuitous and meaningless. It suited his mood. He switched from one sordid video to another, finding himself aroused but uninterested in doing anything about it. It was a way of torturing himself as some kind of perverse punishment for his situation, for his previous indulgences. He wanted to sully the pious performance he'd been involved in, destroy any attempt at piety because it hadn't rewarded him or lifted his spirit. In fact it had made him miserable so he would add to that misery.

Eventually when he was sufficiently sick of himself he closed down the machine, went to the fridge and ferreted around for something to eat. He took a pack of mini pork pies, some cold roast potatoes and tomato ketchup and sat at the kitchen table. He ate greedily, smothering everything by rolling each bite in the pool of ketchup he'd squeezed onto the plate. It felt glutinous and disgusting.

When he'd finished all the pies and potatoes he still wasn't satisfied. What else could he abuse himself with? A plastic container in the fridge revealed half a chocolate cake. He needed double cream, but there wasn't any. He found ice cream in the freezer and scooped a large dollop onto the cake then proceeded to cram it in his mouth. It was rich and sweet and sickly but he persevered 'til well nigh gorged with sucked and glutted offal'. Milton's words from Paradise Lost describing the devil came to him. And he wanted to be the devil, wanted debauchery and self-destruction.

He went to bed feeling ill, stomach distended, and wondered what Maggie was doing. Perhaps out at a club with some of the cast, with the Bernardo guy, what was his name? Sam? 'Hey man!' Fuck you, Sam.

Chapter 39

She had no idea how many days she had been at Joe's. What with being permanently exhausted and trying to cope with the endless things that needed doing, she ceased to realise the passage of time. She had anticipated that it wasn't going to be easy but hadn't anticipated the confusion. She found she hadn't a clue how to look after a baby. Yes, she had picked up in hospital the rudiments of feeding and nursing, of hygiene and handling, but then, when things happened she panicked. Sometimes he seemed not to breathe for ages and she rushed to…to do what? Lift him? Jostle him to breathe? And then he'd take a long breath and she'd almost cry with relief. But it was exhausting, the worry of not knowing. She eventually turned her phone on, charging it up from Joe's solar powered trickle feed, and looked things up off the internet, but her limited data allowance eventually blocked her.

She used her bankcard at the local supermarket to get to her savings to pay for necessities but her savings weren't extensive. She needed to upgrade her phone tariff but couldn't afford it and in any case the account was in Gustav's name. Joe only had an ancient Nokia, pre Smartphone, he just used for messages. There was no computer. He said he didn't need it and couldn't afford it.

Within days of going back to Joe's the baby became stressed, not settling to feed, playing with the nipple but not latching on and then crying. At first Signe was patient, trying to follow the nurse's instructions but quickly finding it impossible. He just refused to accept it and arched his back and screamed, going puce in the face. She was at her wits end. He was obviously hungry. Did she not have milk anymore? Was there something wrong with him? He seemed to be in pain, flailing his arms and twisting his head, distracted and angry. What was she doing wrong?

Joe hummed and looked worried and then disappeared into the workshop and she heard him sawing and banging. She couldn't talk to him, it was like he couldn't cope with problems, well not of that nature. He could cope with things he knew about and knew how to do, cooking, cleaning. But babies were outside his capacity, he just wanted to watch them. Signe felt it was all her fault. She was a woman, she should know how to deal with these things. Why was it all going wrong? Had Mary had these problems? The bible never mentioned it. All the pictures showed Jesus peacefully lying in the manger or sitting on the Virgin's knee making the sign of the Cross.

But she was dreaming again. This wasn't how it was, the delusion was over. She knew now and understood. This was no miracle baby, no Son of God, no immaculate conception. What had she been thinking? What romantic nonsense had filled her mind to imagine this was other than a purely biological event? As she fought to keep her patience with this screaming ball of fury in her arms, the dead weight of her predicament settled on her spirit, deadening her desire to go on. The future extended before her in all its tragic reality, another digit in the stats of family breakdown, teenage pregnancy, single parenthood. The alternatives seemed impossible – living at home with the baby, suffering the indignity of social comment, abandoning her studies, abandoning the Bridgettines.

The Bridgettines. How she longed for that solitude, that order, away from this nightmare with this angry baby. But she'd never get there now. She wanted to pray, to be at one with Jesus, with her Saviour, like at the concert, not struggling to satisfy this infant from hell that plagued her. She'd called him Jesú in the hospital, that's how they'd registered him. Jesú, the name stuck in her throat now, mocking her.

She'd whisk him onto her shoulder, shushing and patting his back, bouncing him as she walked up and down the room, trying desperately to staunch this yelling. Sometimes he'd fall exhausted into a sleep and she'd collapse with him in her arms on a chair, too tired to do more than hold him to her. Then he'd be screaming again. How wasn't he exhausted? She was. Utterly exhausted. His red face and struggling body reminded her of a small devil goading her with the memory of that moment. 'This is the fruit of your transgression.' How many times had she dreamt of living that moment again, that day again, of not having gone to the concert, of not ever having seen that face that had tempted her, that had masqueraded as her Lord and cheated her?

Crying she'd attempt again to satisfy him with her breast, coaxing him gently at first but quickly becoming desperate with lack of patience and sleep, she'd jab his grimacing mouth with her nipple despite the searing pain of it. She'd imagine it her penance. She would suffer it as her Agony. Her nipples would bleed as she rammed them uselessly at his mouth, the dried, cracked tissue splitting again, but still she'd persevere until they'd both be screaming at each other and she'd smeared his face with her blood.

Humming, humming. Is that all he could do? She hated his humming. Why couldn't he talk to her like anyone else instead of faffing about and humming? She wanted to scream and tell him to shut up or ... but she couldn't, had to stifle the desire, clenching her jaw to stop the sound escaping. It was all that she could do to stop herself crushing the baby in her frustration. Why did it scream? SHUT UP. SHUT UP.

There was a knock on the door. Joe's friends. He'd said they'd come. Signe tried hurriedly to arrange herself, tidy herself and the baby. It was impossible, everything was a mess.

"Hi, I'm Cassie and this is Pauls. Hi Joe, how's it going? Look at this little fella!" She was much younger than Joe, maybe twenty five, but Signe was only guessing. They seemed to be a couple. She was loose-limbed, had a spreading manner, relaxed and confident. He was demure, hanging back, letting her take the lead. Signe smiled in response to their open greetings, feeling suddenly swamped by the presence of two people she didn't know. Jesú had unexpectedly fallen silent, but his tear-stained face told a story. Cassie asked if she could hold him.

"Yes of course," Signe stammered and felt a weight lift from her which was more than his four odd kilos. It was like a burden of responsibility had floated from her and it felt wonderful. She sighed involuntarily and a short laugh escaped her before it caught in her throat as a sob and she had to turn to regain herself. She covered it by blowing her nose in a tissue before turning back again to see Cassie so easily holding him in the most natural way.

"He's a handsome boy isn't he Pauls?" Cassie was smiling at him and making popping noises with her lips.

"Sure."

"Has he got a name yet?" Cassie continued.

"Jesú." Signe replied, abashed.

"Oh goodness, wow. That's lovely."

"He was born on Christmas day," Signe explained.

"Ya ya, I know, Joe told us all about it. Quite a drama."

Joe was humming in the background, teetering on the edge of the group, unsure what to do. "Hee hee, yes it was a bit crazy."

There was a short lull, one of those moments when no one says anything and it's a bit awkward, before Joe said, "Shall I make coffee?" which broke the tension. He shuffled off to prepare it in response to their unanimous 'yes'.

"So, how are you getting on?" Cassie said. They sat wherever they could find a convenient place, Pauls awkwardly unsure what to do with a large plastic bag he was holding. "Oh yes, we got you some clothes from the charity shop," Cassie added. "Thought you could do with some first size stuff."

Pauls gestured the bag across to Signe who dragged it towards her.

"That's really kind, thanks." She began going through the heap of soft cottony outfits in various shapes and colours, not because she was interested but because she felt she should be seen to be.

"They're lovely," she said, hoping it sounded grateful.

"Some of those are expensive makes; it's amazing what people get rid of."

"Right. Well I hope they didn't cost you a lot," Signe felt guilty now.

"Oh no, they sell them really cheap 'cos they get tons of it in." Cassie smiled reassuringly and dandled Jesú lightly on her knee. He seemed contented for the first time in ages. How was it Cassie could calm him? "You know what they say, 'one person's rubbish is another's gold'."

Signe laughed weakly.

"So, here we are." Joe fussed about with mugs, milk and sugar. "Kim said he'd be here. I expect he's forgotten the time. He lives in his own time zone, hee hee."

"Ya," Cassie laughed, "well it doesn't matter, we're used to waiting for him." She adeptly managed to drink coffee elegantly whilst balancing the baby with her other arm. Signe wondered if she worked with babies or if she had one of her own. She seemed to be an expert. Every moment she was waiting for him to contract his face and scream.

"D'you mind if I...?" Pauls gestured the roll-up in his fingers, a rather fat spliff, which was leaking fibre from one end.

"No, of course," Joe replied, then quickly looked to Signe, "if that's um..."

"I don't mind," Signe said.

A coil of smoke wreathed Pauls' head and Signe soon detected the familiar smell she'd tasted from Mia's joint the morning she'd arrived back. It was sweet and earthy. She liked it even though she knew it was wrong. Pauls passed it to Cassie who took a deep drag and offered it to Signe. There was a fleeting moment of indecision when Signe's mind argued with itself but her hand was already taking the fat little sausage awkwardly in her fingers. She didn't care anymore. What did it matter?

She took a long draw, feeling the heat in her mouth, removed the butt and gasped inwards. She thought she would choke but swallowed hard, aware of her smarting eyes, and breathed out. Her chest burned and she felt a rush of pain in her head like an ice-cream headache, but that quickly cleared. She offered the joint to Joe but he shook his shaggy head, "I can't take that stuff, it gives me indigestion, hee hee."

Pauls took it back and took a practised pull, inhaling deeply.

"What do you think?" he exhaled, smoke emanating from nostrils and mouth simultaneously. Signe was at that moment experiencing what she believed to be the 'hit', a warm fuzziness engulfing her head and bringing with it a tremendous release.

"It's nice," she said, her voice sounding deeper to her.

"It's the best you can get," Pauls smiled. "We Dutch know all about it; we're the experts. I call it my frankincense mixture. Nice aroma, yes?"

"It's the only thing you are expert in," Cassie put in. Signe saw the signs of an imminent outburst as Jesú's back arched and his face crumpled into its usual screaming mask.

"Oh my goodness, that came out of nowhere." Cassie was shocked.

"He's like this most of the time. I really don't know why." Signe felt herself opening up and able to express this without feeling it was her fault. She didn't even mind if it was.

"What a pair of lungs. He's really angry."

"Cass, just hold him there, let me…do you mind?" Pauls looked to Signe.

No, if you think you can do something."

"Just a bit of massage. I did some training once. It might not help, but you never know." He passed Signe the joint and rubbed his hands together, then very gently cupped them around the baby's head. He kept bawling and struggling, but Pauls quietly moved his fingers minutely around the skull, massaging almost without any movement. He closed his eyes, concentrating. Signe took another drag of the joint as she was holding it and felt the reflex to cough so strongly, but managed again to stop herself. She held in the smoke, wanting to extract as much effect as possible, wanting more of that warming confidence and relaxation. She breathed out at last and revelled in the illicit act. She had taken this drug into her body and the fix felt good, more so because it was wicked and she no longer cared.

She was aware that Jesú's screams had lessened, were subsiding to a less intense crying. Pauls continued to hold his head, now not seeming to move at all, just holding. Cassie made a face at Signe indicating something was happening. They sat silently, Signe taking a smooth mouthful of coffee and deciding she really liked this other drug too. A wave of contentedness washed over her and it seemed that everything was okay after all; the baby, this life, this weird dwelling and Joe humming there smiling stupidly. It was cool and she felt chilled.

Very soon Jesú was quiet, just hupping slightly in post-crying reflex. Pauls kept his hands on his head, moving them now gently here and there, testing, feeling softly with his finger pads. After a bit he seemed satisfied and removed them.

"He had a lot of tension in his head. I could feel it all very tight, stressed. I think we relieved it now quite a bit."

"Why tension," Signe said hazily.

"I dunno. Maybe there was stress in the birth. I didn't study for too long, but we did quite a bit of head massage. It was really interesting." He took the joint back and relit it. "The body's like, linked up electronically. It's amazing. There are, like, pressure points everywhere that can release tension and stress. Reflexology, kind of. Hmm, seems to have worked a bit."

Cassie was holding Jesú on her shoulder now quiet as could be, his mouth sucking on his fist. "Wow, Pauls, why aren't you doing this professionally?"

"Nah, I couldn't go through all that Cass, it was endless. So much technical stuff, you know like tons of exams and shit."

"Yeah, but you're really good at it. You could just do some for people part- time, you know, advertise locally."

"You've got to have a licence and all that stuff. It's all really tight you know, and then you've got to have premises. It costs a lot to set that up."

There was a pause. "Well, thanks so much," Signe said. She really liked these people. They were cool. They didn't hassle her with questions or anything.

"You're welcome."

There was a knock on the door. "Ah, Kim", "Kim's here", "At last," they variously exclaimed and Joe opened the door.

"Hey man, how's it going?" A slight, wispy oriental guy hopped into the room, smiling and greeting everyone. "Hey Maria, good to see you. How you doing? Congratulations and all that."

"Thanks, well, yah, it kind of all happened." Everything was velvety, soft and rounded. She felt so comfortable slouched in the chair, letting it all coalesce around her. There didn't seem to be any hurry, it all just ebbed and flowed.

"So this is the baby," Kim said. "Oh he's sleeping."

"Wasn't ten minutes ago!" Cassie said smiling.

"No, he was yelling like they could hear him in Copenhagen!" Pauls added.

"Ha, no way." Kim settled in, accepting a coffee from Joe. "Oh, I have this for you. It's a tincture, essence of myrrh to heal your wound. Don't rub it on the baby though – too strong. Ha! So what's been happening with you guys?"

The conversation took off gently, talk of the baby and Signe coping in Joe's place merging into more general conversation. She was vaguely aware of talk of events, meetings, people, all of which didn't mean anything to her and she slipped into a soft dream in which she was floating through clouds, moving from one level to another and occasionally seeing snatches of the earth far, far below. She was slightly concerned at the height but a part of her felt that the further away she went the nearer to home she was getting. It didn't make any sense but it was kind of comfortable. She didn't know if she slept, but when she was aware again the conversation had shifted and Cassie was giving her the baby, "I think he's hungry."

Blearily Signe went and sat on the bed to feed him. He was calm and fed quietly and hungrily. It was such a relief. She changed him and put him in one of the charity shop outfits. He looked cute and she thought she liked him again.

He was passed around the group and seemed to enjoy the attention. Signe enjoyed not having to hold him. When he seemed tired they put him in the rocking cradle Joe had made and which they all admired, and rocked him to sleep.

Joe had prepared food and they all perched around eating and sharing some wine Kim had brought. Signe decided she liked wine too. It made everything less worrying, more bearable, so why not?

"So how do you guys all know each other?" she asked, feeling relaxed and confident.

"The market," Kim immediately replied, "we all do the market. Joe sells his wooden stuff, Cassie does her clothes and I do herbal remedies. So we're like a family down there, aren't we Joe."

"Hee hee, yes you could say that."

"Of course Pauls sells stuff too, but he doesn't do that too conspicuously, not on a stall anyway." They all laughed and prodded Pauls who said "Yeah yeah, alright, we've all got to make a living somehow."

For Signe the evening passed away in a cosy haze of half remembered conversation. She didn't know quite how it ended but was vaguely aware of collapsing into bed at some point, but whether they had left by then or not she wasn't sure.

When she woke in the morning her overriding feeling was regret. Not one, but many. They seemed to be lining up one behind the other. Jesú began to squawk and she had to drag herself unwillingly to deal with him. Her nipples weren't sore any more but it was a drudge to have to go through the motions of it all again. She no longer felt that reciprocal glow when he fed, it just felt like being drained, as if all her energy was being sapped. It was as much as she could do to keep awake to finish changing him before giving him the other breast and falling asleep again.

When she woke he was still attached to her nipple but asleep again himself. Joe must have gone into town as she couldn't hear him. It was mid-morning and the sky was dull and low. The fire was out and it was chill in the cabin. She tried to light it, but didn't know where all the things were, the right kindling and lighting paper. She did what she could but her effort flamed for a bit and then as quickly died.

She felt despondent. She didn't want to do anything. She grabbed some bread that was to hand and dolloped some jam on it and went back to bed. Jesú slept in the cradle, exhausted too it seemed. Signe curled up under the duvet and gazed at the roof. Her mouth was crusty and not because of the bread; she'd fallen asleep without brushing her teeth the previous night. She was listless. She'd stay in bed, it was too cold without the fire. She wanted to sleep, return to oblivion, but couldn't. She wanted Irma, to lie in her bed, feel the warmth of her body and sleep on her chest. She stared at fixed points in the room but saw only herself carrying a baby down an endless road.

She was suddenly startled by a screaming commotion on the roof. Something was scratching and banging and squawking. Signe was terrified, not understanding what was happening, thinking a monster was trying to break through the roof. There was a skittering down the roof and a shadow blinked across the light from the window with more shrieks. Signe knelt on the bed and looked out of the window. Thrashing in the snow quite close was a whirl of creamy white feathers beating and squawking, pinned down by a large hawk. It was a dove Signe soon realised, desperate in its death throes, lashing, gasping for life under the unmoved unmoving grip of the hawk, which looked about occasionally, between jabbing at its neck with its hooked beak.

Signe watched despite the cold, mesmerised by the icy calmness of the hawk and the hot desperation of its prey. Within a minute the fluttering had stopped and a trickle of blood oozed gently from the lacerations to its neck. The hawk adjusted its position, sure of its kill now, but still with one talon braced on the dying bird. It looked around dispassionately, cocking its head to look up into the adjacent trees, observing the path and the view to the road.

Seemingly satisfied that it wasn't going to be disturbed it tore open the breast of the dove with one stroke and ripped back the downy soft feathers. It then hacked beakfuls of flesh and swallowed them whole, sprinklings of blood dotting the surrounding snow. It worked efficiently, only pausing to look around again, its keen eyes panning every angle for danger or competition, but, reassured, continuing to gorge on its kill. Signe couldn't drag herself away. There was something fascinating about the ruthlessness of it, the lack of compassion, that stunned her.

Within a short time the hawk had completely devoured the breast of the dove and had also torn out the entrails. As suddenly as it had appeared it was gone, darting off low through the trees at speed.

Signe looked at the mess on the snow; feathers, blood, spatterings of flesh and guts in an aura around the carcass. She felt an ache in the pit of her stomach, a dead weight. That beautiful innocent bird, a miracle of nerves and muscles, instincts and incredible design, had been destroyed in five minutes and discarded. She couldn't cry, it was deeper than that, more fundamental. It wasn't the kind of sadness that could weep out of you. It was the type that bore into your core and dried you up.

Time dragged endlessly. Her days were a succession of repeating duties. The grey cold weather crept into her body even though Joe kept the place warm generally. Grey still days of lowering cloud sat heavily outside the window numbing her mind, deadening spirit.

She became proficient at rolling joints. Pauls had left her his whole pouch. "This is for Signe – she seemed to like it" Joe related to her the evening after their visit. She relied on that release, craved its sure companionship to cope with the every day. She'd sit and smoke and her mind would wander, dwelling on her failure, her loss, her present drudge. The inhale deadened the pain but pulled her into its embrace, blunting the sharpness of detail but weighting the burden of inevitability. She was lost, adrift in a morass of clinging self-pity. She'd done all this herself, through her own stupidity and now, who was she? The morass slowly circled and she could feel the vortex forming, an irresistible attraction dragging her downwards. She was no-one, with no divine destiny, no special relationship, no divinity. What did it all mean now, this life, this child? Inhale, hold it down, absorb the smothering numbness and then release. Smoke-laden breath and wave of mind- smoothing calm. No God, no thought, no thing that matters. Nothing.

Someone had found a baby buggy thing for free on an exchange website and given it to them. Signe would walk out with Jesú along the path and up the steep road where she'd slipped and fallen and up to the pond where she'd met Joe. The weather had suddenly thawed as can often happen and the snow had gone. The temperature was hovering around two degrees and sometimes there were sunny days. She would sit on a bench by the pond, the baby asleep in the buggy and gaze into the cold water. The image of Ophelia in that Millais painting would come into her mind. There she was, floating in the water, her hair spread out on its surface which was sprinkled with flowers. Alone in her chastity, she seemed an embodiment of purity, the clear water cleansing all her earthly torments; Hamlet's cruelty, her father's intrigue, the whispering of the court. She had escaped all that and taken her integrity to her watery grave.

Signe longed for purification, to be able to put the clock back, to get it right next time. But she knew that was impossible. She gazed into the still depths of the pond, drawn to the darkness of its cool waters. She pulled on the joint, practised now, the sweet-musk smoke permeating her nostrils as she drew down the heavy frankincense mixture. It would be sweet also, a sweet release from this sad mess of a life of hers. It wouldn't matter, would free the world of one person too many. Suicide, a mortal sin? That didn't matter either. She couldn't believe any more.

Another drag, hold it down, don't cough. Sweet pleasure, soft caress flooding her body, numbing her mind.

Step across, slip down, rest into the icy coldness, like a pure cold sheet on a naked body, chaste and spotless. Lie back and feel the water searching through the clothes to the skin, freezing it with a cold caress. Let the water flood your face, flushing your eyes and filling your nostrils. Breathe out then take a long drag, sucking the heavy liquid deep into the lungs. Don't choke, hold it down, enjoy the cleansing atmosphere of fluid encapsulating you outside and inside, as in the womb. Back to innocence and oblivion.

Life rewinding in vivid snapshots.

A distant crying, a rush of noise.

The long tunnel and the bright light.

Postlude

After Easter he didn't have any work immediately, just some coaching, a couple of singing lessons and a whole lot of music to learn, so was therefore at home mostly. He decided to spend some time sorting out his papers which had been accumulating on his desk. There were business receipts that needed filing, invoices from his agent and house bills which needed paying. Whilst at it he decided to go through the drawer in the desk which was a mess. Almost immediately he came across the programme from the Passion in Gothenburg and opening it the postcard of the statue fell out. He picked it up and gazed at that mesmerising image. It glowed back at him, resonating again from all those months ago. Who was she, this enigmatic siren lying nude on a raft with the ugly faces in the water beside her? He turned the card over and read again the title and provenance.

'Näckrosen'

Designed by Per Hasselberg

Made by Christian Eriksson

On an impulse he turned on the computer and while it booted up went and made a cup of coffee. Why hadn't he thought to do this before, search the net to find out about the sculpture? Too many things happening after he came out of prison. Entering 'Näckrosen' he was presented with pictures of Näckrosen station on the metro line in Stockholm, and learned that it meant water lily. But there was also an image of a green sculpture in the snow which looked similar. He clicked on it and came up with associated images which included 'his' statue. Scrolling down he found that this sculpture had been reproduced a number of times in different materials. But who was she?

He clicked on Per Hasselberg and came up with a Wikipedia entry which was all in Swedish of course. Clicking on the translate option he learned that he was actually Karl Petter Hasselberg, born Åkesson in 1850, died 1894. The bulk of his work was female nudes. Matt skimmed through his biography, how he had studied in Paris and won the gold medal there for his piece Snöcklacken, Snowdrop. But there was a paragraph near the end which made the hairs of his neck stand up.

'During his years in Paris Per Hasselberg met artist Eva Bonnier and they began a relationship and got engaged, but the engagement was broken. Per Hasselberg began a relationship with his model for Water Lilly, Signe Larsson, who in 1893 gave birth to their daughter Julia. Per Hasselberg died in 1894 in the wake of years of diabetes when the daughter was adopted by Eva Bonnier.'

Signe Larsson. The name of the girl in Gothenburg, the girl he... It couldn't be, he must be imagining it. He got the papers out, knowing even as he looked for them that he was right. It was the same name, spelt the same way. He looked up Larsson, anticipating it was a common name and of course came up with Stieg Larsson the author of 'The Girl with the Dragon Tattoo' from the Millennium Trilogy, as well as hundreds of others. Of course it was a common name. He looked up Signe, plenty of those too, spelt also Signy. Further research revealed that Signe was a princess in Norse legend who took her life after the death of her lover.

He entered Eva Bonnier and came up with a series of thumb prints of paintings by her, including a self-portrait, which he could see were accomplished works, and then, at the end, a haunting picture of a young girl with the saddest eyes he'd ever seen, entitled Julia Hasselberg, circa 1906. Her features were so similar to the girl in the audience, whose pained expression had first entranced him, that Matt was spooked. The daughter of the statue and the statue's creator, adopted by his ex-fiancé. He quickly deduced she would have been about thirteen.

He looked again at the post card of the statue and noticed the similar full lips and shape of the nose. The eyes, though closed, were also bulbous and heavily lidded. The girl in the portrait however had a much higher forehead and longer face below the mop of hair, just like the photo of Per Hasselberg in the Wikipedia entry, but apart from this the likeness was uncanny.

He was taking a long pull from his rapidly cooling coffee when his phone bleeped a message. It was from Maggie. He hadn't heard anything from her for a couple of days. 'Hi babe. Missing you. When are you going to come up and see me again? How you doin'? Love you. M x.'

Its brevity and distant tone struck him. It appeared to be a duty message, touching base but not really communicating. *Is she seeing that Sam guy?*

He turned back to the computer screen and tried to fathom that look of wistful sadness in the girl's eyes, the girl Julia Hasselberg. He seemed to know those eyes as, when he looked once more at the image of the statue, he sensed he knew those curves and crevices, those arching limbs, that polished torso. *This belief has it that we interact with some souls over many lifetimes.* Knew them not just from a viewing in a gallery, but intimately, intensely, profoundly. *You may have encountered your twin flame.* It was like he'd always known them, for a long time, from another time, from another life. *In a previous life you worked with your hands, created things...*

He looked back at the picture of the girl with sad eyes, Julia Hasselberg, so young and innocent and heartbroken. He thought of George, his death, the teenager he'd loved and left behind. Is this how she felt now? And had he done it again and again? Was she just one of many? He heard George's words 'Well you know what they say Matthew, history repeats itself'. Is that possible? Had he gone completely crazy and was now imagining things that were totally against all scientific and rational thought? *There are more things in heaven and earth, Horatio, Than are dreamt of in your philosophy.*

Dawkins and Darwin don't desert me now.

He finished his coffee and went and poured some more and gave it a quick blast in the microwave. Back at the computer habit made him click on Gmail to check his emails, something he normally did first thing in the morning, but the action helped him focus on reality again. He saw the usual notifications from various sources, a couple from his agent, a bank statement, a charity petition and, his pulse quickened, an email from Caterina.

'My dearest Matthew. Please forgive me, I haven't been in touch for so long but I have been so busy with work and travelling – I only just got back for Easter with Tanya before I had to go away again for a recording. I hope you are well and happy and that you are doing lots of excellent work like a good boy.

I'm sorry this has to be a short note but I wanted you to know before anyone else that I got married to an old friend two days after Easter. I have known him for a long time and we have been great friends. He is older than me and is the manager of a large company here in Finland. As I am sure you'll appreciate this is so good for Tanya and provides security for both of us in this uncertain profession.

Matthew, I have so enjoyed our time together and want you to know I will always remember you with such great affection and I hope you will understand that I needed to do this as the sensible thing for my little girl. I know you will have a wonderful career and who knows, maybe we meet again for a performance soon.

I look forward to hopefully singing with you again, and send you my best wishes and my love always,

Caterina x'

Matt stared at the screen, then slowly closed down Gmail.

A long time ago, he remembered, when he was at school, someone had tripped and slammed into him during a game of football and the wind had been completely knocked out of his lungs so that he couldn't breathe. This was the same feeling, the shooting pain in his chest which stopped him breathing.

A door that had occasionally opened onto a garden of paradise had closed and been locked up forever.

He got up and turned to look out of the window but couldn't see anything. The silence in the flat crowded around him and he longed for some distraction. He walked across to the old midi system and flicked on Radio 3 and was plunged into a dense, dark orchestration, heavy and German sounding. Stepping bass brass under flittering arpeggio strings. Heavy, dissonant, agonised. *Bruckner? Possibly.* It suited his mood.

He sat again, the picture of the girl still there on the screen.

What had he expected? That Caterina would always be there for him in some kind of available state? Yes, it would have been on her terms, but had he really believed she would keep herself for him, she with the world at her feet? But it had been such a special love, not of this world, something so precious and unique that he now struggled to understand how she could cut off that possibility as her email indicated. Had it just been a wonderful distraction for her, a redeeming of her youth and a chance to be 'wicked'? Had she not felt it in the same way, been rocked by the intensity of the experience?

The aching strings of the orchestra were suddenly high and sobbing, softly lamenting. Then horns calling beneath, oboes answering.

There was a loud rap on the front door which startled him out of his reverie. He trudged down the stairs and opened the door.

"Mr Chamberlain?"

"Yup."

"Registered letter. So here we are, today's the 25th, if you could just sign on the screen. That's it. Thanks, bye."

Matt stood in the doorway holding the envelope as the postman pushed on down the street in his high viz. The postmark was Stockholm and there was an official-looking crest with writing in Swedish under it.

25th March. Exactly a year since the Passion in Gothenburg.

He walked back upstairs and sat down again as the orchestral texture piled denser and increasingly dissonant. Finally there was a long held note with a tugging suspension which at last resolved and the piece ended. Then Neil Sideburns' voice informed the listeners that was the end of Sibelius's Symphony number seven.

Sibelius, of course. It would have to be.

"And now," he continued, "although we are no longer in Holy Week, I've had so many requests for this particular aria from the St Matthew Passion we broadcast last week from Ghent, that I will just have to play it again."

The computer screen had switched over to rest mode and the girl's face was now traversed by colour-changing bubbles bumping into each other and bouncing across the image. Matt sat transfixed, staring at them, as that soaring soprano once again seared his senses with its crystalline tone and burnished clarity.

"Aus Liebe will mein Heiland sterben." Out of love my Saviour now is dying.

The bubbles became bleary as his eyes focused beyond them and images of Caterina in a black velvet bodice studded with diamantes above a full-length black silk skirt filled his mind. Her face was radiant, perfect.

He remained motionless, the letter in his hand, suffering that unparalleled sound until the final cadence.

"The voice of Caterina Jokela in the Aus Liebe from Bach's St Matthew Passion in a performance with Collegium Brugense, conducted by Henk Wederstraum, broadcast on Good Friday."

He broke open the envelope and read.

Acknowledgements

My thanks go to everyone who has had to put up with me wittering on about this book for the past seven years and for indulging my self-indulgence.

Particular thanks to Peter and Eva McMullen for advice on things Swedish and editorial comment; to Clarissa Meek and John Brackenridge for their great encouragement; to Joyce and Richard, Michelle and Andy in the book club for reading the first draft and their positive comments; huge thanks to Nina Gatward and Colin Spencer for painstaking reading, feedback, advice and encouragement; to Nan Salén of Ulf Carlzon AB for kindly given legal advice; to Simon Guirao and Ansy Boothroyd, fellow writers on a similar trajectory who have shared their griefs, empathised with mine and been stalwart supports both with advice and experience, and with editorial comment respectively; to Tyrel Broadbent for coming up with such a beautiful cover; to Barney Meek for endless computer support and formatting, and patience in dealing with a technologically inept father and to Lynne, my long-suffering wife, who has to put up with me and this book - just one of my many projects which take over our lives – and who has generously given me the space, opportunity and love to be able to complete it.